Keith Waterhouse is one of our most versatile and prolific writers. His long-running newspaper column, now appearing twice weekly in the *Daily Mail*, has six times won major press awards, while his hit play *Jeffrey Bernard is Unwell* won the *Evening Standard* Comedy of the Year Award for 1990. Other stage successes include *Mr and Mrs Nobody* and *Bookends*, which, together with *Jeffrey Bernard is Unwell*, have been published by Penguin in one volume, and *Our Song*. His widely acclaimed novels include *There is a Happy Land* (1957), *Billy Liar* (1959), *Jubb* (1963), *Maggie Muggins* (1981), *In the Mood* (1983), *Our Song* (1988), *Bimbo* (1990) and *Unsweet Charity* (1992). In collaboration with Willis Hall he has written extensively for film, theatre and television, their credits including *Billy Liar*, *Whistle Down the Wind*, *A Kind of Loving*, and the long-running TV series *Budgie* and *Worzel Gummidge*. Six collections of his journalism have been published, the latest being *Sharon & Tracy & the Rest*. His highly praised *English Our English* (1991) is published by Viking and *Waterhouse on Newspaper Style* (1989) is published by Penguin.

Keith Waterhouse was made a CBE in 1991.

WITHDRAW FROM
NEWCASTLE UPON TYNE
CITY LIBRARIES

KEITH WATERHOUSE

BILLY LIAR
BILLY LIAR ON THE MOON

NEWCASTLE UPON TYNE

WITHDRAW FROM
NEWCASTLE UPON TYNE
CITY LIBRARIES

PENGUIN BOOKS
IN ASSOCIATION WITH MICHAEL JOSEPH

FOR CIRCULATION

PENGUIN BOOKS

Published by the Penguin Group
Penguin Books Ltd, 27 Wrights Lane, London W8 5TZ, England
Penguin Books USA Inc., 375 Hudson Street, New York, New York 10014, USA
Penguin Books Australia Ltd, Ringwood, Victoria, Australia
Penguin Books Canada Ltd, 10 Alcorn Avenue, Toronto, Ontario, Canada M4V 3B2
Penguin Books (NZ) Ltd, 182–190 Wairau Road, Auckland 10, New Zealand

Penguin Books Ltd, Registered Offices: Harmondsworth, Middlesex, England

Billy Liar first published by Michael Joseph 1959
Published in Penguin Books 1962

Billy Liar on the Moon first published by Michael Joseph 1975
Published in Penguin Books 1977

This omnibus edition published in Penguin Books 1993
1 3 5 7 9 10 8 6 4 2

Billy Liar copyright © Keith Waterhouse, 1959
Billy Liar on the Moon copyright © Keith Waterhouse, 1975
All rights reserved

Printed in England by Clays Ltd, St Ives plc

Except in the United States of America, this book is sold subject
to the condition that it shall not, by way of trade or otherwise, be lent,
re-sold, hired out, or otherwise circulated without the publisher's
prior consent in any form of binding or cover other than that in
which it is published and without a similar condition including this
condition being imposed on the subsequent purchaser

NEWCASTLE UPON TYNE
CITY LIBRARIES
WITHDRAWN FROM
NEWCASTLE UPON TYNE
MORLEY CITY LIBRARIES

C 1 7 3 3 7 8 2 0098
7 FEB 1994
F ≠6.99
6/94 HH

FOR CIRCULATION
Wa – WV
12/94

+ By →
+ @ – Hth 4/00
Hc UKB

CONTENTS

BILLY LIAR

I

LYING in bed, I abandoned the facts again and was back in Ambrosia.

By rights, the march-past started in the Avenue of the Presidents, but it was an easy thing to shift the whole thing into Town Square. My friends had vantage seats on the town-hall steps where no flag flew more proudly than the tattered blue star of the Ambrosian Federation, the standard we had carried into battle. One by one the regiments marched past, and when they had gone – the Guards, the Parachute Regiment, the King's Own Yorkshire Light Infantry – a hush fell over the crowds and they removed their hats for the proud remnants of the Ambrosian Grand Yeomanry. It was true that we had entered the war late, and some criticized us for that; but out of two thousand who went into battle only seven remained to hear the rebuke. We limped along as we had arrived from the battlefield, the mud still on our shredded uniforms, but with a proud swing to our kilts. The band played 'March of the Movies'. The war memorial was decked with blue poppies, the strange bloom found only in Ambrosia.

I put an end to all this, consciously and deliberately, by going 'Da da da da da da da' aloud to drive the thinking out of my head. It was a day for big decisions. I recalled how I could always cure myself when I got on one of those counting sprees where it was possible to reach three thousand easily without stopping: I would throw in a confetti of confusing numbers or, if they didn't help, half-remembered quotations and snatches of verse. 'Seventy-three.

Nine hundred and six. The Lord is my shepherd, I shall not want, he maketh me to lie down. Four hundred and thirty-five.'

It was a day for big decisions. I had already determined, more for practical reasons than out of any new policy, to clip the thumb-nail which I had been cultivating until it was a quarter of an inch long. Now, lying under the pale gold eiderdown, staring up at the crinoline ladies craftily fashioned out of silver paper and framed in passe-partout (*they* would be coming down, for a start) I began to abandon the idea of saving the clipping in an ointment box; I would throw it right away, without a backward glance, and from now on short nails, and a brisk bath each morning. An end, too, to this habit of lying in bed crinkling my toes fifty times for each foot; in future I would be up at seven and an hour's work done before breakfast. There would be no more breath-holding, eye-blinking, nostril-twitching, or sucking of teeth, and this plan would start tomorrow, if not today.

I lay in bed, the toe-crinkling over; now I was stretching the fingers of both hands to their fullest extent, like two starfish. Sometimes I got an overpowering feeling that my fingers were webbed, like a duck's, and I had to spread them out to block the sensation and prevent it spreading to my feet.

My mother shouted up the stairs: 'Billy? Billy! *Are* you getting up?' the third call in a fairly well-established series of street-cries that graduated from: 'Are you awake, Billy?' to 'It's a quarter past nine, and you can stay in bed all day for all I care', meaning twenty to nine and time to get up. I waited until she called: 'If I come up there you'll *know* about it' (a variant of number five, usually 'If I come up there I shall *tip* you out') and then I got up.

I put on the old raincoat I used for a dressing-gown, making the resolution that now I must buy a real dressing-gown, possibly a silk one with some kind of dragon motif, and I felt in my pocket for the Player's Weights. I was trying to bring myself up to smoke before breakfast but this time even the idea of it brought on the familiar nausea. I shoved the cigarettes back in my pocket and felt the letter still there, but this time I did not read it. '*He scribbled a few notes on the back of a used envelope.*' The phrase had always appealed to me. I had a pleasing image of a stack of used envelopes, secured by a rubber band, crammed with notes in a thin, spidery handwriting. I took the used envelope out of my pocket with the letter still in it and thought up some jottings. '*Calendars. See S. re job. Write Boon. Thousand??? See Witch re Captain.*' Most of these notes were unnecessary, especially the bit about seeing Witch re Captain; that, along with the calendars, always a part-time worry, and the other bit about seeing S. re job, had kept me awake half the night. As for Thousand??? this was a ghost of idle thinking, the last traces of a plan to write a thousand words each day of a public-school story to be entitled *The Two Schools at Gripminster*. Having conceived the plan in early August, I was already thirty-four thousand words behind on the schedule. There were long periods of time when my only ambition was to suck a Polo mint right through without it breaking in my mouth; others when I would retreat into Ambrosia and sketch out the new artists' settlement on route eleven, and they would be doing profiles of me on television, 'Genius – or Madman?'

I put the ballpoint away and shoved the envelope back in my pocket, and on the cue of cry number seven, by far my favourite ('Your boiled egg's stone cold and *I'm* not cooking another') I went downstairs.

Hillcrest, as the house was called (although not by me) was the kind of dwelling where all the windows are leaded in a fussy criss-cross, except one, which is a porthole. Our porthole was at the turn of the stairs and here I paused to rub the heel of my slipper against the stair-rod, another habit I would be getting out of henceforth. Shuffling there, I could see out across the gravel to the pitch-painted garage with its wordy, gold-painted sign: 'Geo. Fisher & Son, Haulage Contractors, Distance No Object. "The Moving Firm." Tel: 2573. Stamp, Signs.' The sign was inaccurate. I was the son referred to, but in fact the old man had gone to great trouble to keep me out of the family business, distance no object. What really got on my nerves, however, was the legend 'Stamp, Signs' which was almost as big as the advertisement itself. Eric Stamp had been the white-haired boy of the art class when we were at Stradhoughton Technical together, and was now my colleague at Shadrack and Duxbury's. It was his ambition to set up in the sign-writing business full-time, and I for one was not stopping him.

Anyway, the fact that the garage doors were not open yet meant that the old man was still at home and there were going to be words exchanged about last night's outing. I slopped down into the hall, took the *Stradhoughton Echo* out of the letter-box, where it would have remained all day if the rest of the family had anything to do with it, and went into the lounge. It was a day for big decisions.

The breakfast ceremony at Hillcrest had never been my idea of fun. I had made one disastrous attempt to break the monotony of it, entering the room one day with my eyes shut and my arms outstretched like a sleep-walker, announcing in a shaky, echo-chamber voice: 'Ay York-shire breakfast scene. Ay polished table, one leaf out, covahed diagonally by ay white tablecloth, damask, with grrreen stripe bordah. Sauce-stain to the right, blackberry stain to the centre. Kellogg's corn flakes, Pyrex dishes, plate of fried bread. Around the table, the following personnel:

fathah, mothah, grandmothah, one vacant place.' None of this had gone down well. I entered discreetly now, almost shiftily, taking in with a dull eye the old man's pint mug disfigured by a crack that was no longer mistaken for a hair, and the radio warming up for 'Yesterday in Parliament'. It was a choice example of the hygienic family circle, but to me it had taken on the glazed familiarity of some old print such as *When Did You Last See Your Father?* I was greeted by the usual breathing noises.

'You decided to get up, then,' my mother said, slipping easily into the second series of conversations of the day. My stock replies were 'Yes', 'No, I'm still in bed', and a snarled 'What does it look like?' according to mood. Today I chose 'Yes' and sat down to my boiled egg, stone cold as threatened. This made it a quarter to nine.

The old man looked up from some invoices and said: 'And you can start getting bloody well dressed before you come down in a morning.' So far the dialogue was taking a fairly conventional route and I was tempted to throw in one of the old stand-bys, 'Why do you always begin your sentences with an "And"?' Gran, another dress fanatic who always seemed to be fully and even elaborately attired even at two in the morning when she slunk downstairs after the soda-water, chipped in: 'He wants to burn that raincoat, then he'll have to get dressed of a morning.' One of Gran's peculiarities, and she had many, was that she would never address anyone directly but always went through an intermediary, if necessary some static object such as a cupboard. Doing the usual decoding I gathered that she was addressing my mother and that he who should burn the raincoat was the old man, and he who would have to get dressed of a morning was me. 'I gather,' I began, 'that he who should burn the raincoat –' but the old man interrupted:

'And what bloody time did you get in *last* night? If you can call it last night. This bloody morning, more like.'

I sliced the top off my boiled egg, which in a centre favouring tapping the top with a spoon and peeling the bits off was always calculated to annoy, and said lightly: '*I* don't know. 'Bout half past eleven, quarter to twelve.'

The old man said: 'More like one o'clock, with your half past bloody eleven! Well you can bloody well and start coming in of a night-time. I'm not having *you* gallivanting round at all hours, not at your bloody age.'

'Who *are* you having gallivanting round, then?' I asked, the wit rising for the day like a pale and watery sun.

My mother took over, assuming the clipped, metallic voice of the morning interrogation. '*What were you doing down Foley Bottoms at nine o'clock last night?*'

I said belligerently: 'Who says I was down at Foley Bottoms?'

'Never mind who says, or who doesn't say. You *were* there, and it wasn't that Barbara you were with, neither.'

'He wants to make up his mind who he *is* going with,' Gran said.

There was a rich field of speculation for me here. Since my mother had never even met the Witch – the one to whom she referred by her given name of Barbara – or Rita either – the one involved in the Foley Bottoms episode, that is – I wondered how she managed to get her hands on so many facts without actually hiring detectives.

I said: 'Well you want to tell whoever saw me to mind their own fizzing business.'

'It *is* our business,' my mother said. 'And don't you be so cheeky!' I pondered over the absent friend who had supplied the Foley Bottoms bulletin. Mrs Olmonroyd? Ma Walker? Stamp? *The Witch herself?* I had a sudden, hideous notion that the Witch was in league with my mother and that they were to spring some dreadful *coup* upon me the following day when, with a baptism of lettuce and pine-apple chunks, the Witch was due to be introduced to the family at Sunday tea.

Gran said: 'If she's coming for her tea tomorrow she wants to tell her. If she doesn't, I will.' My mother interpreted this fairly intelligently and said: 'I'm *going* to tell her, don't you fret yourself.' She slid off down a chuntering landslide of recrimination until the old man, reverting to the main theme, came back with the heavy artillery.

'He's not bloody well old enough to stay out half the night, I've told him before. He can start coming in of a night, or else go and live somewhere else.'

This brought me beautifully to what I intended to be the text for the day, but now that the moment had come I felt curiously shy and even a little sick at the idea of my big decisions. I allowed my mother to pour me a grudging cup of tea. I picked up the sugar with the tongs so as to fall in with house rules. I fingered the used envelope in my rain-coat pocket, see S. re job. I cleared my throat and felt again the urge to yawn that had been with me like a disease for as long as I could remember, and that for all I knew *was* a disease and a deadly one at that. The need to yawn took over from all the other considerations and I began to make the familiar Channel-swimmer mouthings, fishing for the ball of air at the back of my throat. The family returned to rummage among their breakfast plates and, aware that the moment had gone by, I said:

'I've been *off*ered that job in London.'

The replies were predictable, so predictable that I had already written them down, although not on a used enve-lope, and had meant to present the family with this wryly-humorous summing-up of their little ways as some kind of tolerant benediction on them after they spoke, which according to my notes was as follows:

Old man: 'What bloody job?'

Mother: 'How do you mean, you've been offered it?'

Gran: 'What's he talking about, I thought he was going to be a cartooner, last I heard.'

Another of Gran's whimsicalities was that she could not, or more likely would not, remember the noun for the person who draws cartoons. She threw me a baleful glare and I decided not to bring out the predictions but to carry on as I had planned the night before or, as the old man would have it, the early hours of the morning, tossing and turning under the pale gold eiderdown.

'That job with Danny Boon. When I wrote to him,' I said.

I had often likened the conversation at Hillcrest to the route of the old No. 14 tram. Even when completely new subjects were being discussed, the talk rattled on along the familiar track, stopping to load on festering arguments from the past, and culminating at the terminus of the old man's wrath.

'What job with Danny Boon?' This line – together with a rhubarb-rhubarb chorus of 'What's he talking about, Danny Boon' – was optional for the whole family, but was in fact spoken by my mother.

'The job I was *tell*ing you about.'

'What job, you've never told *me* about no job.'

It was obviously going to be one of the uphill treks. The whole family knew well enough about my ambition, or one of my ambitions, to write scripts for comedy. They knew how Danny Boon, who was not so famous then as he is now, had played a week at the Stradhoughton Empire. They knew, because I had told them four times, that I had taken him some material – including my 'thick as lead' catchline

12

which Boon now uses all the time – and how he had liked it. ('Well how do you know he'll pay you anything?' my mother had said.) They knew I had asked him for a *job*. Thank God, I thought, as I pushed my boiled egg aside with the yolk gone and the white untouched, that they don't ask me who Danny Boon is when he's at home.

'Why does he always leave the white of his egg?' asked Gran. 'It's all goodness, just thrown down the sink.'

The remark was so completely irrelevant that even my mother, always a willing explorer down the back-doubles on the conversational map, ignored it. Shouts of 'What about your job at Shradrack and *Dux*bury's?' and 'Who do you think's going to *keep* you?' began to trickle through but I maintained my hysterical calm, wearing my sensitivity like armour. Above everything I could hear the querulous tones of Gran, going over and over again: 'What's he on about? What's he on about? What's he on about? What's he on about?'

I took a deep breath and made it obvious that I was taking a deep breath, and said: 'Look, there is a comedian. The comedian's name is Danny Boon. B-double O-N. He does not write his own scripts. He gets other people to do it for him. He likes my material. He thinks he can give me regular work.'

My mother said: 'How do you mean, he likes your material?'

I brought out the heavy sigh and the clenched teeth. 'Look. This pepper-pot is Danny Boon. This salt-cellar is my material. Danny Boon is looking for material –' I turned the blue plastic pepper-pot on them like a ray-gun. 'He sees my flaming material. So he flaming well asks for it.'

' 'Ere, rear, rear, watch your bloody language! With your flaming this and flaming that! At meal-times! You're not in bloody London yet, you know!'

13

'He's gone too far,' said Gran, complacently.

I went 'Ssssssss!' through my teeth. 'For crying out loud!' I slipped back a couple of notches into the family dialect and said: 'Look, do you wanna know or don't you? Cos if you do ah'll tell you, and if you don't ah won't.'

They sat with pursed lips, my mother heaving at the bosom and the old man scowling over his bills and the Woodbine ash filling up his eggshell. The radio took over the silence and filled it for a moment with some droning voice.

'Try *again*,' I said. I took another deep breath, which developed into a yawning fit.

'You just eat your breakfast, and don't have so much off,' my mother said. 'Else get your mucky self washed. And stop always yawning at meal-times. You don't get enough sleep, that's all that's wrong with you.'

'And get to bloody work,' the old man said.

I pushed back the polished chair, about whose machine-turned legs I had once had so much to say, and went into the kitchen. It was five minutes past nine. I leaned against the sink in an angry torpor, bombing and blasting each of them to hell. I lit a stealthy Player's Weight, and thought of the steel-bright autumn day in front of me, and began to feel better. I breathed heavily again, this time slowly and luxuriously, and began to grope through the coils of fuse-wire in the kitchen drawer for the old man's electric razor. I switched on, waited for a tense second for the bellowed order from the lounge to put the thing away and buy one of my own, and then began my thinking.

I was spending a good part of my time, more of it as each day passed, on this thinking business. Sometimes I could squander the whole morning on it, and very often the whole evening and a fair slice of the night hours too. I had two kinds of thinking (three, if ordinary thoughts were counted) and I had names for them, applied first jocularly and then mechanically. I called them No. 1 thinking and No. 2 thinking. No. 1 thinking was voluntary, but No. 2 thinking was not; it concerned itself with obsessional speculations about the scope and nature of disease (such as a persistent yawn that was probably symptomatic of sarcoma of the jaw), the probable consequences of actual misdemeanours, and the solutions to desperate problems, such as what would one do, what would one actually *do*, in the case of having a firework jammed in one's ear by mischievous boys. The way out of all this was to lull myself into a No. 1 thinking bout, taking the fast excursion to Ambrosia, indulging in hypothetical conversations with Bertrand Russell, fusing and magnifying the ordinary thoughts of the day so that I was a famous comedian at the Ambrosia State Opera, the only stage personality ever to reach the rank of president.

Propped up against the gas-stove, buzzing with the old man's razor, I began to do some No. 1 thinking on the subject of the family. This usually took a reasonably noble form: riding home to Hillcrest loaded with money, putting the old man on his feet, forgiving and being forgiven. My mother would be put into furs, would feel uneasy in them at first, but would be touched and never lose her homely ways. Grandma married Councillor Duxbury and the pair of them, apple-cheeked, lived in a thatched cottage high up in the dales, out of sight. That was the usual thing. But this morning, in harder mood, I began to plan entirely new parents for myself. They were of the modern, London, kind. They had allowed, in fact en*couraged* me to smoke from the age of thirteen (Markovitch) and when I came home drunk my No. 1 mother would look up from her solitaire and groan: 'Oh God, how dreary! Billy's pissed again!' I announced at breakfast that I was going to start out on my own. My No. 1 father – the old man disguised as a company director – clapped me on the back and said: '*And* about time, you old loafer. Simone and I were thinking of kicking you out of the old nest any day now. Better come into the library and talk about the money end.' As for Gran, she didn't exist.

The thinking and the shaving finished concurrently. I switched off and began brooding over the matter of the black bristles under my chin which, shave as I might, would never come smooth. I dropped back into my torpor, a kind of vacuum annexe to the No. 2 thinking, and began scraping the back of my hand against the bristles, listening to the noise of it and wondering whether there was something wrong with me. The old man came through into the kitchen, putting on his jacket on his way to the garage.

'And you can buy your own bloody razor and stop using mine,' he said without stopping. I called: '*Eighty-four!*' supposedly the number of times he had used the word 'bloody' that morning, a standing joke (at least, with me), but he had gone out. The business of going to London was shelved, forgotten or, as I suspected, completely uncomprehended.

I went through the lounge and upstairs. My mother, as I passed her, chanted automatically: 'You'll-set-off-one-of-these-days-and-meet-yourself-coming-back,' one of a series of remarks tailored, I liked to fancy, to fit the exact time taken by me from kitchen door to hall door. There had been a time when I had tried to get the family to call these stock sayings of hers 'Motherisms'. Nobody ever knew what I was talking about.

Swilling myself in the bathroom, I found the business of the bristles on my chin leading, as I had known it would, into a definite spasm of No. 2 thinking. I wondered first if I were developing ingrowing hair, like those people whose throats tickle every six weeks and who have to go into hospital to get it removed, and then I ran through the usual repertoire, polio, cancer, T.B., and a new disease, unique in medical history, called Fisher's Yawn. Nowadays these attacks, occurring more or less whenever I had a spare minute, usually culminated at the point where I began to wonder what would happen if I were taken to hospital, died even, and they found out about the calendars.

My mother shouted up the stairs: 'You'll never get into *town* at this rate, never mind London! It's after half past nine!' but by now the calendar theme had me in its grip, and I staggered into my bedroom, gasping and clawing for breath, doing some deep-level No. 2 thinking on the subject.

It was now September. The calendars had been given to me to post about two weeks before Christmas of the previous year. This meant that this particular problem had been on the agenda for over nine months or, as I sometimes worked it out, six thousand five hundred and twenty-eight hours. The calendars were stiff cardboard efforts measuring ten inches by eight, each bearing a picture of a cat looking at a dog, the legend 'Rivals' and, overprinted in smudgy olive type, 'Shadrack and Duxbury, Funeral Furnishers. Taste' – then a little star – 'Tact' – and another little star – 'Economy'. They were prestige jobs for Shadrack's contacts, people like the directors of the crematorium and parsons who might ring up with a few tip-offs, and for good customers like the Alderman Burrows Old People's Home, with whom Shadrack and Duxbury's had a standing account. I had omitted to post them in order to get at the postage money, which I had kept for myself. I had hidden the calendars in the stockroom in the office basement for a while and then, tired of the hideous reel of No. 2 thinking where Shadrack lifted the coffin lid and found them, had gradually transferred them home. A few I had already destroyed, taking them out of the house one by one at night and tearing them to shreds, dropping them in a paper-chase over Stradhoughton Moor and sweating over an image of the police picking them up and piecing them together. I had got rid of fourteen in this way. The rest were in a tin trunk under my bed. There were two hundred and eleven of them.

I dressed, making another mental note to look up *Every Man's Own Lawyer* and find out the penalties for this particular crime. 'Pay attention to me, Fisher. I have thought very carefully about sending you to prison. Only your youth and the fact that your employers have spoken so highly of your abilities . . .' Tying my tie, I began to imagine myself in Armley Jail, impressing the governor with my intelligence, making friends with the padre; and for a short while I was back on the No. 1 thinking, a luxury I could ill afford at half past nine on a working morning.

'Billy! If you're not out of this house in five minutes I shall push you out!'

I put on my jacket and pulled the old japanned trunk from under the bed. The piece of stamp edging was still in position across the lid. A long while ago, when it had contained no more than the scribbled postcards from Liz and a few saccharine notes from the Witch, I had started to call this trunk my Guilt Chest. Any grain of facetiousness there had been in this description had long since disappeared.

I lifted the lid gingerly, jolted and disturbed as usual by the vast number of calendars there seemed to be, stacked dozens deep in their thick brown envelopes, addressed in my own broad handwriting to Dr H. Rich, P. W. Horniman, Esq., J.P., Rev. D. L. P. Tack, the Warden, Stradhoughton Workpeople's Hostel. Besides the calendars, nestling in their own dark hollow of the Guilt Chest, were the love-letters, the bills the old man had given me to post, the aphrodisiac tablets that Stamp had got for me, the cellophaned, leggy copy of *Ritzy Stories*, and the letter my mother had once written to 'Housewives' Choice'. I could picture her sitting down with the Stephens' ink bottle and the Basildon Bond, and I could never explain to myself why I had not posted the letter or why I had opened it under cover of the Guilt Chest lid. '*Dear Sir, Just a few lines to let you know how much I enjoy Housewife's "Choice" every day, I always listen no matter what I am doing, could you play (Just a Song at Twilight) for me though I don't suppose you get time to play everyone that writes to you, but this is my "favourite song". You see my husband often used to sing it when we a bit younger than we are now, I will quite understand if you cannot play. Yours respectfully (Mrs) N. Fisher. PS. My son also write songs, but I suppose there is not much chance for him as he has not had the training. We are just ordinary folk.*' The debates I had had with my mother on the ordinary-folk motif, in long and eloquent streams of No. 1 thinking, would have filled 'Housewives' Choice' ten times over.

Snapped together by a rubber band, like the used envelopes I had fancied for myself, was the thin pack of postcards that Liz had written to me on her last expedition but one. They were matter-of-fact little notes, full of tediously interesting details about the things she had seen in Leicester, Welwyn Garden City, and the other places where whatever urge possessing her had taken her; but at least they were literate. I felt mildly peculiar to be treasuring love-letters for their grammar, but there was nothing else I could treasure them for. Sometimes I could think about Liz, think properly on the ordinary plane, for a full minute, before we were both whisked off into Ambrosia, myself facing trial for sedition and she a kind of white-faced Eva Peron in the crowd.

I took one of the calendars out of the Guilt Chest and stuffed it under my pullover. If I was going to London in a week it meant that I had one hundred and sixty-eight hours to dispose of two hundred and eleven calendars. Say, for safety, two calendars an hour between now and next Saturday. I took out another three and crammed them half under my pullover and half under the top of my trousers. Rummaging in the Guilt Chest, I spotted the flat white packet of supposed aphrodisiacs, the 'passion pills' as Stamp, shoving them grubbily into my hand in a fit of remorse, fear, and generosity, had called them. I put Liz out of my mind and began thinking about Rita and then, making a definite decision, about the Witch. I put the passion pills in my side pocket and bent to close the Guilt Chest, the calendars stiff under my ribs and the sharp corners showing through the cable-weave of my pullover. I replaced the stamp edging, four inches from the handle on the right-hand side, pushed the trunk carefully under the bed and went downstairs, feeling like a walking Guilt Chest myself. In the hall I put on my outdoor raincoat and buttoned it to the waist before going into the lounge.

'He'll be *buried* in a raincoat,' said Gran, almost, in fact completely, automatically. She was rubbing viciously at the sideboard with a check duster, a daily gruelling which she imagined paid for her keep. It was to the sideboard that she addressed herself, because my mother was in the kitchen.

It was long past any time at all for a working morning. The last late typists, their bucket bags stuffed with deodorants and paper handkerchiefs, had clacked past on their way to the bus shelter. A morning hush had settled over the house. There were specks of dust in the sunlight and the stiff smell of Mansion Polish. The radio emphasized the lateness with an unfamiliar voice, talking about some place where they had strange customs; it was like going long past one's station on the last train.

I called: 'I'm off, mother!'

'Well don't hurry yourself, will you?' she called back, following her voice into the lounge. I paused with my hand running up and down the brown bakelite finger-plate on the door.

'Might as well give my notice in today, if I'm going to London,' I said. My mother pressed her lips together in a thin purple line and began bundling up the tablecloth, taking it by the corners to keep the crumbs in.

'You want to make up your mind what you *do* want to do!' she said primly.

'I *know* what I'm going to do. I'm going to work for Danny Boon.'

'Well how do you know, you've never done that sort of thing before. You can't switch and change and swop about just when you feel like it. You've got your living to earn now, you know!'

She was trying to talk kindly, making a real effort at it but drawing the effort back, like someone whispering across a bridge. I was touched, fleetingly. I said, trying hard myself: 'Any road, we'll talk about it later,' a gruff and oblique statement of affection that, I could see, was received and understood.

I left the house, ignoring the old man who was messing about with the lorry in the road outside. If I can walk all the way down Cherry Row without blinking my eyelids, I told myself, it will be all all right. I kept my eyes wide and burning long past Greenman's sweet-shop, past the clay cavities where the semis were not built yet; then Mrs

Olmonroyd came past, spying. I clapped my eyes shut and wished her a civil good morning. I felt the calendars under my jacket and wondered why I had brought them out and what I was going to do with them, and what I was going to do about everything.

'THE very name of Stradhoughton,' Man o' the Dales had written in the *Stradhoughton Echo* one morning when there was nothing much doing, 'conjures up sturdy buildings of honest native stone, gleaming cobbled streets, and that brackish air which gives this corner of Yorkshire its own especial *piquancy*.' Man o' the Dales put piquancy in italics, not me.

My No. 1 thinking often featured long sessions with Man o' the Dales in whatever pub the boys on the *Echo* used, and there I would put him right on his facts. The cobbled streets, gleaming or otherwise, had long ago been ripped up with the tramlines and relined with concrete slabs or tar-macadam – gleaming tarmacadam I would *grant* him, stabbing him in the chest with the stocky briar which in this particular role I affected. The brackish air I was no authority on, except to say that when the wind was in a certain direction it smelled of burning paint. As for the honest native stone, our main street, Moorgate, was – despite the lying reminiscences of old men like Councillor Duxbury who remembered sheep-troughs where the X-L Disc Bar now stands – exactly like any other High Street in Great Britain. Woolworth's looked like Woolworth's, the Odeon looked like the Odeon, and the *Stradhoughton Echo*'s own office, which Man o' the Dales must have seen, looked like a public lavatory in honest native white tile. I had a fairly passionate set-piece all worked out on the subject of rugged Yorkshire towns, with their rugged neon signs and their rugged plate-glass and plastic shop-fronts, but so far nobody had given me the opportunity to start up on the theme.

'Dark satanic mills I can put up with,' I would say, pushing my tobacco pouch along the bar counter. 'They're part of the picture. But' – puff, puff – 'when it comes to dark satanic power stations, dark satanic housing estates, and dark satanic teashops –'

'That's the trouble with you youngsters,' said Man o' the Dales, propping his leather-patched elbows on the seasoned bar. 'You want progress, but you want all the Yorkshire tradition as well. You can't have both.'

'I want progress,' I retorted, making with the briar. 'But I want a Yorkshire tradition of progress.'

'That's good. Can I use that?' said Man o' the Dales.

Anyway, satanic or not, it was the usual Saturday morning down in town, the fat women rolling along on their bad feet like toy clowns in pudding basins, the grey-faced men reviewing the sporting pinks. Along Market Street, where the new glass-fronted shops spilled out their sagging lengths of plywood and linoleum, there were still the old-fashioned stalls, lining the gutter with small rotten apples and purple tissue paper. The men shouted: 'Do I ask fifteen bob, do I ask twelve and a tanner, I do *not*. I do not ask you for ten bob. I do not ask you for three half crowns. Gimme five bob, five bob, five bob, five bob, five bob.' Frowning women, their black, scratched handbags crammed with half-digested grievances, pushed through the vegetable stalls to the steps of the rates office.

Off Market Street there was a little alley called St Botolph's Passage, the centre of most of Stradhoughton's ready-money betting. Besides the bookies' shops, the stinking urinal, the sly chemist's with red rubber gloves and big sex books in the window, and the obscure one-man businesses mooning behind the dark doorways, there was a pub, a dyer's and cleaner's, and Shadrack and Duxbury's tasteful funerals. Many were the jokes about St Botolph and his passage, but even more were those about the dyers and the undertakers.

The exterior of Shadrack's, where I now paused to take my traditional deep breath before entering, showed a conflict of personalities between young Shadrack and old Duxbury, the two partners. Young Shadrack, taking advantage of Duxbury's only trip abroad, a reciprocal visit by the town council to Lyons (described by Man o' the Dales as the Stradhoughton of France), had pulled out the Dickensian windows, bottle-glass and all, and substituted modern plate-glass and a shop sign of raised stainless-steel lettering. Thus another piece of old Stradhoughton bit the dust and the new effect was of a chip shop on a suburban housing estate. Councillor Duxbury had returned only just in time to salve the old window-dressing from the wreckage, and this remained: a smudgy sign by Stamp reading 'Tasteful Funerals, "Night or Day Service"' (which, as my other colleague Arthur had said, needed only an exclamation mark in brackets to complete it) and a piece of purple cloth on which there was deposited a white vase, the shape of a lead weight, inscribed to the memory of a certain Josiah Olroyd. The reason Josiah Olroyd's vase was in Shadrack's window and not in the corporation cemetery was that his name had been misspelled, and the family had not unreasonably refused to accept the goods ordered. The Olroyd vase always served to remind me of a ghastly error with some coffin nameplates in which I had been involved, a business that was far from finished yet, and it was with this thought uppermost in a fairly crowded mind that, ninety minutes late, I entered Shadrack and Duxbury's.

The shop-bell rang and, behaving exactly like a Pavlov

dog, Stamp got up and began, elaborately, to put on his coat.

'Must be going-home time, Fisher's come,' he said.

I ignored him and addressed Arthur.

'Is buggerlugs in?' I jerked my head towards Shadrack's door.

'Just come in this minute,' said Arthur. 'You can say you were in the bog.'

I hissed with relief and flopped down at my desk, between Stamp and Arthur. Every day, sitting tensed at the front of the bus, pushing it with my hands to make it faster, I had this race to the office with Shadrack. Duxbury didn't matter; he never came rolling in until eleven and in any case he was so old that he could never remember who worked for him. It was Shadrack, with his little notebooks, and the propelling pencil rattling against his teeth, who gave all the trouble. 'It's been noticed that you were half an hour late again this morning.' He always said 'It's been noticed'. 'It's been noticed that you haven't sent those accounts off yet.'

'I'm off to tell him what time you came in,' sniggered Stamp, and I was obliged to murmur 'You do', the passing acknowledgement of his feeble jest. Stamp called himself a 'clurk' and did not go very much beyond jokes of the Mary-Rose-sat-on-a-pin-Mary-Rose variety. He now started on his morning performance.

'Hey, that tart on telly last night! Where she bent forward over that piano! *Coarrrr!*'

It was the first duty of Arthur and myself to nip this quietly in the bud.

'What make?' said Arthur innocently.

'What make what?'

'What make was the piano?'

Stamp sneered: 'Oh, har har. Some say good old Arthur.

26

We got down to our work, what there was of it. Shadrack and Duxbury's was dull and comfortable as offices go. It was done throughout in sleepy chocolate woodwork, which Shadrack, dreaming of pinewood desks and Finnish wall papers, had not yet got his hands on. Our task was to do the letters, make up the funeral accounts, run the errands, and greet prospective customers with a suitably gloomy expression before shuffling them off on to Shadrack. September was a quiet month and Saturday was a quiet morning; we all had our own pursuits to work on. Stamp, head on one side, tongue cocked out of the corner of his mouth, spent most of his time making inky posters for the youth club. *'Have you paid your "subs"? If not, "why not"! ! !'* Arthur and I would sit around trying to write songs together, or sometimes I would tinker with *The Two Schools at Gripminster.*

'You couldn't see what make it was, she was bending too far over it,' Stamp said at last. I did not look at him, but I knew that he was describing a bosom with his hands.

'Penny's dropped,' Arthur said.

'Penny-farthing more like,' I said. 'It's been earning interest while he thought that one up.'

'Write that one down,' Arthur said.

'Joke over,' said Stamp.

There was nothing in the in-tray. I got *The Two Schools at Gripminster* out of my desk drawer and stared vacantly at what I had written of my thirty-four thousand words. *' "I say, weed! Aren't you a new bug?" Sammy Brown turned to greet the tall, freckle-faced boy who walked across the quad towards him. Sammy's second name was appropriate – for the face of this sturdy young fellow was as brown as a berry. W. Fisher. William Fisher. The Two Schools at Gripminster, by William Fisher. William L. Fisher. W. L. Fisher. Two-School Sammy, by W. L. P.*

Fisher. *Two Schools at Gripminster: A Sammy Brown Story* by W. L. P. Fisher. *The Sammy Brown Omnibus.* W. *Lashwood Fisher.* W. *de L Fisher.*' I looked at it for some time, thought '*William Fisher: His Life and Times*' but did not write it down, then put the paper back in the drawer. The four chunky calendars under my pullover hurt my chest when I leaned forward over the desk. I began thinking of Danny Boon and the letter I had better write to him, and about Shadrack and the letter I had better write to *him*.

'I've got something unpleasant to say to our Mr Shadrack this morning,' I said to Arthur.

'You've got something unpleasant to say to our Mr Shadrack this morning?' repeated Arthur, dropping into the Mr Bones and Mr Jones routine in which we conducted most of our exchanges. I decided not to tell Arthur just yet about the London business but to while half an hour away in the usual manner. 'Anything I say to Mr Shadrack would be unpleasant,' I said.

'Kindly leave the undertaker's,' Arthur said.

'Tell me, Mr Crabtree, what are the Poles doing in Russia?'

'I don't know, Mr Fisher, what are the Poles doing in Russia?'

'Holding up the telegraph wires, same as everywhere else.'

'That's not what these ladies and gentlemen have come to hear.'

I jumped to my feet, clutching the ruler from my desk. 'Have a care, Mr Crabtree! If I fire this rod it'll be curtains for you!'

'Why so, Mr Fisher?'

'It's a curtain rod.'

'I don't wish to know that.'

Stamp plodded in: 'Same here, it's got whiskers on it, that one.' We had explained to him fifty times over that that was the whole bloody *point*, but the idea would not sink in. It always led Stamp to his own jokes.

'If a barber shaves a barber, who talks?'

Arthur and I, deadpan, said: 'Who?'

'Joke over,' Stamp said, weakly. He went back to the poster he was doing for a pea-and-pie supper out Treadmill way. Arthur started typing out the new song we had written. I got going on the letter.

Dear Mr Boon,
  Many thanks for your letter of September 2 –
Dear Mr Boon,
  Yes! I should be delighted to come to London –
Dear Mr Boon,
  I will be in London next Saturday –

The idea of being in London next Saturday, put down on paper and staring me in the face, filled my bowels with quick-flushing terror. For as long as I could remember, I had been enjoying rich slabs of No. 1 thinking about London, coughing my way through the fog to the Odd Man Out Club, Chelsea, with its chess tables and friendly, intelligent girls. I was joint editor, with the smiling 'Jock' Osonolu, a Nigerian student, of the club's sensational wall-sheet, modelled somewhat on the lines of the Ambrosia *Times-Advocate*. I would live in a studio high over the Embankment, sometimes with a girl called Ann, a Londoner herself and as vivacious as they come, but more often with Liz, not Liz as she actually existed but touched up with a No. 1 ponytail to become my collaborator on a play for theatre in the round. Sometimes I could see myself starving on the Embankment, the tramp-poet; and now, sitting at my desk, the idea of *actually* starving on the Embankment suddenly presented itself to me. I switched over into the No. 2 thinking with a grinding of the points inside my stomach and there I was, feeling for the actual pangs of hunger and counting the hot pennies in my pocket. Five shillings left, one egg and chips leaves three and nine, doss down at Rowton House, two and nine. Evening paper two-pence-halfpenny, breakfast a tanner, call it two bob, two bob, two bob. I do not ask for ten bob, ladies, I do not ask you for three half crowns. Gimme two bob, two bob, two bob, two bob, and back I was on the No. 1, the poet stall-holder of Petticoat Lane.

The door-bell tinkled and we put on our funeral faces but it was nobody, only Councillor Duxbury. He crossed the floor to his own office with an old man's shuffle, putting all his thought into the grip of his stick and the pattern of the faded, broken lino. A thick, good coat sat heavily on his bowed back, and there were enamelled medallions on his watch-chain. At the door of his room he half-turned, moving his whole body like an old robot, and muttered: 'Morning, lads.'

We chanted, half-dutifully, half-ironically: 'Good morning, Councillor Duxbury,' and directly the door was closed, began our imitation of him. 'It's *Coun*cillor Duxbury, lad, *Coun*cillor Duxbury. Tha wun't call Lord Harewood mister, would tha? *Coun*cillor, that's mah title. Now think on.'

'Ah'm just about thraiped,' said Arthur in broad dialect. The word was one we had made up to use in the Yorkshire dialect routine, where we took the Michael out of Councillor Duxbury and people like him. Duxbury prided himself on his dialect which was practically unintelligible even to seasoned Yorkshiremen.

'Tha's getten more bracken ivvery day, lad,' I said.

'Aye, an' fair scritten anall,' said Arthur.

30

'Tha mun laik wi' t' gangling-iron.'

'Aye.'

We swung into the other half of the routine, which was
Councillor Duxbury remembering, as he did every birthday
in an interview with the *Stradhoughton Echo*. Arthur
screwed up his face into the lined old man's wrinkles and
said:

'Course, all this were fields when I were a lad.'

'– and course, ah'd nobbut one clog to mah feet when ah
come to Stradhoughton,' I said in the wheezing voice.

'Tha could get a meat pie and change out o' fourpence –'

'Aye, an' a box at t' Empire and a cab home at t' end on
it.'

'Ah had to tak' a cab home because ah only had one clog,'
said Arthur.

'Oh, I'll *use* that,' I said, resuming my normal voice.

'*Bastard.*'

'Bar-steward,' said Stamp, automatically.

Every Saturday night I did a club turn down at one of
the pubs in Clogiron Lane, near where we lived. It was a
comedy act, but not the kind of thing Danny Boon would
be interested in: a slow-burning, Yorkshire monologue that
was drummed up mainly by Arthur and me at these sessions
in the office. Arthur was more interested in the singing side.
He did a turn with the band at the Roxy twice a week,
Wednesdays and Saturdays, trying vainly to get them to
play the songs we had written between us. When my own
turn was finished I would hurry over to the Roxy to listen to
him, pretending that I was whisking from one theatre to
another to catch a promising act that I was thinking of
booking.

As for Stamp, he did nothing at all except loll about in
the Roxy, waving his arms about and mouthing 'Wood-
chopper's Ball' when the band played it.

'Saw that bint you used to knock about with 's morning,' he said, when the Duxbury routine was over.

'You what?'

'That bint. Her that always used to be ringing you up.'

I ran flippantly back through the sequence of disasters, Audrey, Peggy, Lil, that bint from Morecambe. A depression grew inside me as I traced them back almost to my schooldays. When I recognized the depression, I knew whom he was talking about.

I said lightly, knowing what was coming: '*What* bint, for Christ sake?'

'That scruffy-looking one. Her that always wore that suède coat.'

I poured unconcern into my voice. 'Who – Liz What's-her-name?'

'Yer, Woodbine Lizzy. Shags like a rattlesnake, doesn't she? She hasn't got a new coat yet.'

So Liz was back in town. I liked the phrase 'back in town', as though she had just ridden in on a horse, and I toyed with it for a second, so as not to think about her. Drive you out of town. City limits. Get out of town, Logan, I'm warning you for the last time.

It was a month ago since she had left last, with only a chance good-bye, and this time there had been no postcards. It was part of the nature of Liz to disappear from time to time and I was proud of her bohemianism, crediting her with a soul-deep need to get away and straighten out her personality, or to find herself, or something; but in less romantic moments I would fall to wondering whether she was tarting round the streets with some American airman. I had no real feeling for her, but there was always some kind of pain when she went away, and when the pain yielded nothing, I converted it, like an alchemist busy with the seaweed, into something approaching love.

'Where did you see her?' I asked.

'*I* don't know. Walking up Infirmary Street,' said Stamp. 'Why, frightened she's got another boy friend?' he said in his nauseating, elbow-prodding way.

I said carefully: 'Thought she'd gone to Canada or somewhere,' naming the first country that came into my head.

'What's she come back for, then?' said Stamp.

I was trying to find a cautious way of going on with it when Arthur came to the rescue. He had been handling the switchboard.

'Never use a preposition to end a sentence with,' he said.

I often told myself that I had no friends, only allies, banded together in some kind of conspiracy against the others. Arthur was one of them. We spoke together mainly in catchphrases, hidden words that the others could not understand.

'I must ask you to not split infinitives,' I said gratefully, in the light relieved voice.

'Hear about the bloke who shot the owl?' said Arthur. 'It kept saying to who instead of to whom.'

'Shouldn't it be Who's Whom instead of Who's Who?' I said, not for the first time that week. Even our ordinary conversations were like the soft-shoe shuffle routine with which we enlivened the ordinary day. I was perfectly aware that I was stalling, and I turned back to Stamp.

'Did you speak to her?'

'Speak to who?'

'To whom. Woodbine Lizzy,' I said, burning with shame for using the nickname Stamp had given her.

'No, just said hullo. She was with somebody,' he said, as though it did not matter. But it was my first bit of emotional meat this morning, and I was determined to make it matter, and to get the pain back inside where it belonged.

'Who was she with?'

33

'*I* don't know, I don't ask people for their autographs. What's up, are you jealous, eh? Eh?' He pronounced the word 'jealous' as though it were something he had dug up out of the garden, still hot and writhing.

The door-bell tinkled again. 'Shop,' called Arthur softly, getting up. A small woman, all the best clothes she had collected together on her body, peered round the door. 'Is this where you come to arrange for t' funerals?'

Arthur walked respectfully over to the counter.

'Ah've been in t' wrong shop. Ah thought it were next door.' She leaned heavily on the counter, her arms folded against it, and began to spell out her name.

I got up, stiffly, feeling the calendars under my pullover, and the waft of cold air when I separated them from my shirt. 'Off for a slash,' I muttered to Stamp and went downstairs among the cardboard boxes of shrouds and coffin handles. I pottered aimlessly among the wreath-cards and the bales of satin lining, looking for something worth having, and then went into the lavatory.

The lavatory at Shadrack and Duxbury's had a little shaving mirror on the door, where Shadrack could inspect his boils. More as a matter of routine than anything else, I put my tongue out and looked at it. There were some lumps at the back of my throat that I had never noticed before. Putting the subject of Liz on one side, I began putting my tongue between my fingers, seeing if the lumps got worse farther down and wondering if this were the beginning of gingivitis which Stamp, with some justice, had suffered the year before. The sharp pain in my chest I located as the edge of the calendars shoving against my ribs. I checked the bolt on the door again, and took the calendars out from under my pullover. They were dog-eared now, with well-established creases across the envelopes. The top one was addressed to an old mother superior at the nunnery down by the canal. I took out the calendar and folded the envelope in four, a surprising bulkiness. I rammed the envelope into my side-pocket, where the passion pills were, and held the calendar in my hands, the other three grimly gripped under my arm.

There was a brown-printed page for each month. The months tore off, and at the bottom of each month was a quotation. I knew some of them by heart. *'The only riches you will take to heaven are those you give away'* – January. *'Think all you speak, but speak not all you think'* – February. *'It takes sixty muscles to frown, but only thirteen to smile. Why waste energy'* – April. I tore off the leaves one by one and dropped them into the lavatory. When I had reached October, *'It is a gude heart that says nae ill, but a better heart that thinks none,'* I decided that that was enough for the time being and pulled the length of rough string that served for a chain. As the screwed-up pieces of paper swam around in the water I tried hurriedly to count them, January to October inclusive, ten pages, in case I had dropped one on the floor for Shadrack to find and investigate. The water resumed its own level. To my horror, about half a dozen calendar leaves, soggy and still swimming, remained. I began gnawing at my lower lip and checking the signs of panic, heart, sweaty palms, tingling ankles, like a mechanic servicing a car. I flushed the lavatory again but there was only a heavy zinking noise and a trickle of water as the ballcock protested. I perched myself on the side of the scrubbed seat and waited, staring at the mother superior's calendar. *'Those who bring sunshine to the lives of others cannot keep it from themselves'* – November.

I could hear Councillor Duxbury clumping about upstairs, aimlessly opening drawers and counting his money. Without much effort, I drifted into Ambrosia, where the Grand Yeomanry were still limping past the war memorial, their left arms raised in salute. *'It is often wondered how the left-hand salute, peculiar to Ambrosia, originated. Accounts differ, but the most widely-accepted explanation is that of the seven men who survived the Battle of Wakefield all, by an amazing coincidence, had lost their right arms. It was necessary for them to salute their President –'*

The stairs creaked and there were footsteps on the stone floor outside. Somebody rattled the loose knob of the lavatory door. I waited for them to go away, but I could hear the heavy breathing. I began to start up a tuneless whistling so that they would know the booth was engaged, and to back-track through my recent thoughts to check that I had not been talking to myself. The door-rattling continued.

'Someone in here,' I called.

I heard the voice of Stamp: 'What you doing, man, writing your will out?'

It was the kind of remark Gran would shout up the stairs at home. 'Piss off,' I shouted, as I would dearly have loved to shout at Gran in the same situation. Stamp began pawing at the door. If there had been a keyhole he would have been peeping through it by now.

'No writing mucky words on the walls!' he called. I did not reply. Stamp began quoting, *'Gentlemen, you have the future of England in your hands.'* The last few words were breathless and accompanied by a scraping noise on the floor, and it was obvious that he was jumping up and down, trying to peer over the top of the door. 'Naff off, Stamp, for Christ sake!' I called. I stood up. The soggy little balls of paper were still in the lavatory but I dared not pull the chain again while Stamp was still there. I picked up the other calendars from the floor where I had put them and stuck them back inside my pullover, trying not to let the stiff paper crackle. Outside, Stamp began grunting in what he imagined to be an imitation of a man in the throes of constipation.

'Bet you're reading a mucky book,' he said in a hoarse whisper through the door. I let him ramble on. 'Bet y'are, bet you're reading a mucky book. *"His hand caressed her silken knee —"* ', and excited by his own fevered images, he began to mouth obscenities through the cracks in the deep green door.

There was another sound on the stairs, this time the furry padding of light suède shoes, and I could imagine the yellow socks and the chocolate-brown gaberdines that went with them. I heard the nasal, nosey voice of Shadrack: 'Haven't you anything to do upstairs, Stamp?' and Stamp, crashing his voice into second gear to simulate something approaching respect, saying: 'Just waiting to go into the toilet, Mr Shadrack.'

'Yes, it's thought some of you spend too much time down here. Far too much time,' said Shadrack. He picked at words as other people picked at spots.

Shadrack was not the stock cartoon undertaker, although he would have made a good model for other stock cartoons, notably the one concerning the psychiatrist's couch. He was, for a start, only about twenty-five years old, although grown old with quick experience, like forced rhubarb. His general approach and demeanour was that of the second-hand car salesman, and he had in fact at one time been one in the south. He was in the undertaking business because his old man was in it before him and old Shadrack had been, so to speak, young Shadrack's first account. After that he rarely attended funerals and would indeed have found it difficult in view of the R.A.F. blazer and the canary-coloured pullover which, sported being the word, he sported. But he was useful to the firm in that, besides having inherited half of it, he could get round old ladies.

He was a member of most churches in Stradhoughton and to my certain knowledge was a card-carrying Unitarian, a Baptist, a Methodist, and both High and Low Church.

'You'd better get up into the office,' I heard him say to Stamp. 'I've got to go out.'

Stamp shuffled off, murmuring inarticulate servilities. I called: 'Is that you, Mr Shadrack?'

He either did not hear or did not choose to hear, but started fidgeting among the coffin handles, just outside the lavatory door.

'Is that Mr Shadrack?'

'Yes, there's someone waiting to come in there,' he said testily.

'Shan't be a minute,' I called in the high monotone of a man hailing down from the attic. 'I was wondering if I could see you before you go out?'

'What?'

The voice I had chosen was beginning to sound ridiculous. 'Was wondering if I could *see* you, 'fore you go out.'

Shadrack called back: 'Yes, I've been thinking it's about time we had a little talk.' Perched in my cold cell, I wondered miserably what he meant by that and skimmed quickly through a condensed inventory of the things he might know about.

'Well I can't see you now, Fisher, I've got to arrange a funeral. You'll have to come back after lunch.'

Every Saturday afternoon, after the firm had closed for the day, Shadrack started messing about with a drawing-board he kept in his office. He was trying to design a contemporary coffin. So far he had not had the nerve to try and interest Councillor Duxbury in the project, the Councillor being an oak and brass fittings man, but he spent a lot of time drawing streamlined caskets, as he called them, on yellow scratchpads. One thing he had succeeded in doing was fitting out the funeral fleet, including the hearse, with a radio system. When there was a funeral Shadrack would sit in his office saying 'Able-Peter, Able-Peter, over' into a microphone. So far as I could remember, nobody ever answered him, and I could not think what he would have said if they had, except: 'Divert funeral to Manston Lane Chapel, over.' He kept a copy of *The Loved One* in his desk, but only to get ideas.

I called: 'Righto, Mr Shadrack.' I did not know whether he had gone back upstairs or whether he was still prowling about outside. Not to take chances, I flushed the lavatory again. When the water had flowed away there were two little balls of paper still floating about. I took the thick, folded envelope out of my pocket and, my face disfigured by nausea, scooped the two soggy leaves of calendar out of the lavatory. I stuffed them inside the envelope and crammed it into my pocket. Then I unbolted the door. Shadrack was standing immediately behind, and he glanced me up and down like a customs officer as I passed.

Upstairs, Arthur had his raincoat on, waiting to go out for coffee. Before I could speak, Stamp called: 'Here he is! Reading mucky books in the bog!' I reached for my own raincoat. Stamp shouted, hoarsely so that Shadrack could not hear downstairs, 'Let's have a read! What you got, *Lady Chatterley's Lover*?' He dived forward and began scragging me around the stomach. He felt the stiff calendars under my pullover and bellowed in triumph: 'He has! He has! He's got a mucky book under his jersey! *Coarrr!* Dirty old man!'

I seized his wrists and snapped: '*Take* your frigging mucky hands off my pullover, stupid-looking crow!'

'Give us your mucky book,' pleaded Stamp, wheezing in his joke-over way.

Arthur was twiddling the door-handle impatiently. 'Are you coming out for coffee?' I pulled my coat on.

'Don't be all day, you two, I want some,' said Stamp.

'Get stuffed,' I said.

'Don't take any wooden bodies,' Arthur called from the door.

'Get stuffed,' said Stamp.

3

STRADHOUGHTON was littered with objects for our derision. We would make Fascist speeches from the steps of the rates office, and we had been in trouble more than once for doing our Tommy Atkins routine under the war memorial in Town Square. Sometimes we would walk down Market Street shouting 'Apples a pound pears' to confuse the costermongers with their leather jackets and their Max Miller patter.

The memorial vase to Josiah Olroyd in Shadrack's window always triggered off the trouble at t' mill routine, a kind of serial with Arthur taking the part of Olroyd and I the wayward son.

As we begun to walk down St Botolph's Passage, Arthur struck up: 'Ther's allus been an Olroyd at Olroyd's mill, and ther allus will be. Now you come 'ere with your college ways and you want none of it!'

'But father! We must all live our lives according to our lights –' I began in the high-pitched university voice.

'Don't gi' me any o' yon fancy talk!' said Arthur, reflecting with suspicious accuracy the tone of the old man at breakfast. 'You broke your mother's heart, lad. Do you know that?'

'Father! The men! They're coming up the drive!'

We turned into Market Street swinging our arms from side to side like men on a lynching spree. Arthur held up an imaginary lantern.

'Oh, so it's thee, Ned Leather! Ye'd turn against me, would ye?'

In the university voice: 'Now, Leather, what's afoot?' –
and before Arthur could seize the part for himself, I
switched accents and got into the character of Ned Leather.
'Oh, so it's the young lord and master up from Oxford and
Cambridge, is it? We'll see about thee in a minute, im-
pudent young pup!'

Arthur, piqued as always because I had got the Ned
Leather dialogue for myself, dropped the routine. We
walked in silence past the pork butchers and the dry-
cleaning shops stuffed with yellow peg-board notices, and
turned into Moorgate. I was in a fairly schizophrenic state
of mind. I was looking into the distance to catch a glimpse
of Liz in her green suède jacket, but at the same time
tensing myself ready to meet Rita, who worked in the café
where we had our morning break. Digging my hands into
my pockets I could feel Stamp's little box of passion pills,
and this reminded me of the Witch. I was thinking con-
fusedly about all three of them when Arthur began clearing his throat to adjust his voice into ordinary speech. I
had noticed before that when he had something unpalat-
able to say he would preface it with a bit of clowning from
either the trouble at t' mill or Duxbury routines.

'My mother's been saying how nice it would be if our
families could get together,' he said at length.

'God forbid,' I said.

A star feature of my No. 2 thinking was a morbid dread
of Arthur's mother meeting *my* mother. I had once told
Arthur's mother, in a loose moment, that I had a sister
called Sheila.

'And she wants to send some old toys to the kids as
well,' said Arthur.

'All contributions gratefully received,' I said, still flip-
pant.

I wondered to myself why I had ever started it. In the

42

odd bored moments, waiting for Arthur to tie his tie in the quiet ticking house where he lived, I had got Sheila married to a grocer's assistant in the market called Eric. Eric, prospering, now had three shops of his own, two in Leeds and one in Bradford. As conversation lagged between me and Arthur's mother, I had given Eric and Sheila two children; Norma, now aged three, and Michael, aged one and a half. Michael had unfortunately been born with a twisted foot, but medical skill on the part of one Dr Ubu, an Indian attached to Leeds University, had left him with a hardly noticeable limp. Arthur had often asked me to kill my sister off and put the kids in a home, but the long-drawn-out mourning and a Shadrack and Duxbury funeral were beyond me. I felt indignant that his mother should take so much interest in a family of what, after all, were total strangers to her.

'Anyway, don't let your mother come near *our* house,' I said. 'I've told 'em she's in hospital with a broken leg.' This was the truth, not the truth that Arthur's mother was in hospital, but the truth that I, to tide me over some awkward moment, had said she was.

'The trouble with you, cocker, is you're a pathological bloody liar,' said Arthur.

'Well, I've seen the psychiatrist and –'

'Kindly leave the couch.'

We resumed our silence, this one more uncomfortable than the last. I saw that we had a hundred yards to go before the café, and I switched into the No. 1 thinking for a brief morning bulletin. My No. 1 mother was on: 'Billy, is this another of your *ghastly* practical jokes?' The idea of switching in brought a radio into my mind, a little white portable singing among the rubber-plants on the low-slung shelves as I mixed the drinks before dinner. My No. 1 mother said: 'Do for God's sake turn off that bloody

43

box!' but this brought me back to the Vim-scoured face of my actual mother and her letter to 'Housewives' Choice'. Cornered between the Guilt Chest and the spectre of *Arthur's* mother it was with some relief that I saw that we were outside the glassy, glacial doors of the Kit-Kat café and its monstrous, wobbling plaster sundae.

The Kit-Kat was another example of Stradhoughton moving with the times, or rather dragging its wooden leg about five paces behind the times. The plaster sundae was all that was supposed to be left of a former tradition of throbbing urns, slophouse cooking, and the thin tide of biscuit crumbs and tomato pips that was symbolic of Stradhoughton public catering. The Kit-Kat was now a coffee bar, or thought it was. It had a cackling espresso machine, a few empty plant-pots, and about half a dozen glass plates with brown sugar stuck all over them. The stippled walls, although redecorated, remained straight milkbar: a kind of Theatre Royal backcloth showing Dick Whittington and his cat hiking it across some of the more rolling dales. Where the coffee-bar element really fell down, however, was in the personality of Rita, on whom I was now training the sights of my anxiety. With her shiny white overall, her mottled blonde hair, and her thick red lips, she could have transmogrified the Great Northern Hotel itself into a steamy milkbar with one wipe of her tea-cloth.

'You know, dark satanic mills I can put up with,' I said as we climbed on the wobbling stools. 'But when it comes to dark satanic power stations, dark satanic housing estates, and dark satanic coffee bars –'

'Put on another record, kid, we've heard that one before,' said Arthur in a surprisingly coarse voice.

The Kit-Kat was full of people of the Stamp variety, all making hideous puns and leaning heavily on the I've-stopped-smoking-I-do-it-every-day kind of conversation.

44

Rita was serving chocolate Penguins to a mob of cyclists at the other end of the bar. She waved, tinkling her fingers as though playing the piano, and I waved back.

'Watch your pockets, fellers! See if they measure you up!' This was the standard greeting from the Stamp crowd for any of us from Shadrack and Duxbury's, and the reply was: 'Drop dead.' – 'Will you bury me if I do?' – 'Free of charge, mate,' and that was the end of the responses.

'No, look, seriously though, you haven't said our old woman's broken her leg, have you?' said Arthur.

'Course I have.'

'She'll go bloody bald, man! What if I'd called at your house and your old woman had asked after her?'

'You would have risen to the occasion,' I said mock-heroically.

'The liefulness is terrific,' said Arthur, entering reluctantly into the mood of banter.

I toyed with the Perspex-covered menu, advertising onion soup that did not exist. 'Think Stamp really *did* see Liz this morning?' I said.

'*I* don't bloody know, man,' Arthur said, adding irrelevantly: 'I've lost track of your sex-life.'

'No, I was just wondering,' I said.

Arthur nodded furtively up the bar towards Rita, who was still engaged in primitive verbal by-play with the cyclists. 'Listen,' he whispered hoarsely. 'Which one of 'em are you supposed to be engaged to – her or the Witch?'

'That's an academic question.'

'Well you can't be engaged to them both at once, for Christ sake,' said Arthur.

I turned a wryly-haunted face to him. 'How much have you got *says* I can't?'

45

'Jesus wept!' said Arthur.

The position with Rita was that I had had my eye on her ever since she moved into the Kit-Kat from a transport café in the Huddersfield Road, her natural habitat. A life of mechanical badinage with lorry drivers had left her somewhat low on the conversational level, but she was a good, or at least a stolid, listener. The previous night, in an eloquent mood, I had proposed marriage and Rita, probably thinking it bad manners to refuse, had accepted. The only complicated thing was that I was already engaged to the Witch, so that Rita's status was roughly that of first reserve in the matrimonial team.

'Well which one of them's got the naffing *engagement* ring?' whispered Arthur.

I said: 'Well, the Witch had it, only I've got it back. I'm supposed to be getting it adjusted at the jeweller's.' The Witch's engagement ring in its little blue box, I now remembered, was among the items of loot in my jacket pockets. I wondered in a fleeting panic what they would make of it all if I was knocked down by a bus and my possessions were sent home to Hillcrest.

'Who's next on the list – Woodbine Lizzie?' said Arthur.

'No,' I said. 'We can accept no further engagements.'

'Write that down,' said Arthur.

At the other end of the counter, Rita's conversation with the cyclists ended abruptly as one of them stumbled over the tight boundaries of propriety. She pitched her mill-tinged, masculine voice at its most raucous to call back 'Gerron home, yer mother wants yer boots for loaftins!' as she turned away and sauntered down the bar, running the gauntlet of standard raillery as she came to greet us. There was no doubt at all that the Stamp crowd had something to whistle about. Rita was a natural for

46

every beauty contest where personality was not a factor. She had already been Miss Stradhoughton, and she had been voted The Girl We Would Most Like To Crash The Sound Barrier With by some American airmen.

Arthur slumped himself ape-fashion across the bar. 'Gimme two cawfees, ham on rye, slice blueberry pie,' he drawled, a snatch from the two Yanks in a drugstore routine which we were still perfecting.

'Oo, look what's crawled out of the cheese,' said Rita. 'Marlon Brando.'

'If I fire this rod it'll be curtains for you, sister,' said Arthur out of the side of his mouth.

'Yer, cos it's a curtain rod. Tell us summat we don't know.'

'Well come on, love, pour us a coffee,' I said, speaking for the first time.

'Gerroff yer knees,' said Rita without rancour, strolling over to the espresso machine. So far there had been no sign from anybody, her, me, or anybody else, that we were engaged to be married.

Someone out of the Stamp crowd, preparing to leave, called out: 'Coming to the Odeon tonight, Rita, back row, eh?' Without turning round she called back: 'They wun't let you in, it's an "A" picture.'

Everybody I knew spoke in clichés, but Rita spoke as though she got her words out of a slot machine, whole sentences ready-packed in a disposable tinfoil wrapper. There was little meaning left in anything she actually said; her few rough phrases had been so worn through constant use that she now relied not on words but on the voice itself, and the modulation of the animal sounds it produced, to express the few thick slabs of meaning of which she was capable. In moments of tenderness a certain gruffness, like Woodbine smoke, would curl into her throat, but she had

47

long ago forgotten, and probably never knew, the vocabulary of human kindness.

She slopped the coffee in front of us, Joe's Café style,
and rested her elbows on the counter, her bosom – itself
a cliché, like a plaster relief given away by the women's
magazines – protruding over the bar. She now thought it
necessary to make some delicate reference to the fact that
we had had a momentous time of it the night before.

'What time did you get in last night?' she said.

' 'Bout one o'clock,' I said. 'Our old man went crackers
this morning. Should've heard him.'

'Me mam did as well. I've got to stop in on Monday.
Why, did you miss your bus or summat?'

'Yer – 'ad to walk,' I said, falling chameleon-like into
her own tongue.

'Why didn't you take a taxi, old man, old man?' said
Arthur in his Western Brothers voice.

'Oo, hark at Lord Muck,' said Rita. 'You should have
gone to Town Square, got an all-night bus.'

This was the sequence and rhythm of daylight love-play
as she knew it, a kind of oral footy-footy that was the
nearest she could get to intimate conversation.

'No, I like walking,' I said.

Rita said, 'Tramp, tramp, tramp, the boys are marching,'
in the derisory tone she used to apologize for putting her
tongue to a quotation. 'Anyway, you're lucky, you can
always get your shoes mended free.'

I was puzzled by the remark until I remembered, dredg-
ing among the fallen platitudes of the night before, an invitation I had made to Rita to come to Sunday tea. The
invitation had been make-weight, a kind of free coupon
along with the proposal, but in the course of it I had told
her that the old man was a cobbler with a shop down
Clogiron Lane.

48

'Oh, yer,' I said. 'Are you still going to the Roxy to-night?'

'Yer.'

'Have I to see you inside, or outside?'

'Are you kidding?'

'Just thought I'd get away without paying,' I said. It was standard, ready-to-use repartee, expected and indeed sought after. 'See you outside then, 'bout nine o'clock. Are you still coming for your tea tomorrow?'

'Yer, if you like. Anyway, we'll fix that up tonight,' she said.

Rita did not know it, but the matter was already fixed. The old man would be called away to inspect a load of Government surplus rubber heels in Harrogate, my mother would take the opportunity of a lift to visit my Aunt Polly in Otley or somewhere, and the tea would be postponed. I had not yet tackled the problem of the Roxy, to which I was also supposed to be going with the Witch. Arthur, by my side, was covering his face with his hands and making quiet cawing noises in a pantomime of amazement. I gave him a quick kick on the foot and felt in my pocket for the little blue box with the Witch's engagement ring in it.

'Try this on for size,' I said, sliding it casually across the counter.

'What, is it for me?' said Rita in her gormless way.

'Who do you think it's for, your mother?'

She opened the box and put the cheap, shiny engagement ring on her finger, as though expecting a practical joke. 'Just fits,' she said grudgingly. 'Why, you haven't *bought* it, have yer?'

'No, he knocked it off out of Woolworth's window,' said Arthur, who had started whistling tunelessly and looking up at the ceiling.

49

'Oo, it can speak!' jeered Rita. She changed her voice to find the unfamiliar tone of gratitude. 'Anyway, ta. I *won't* wear it now, cos you know what they're like in here.' I could see the picture of marriage forming in her mind, the white wedding, the drawers crammed full of blankets, the terrace house with the linoleum squares, the seagrass stools, and the novel horseshoe companion-set in satin-brass. I felt pleased to have brought her this temporary pleasure, but there was no time to lose, and already I was racing ahead with the No. 1 thinking, breaking the engagement with the big speech about incompatibility.

The glass doors of the Kit-Kat rocked open, and one of the burly lorry drivers with whom Rita had had barren and wintry affairs in the past shambled in. 'Look what the cat's brought in,' said Rita loudly. She slipped the engagement ring into her overall pocket and re-set her face into gum-chewing nonchalance.

I was smiling as we walked back to the office. 'What have *you* got to grin about?' said Arthur.

'Those who bring sunshine into the lives of others cannot keep it from themselves,' I said.

'You what?'

'A quotation from Messieurs Shadrack and Duxbury's calendars,' I said. The calendars were still warm and sharp under my pullover, but they had become a part of my clothing, like an armoured vest.

'You're going to be up for bloody bigamy, mate, that's what you're going to be up for,' said Arthur.

I tried to look as though I knew more than he did about my affairs, and we walked on along Moorgate.

'Have I told you I'm leaving?' I said, putting it as casually as I could.

'Yes, we've heard that one before as well,' said Arthur.

I wondered whether to tell him at all, or whether just

to vanish, turning up self-consciously in a camel-hair coat years later like somebody coming home in uniform.

'I'm going to London,' I said.

'What as – road-sweeper?'

'Ay road sweepah on the road – to fame!' I cried in the grandiloquent voice. When it came to the point, I was embarrassed about telling him. I added, in a shuffling kind of way: 'I've got that job with Danny Boon.'

'You haven't!'

'Yup. Scriptwriter, start next week.'

'Jammy bugger! Have you though, honest?'

'Course I have. Don't tell anybody, though, will you?'

'Course I won't. When did you fix *that* up, then?' Arthur was finding it hard to keep the traces of envy out of his voice.

'He sent me a letter.'

Arthur stopped abruptly in the middle of the street and gave me what my mother would have described as an old-fashioned look.

'*Let's* see it,' he said, holding his hand out resignedly.

'What?' I remembered where I had left the letter, in the pocket of the raincoat I used for a dressing-gown, and I wondered if my mother was snooping round reading it.

'Come on – letter,' said Arthur, clicking his fingers.

'I haven't got it with me.'

'No, thought not. I'll believe it when I see it.'

'All right, you wait till next week,' I said, trying hard to get into the spirit of jocular injured innocence, but succeeding only in the injured innocence.

'What's he paying you, then?' He was as bad as my mother.

'Wait till next week.'

'No, what's he paying you?'

'Wait till next week. You don't believe me, so wait till next *week*.'

We were back in St Botolph's Passage. I started on an indignant sliver of No. 1 thinking. 'The Danny Boon Show! Script by Billy Fisher, produced by –' Before I could get any further with this, I detected the pale shape of Stamp, hopping about in Shadrack's doorway, making an elaborate show of tutting and looking at his watch.

'Where've you been for your coffee – Bradford?'

'No, Wakefield,' I said, bad-tempered. Stamp buttoned his splitting leather gloves.

'The Witch has been ringing up for you,' he said. 'She rang up twice. I'm off to tell Rita you're two-timing her.'

'Piss off,' I said.

'Anyway, she said if she doesn't ring back, she wants to meet you at one o'clock, usual place.'

'She'll be lucky.'

'*Does she shag?*' said Stamp, speaking the phrase as though it were a headline. I snarled at him, half-raising my elbow, and went into the office.

4

AT the far end of St Botolph's Passage, past the green wrought-iron urinal, was a broken-down old lych-gate leading into the churchyard. St Botolph's, a dark, dank slum of a church, was the home of a Ladies' Guild, a choir, some mob called the Shining Hour, and about half a dozen other organizations, but so far as I knew it had no actual congregation except Shadrack, who went there sometimes looking for trade. The churchyard itself had long ago closed for business and most of the people in it had been carried away by the Black Death. It had a wayside pulpit whose message this week was: 'It is Better To Cry Over Spilt Milk Than To Try And Put It Back In The Bottle,' a saw that did not strike me for one as being particularly smart.

I reached the lych-gate at one o'clock, straight after work. The Witch was fond of the churchyard as a rendezvous. We had first met at the St Botolph's youth club and she was a great one for the sentimental associations. She was also very fond of the statues of little angels around the graves, which she thought beautiful. She shared with Shadrack a liking for the sloppy bits of verse over the more modern headstones. I would have liked to have seen her as Stradhoughton's first woman undertaker.

I sat down on the cracked stone bench inside the porch and collected at least some of my thoughts together. The first thing was to get the stack of creased calendars out from under my pullover. My stomach felt cramped and cold where they had been. I pulled the envelope of soggy paper gingerly out of my jacket pocket. Then I bundled the whole lot together and shoved it under the porch seat, where no one would ever look. That seemed to dispose of the calendars. I took out of my pocket the folded carbon copy of a letter I had written to Shadrack on the firm's notepaper when I got back from the Kit-Kat.

Dear Mr Shadrack,

With regret I must ask you to accept my resignation from Shadrack and Duxbury's. You probably know that while enjoying my work with the Firm exceedingly, I have always regarded it as a temporary career. I have now succeeded in obtaining a post with Mr Danny Boon, the London comedian, and I do feel that this is more in line with my future ambitions.

I realize that you are entitled to one week's notice, but under the circumstances I wonder if it would be possible to waive this formality. May I say how grateful I am for all the help you have given me during my stay with the Firm.

My best personal regards to yourself and Councillor Duxbury.

I was rather pleased with the letter, especially the bit about being grateful for Shadrack's help, but still apprehensive about the interview it would be necessary to have with him when I had finished with the Witch. I speculated idly on what he was getting at by saying it was about time we had a little talk. I looked out at the church clock and thought: never mind, in one hour it will all be over. I put the letter away again and began thinking about the Witch, the slow and impotent anger brewing up as it always did whenever I dwelt on her for any length of time.

The point about the Witch was that she was completely sexless. She was large, clean, and, as I knew to my cost,

54

wholesome. I had learned to dislike everything about her. I did not care, to begin with, for her face: the scrubbed, honest look, as healthy as porridge. I disliked her for her impeccable shorthand, her senseless, sensible shoes, and her handbag crammed with oranges. The Witch did nothing else but eat oranges. She had in fact been peeling a tangerine when I proposed to her during a youth-club hike to Ilkley Moor, and her way of consummating the idea had been to pop a tangerine quarter in my mouth. She had not been very much amused when I said, 'With this orange I thee wed'.

What I most disliked her for were the sugar-mouse kisses and the wrinkling-nose endearments which she seemed to think symbolized some kind of grand passion. I had already cured her of calling me 'pet lamb' by going 'Jesus H. Christ!' explosively when she said it. The Witch had said sententiously: 'Thou shalt not take the name of the Lord thy God in vain.' I disliked her for her sententiousness, too.

Part of the booty in my raincoat pockets was a dirty, crumpled bag of chocolates that had been there for months. I had bought them when Stamp handed over his white box of passion pills. 'You'll need snogging fodder to go with them,' he had explained. I took the chocolates out and inspected them. There had originally been a quarter of a pound, but as one opportunity after another slipped by, I had started to eat the odd chocolate and now there were only three left at the bottom of the bag, squashed and pale milky brown where they had melted and reset.

I put the paper bag on my knee. Fumbling about in my side-pocket I found Stamp's little box. That too was squashed almost flat by now, and most of the pills had rolled out into my pocket. I took one out, a little black bead that looked inedible. I wondered again where Stamp had got them and why he had given them to me, and also whether I could be prosecuted for what I was doing. 'Fisher, pay attention to me.' I fished around for the most presentable chocolate I could find, and tried to break it in half. It would not break properly. The chocolate covering splintered like an eggshell. It was an orange cream. I stuffed the round black bead into it and tried to press the chocolate whole again. The result was a filthy, squalid mess. I ate one of the remaining chocolates, and then the second, leaving only the doctored orange cream in its grimy paper bag.

I lit a cigarette and stood up, and stretched. Looking down St Botolph's Passage, I saw the Witch picking her way disdainfully through the swaying little groups of betting men who were beginning to congregate.

I felt the usual claustrophobia coming on as she marched up to the lych-gate, swinging her flared skirt like a Scot swings his kilt; an arrogant and not a sexy swing. I disliked the way she walked.

'Hullo,' the Witch said, coldly. She was always cold whenever we were anywhere that resembled a public place. Later on she would start the ear-nibbling, the nose-rubbing, and the baby talk. I said: 'Hullo, dalling.' I could not say darling. I was always trying, but it always came out as dalling.

We sat down together on the hard stone bench, under the spiders' webs. She eyed my Player's Weight viciously.

'How many cigarettes today?'

'Two,' I said.

'That's a good boy,' the Witch said, not quite half jokingly. She had got hold of some idea that I was smoking only five a day.

'Did you have a busy morning, dalling?' I said, giving her the soulful look. The Witch raised her eyeballs and blew upwards into her nostrils, a habit for which I was fast getting ready to clout her.

'Only about thirty letters from Mr *Turn*bull. Then he wanted me to type out an ag*ree*ment. ...' She rattled on in this vein for a few minutes.

'Did you talk to any *men* today?' I asked her. This was another idea she had. I was supposed to be jealous if she spoke to anybody else but me.

'Only Mr Turnbull, and Stamp when I rang up. Did you talk to any *gurls*?'

'Only the waitress when we went out for coffee.'

The Witch put on a mean expression. 'Couldn't your friend have spoken to her?' she pouted. She wouldn't speak Arthur's name, because even *that* was supposed to make me jealous.

'Dalling!' I said. 'Have you missed me?'

'Of course. Have you missed *me*?'

'Of course.'

That seemed to be the end of the inquisition. I grubbed around in my pocket and produced what was left of the chocolates. 'I saved this for you,' I said.

The Witch peered doubtfully into the sticky, brown-stained depths of the paper bag.

'It looks a bit *squashed*,' she said.

I took the chocolate between my fingers. 'Open wide.' She opened her mouth, probably to protest, and I rammed the chocolate in.

'Nasty!' said the Witch, gulping. I craned my neck, pretending to scratch my ear, and glanced out of the porch at the church clock. Stamp's passion pills were supposed to take effect after a quarter of an hour at most. He had once given me a description of a straight-laced, straight-faced Baloo who ran a Wolf Cub pack over in Leeds, and she had started pawing his jacket and whimpering only five minutes after he had slipped her a passion pill in the guise of an energy tablet.

'What were you ringing up about this morning? Anything?'

'Just wanted to talk to you, pet,' said the Witch, wriggling herself into a position of squeamish luxury. 'I've seen the most marvellous material to make curtains for our cottage. Honestly, you'll love it.'

Eating oranges in St Botolph's churchyard on the long crisp nights, or sometimes in the public shelter at the Corporation cemetery, another favourite spot, we had discussed at length the prospect of living in a thatched cottage in the middle of some unspecified field in Devon. At times, in the right mood, I could get quite enthusiastic over this rural image, and it had even figured in my No. 1 thinking before now. We had invented two children, little Barbara and little Billy – the prototypes, actually, of the imaginary family I had told Arthur's mother about – and we would discuss their future, and the village activities, and the pokerwork mottoes and all the rest of it.

'It's a sort of turquoise, with lovely little squiggles, like wineglasses –'

'Will it go with the yellow carpet?'

'No, but it'll go with the grey rugs in the kiddies' room.'

'Dalling!'

The yellow carpet and the grey rugs we had seen in a furniture-shop window on one of the interminable expeditions round Stradhoughton that the Witch sometimes dragged me on. They had all long ago been sold, but many had become part of the picture of the cottage, along with the Windsor chairs, the kettle singing on the hob, the bloody cat, and also the crinoline ladies from my bedroom wall at home.

We continued on these lines for a few minutes, until

at a reference to the wedding ceremony in some village church that would precede it all, the Witch stiffened.

'Have you got my engagement ring back yet?'

'Not yet, crikey! I only took it in this morning!' The Witch had parted with it suspiciously and reluctantly, not really convinced that it needed making smaller.

'I feel unclothed without it,' she said. She could not bring herself to say 'naked', yet, from her, 'unclothed' sounded even more obscene than she imagined nakedness to be. The reference reminded me that her time was nearly up.

'Let's go in the churchyard, away from all the people,' I said, standing up and taking her cold, chapped hands.

She looked doubtful again, into the dead-looking grave-yard. 'It's a bit *damp*, isn't it?'

'We'll sit on my raincoat. Come on, dalling.' I was almost dragging her to her feet. She got up half-heartedly. I put my arm around her awkwardly, and we walked up the broken tarmacadam path that was split down the middle like the crust of a cottage loaf, round to the back of the old church. Behind some ancient family vault was a black tree and a clump of burnt-looking, dirty old grass. Some-times I could persuade the Witch to sit down there, when she was not inspecting the vault and reading out aloud: 'Samuel Vaughan of this town, 1784; alfo his wife Emma, alfo his fon Saml, 1803.' I threw my raincoat on the shoddy grass and sat down. The Witch remained standing and I pulled her impatiently, almost forcibly, to her knees. By now, even allowing extra time for a difficult case, Stamp's pill should be working.

I stared at her gravely. 'I love you, dalling,' I said in the stilted way I couldn't help.

'Love *you*,' said the Witch, the stock response which she imagined the statement needed.

'Do you? Really and truly?'

'Of course I do.'

'Are you looking forward to getting married?'

'I think about it every minute of the day,' she said. I disliked the way she talked, tempering her flat northern voice with the mean, rounded vowels she had picked up at the Stradhoughton College of Commerce.

'Dalling,' I said. I began stroking her hair, moving as quickly as possible down the side of her face and on to her shoulder. She started the nose-rubbing act, and I seized her roughly and began kissing her. My lips on hers, I decided that I might as well try to get my tongue into her mouth but she kept her lips hard and closed. She pulled her face away suddenly so that my tongue slithered across her cheek and I was licking her, like a dog. It was not a very promising start.

'Don't ever fall in love with anybody else,' I said in the grave, sad voice. 'Love you, pet,' she said, leaning forward and nibbling my ear. I caught hold of her again and started fumbling, as idly as I could manage it, at the square buttons of her neat blue suit. The Witch struggled free again.

'Let's talk about our cottage, pet,' she said.

I counted seven to myself, seeing the red rash in front of my eyes. Obviously the pill was not working yet, or perhaps in the Witch's case I should have given her three or four.

'What about our cottage?' I said in the dreamy voice, containing myself.

'About the garden. Tell me about the garden.'

'We'll have a lovely garden,' I said, conjuring up a garden without much trouble. 'We'll have rose trees and daffodils and a lovely lawn with a swing for little Billy and little Barbara to play on, and we'll have our meals down by the lily pond in summer.'

'Do you think a lily pond is *safe*?' the Witch said

anxiously. 'What if the kiddies wandered too near and fell in?'

'We'll build a wall round it. No we won't, we won't have a pond at all. We'll have an old well. An old brick well where we draw the water. We'll make it our wishing well. Do you know what I'll wish?'

The Witch shook her head. She was sitting with her hands folded round her ankles like a child being told a bedtime story.

'Tell me what you'll wish, first,' I said.

'Oh – I'll wish that we'll always be happy and always love each other. What will *you* wish?' the Witch said.

'Better not tell you,' I said.

'Why not, pet?'

'You might be cross.'

'Why would I be cross?'

'Oh, I don't know. You might think me too, well, forward.' I glanced at her face for reaction. There was no reaction, and in fact when I looked at her again she seemed to have lost interest in the wishing well. I tried the lip-biting trick, combined with the heavy breathing.

'Barbara –' I began, making a couple of well-feigned false starts. 'Do you think it's wrong for people to have, you know, feelings?'

The Witch looked at me, too directly for my liking. 'Not if they're genuinely in love with each other,' she said.

'Like we are?'

'Yes,' she said, with less certainty.

'Would you think it wrong of me to have – feelings?'

The Witch, speaking briskly and firmly as though she had been waiting for this one and knew what to do about it, said: 'I think we ought to be married first.'

I looked at her sorrowfully. 'Dalling.' I got hold of the back of her neck and kissed her again. This time, making a bold decision, I put my hand on the thick, salmon-coloured stocking, just about at the shin. She stiffened, but did not do anything about it. I moved the hand up, the voice of Stamp floating into my mind, '*His hand caressed her silken knee.*' As soon as I reached her knee the Witch tore herself free.

'Are you feeling all right?' she said abruptly.

'Of course, dalling. Why?' I said, not moving my hand.

She looked pointedly down at her knee. 'Look where your hand is.'

I moved it away, sighing audibly.

'Dalling, don't you *want* me to touch you?'

The Witch shrugged.

'It seems – indecent, somehow.' I leaned forward to kiss her again, but she side-stepped abruptly, reaching for the leather shoulder-bag that she always carried with her.

'Would you like an energy tablet?' I said.

'No, thank you. I'm going to have an orange.'

I saw the red rash again and felt the old, impotent rage. I jumped to my feet. '*Ai'm* going to have an *or*-rainge!' I mimicked in a falsetto voice. '*Ai'm* going to have an *or*-rainge!' On a sudden urge I booted the leather handbag out of her hand and across the grass. It came to rest by an old gravestone, spilling out oranges and shorthand dictionaries.

'Billy!' said the witch sharply.

'You and your bloody oranges,' I said.

She sat there looking straight in front of her, obviously wondering whether it was going to be worth her while to start crying. I bent down and touched her hair.

'Sorry, dalling,' I said. I put on a shamefaced look and slunk off after her handbag. I started collecting her oranges and things together, looking closely into her open handbag to see if there were any letters from men I might be able to use. There was nothing but her lipstick and a few coins, but on the grass close by I saw something small and gleaming. I recognized it as a miniature silver cross that the Witch used to wear around her neck. Until a few months ago she had never been without it, then she had revealed that it was a present from some cousin called Alec who lived in Wakefield. Under the jealousy pact between us I had made her promise to give it back to him, and according to her story she had done so.

I looked back sharply at the Witch, but she was occupied, dabbing at her eyes with her handkerchief. I slipped the little silver cross quickly into my pocket, picked up her handbag, and strolled back to where she was sitting.

'Sorry, dalling,' I said again. She reached up and squeezed my hand, sniffing deeply to prove that she had finished crying.

'Let's go,' she said.

'All right.'

We walked back along the crumbling church path, through the lych-gate, and into St Botolph's Passage. I was beginning to say, 'You know, darling, I think you have feelings, too, deep down,' but the Witch had already resumed the formal attitude she assumed for public appearances. I let the matter drop.

'Are we going looking at the shops this afternoon?' she said as we paused at the corner of Market Street.

My heart sank. On Saturdays, as well as taking her to the Roxy at night, I was expected to meet her two or three times during the day – at lunch-time, during the afternoon, and possibly before I went to the pub for my club turn in the evening. She always said it made her feel wanted, although she had little idea what I wanted her for.

Today I was hoping to get out of the afternoon session.

'I'd love to, only I've got to go and see Shadrack this

afternoon, and I don't know what time I'll get through.'

'Please?' She would have said 'Pretty please' if she had had the nerve.

'All right, dalling. About four o'clock. Only wait for me if I'm late.'

'All right, pet.'

Fingering her little silver cross in my raincoat pocket, I watched her down Market Street until her swinging skirt was out of sight.

5

IN the cold sun, on a Saturday afternoon, St Botolph's Passage was just about bearable. It was alive with fat men in dark suits, puffing and blowing over folded racing papers and chucking clean, empty packets of twenty down on the uneven paving stones. Men in raincoats came and went in the vicinity of the shady chemist's, and a swaying, red-faced group continued an argument outside the pub, one of them saying the same sentence over and over again like a blocked gramophone. It seemed to be the same group every Saturday, having the same argument. 'Have you ever realized,' I said to Man o' the Dales – puff, puff – 'that your blunt Yorkshire individuals are in fact inter-changeable, like spare wheels on a mass-produced car?' At the end of the passage, by Market Street, there was even a violinist with his hat on the floor, playing 'Pennies from Heaven'. Shadrack and Duxbury's was the only shop with the blinds down, but the door was open and the bell rang quietly when I went in.

The office was cold and dusty now, and looking more like a funeral parlour than usual with the roller blind filtering a green, dead light over the empty desks. I stood hesitating, gaping dozily at the washed-looking photo-graph of Councillor Duxbury doffing his bowler in front of a horse-driven hearse. It was very quiet. I had a quick, happy notion that they had abandoned the office for ever, or dropped dead in their own coffins or something, but then I saw the thin red glow of the convector heater shin-ing under Shadrack's door. I went over reluctantly and knocked. He was not there. It was probable that he was out in Market Street, selling a Morris Thousand to some fruiterer or other. Shadrack had never quite abandoned his previous trade.

I sauntered over to my desk and sat down heavily, feeling happier because Shadrack was not there. It was, after all, not beyond the range of possibility that he had been run over by a bus. I lit one of my cigarettes and aimlessly opened the drawer of my desk. I stared vacantly into it for a moment, and then made a decision. My desk drawer was a sort of town branch of the Guilt Chest; there were few documents in it that did not cause even a passing spasm of anxiety. I began, briskly, to sort through them, tearing up the unposted funeral accounts first, then the obscene verses about Councillor Duxbury, and the rough notes for a long love letter I had once written to the Witch, daringly mentioning her breasts by name. There were about eight first pages of *The Two Schools at Gripminster*. I stacked them together, tore them through the middle, and dropped them in the wastepaper basket. There seemed to be whole sheafs of quarto with nothing written on them but my name in a variety of handwriting styles. I threw those away too. There was a fragment of dialogue entitled *Burglar Scene*, that I had once thought just right for Danny Boon:

BOON: If I fire this rod it'll be curtains for you.

FEED: W-why?

BOON: It's a curtain rod. Of course, I'm a very respectable man, you know, a very respectable man. My wife and I are in the iron and steel business.

FEED:

BOON: She does the ironing while I do the stealing.

I put this in my pocket together with the beginnings of the letter I had tried to write to Danny Boon. At the back of the drawer there was an old, yellowing piece of foolscap on which I had tried to list all the things that were worrying me at the time. The idea was that I should tick off each item as it ceased to be an anxiety, and when I had finished there would be nothing left to worry me any more.

I looked at the list again, apprehensively. 'Cal. Witch (Capt). Ldn. Hswvs Choice. Namepl. A's ma (sister).' There was nothing on the long list that I could honestly cross off and forget about. I made a decision, and ripped the piece of paper into four, dropping the pieces in the wastepaper basket. There was nothing left in the desk except the long ink stain, the stubs of pencil, and the word 'LIZ' which I had blocked in in careful crayon. I got up and tried to open Stamp's desk, but it was locked. I paced round the office, whistling through my teeth.

One of the habits I was going to get out of was a sort of vocal equivalent of the nervous grimace, an ever-expanding repertoire of odd noises and sound effects that I would run through in time of tension. Alone in my bedroom, seeking refuge in a telephone box, or walking purposefully, purposelessly home along Clogiron Lane late at night, I would begin to talk to myself, the words degenerating first into senseless, ape-like sounds and then into barnyard imitations, increasing in absurdity until I was completely incoherent, thereupon I would switch back into human speech with a kind of thought-stream monologue on whatever problem was uppermost in my mind at the time.

I did this now, dropping my cigarette end into Stamp's inkwell.

'London is a big place, Mr Shadrack,' I began, mumbling to myself. 'A man can lose himself in London. You know that? Lose himself. Loo-hoo-hoose himself. Loooooooose himself. Himself Him, himmmmmnnn, himnnn, himself. Ah-him-ah-self!' Wandering about the office, I started on

the odd sounds and the imitations of animals. 'Hyi! Hyi!
Yi-yi-yi-yi-yi. Grrruff! Grrruff! Maaa-aaa. Maa-aaa!
Maaaaaa! And now –' – taking in a fragment of one of the
routines I went through with Arthur from time to time –
'and now as Sir Winston *Chur*chill might have said it.
Nevah! In the field! Of human conflict! And this is the
voiceofemall, Wee Willy Fisher, saying maa-aaa! Maaaa!
Maaaaa! Grmp. Grmp. What a beautiful little pig. Hay
say, whhat ay *beau*tiful little pig.' I began to repeat this
sentence in a variety of tones, stresses and dialects, ranging
from a rapid Mickey Mouse squeak to a bass drawl, and
going through all the Joycean variations. 'What a batiful
lattle pahg. Ah, whet eh behtefell lettle peg.'

I was standing at the open door of Shadrack's office. The
room was beginning to echo with my voice. I stopped for a
moment and toyed with the idea of going in and having a
quick run through Shadrack's desk, but my ankles tingled
at the thought. I had a short flash of No. 2 thinking, trapped
in Shadrack's swivel chair with the drawer of his desk
jammed open. For relief, I turned back to my verbal doodling and began to call his name.

'Mr Shadrack? Mr Shadrack? Ha-*mees*ter Shadrack!
Mee-hee-heester Shadrack! Shadrack! Shadrack!' Each
time I called, the 'rack' sound bounced back off his
streamlined convector stove. '*Shad*rack! Shar-har-har-har-
*had*rack! Shaddy-shaddy-shaddy-shaddy-*shad*rack! Hoy!
Shadders!'

I was just drawing breath for the second run when
Shadrack, who had undoubtedly been listening for the
past ten minutes, came into the office through the door that
led down to the lavatory. I stuck a finger in my throat and
began going 'Ar! Ar! Arrgh! Sharrgh!' trying to falsify
his memory of what he had heard. My first real thought was
one of relief that I had not been going through his desk;

my second was to turn on him the Ambrosian repeater gun, rather like a machine-gun, which I kept permanently manned for such occasions as this.

'Oh, it's you, is it?' said Shadrack, but without any indication that these words explained, or excused, the din I had been making. Had he heard everything, or had he just come up from downstairs? Even downstairs he could not have failed to hear. Four moves flashed through my mind like a drowning man's life story. One, pretend was singing. Two, pretend not seen him and continue, making it sound like singing. Three, pretend rehearsing play. 'And yet, Lady Alice, even pigs have feelings.' Four, on the No. 1 level, 'I'm glad you heard that, Shadrack. I've been wanting you to hear my views for a long time.'

'Hope my singing didn't put you off,' I said.

'Curious din you were making,' said Shadrack. 'You'd better come into the office.'

I followed him into his private sanctum, humming in an embarrassed way.

Shadrack's office was furnished in what he imagined to be American executive style, in so far as he could afford it. He had a metal desk completely free of everything except a black ebony ruler, an unacceptable object to me ever since he had discovered me, or I think discovered me, conducting with it from a record of 'Abide With Me' which he kept on the record-player, another item of luxury. I turned the Ambrosian repeater gun on him again for good measure. On a low, coffee-bar sort of table there were the plans and drawings of the glass-fibre coffin he was working on, and a yellow pad on which he was doodling his ideas for a streamlined hearse. Beyond this, a couple of grey contemporary chairs, the first ever seen in Stradhoughton, and on the wall a boxed print of one of those Chinese horses.

'Come in, siddown, make 'self at home,' said Shadrack.

He smiled with his bad teeth, and produced from his blazer pocket a matchbox-sized model, made out of Perspex, of his wedge-shaped coffin. 'Y'know, by the time we're burying you, you'll be going off in one o' these. You know that?'

'Really?' I said, trying to sound interested. I was not fooled by his manner, the well-known friendly word, the boss relaxing on his Saturday afternoon off. I perched on one of the grey chairs and cleared my throat. 'Arrgh! Sharrgh!'

'Y'see, people don't realize. It's all clean lines nowadays. All these frills and fancies are going out. It's all old.'

'Hm,' I said.

'Same as I tell Councillor Duxbury. You've got to move with the times. It's no use living in one style and dying in another. It's an anarchism.'

'Anachronism,' I said, before I could stop myself.

'Yes, well.' Shadrack turned abruptly to the olive-green filing cabinet and took out a manilla file. He held it up and tapped it. 'Anyway, that's my worry. S'pose you want to talk to me about this letter of yours, do you?' I had an absurd feeling of importance that I should have written a letter and that he should have put it in a file. He put the file, open, on the desk, and I saw that there were several other papers underneath my letter of resignation. I fell to wondering if this was some kind of personal dossier, filled with reports from Stamp and the Witch, and secret spidery mumblings from Councillor Duxbury.

Shadrack perched on the desk, adjusting his tapered slacks and shooting his cuffs. 'So y're thinking of leaving us, hey, is that it?'

'Yes, well, I *was* thinking, now this opportunity's come up. . . .' I trotted out a wretched, shambling imitation of the speech I had prepared.

70

Shadrack picked up my letter and examined it. I tried to see what the next paper on the file was. It was one of his yellow memo-sheets with a lot of his writing on it. He frowned over the letter as though he could not read.

' "... now succeeded in obtaining a post with Mr Danny Boon...." ' he quoted, and I had an idea that he was going to go through the letter, point by point, getting me to expand. 'Now that's the chap who was on telly the other night, isn't it?'

'That's right,' I said in the encouraging voice.

'Yes, vair vair clever fellow. And you say you're going to work for him?'

'Yes, well, he liked some of the material I sent him and –'

'That's your ambition is it, script-writing?' He was the eager questioner, off-duty, Saturday afternoon.

'Oh, yes, always has been,' I said, beginning to relax and sit back in my chair. 'And of course, there's quite a lot of money in it if you go about it the right way.'

'You get paid by the joke, then, or what? Or do you get a salary coming in each week?'

'Well, it's vair vair difficult to say,' I said. I had noticed before that I often tended to start imitating the person I was talking to. But Shadrack had lost interest. While I was scrabbling away trying to think of something to tell him, he began murmuring 'Ye-es, ye-es' absent-mindedly and shuffling the papers in the file. His expression changed to a business one. He got up off the desk and stood behind his chair, putting his full weight on it and swivelling it from side to side.

'Ye-es. Well this letter,' Shadrack began, and it was obvious that we were getting down to the serious business. I looked up intelligently.

'Now you don't need me to tell you that it's vair vair unsatisfactory, a letter like this. Now do you?'

I mumbled, trying to get some action into my voice: 'Oh, I'm sorry to hear that?'

'Vair unsatisfactory. Fact I'd go so far as to say it's unprofessional, Fisher. Vair vair unprofessional.'

Shadrack had a thing about the undertaking business being a profession. I cleared my throat and said: 'Well, I suppose I've got to leave some time –'

'Yes, we realize that. We all realize that. Don't doubt it. Nobody wants to stand in your way, don't think that, and I wish you the vair vair best of luck. But it's felt that you might have gone about it in a more sa'sfactory manner.'

'Oh, in what way?' It sounded like something out of amateur dramatics, the way I said it.

'Well we were hoping, we were *hoping*, that you'd try and get one or two things cleared up before you took a step like this.'

An icy chill, a familiar enough visitor by now, seized me somewhere under the heart. I cleared my throat again and said faintly: 'What –?'

'Y'see, I don't mind telling you that we're vair vair disappointed you've not been to see us be*fore* this. I mean before you wrote this letter. I mean don't think I want to make things *awk*ward for you, far from it, but it has been felt you owe us one or two little explanations.'

It was difficult not to look as though I understood what he was talking about. I said, trying to keep up the equal partners voice of a few moments before, 'Well, I know my work probably hasn't been as good as it might have been. I mean, that's one of the reasons why I think I ought to leave.'

'It's not a question of work,' said Shadrack. 'It's not a

question of work at all. It's just a question of what you pr'pose to do about one or two things.'

He looked at me levelly, trying to gauge how much of the message was coming across. Then he said, almost gently: 'Y'see, there's those calendars to be explained, for one thing. I mean, we've never had any sa'sfactory explanation about *that*, now have we?'

I stared back at him, licking my lips. It was no surprise to me that Shadrack actually knew about the calendars. He was bound to suspect, if not to know. I had just been hoping that natural delicacy or some kind of feeling of hopelessness would have prevented him from bringing the subject up. There were many things, in fact, on which I leaned heavily on the reluctant, brooding tact that was Shadrack's speciality. I decided that my best policy was to say nothing, and indeed I had nothing to say.

'I mean, they cost a lot of money to produce, a *lot* of money. We can't understand what you did with them.'

I felt bound to make some sort of an effort. 'Well, there was a bit of a misunderstanding –' I began, a story about a fire at the post-office beginning to cobble itself together in my mind.

'It wasn't a misunderstanding, it's just that two or three hundred calendars didn't get posted. To *my* knowledge. I mean, I know you want to leave, I think it's the best thing you could do. I think you're taking a very wise step. We all realize that. But y'see, we've got to get this cleared up and implemented.'

I didn't know, and neither did he, what he meant by 'implemented'. Shadrack had a habit of hoarding words and dropping them into a sentence when they got too heavy for him. It was obvious now that he was going to go on and on about the calendars, probably for half the afternoon, simply because he had never studied the art of

73

changing the subject. I decided that I was supposed to make some constructive suggestion.

'Well, of course, if it's a question of paying for them –'

'Ah. Aha! Wait a minute. Wait just one little minute. It's not as easy as that. It's not – as – easy – as – that. Y'see, there's the goodwill to consider. What about the goodwill? Those calendars were for goodwill, we can't understand why you didn't send them out. I mean that's what they're there for. I mean, we don't buy calendars so that you can just go out and chuck them on the fire, y'know. That's not what we're in business for.'

He was getting warmed up now. He had stopped fiddling about with his chair and was sitting down, leaning forward over the desk, messing about with the ebony ruler. His eyes glistened.

'No, that won't do at all. I'm afraid you don't seem to apprec'ate it's a vair vair serious business. And then of course there's this other matter.'

'What other matter?' I said dully.

'I think you know vair well what matter. It's no good sitting there saying what matter. There's this matter of the nameplates, isn't there?'

Here I had no advantage at all, and for the first time my mouth sagged. I had suspected, when I considered the thing seriously, that Shadrack knew about the calendars. I felt that he knew something about the irregularities in the postage book, a subject I was surprised had not been ventilated earlier in the conversation. I was fairly sure that he knew about the offensive imitations of Councillor Duxbury but was too inarticulate to mention them. But I would have sworn, willingly, that he knew nothing about the nameplates.

In a way, the nameplates were just as serious as the calendars, if not more so. There were two of them, and I

74

had hidden them in a box of shrouds down in the stockroom. The whole thing had happened during Shadrack's holiday in the summer. I had been supposed to order a coffin nameplate for the funeral of a preacher who had dropped dead in the aisle at Bridle Street Methodist Church. By mistake, thinking about something else, I had put the letters 'R.I.P.' on the engravers' instructions, with the result that they had turned out what was in effect a Catholic nameplate for a Methodist body. I had got the thing hurriedly remade, but too late for the funeral. By a miracle neither Councillor Duxbury nor the relatives had noticed it was missing, and the Methodist minister had been buried in an unidentified coffin. There was nothing to do with the nameplates but hide them, and I had often worried about them, sometimes going into the theological aspects of the affair and wondering if I had committed anything to do with the unforgivable sin. But I would have sworn that Shadrack knew nothing about it.

'Y'see, that's another matter we've got to get cleared up. I don't see how you can leave without getting *that* cleared up.'

He did not make it evident whether or not he knew where the nameplates were. Perhaps he knew only that the body had been buried without a nameplate. I had lived in fear, for some time, of an exhumation order. I decided to sneak downstairs when he let me go and stuff the nameplates under my pullover.

'Well, I can only say I'm sorry if there's been any inconvenience,' I said.

'Inconvenience? Inconvenience? Ha!' He gave a short snort, and entered one of his caves of rhetoric. 'It's not a question of inconvenience, it's a question of what you pr'pose to do about it. S'posing the relatives had found out, what sort of a fool d'y'think I'd have looked then?

S'posing Councillor Duxbury had found out?' (I felt a slight ray of hope that he was shielding me from Councillor Duxbury.) 'Y'see, I'm vair much afraid that you've been spending too much time acting the fool. You seem to think you're on the music halls, not in a funeral furnishers.'

I was beginning to be possessed by the inward, impotent rage. What did the man want me to *do*? Atone for my sins? Work for another year as penal servitude? Pay for the calendars and the nameplates? Get the goodwill back?

Shadrack looked at the yellow paper in his file where, I was quite ready to believe, he had a list of my misdemeanours scribbled down, like a charge sheet. I expected him to tick them off and start each charge with 'That he did unlawfully . . .'

'Yes, there's been too much acting the fool in this office. We'll have to get some other system. Y'see, then there's those verses, you never wrote *those* out, now did you?'

Shadrack had once caught Arthur and me writing songs in the firm's time, and had set us to work making up little verses for the In Memoriam column of the *Echo,* a chore he handled for the bereaved on a commission basis. The nearest we had got to the job was an obscene poem about Councillor Duxbury and a couple of lines about Josiah Olroyd in the window: 'Josiah Olroyd has gone to join his Maker. Come inside and join Josiah Olroyd.' Shadrack knew about them both. I was relieved that he was getting on to the minor misdemeanours, but I knew that even those could keep him talking for hours.

'Then there's all that office paper you've been using for your bits and pieces. I mean, that costs money as well.'

'I'll pay for it.'

'It's not a question of paying for it –' In the outer office, the telephone began to ring. Shadrack picked up his extension and found that it was not connected. It was my responsibility to see that it was, last thing on Saturday morning, and he shot me a look of exasperation as he rose to his feet.

'Anyway, under the circumstances I have to tell you, I have to tell *you*, Fisher, that under no circ'stances can we accept your resignation at the moment. Not at the moment. Not until we've got this straightened out. We may even have to take some kind of legal action, I don't know.'

He strode out of his office and went over to the switchboard. 'Shadrack and Duxbury?' I got up and stood in the doorway, running over the bit about legal action and testing it for strength.

Shadrack began talking to some mourning wife in his soupy, funeral voice. I just stood there. He put his hand over the mouthpiece and said: 'Well we'll talk about this another time.' I walked unsteadily to the outer door, twisted the door-handle for a moment, and walked out into St Botolph's Passage. For the first time since breakfast I felt my elusive yawn coming on, and I leaned against Shadrack's window, gasping and gulping. My forehead was sweating, but I was relieved that I had jumped another hurdle. I remembered that I had not gone downstairs after the name-plates, but decided that after all there was little point in it.

I lit a cigarette and started walking down towards Market Street, trying to translate the interview into No. 1 thinking. 'Now look here, Mr Shadrack, there's such a thing as slander —'

It didn't work. I set off home. My No. 1 mother said: 'For God's sake, Billy, why don't you tell the boring little man to stick the job up his jacksy?'

6

I REACHED Hillcrest at about half past two to find lunch over and my mother in the kitchen, making notes for a scene about my not being home for meals. It was bacon and egg again, the traditional Saturday feast; the eggshells were in the sink-tidy and there was an air of replete doom about the house. Gran was mumbling to herself in the lounge. The old man was mending something in the garage, or thought he was.

'What time do you call this?' my mother asked as I opened the kitchen door. I knew my part in this little passage and replied: 'Twenty-seven minutes past two, though you may have another phrase for it,' reflecting that my answers were becoming as stereotyped as her questions. 'I've had an exciting morning,' I added, trying to get some uplift into the conversation.

My mother was not having any. 'You seem to think I've nothing else to do but cook, cook, cook,' she said, slipping with disturbing ease into a monologue so familiar to me that I could have chanted it with her, like those two men doing imitations on the radio. 'You come in when you like and expect to find a meal waiting for you, you don't seem to think I'm entitled to five minutes' peace.'

'Peace –' I began, not troubling to think what I was going to say; anything obscure would pass for something clever. My mother cut me short.

'I've not sat down all morning. If I'm not sick!'

From the lounge, Gran shouted: 'If that's our Billy,

there's his old raincoat been in the bathroom all morning. It's about time he started hanging his things up.'

I called back: 'What if it isn't our Billy, where has his old raincoat been then?' a grammatical pleasantry whose full subtlety I did not expect to be appreciated. I anticipated, and got, no reply. The old man came into the kitchen from the garage, carrying a shelf.

'And you can start coming home on a dinner-time, instead of gadding round town half the bloody day,' he said, without even looking at me.

'Good afternoon, father,' I said with heavy civility. I was beginning to wonder why I had come home at all.

'And stop being so bloody cheeky. I've just about had enough of it.'

'He wants to give him a good hiding, teach him some manners,' called Gran from the lounge.

I began to feel angry, like a caged animal being taunted with sticks. This feeling, a regular enough occurrence in this house, had several outlets. One course open to me was to revert to what I felt must be my former self or my real self or something, an abusive shadow of the old man. Another, less dangerous move was to introduce the mood of polished detachment.

'What are manners –?' I began, examining my fingernails. But I had underestimated the strength of the old man's frustration or whatever it was.

'Talk bloody sense, man!' he roared. 'By Christ, if this is what they learned him at technical school, I'm glad I'm bloody ignorant!'

'Ah, a confession!' I murmured, but without any idea that he should hear me. The old man gave me a steady, threatening look. Aloud, I said, 'I'm going upstairs.'

'And keep out of them bedrooms!' Gran called from the lounge.

The bedrooms were nothing to do with her. She was only the permanent guest. I whipped round in a sudden gust of fury.

'*Stick the bedrooms up your –*' I began, then checked myself on the absolute verge of disaster, so abruptly that I physically teetered on my toes.

'You what!' The old man dropped his shelf on the floor and came almost running across the kitchen, face to face with me. 'What did you say? What was that? What did you say?' He grabbed my collar and put his fist close against my face.

'These melodramatics –'

'Don't melodram me with your fancy talk!' I was seized, not with fear or anger but with sheer helplessness at the thought that these were beautiful Josiah Olroyd lines and I could not point them out to anybody, or even scoff.

'I merely said –'

'Talk bloody properly! You were talking different a minute ago, weren't you? What did you just say to your grandma? What did you say?'

'Well, don't pull him round, that shirt's clean on,' my mother said, anxiously.

'I'll clean shirt him! I'll clean shirt him round his bloody earhole! With his bloody fountain pens and his bloody suède shoes! Well he doesn't go out tonight! *I* know where he gets it from. He stops in tonight, and tomorrow night anall!'

I stood by the sink, looking weary, seeking some facial expression that was not outside the histrionic experience of the family. I searched for something to say that would not sound clever or impertinent. From the lounge I heard Gran muttering, 'Cheeky young devil!' but her voice sounded thick and strange.

'Look –'

'Don't look me! With your look this and look that! And you get all them bloody papers and books and rubbish thrown out, anall! Before I chuck 'em out first, and you with 'em!'

The only way into the conversation was to counterfeit the old man's blunt and blunted way of talking. I set my lips into the same loose, flabby shape and said in the rough voice: 'What's up, they're not hurting you, are they?'

'No, and they're not bloody hurting you, eether,' the old man said, taking over, in his mind anyway, the role of family wit.

He went back across the kitchen and picked up the shelf where he had dropped it. I stood there straightening my tie, not speaking. My mother looked at me, her 'You've done it now' look. The old man turned back.

'Anyway, I've finished with him. He knows where his suitcase is. If he wants to go to London he can bloody well go!'

'Oh, but he's not!' my mother said sharply. She had been dithering for some time, wondering which side she was on, and now she came down on mine, or what she thought was mine.

'I've finished with him! He can go!'

'Oh, but he's not!'

'He's going. He's going out.' The idea was building up attractively in the old man's mind. 'He's going!'

'Oh, but he's not. Oh, but he's not. Oh, but he's not.'

'Look,' I said. 'Can I settle this –'

This time the old man ignored me.

'It's ever since he left school, complaining about this and that and t' other. If it isn't his boiled eggs it's summat else. You have to get special bloody *wheat* flakes for him cos he's seen 'em on television. Well I've had enough. I've had enough. He can go.'

'Oh, but he's not! Now you listen to me, Geoffrey. He's not old enough to go to London, or anywhere else. You said yourself. He doesn't think. He gets ideas into his head.'

'Well he's going, he can get *that* idea into his head.'

'Oh, but he's not. Not while *I'm* here.'

The old man's anger died down as quickly as it had flared up. 'He wants to get into t' bloody army, that's what he wants to do,' he said.

'Yes, and you want to get into t' bloody army as well,' my mother said.

This exchange of epigrams seemed to mark the end of the conversation. I turned to go.

'Where's he going *now*?' the old man said.

'I'm going to be sick,' I said viciously.

I went into the lounge, expecting Gran to toss her widow's mite into the controversy as I passed. I glanced at her as I walked towards the hall door, and saw at once, with a quick sense of panic, why she was so silent.

I shouted: 'Mother! Quick!' and looked up at the ceiling rather than at my grandmother. She was sitting in her armchair in a curiously rigid position, her yellow face convulsed, her neck ricked back. Specks of foam appeared on her lips and her watering eyes were bulging. She was trying to cry out, but no sounds came. Her skinny hands gripped the arms of her chair and her back was arched as though she had frozen in the act of getting up.

My mother and the old man came rushing into the room. 'Now look what you've done!' my mother cried. The old man dashed over to open the window.

He shouted: 'She's having a bloody fit, can't you see? Get t' smelling salts! Go on, then, frame yourself!'

Glad to get out of it, I galloped upstairs for the smelling

salts. Gran's fits, occurring nowadays with increasing regularity, always filled me with dread and, I could not help it, disgust. I had a horror that I would one day be alone with her in the house when she threw one, and I was often haunted by the thought of what I would do in these circumstances. Rummaging around in my mother's dressing-table for the smelling salts, automatically conning the contents of the drawer to see if she had found anything of mine and hidden it, I realized that emerging from my panic was the old thought that perhaps this time Gran would die and there would be no more scenes. I tried to push the thought out by the counting and quoting method: *'Seventy-four, ninety-six, the Lord is my shepherd I shall not want.'* Calming a little, I no longer hoped that she was dead but that she was all right, or at least looking all right on the face of it, with the foam wiped off her lips and everything looking normal. I found the green bottle of smelling salts and went downstairs. At the turn of the stairs, scraping my shoe against the loose stair-rod, I told myself that I would count five and that at the end of that time she would have recovered, and I would go in.

I counted slowly, one, two, three, four, five, six. The hall door opened suddenly and the old man was peering round urgently. 'Come on, what you bloody doing?' I jumped the remaining stairs and handed him the bottle. 'Still feel sick,' I muttered. He shut the door in my face.

I walked slowly back upstairs, trying to *make* myself feel sick, but with no success. I went into my room and lay shivering on the bed. I strained my ears to listen for the voices downstairs, and told myself that I could hear the faint voice of Gran, and that that meant she was all right now. To get the incident out of my head I tried out a piece of No. 1 thinking, concerning my own death and the grief of the family. It tapered out and, feeling more at ease, I began to think aggressively, and then constructively, casting myself slowly into the role of master of the house. There was an insurance man bullying Gran into taking out a funeral policy, but she was too dim to know what it was all about. I came in just as the insurance man was becoming sneering and abusive. 'Would you mind, sir? This lady happens to be my grandmother.' – 'And who are you?' – 'Let us say that I have some experience in these matters.'

By now there were definitely voices downstairs, and I heard the old man going out into the garage. He wouldn't be going into the garage if everything were not all right. I breathed in deeply and began to sing quietly to myself. I rolled myself off the bed, stood around indecisively for a moment, then kneeled down and dragged the Guilt Chest out, checking the stamp-edging only perfunctorily and not worrying overmuch whether they had been in it or not. It was time for another decision. I opened the wardrobe and got down the biggest sheet of brown paper I could find. I spread it out over the bed. Then I fell once again into a mild stupor, putting the recent conversation downstairs into some kind of glassy-eyed perspective. Brooding over Gran's complaint about my old raincoat in the bathroom, I remembered with a jolt the letter still there in it. I bounded into the bathroom and felt for it in my raincoat-cum-dressing-gown pocket. It was still there. I took it out and tried to remember the way I had folded it. They would surely have mentioned the matter if they had opened it and read it. I smoothed the letter out, and fluff fell out of the creases. I read it again.

Dear Mr Fisher,

   Many thanks for script and gags, I can use some of the gags and pay accordingly. As for staff job, well, I regret to tell you, I do not have 'staff' beside my manager, but several

*of the boys do work for me, you might be interested in this.
Why not call in for a chat next time you are in London?
Best of luck and keep writing,*

                              Danny Boon

Read in this light with the old man's threat to kick me
out tentatively expressed if not actually confirmed, it did
not seem after all much to go on. The thought of being in
London began to fill me, once again, with apprehension. I
walked back into the bedroom and took out the pound notes
that I had been hoarding in my wallet. There were nine of
them. I emptied my loose change out on to the sheet of
wrapping paper on the bed: fourteen and sixpence. Nine
pounds fourteen and sixpence. But I could not do the complicated sum of subtracting rail fares, rents, meals, and the
rest of it. I put the money away and turned back to the
Guilt Chest.

Carefully, I winkled out a stack of about three dozen
calendars and piled them on the sheet of brown paper.
There seemed to be room for more. I got another dozen,
and then wrapped the whole lot up, finding a length of
string in the elephant-shaped vase on the bedroom mantelpiece. They made a heavy parcel, heavier than I had expected. I closed the Guilt Chest, putting the stamp-edging
in a new position, and went downstairs, humping my parcel
with me. In the hall I picked up a gramophone record
that had been there for days, waiting to go back to the
shop.

I went nervously into the lounge. Gran was sitting in her
chair with a shawl over her shoulders, drinking weak tea
and moaning composedly to show that she was still not herself. I breathed heavily with relief and went through into
the kitchen, where my mother had started making scones.

'Is she all right,' I said gruffly.

                         85

'As all right as she'll ever be,' my mother said wearily, in her martyr's voice. I decided to let it go at that.

She nodded towards the parcel under my arm.

'What's that?'

'Books. Papers. Records,' I said.

'Where are you going with them?'

'Chucking them out, like he told me to,' I said, using my own martyr's voice.

'Don't be silly,' my mother said easily, and went on baking. I walked out of the house. The old man was still messing about in the garage.

Instead of walking down Cherry Row I walked up it, into Valley Gardens, along Valley Gardens into Moorside Gardens, and along Moorside Gardens past the builders' huts and over the rubbish tip that led steeply down into Stradhoughton Moor.

Stradhoughton Moor was a kind of pastoral slum on the edge of the town. It was fringed on Moorside by the dyeworks, Stradhoughton Town football ground, and some public lavatories. The centre of the Moor was paved with cinders, where generations had tipped their slag and ashes, and where the annual fairs were held. There was a circumference of sparse yellow grass where the old men walked in summer, and I took the path they had worn towards a pocket of stone cottages, mostly condemned, that huddled miserably together in a corner of the Moor. Behind the cottages Stradhoughton Moor rose steeply again, out of an ashpit, to meet the scraggy allotments and, beyond them, the real moors of Houghtondale, such as were illustrated in the Council yearbook. I intended to drop my parcel of calendars down a pothole.

I enjoyed walking here. Given a quiet day I could always talk to myself, and it was easy to picture the clifflike, craggy boundaries of the Moor as the borders of Ambrosia.

The sun was still out, in a watery sort of way, and there was a hard, metal-grey shine on the afternoon. The faint waves of shouting, and all other noises, sounded remote and not very real, as though heard through a sheet of glass.

In Ambrosia, we were settling down to a shaky peace. The reactionary, Dr Grover, weakened it was true by his Quisling record but still a power to be reckoned with, had got hold of some letters I had written to Arthur, outlining our plans for taking over the state. Liz, potentially the country's first home secretary, was abolishing the prisons.

I had reached the broken-down cottages by now. 'Mr President,' I said aloud, negotiating the ashpit and wondering whether to drop the parcel of calendars in it to be found, soggy and disintegrating, like a baby's body in a shoe box. 'Democracy is a stranger to Ambrosia. And yet this is a country of democrats. You know what this is?' – I held up the gramophone record I had brought out with me – 'It is a ballot paper. Mr President, I will not rest until we have democracy *by vote* in this, er, ancient land of ours.'

I scrambled up the ashpit, until I had reached the top of the Moor and was standing on the verge of grass surrounding the allotments. I looked down over the acre of cinders, across the lines of washing and the terrace-end pubs, the grandstand roof of the football ground advertising Bile Beans, and the black stone police station.

'We will rebuild –' I began in the ringing voice. I heard a slight crunching noise behind me, and turned round. A rough path of stone chippings led through the plots of beetroot and big blue cabbages towards the tufty moorland. Staggering along the path like some lost shepherd, doubtless living out his own private dreams as Dr Johnson or George Borrow or somebody, came Councillor Duxbury himself, dabbing his streaming eyes and clutching his gnarled old stick.

My heart missed a beat, and I wondered quickly how many beats it had missed this day, and whether it could only miss so many before you were dead, and if so how far was I off the total. There was nothing to dodge behind, unless I cared to jump back into the ashpit, but in any case he had seen me. I composed my face to look as though I wasn't doing anything, and tightened my grip of the suddenly enormous parcel of calendars under my arm.

Councillor Duxbury came flapping down the stone path, raising his stick in salute.

'Afternoon, lad!' he called in his rich, so-called Yorkshire relish voice.

'Afternoon, Councillor!' I called in the robust voice.

'It's a sunny 'un, this! 'Appen tha's watching t' football?'

'Nay, ahm' just bahn for a walk ower t' moor.' I always talked to Councillor Duxbury in his own dialect, half-mockingly, half-compulsively, usually goading myself into internal hysterics when I thought how I would reproduce the conversation to Arthur later.

'What's ta got theer, then? T' crown jewels?' He pointed with his stick at my parcel, his old face set in the serious, deadpan expression that had won him his tiresome reputation as a wag in the council chamber.

'Nay, old gramophone records,' I said, wildly producing the one record I did have, as proof. He did not ask me where I was taking them.

'Aye, ther' were nowt like that,' he said. His memory had been jogged so many times by *Echo* interviews that he now regarded every statement as a cue for his reminiscences, and no longer bothered to add 'when I were a lad' or 'fot'ty year ago'. 'Ther' were nowt like that. We had to make our own music if we wanted it, else go without.' He rattled on as though he were himself an old gramophone that has just been kicked back into action. I was not sure that he knew who I was. Entirely lost in himself he began to mumble about the *Messiah* and I let him, full of frothy self-congratulation because I would be one up on Arthur when the next Duxbury routine came up.

'No, ther' were nowt like that.' He stopped at last to wipe his nose, making a ritual of it with a coloured handkerchief about the size of a bed-sheet. He paused between sniffs and shot me what he imagined to be a playful glance, the expression he always wore when he asked people how old they thought he was.

'Does ta think ah could climb down yon ashpit?'

'Nay, tha'd break thi neck, Councillor!' I said, giving him entirely the wrong answer. He gave me a sour look and said: 'Aye, well ah'sll have to manage it, whether or no. Ah'm bahn down to t' police station.'

My heart missed another beat, or rather ceased operating altogether for a second.

'What's ta bahn down theer for, then?' I told myself optimistically that if it were about me he would be going to the town hall, never mind the local police station. Besides, he didn't know who I was.

Councillor Duxbury chuckled. 'We're pulling t' bugger down.'

I gulped with relief, although my heart was still at it. 'Tha's not, is ta?' I said, packing some incredulity into my voice.

'Aye, we are that. All yon cottages anall, they're going. And they won't get *council* houses for three and six a week, neether.'

I shook my head in sympathy, and saw that he was going into another of his reveries. I transferred my parcel from one arm to the other.

'It's all change,' said Councillor Duxbury. 'All change,

nowadays. T' old buildings is going. T' old street is going. T' trams, they've gone.'

'Aye,' I said, sighing with him. 'It's not t' same wi' t' buses, is it?' One good shove, I thought, and he would be down at the bottom of the ashpit, where he wanted to be.

'It were all horse-drawn trams, and afore that we had to walk. It's all change. T' old mills is going. T' old dialect, *that's* going,' he said. I suddenly realized that he knew perfectly well that I did not talk in dialect all the time, and also that it was ridiculous to imagine that he did not know I worked for him. To prevent him saying whatever he might have been going to say next, I began to talk, looking desperately down over Stradhoughton Moor.

'Well, progress is all very well,' I said. 'But it's a pity we don't have a Yorkshire tradition o' progress.' I was trying to modify the dialect so that I could drop out of it completely within the minute. I nodded down at the police station. 'I don't mind dark satanic mills, but by gum when it comes to dark satanic shops, dark satanic housing estates, and dark satanic police stations –' I broke off, realizing that I had never worked out the end of this sentence. I looked at Councillor Duxbury for the feedline but he was away, staring glassily over the Moor.

'– that's different,' I concluded lamely. He did not seem inclined to speak. 'And yet,' I went on, grabbing half-remembered tufts of my Man o' the Dales conversation, 'and yet we've got to remember, this isn't a religion, it's a county. We've, er –'

I tailed off again. Councillor Duxbury had the fixed expression that old men have when they are lost in their thoughts, or what they claim are their thoughts, not listening to a word I was saying. A quick gust of wind swept around our ankles. I opened my mouth to speak again, remembering another bit, and then suddenly, without moving, he carved straight into my monologue.

'Tha's a reet one wi' them calendars, i'n't ta?'

I blanched, rocked on my heels and nearly fell over the grass edge into the ashpit below. I looked into his face to see if there was any suspicion of a boys-will-be-boys chuckle, but he maintained his deadpan look as though he were telling wry jokes at a masonic dinner.

'By, that's capped me theer, Councillor!' was all I could think of to say.

'Aye, and tha's capped me anall! Ah were reet taken back when Shadrack rang me upon t' telephone. Ah'd ha' thowt a lad like thee would have had more sense.' He spoke easily and not sternly, like a Yorkshire butler filling in plot-lines in a dialect comedy. I fancied that he was peering with keen suspicion at the parcel of calendars, and wondered if it were true that there were wise old men and he was one of them. I didn't know what to make of it. Even if he knew I worked for him, I was surprised that he could distinguish me from Stamp and Arthur. I had a reckless impulse to tell him that I *was* Arthur and that he was getting the two of us mixed up.

I said nothing.

'So tha's going to London, is ta?' he said with mild interest, as though the subject of the calendars had been settled entirely to his satisfaction.

Hopefully, I said: 'Aye, ah'm just about thraiped wi' Stradhoughton.' I remembered too late that 'thraiped' was a word Arthur and I had made up.

'How does ta mean?'

'It's neither muckling nor mickling,' I said, using another invented phrase in my complete panic.

'Aye.' The old man poked the ground with his stick, and said again, 'Aye.' I had no indication what he was thinking about at all. I tried hard to keep talking, but I could not think of a single word of any description.

'Well tha's gotten me in a very difficult position,' he said weightily, at last.

'How does ta mean, Councillor?'

He studied me keenly, and I realized for the first time, with a sinking heart, that he was not as daft as he looked.

'Is ta taking a rise out o' me, young man?'

I felt myself flushing, and found my whole personality shifting into the familiar position of sheepishness and guilt. 'No, of course not.'

'Well just talk as thi mother and father brought thee up to talk, then. Ah've had no education, ah had to educate myself, but that's no reason for thee to copy t' way *I* talk.' He spoke sharply but kindly, in a voice of authority with some kind of infinite wisdom behind it, and at that moment I felt genuinely ashamed.

'Now sither. We'll noan go ower t' ins and outs of it, tha's been ower all that down at t' office. But young Shadrack theer thinks ah ought to have a word wi' thi father about thee. What does ta say to that?'

'I don't know,' I muttered, hanging my head. I wondered how I could ask him, without actually begging for mercy, not to talk to the old man.

'Well don't look as if tha's lost a bob and fun sixpence! Tha's no deead yet!'

I looked up at him and gave him a thin, grateful smile.

'Straighten thi back up! That's better. Now sither. Ah don't know what ah'sll do. Ah'sll have to think about what's best. But sither –' He gripped my arm. I did not feel embarrassed; I was able, even, to look steadily into his eyes. 'Sither. Tha'rt a young man. Tha's got a long way to go. But tha can't do it by thisen. Now think on.'

He released my arm, leaving me feeling that he had said

something sage and shrewd, although I was unable to fathom quite what he was getting at. He was stuffing his handkerchief into his overcoat pocket, preparing to go. I did not want him to go. I did not feel afraid. I felt a kind of tentative serenity and I wanted him to go on with his old man's advice, telling me the things I should do.

'My grandma's poorly,' I said suddenly, without even knowing that I was talking. But he did not seem to hear.

'Ah'm glad to have had t' chance o' talking to thee,' he said. He turned and began to make his way gingerly down the gentlest slope of the ashpit, feeling the way with his shiny stick. Half-way down he turned back awkwardly. 'Think on,' he said.

I looked down after him, only just beginning to realize that for the first time I wanted to tell somebody about it, and that I could very probably have explained it all to him. I had to resist an impulse to call back after him.

I stood there until he was safely on the grass perimeter surrounding the stretch of cinders. I had a feeling, one that I wanted to keep. It was a feeling of peace and melancholy. I was not at all afraid. I walked happily along the rough stone path through the allotments to the quiet moorland beyond, and even while I was burying the calendars the feeling was still with me.

7

THE Witch was already fishing in her handbag for an orange, but I was in a rare mood of optimism, as though I were starting a new life or something. We were on top of the No. 17 bus, bound for the Corporation Cemetery. I was humming quietly, and fingering two or three of Stamp's passion pills in my pocket. The Witch was fuming to herself over the approaches that had been made to her by various men in raincoats while she waited for me in St Botolph's Passage. Luckily for me the experience had put her out of mood for window-shopping.

Half-way to the cemetery, she was still going on about it. 'There *are* some nasty people about.'

'Mm,' I said. 'Have a passion pill.' I held two of the little black beads out in the palm of my hand. 'Energy tablets, they are,' I added hastily, realizing what I had just said. 'We always call them passion pills. They're supposed to give you energy.'

The Witch was digging her thumbnail viciously into the peel of her orange. The bus was passing a row of advertising hoardings.

'Look, there y'are,' I cried excitedly, clutching her sleeve and jabbing at the window. '*Too* late. It was an advert for them. P.P., they're called. That's why they're nicknamed passion pills. You're supposed to take two.'

The Witch, stuffing bits of orange into her mouth, gave me her pitying look. 'What *is* the boy talking about?' she said.

I put on the frank and open grin and held out the two

black pills. 'Very nice with fruit!' I said in the persuasive voice.

The Witch made some heavy weather over a sigh. 'Better humour the boy,' she said with an attempt at mock-resignation. She took the two pills in her mouth and knocked them back with a slice of orange. 'Satisfied?'

I sat back contentedly and lit a cigarette.

'Fifth today.'

'Last one,' the Witch cautioned.

Life seemed temporarily good. We got off the bus at the cemetery gates and walked up the broad red-gravel avenue between the white gravestones. Sometimes, in expansive moments such as this, I could understand what the Witch found so fascinating about this place. In fact it sometimes fascinated *me*. It was open, tidy, and secure, like the campus in an American college musical. After the black, streaky tombs of St Botolph's churchyard there was something pleasantly normal about the symmetrical rows of neat headstones and the tidy oblongs of clean pebbles. All the people here seemed to have died a modern, healthy sort of death.

We strolled on to the grass verge between the graves, making our way to the public shelter outside the red-brick chapel at the end of the long drive. The Witch, completely in her element, darted busily from one grave to another, admiring the angels and the September flowers, and crying 'Oh, look, pet, isn't it *sweet*!' whenever she found a stone crib. From time to time she would stoop reverently over a headstone and read out one of the verses chipped in gold, square lettering.

> *With you dearest Mother and darling dad,*
> *Happy were the years we had,*
> *And it is comfort in our pain*
> *You are now together again.*

I listened to all this benevolently. So far as I was concerned, this was the scene where you see a close-up of a clock and the minute hand moves round a quarter of an hour to show the passage of time. Remembering the fiasco earlier in the day, I decided to give her a good twenty-five minutes this time, and she had quoted enough verses to fill an anthology before we reached the deserted shelter by the mock-Norman door of the burial chapel.

I got her snuggling up to me in the dark corner where we had carved our initials; that was the first step.

'Happy?'

'Mmmmm.'

I kissed her. She responded drowsily.

'Barbara? Tell me, how do you feel?'

'Contented,' she said, squeezing up to me kittenishly.

'You don't feel – you know, restless?'

'No.'

I sat there stroking her sleeve, trying to get some action out of her. I put my mouth close to hers again, but she was messing about making little kissing noises with her lips, and it was impossible to get at her for any length of time.

'Would you like another energy tablet?'

'No thank you, pet. They seem to make me sleepy.'

I grabbed hold of her arms roughly and urgently. She sat up, recognizing the signs.

'Barbara,' I said in the pleading voice. 'Barbara!'

'Don't be angry again, pet,' she pleaded, clutching her handbag full of oranges in alarm.

'I'm not angry, just sad. Barbara – you know you're making me ill, don't you?'

'Poor Billy! Why am I making you ill?'

'Dalling! Have you ever heard of repressions? The nervous reactions that affect men who aren't, well –' – the only ending I could think of for the sentence was a phrase of Stamp's, 'Getting it regular.' I let the thing peter out.

'I know what you mean, pet,' the Witch said, gently but desperately, as though she were soothing a dangerous lunatic. 'But we must be patient. We must. We'd only regret it.' But I was already regretting it. I found myself, quite suddenly, not caring a damn one way or the other, only wondering what I was doing here in a cemetery with a stone woman, anyway.

I muttered 'Forget it' and leaned back in the hard wooden shelter with my eyes closed, calculating how soon I could get away. I had been meaning to scheme out some way of keeping the Witch out of the Roxy tonight, out of the way of Rita, and I decided that it was high time I got to work on it. A tentative plot began to form in my mind; arranging to meet the Witch outside the Odeon, not turning up, and then explaining the whole unfortunate misunderstanding when she came to tea tomorrow. A warning bell sounded in my brain on the idea of the Witch coming to tea. *See Witch re Captain.* The words I had scribbled down hours before suddenly flashed like a neon sign in my head. I sat up again, sharply.

'Dalling!'

'Mmmm?' She was almost asleep.

'Dalling, are you still coming to tea tomorrow?'

The Witch sat up herself and shot me a keen glance, daring me to wriggle out of it.

'Of course. That's why I was hoping you would have got my engagement ring back.'

'Good.'

I swallowed. I had rehearsed this once, but that was days ago. I tried to visualize the stage instructions, looking studiously down at the stone-flagged floor and tracing one of the cracks with my foot.

97

'There's something I want to tell you,' I said in the low voice.

The Witch said nothing but, employing her main defence mechanism, stiffened.

'You know what you were saying about loving me even if I were a criminal?'

'Well?' in her icy voice. We had had a fairly tortured evening once when the Witch had cornered me into admitting that I would love her in every conceivable circumstance — age, infirmity, unfaithfulness (the idea of her being unfaithful had rather charmed me), and criminal record being taken into account. I had had no option but to fire the same litany back at her, and had got so far as to make her agree that even if I shot her father and mother she would still, she thought, love me.

'I wonder if you'll still love me when you've heard what I've got to say,' I said.

The Witch was rapidly withdrawing into a cocoon of formality.

'You see — well, you know that I've got a fairly vivid imagination, don't you?'

'Well you have to have, if you're going to be a script-writer, don't you?' she said smugly. There were occasions when I would have willingly shot *her*, never mind her relations.

'Well *be*ing a script-writer,' I continued ponderously, 'I'm perhaps a bit inclined to let my imagination run away with me. As you know.'

The Witch said nothing, but she was beginning to breathe heavily through her nostrils.

'You see, if — if we're going to have our life together, and the cottage, and little Billy and little Barbara and the wishing-well and all that, there's some things we've got to get cleared up.' I nearly added 'and implemented'.

98

'What things?'

According to my stage instructions I was to give her a frank, honest glance. I was unable to do it, and decided to rely on a frank, honest profile.

'Some of the things I'm afraid I've been telling you.'

The Witch said, in her direct, devastating way: 'Do you mean you've been telling *lies*?'

'Well not lies exactly, but I suppose I've been – well, exaggerating some things. Being a script-writer . . .' Another idea crossed my mind, that of slapping the Witch across the mouth and striding out of the cemetery, never to meet her again. I put it away. 'Well, for instance, there's that business about my father. Him being a sea captain.'

In a weak moment, or rather in a panoramic series of weak moments, I had told the Witch that during the war the old man had been the captain of a destroyer. He had been partly responsible for sinking the *Graf Spee* before being captured – one of the first men to be captured by U-boats, as a matter of fact – and had spent three years in a prisoner-of-war camp. He had been wounded in the leg, which still gave him some trouble.

'You mean he wasn't a sea captain, I suppose?' said the Witch, and I was surprised that *she* didn't seem surprised.

'He wasn't even in the navy,' I said.

'And what about him being a prisoner-of-war? Don't say *that* was all lies.'

'Yes.'

The Witch turned away with a quick movement of the head, bringing tears to her eyes without difficulty. I suspected that she had perfected the whole action in front of a mirror. Its point was to make it quite evident that she was turning away and not just looking away. Reaching out for the most banal remark I could find, I said:

'Are you cross?'

There was a practised silence. The Witch gave it thirty seconds and then said:

'No, I'm not cross. Just disap*po*inted, that's all. It sounds as though you were *ashamed* of your father.'

I sat bolt upright and steamed the heat into my voice. 'I'm *not* ashamed, I'm not, I'm not!'

'Otherwise why say he was a sea captain? What was he?'

I had to stop myself from saying 'A conscientious objector' and starting the whole thing over again. I said: 'He wasn't anything. He wasn't fit. He has trouble with his knee.'

'The knee he's supposed to have been shot in, I suppose.'

'Yes,' and I was now talking belligerently. 'Another thing, we haven't got a budgie.'

I had told her that we kept a yellow budgerigar called Roger. I had regularly given her communiqués about its antics and there had been a highlight when Roger had flown out of his cage and nearly been caught by Sarah, the tabby.

'Or a cat,' I said.

The Witch was shuffling her handbag about and buttoning her coat to give the impression that she was about to leave.

'How many other lies have you been telling me?'

'My sister.' The Witch had roughly the same story about my imaginary sister as I had given to Arthur's mother.

'Don't tell me you haven't got a *sister*.'

'I did have, but she's dead.' This time it was out before I could prevent it. I ran rapidly over this new turn, and within seconds I had established death from tuberculosis, and a quiet funeral. 'If you still want to come tomorrow, they never talk about her,' I said.

'I'm not sure I *shall* be coming, now,' said the Witch. She shuddered elaborately. 'I've always hated – lying.'

A happy thought struck me. In my pocket I still had the

miniature silver cross that had spilled out of her handbag in St Botolph's churchyard – the one she was supposed to have given back to her cousin Alec.

'Have you?' I said. I decided against producing the thing triumphantly and waving it under her nose, for the moment at least. I went into the hard voice and said: 'Look, Barbara, we all have our faults. I have mine. You have yours.

'I don't tell *lies*,' said the Witch.

'Don't you?'

'No!'

'What about that cross or whatever it was that you were supposed to have given back to your cousin?'

'Well, I *did* give it back,' said the Witch. I was satisfied to see the same smooth expression on her face that I wore so regularly myself.

'Did you?' I said cryptically. She looked down at her handbag and back at me.

'I told you I'd given it back and I *gave* it back.'

'All right.' I stood up as though washing my hands of the whole business. From the hard voice into the matter-of-fact voice. 'Look. I've got to go into town now. You probably won't believe anything I say after this, but I may as well tell you that I've been offered a job in London. It depends on your attitude whether I take it or not.'

The Witch got to her feet, contriving a dazed expression. I felt like gripping her by the lapels of her coat and saying coarsely: 'Look, chum, I do all these tricks myself. I *know* them. Pack it in.'

'I shall never know whether you're telling the truth after this,' she said. She walked with me down the gravel drive towards the cemetery gates, almost falling over her own feet in her attempts to look straight in front of her.

As we were passing the last grave I said in the bitter voice: 'Well I know what *my* epitaph will be.'

She did not reply at first, so I let her wait for it. At length she said: 'What?' reluctantly.

' "Here lies Billy Fisher",' I said.

I put just the right amount of ruefulness in my voice, and it took effect. She caught my hand impulsively and said: 'Don't be cross with yourself.'

At the cemetery gates she stopped and held my hands at arm's length, as though for inspection. 'Billy?'

'Yes, dalling?'

'Promise me something?'

'That I'll never lie to you again?' She nodded. 'I'll never lie to you again,' I said.

Holding hands, we walked out of the cemetery. The first person I saw, coming towards us and too near for me to do anything about it, was Arthur's mother, carrying a bunch of pansies.

Out of the side of my mouth I said rapidly: 'Do as I say, explain later!' As Arthur's mother came alongside us, I smiled broadly.

'Hullo, Mrs Crabtree. I don't think you've met my sister. Sheila, this is Mrs Crabtree.'

Arthur's mother looked at me as though I had hit her. It suddenly struck me that I had made the wrong decision. She said indignantly:

'I'm afraid you've picked the wrong person to play your tricks with *this* time. I happen to know Barbara very well.'

The Witch, for public consumption only, gave me her tolerant, more-in-sorrow look.

'I think it's his queer sense of humour,' she said.

'Got to catch a tram,' I gabbled. 'Bus.' A No. 17 was pulling slowly away from the bus stop. I jumped on and galloped up the stairs, getting the Ambrosian repeater gun into position.

8

'WHAT, is *this* for me as well?' asked Rita incredulously.

I nodded, my mouth so full of egg sandwich that my eyes were watering. 'Been robbing a bank,' I chuntered, spluttering food. It was already five o'clock, and the first time I had eaten since breakfast.

'Cugh! Got owt else you don't want?' She was genuinely delighted, more pleased, in fact, than she had been over the engagement ring. She put the silver cross round her neck fumbling under her metallic blonde hair to fasten the slender chain.

'Joan of Arc,' said Arthur.

'Oo, it's woke up again!' She bared her teeth at him, registering exaggerated scorn. Afraid that she had perhaps been sounding too grateful and had made a fool of herself, she said dubiously, peering down at the cross: 'Aren't you supposed to go to church or summat when you wear one of these?'

Arthur said: 'Yes, you've got to take a vow of chastity.'

'Get back in the knifebox, bighead!' Rita picked up my empty plate, a move I recognized as an obscure gesture of affection. 'You can bring me a fur coat tomorrer,' she said genially. She went back to the counter, leaving us sitting at the rockety table in the corner of the Kit-Kat by the huge, throbbing refrigerator.

'The sexfulness is terrific,' Arthur said, watching her go.

I was back in the buoyant, almost hysterical mood.

'Lo, she is the handmaiden of my desires!' I said, raising

a solemn right hand. Arthur took the cue to go into the Bible routine.

'And a voice spake,' he said in a loud, quavering voice. 'And the voice said Lo, who was that lady I saw ye with last cock-crow?'

'And Moses girded up his loins and said Verily, that was no lady, that was my spouse,' I responded.

'Yea, and it was so.'

'Yea, even unto the fifth and sixth generations.'

We finished our coffee and got up, guffawing and blowing kisses at Rita. 'Don't do owt I wouldn't do!' she called, in an unusual mood herself.

We left the glass doors wide open, the doughnut-eaters yelling 'Door!' after us, and walked out into Moorgate and across the road towards Town Arcade.

I had got over the feeling of guilt at meeting Arthur so soon after the hideous *contretemps* with his mother. I had been thinking of telling him about it, in one form or another, but now I was glad that I hadn't.

We walked into Town Arcade shouting: 'Paymer! Paymer! War declared! Paymer!' and our voices echoed under the arched glass roof. The women shoppers, shuffling miserably after each other with their string bags and their packets of cream biscuits, stared at us. 'Paymer, lady?' I called, flourishing an imaginary *Echo*. To my own surprise, I found that I was still carrying under my arm the gramophone record I had taken out of the house hours ago.

'Let's go take the piss out of Maurie,' I said.

Maurie was the owner of the X-L Disc Bar at the top of the Arcade, a slight, dapper little man who looked like an Armenian. He was interested in youth work and all the rest of it, and was always going on about showing tolerance and treating everybody as adults. When we had nothing to do we would go in and bully him. 'Hey, Maurie, this record's got all grooves in it.'

'Wonder if we'll get any buckshee records out of him?' said Arthur. We opened the door with our feet and almost fell into the shop.

On Saturday afternoons the X-L Disc Bar was crowded with girls in gipsy ear-rings and youths in drainpipe trousers. They were the same people that we saw in the Roxy every week, but we never saw them anywhere else in Stradhoughton. They seemed to be transported invisibly from one place to another. They made me feel curiously old-fashioned in my stained raincoat and my crumpled suit, and I put on the intellectual act, sloping one shoulder down and trying to look as though the record under my arm was a copy of *Under Milk Wood*. One of the Kit-Kat crowd, doing a sort of skaters' waltz round the shop, called 'Rag-bones!' but nobody else took any notice.

The Disc Bar would not have made a good subject for Man o' the Dales' Yorkshire Sketchbook. It had been a quite passably modern record shop when Maurie first opened it, but under his policy of live and let live it had been quickly reduced to a glass shambles. The cone-shaped ashtray stands, their bright yellow smudged with black, were already tilted, broken, and abandoned. The showcases, which were supposed to hang in mid-air on steel wires, sagged and lurched so dangerously that they had to be propped up on old packing cases. One of them was broken, a great jagged crack going along one corner. There were scuff marks all along the orange walls.

The girls in their tartan trousers swarmed around the record booths, leaving the doors swinging open untidily, so that half a dozen melodies – the pop songs, the trumpet specialities, and the jazzed-up hymns – met and collided somewhere in the middle of the shop. A boy of about sixteen in a leather lumber jacket was leaning against the counter, juggling with a plastic record sleeve. Little Maurie, in his red braces, was trying to make himself heard. 'Would you mind? I know it's a great temptation, but would you mind?'

Arthur pirouetted across the shop like a dancer, using the peculiar gliding steps that seemed to be more or less obligatory in this centre. He found a cluster of friends from the band that played at the Roxy, and was immediately swallowed up with them in the corner. I stood by myself, hesitating. The odd thing was that he seemed to know everybody and I didn't. In the No. 1 thinking it was sometimes the other way round.

I heard a familiar, grating voice behind me and looked round. It was Stamp, holding up an L.P. and shouting: 'Hey, Maurie, is this a record?' – a joke, if you could call it a joke, that he had used a hundred times before. Stamp was never out of the Disc Bar. Little Maurie was the leader of the youth club whose illiterate posters Stamp was always designing. 'Hey, Maurie! Maurie! Is this a record?' I cuffed his arm so that he almost dropped the L.P. 'No, slipped disc,' I said.

'Oh, they've let *you* out, have they?' jeered Stamp, his eyes narrowing maliciously.

'Yes, they wanted to make room for you,' I said. I was glad to have met even Stamp. I turned away, looking around the shop to see if there was anybody else I knew.

'I say!' Stamp called me back.

'I wouldn't come in on Monday if I were you,' he said.

'I wouldn't come in on *Tuesday* if I were you. Why not?'

He was grinning in the malevolent way he had when he had got hold of a piece of rich bad news. 'I've just been back to the office to get some stuff,' he said. 'Shadrack's adding up your postage book.'

'After you with Shadrack,' I said. I suddenly felt ill. In the light voice: 'Did he say anything?'

'What?'

'Did he *say* anything, dozey! About the frigging postage book?'

'No, he was just muttering to himself. He had all the money and all the stamps out, though. He was adding it all up. How much have you knocked off?'

'Haven't knocked anything off.' Some of Stamp's friends were hovering round, staring at me. 'Only the book's not up to date, that's all,' I said.

'Borstal here we come,' said Stamp. He turned back to his friends, tittering. Over his shoulder, he said casually: 'Your mate's upstairs.'

I knew at once, with a quick vibration running through me, whom he was talking about, exactly as I had known when he mentioned her this morning. I glanced involuntarily up the stairs where the classical department was, all thought of Shadrack going out of my head before it had time even to take root. One of Stamp's friends, a dopey-looking youth in an Italian striped suit, said: *'Git in there, Charlie!'* I walked slowly up the stairs, the noise fading into a cacophonous backwash. Things I had forgotten came back and I was already steeped in the familiar atmosphere, the sense of freshness, relief, absurd comfort, anticipation, and the hint of some elusive scent that I knew for a fact did not exist. I was already telling her, 'I could remember how you *smelled*, even!' The last thing I heard was Stamp shouting, away in the distance, down in the shop, 'Hey, Maurie, this record's got a hole in it!'

The classical department, usually deserted on a Saturday afternoon, had an almost public-library air about it. It was thickly carpeted, with a single glass counter and a row of grey record booths. The rest of it was empty and light and spacious, and quiet. Liz was standing behind the counter, handing a record album to a middle-aged man in a black overcoat. She was talking to him in her comfortable, plummy voice. I knew that she had seen me out of the corner of her eye, and was putting the moment off, the same as I was.

I was trying on expressions, as though I carried a mirror about with me and was pulling faces in it. I tried to look stunned, because after all there was the material for it, and I tried to assemble some kind of definite emotion that I wasn't putting on or concocting out of the ingredients of the atmosphere she carried around with her. I found that what I had was a sensation of singing.

The man picked up the record album and went into one of the record booths, closing the door behind him.

I walked slowly forward to the counter.

'Hullo, Liz.'

'Hullo, Billy.'

I spoke in what I hoped was the low, husky voice, indicating the end of a long journey or something, but she spoke frankly and happily, as though she were delighted to see me and had no reason to hide what she felt.

We grinned at each other, full of relief, like people who have found each other again in a crowd. She was still wearing the same old things, the green suède jacket and the crumpled black skirt. But the crisp white blouse went well with her round, shiny face, the mousy hair, and the eyes that laughed aloud.

'It's been a long time,' I said, knowing it was a cliché, in fact selecting it *as* a cliché, but trying to put some meaning into what I was saying.

She shook her head from side to side, happily, considering the point.

'Oh – a month. Five weeks.'

'I ought to say it seemed like years.'

She grinned again. Liz was the only girl I had ever met who knew *how* to grin, or anything about it. 'Isn't this *grand*?' she said.

'I could even remember how you smelled,' I said.

She gave me a mock bow. 'Thank you, kind sir, she said.'

'When did you get back?'

'Yesterday.'

'Thank you very much for ringing me up and telling me.'

She wrinkled her nose, not in the same way as the Witch but in a friendly, candid way. Liz never gave excuses.

'I would have seen you tonight, anyway,' she said. 'Are you going to the Roxy?'

Who isn't? I thought. I started rapidly disposing of personnel. The Witch, for one, would quite obviously be going into a nunnery or somewhere after this afternoon's business. Rita, if I stood her up, would not dream of paying her own way into the Roxy. I did not care, anyway, knowing that I could tell Liz all about it if I wanted to.

'Yes,' I said. 'But I wish you'd rung me up.'

'I hadn't time.' She grinned broadly again, telling me not to believe her and not to worry because it didn't matter, and it didn't. 'Ask me what I'm doing *here*.'

'What are you doing here?'

'Helping Maurie out for the day.' No time to ring me up, but time to help Maurie out. It still didn't matter. The only thing that crossed my mind was the vague question of how Liz knew Maurie. She seemed to know everybody. It was part of the enigma, one of the things about her that I could never get into the test tube and examine.

'Well what have you been doing all these weeks?' she said, bubbling over with it all. 'How's the script-writing? How are the songs? How's Arthur?' She was the only girl I knew who cared, or who could talk about things as though they really mattered. We began chattering, eagerly interrupting, laughing, grinning at each other as though we knew the whole joke about the world and understood it. We talked until the man in the record booth, whom we had both forgotten, emerged with the record album and paid for it and went away. It was nearly closing time.

'Ask me where I've been all these weeks,' said Liz.

'No,' I said steadily, not laughing this time. It was the one standing challenge between us and I had always told myself that I would never ask. I did not know any longer whether I was afraid to, or whether it was out of some kind of respect for her, or whether it was just an obsession like growing my thumb nail until it was a quarter of an inch long.

'But you might have sent me a postcard,' I said.

'Postcards next time. If there is a next time,' she added softly.

I went downstairs again, waving to her. The crowd had thinned out, leaving a litter of discarded records and cigarette packets on the floor and on the glass showcases. Arthur had gone, and so had his friends from the band. Most of Stamp's crowd had gone too, but Stamp was still there, sniggering with Maurie at the counter.

The old gramophone record still under my arm, I remembered what I had come into the Disc Bar for in the first place. I was loth to approach Maurie without Arthur to back me up, but I decided to do so for Stamp's benefit.

'Hey, Maurie!' I said. 'Can I have the money back on this record?'

He glared at me, a sour look that was unusual for him, and snapped: 'Why?'

'It only *plays* one tune.'

Maurie rang open his cash register. 'Yes, I've been *watch*ing you,' he said venomously. 'I've been *hear*ing about you.' Stamp was leaning on the counter, trying to look as though he didn't know what was going on. 'You're another of these who come in here, thinking you own the shop. Well *I* don't know where you get your money from.'

Maurie always dribbled when he spoke. He sucked in vigorously with his upper lip, retrieving the thin spittle that had been trickling down his chin.

'Well we're having a big clear-out. From now on it's a shop, not a market-place. Take the money and clear out.'

He flung some coins on the scratched glass counter. I had to scrabble at them to pick them up. Stamp was finding it difficult not to break out sniggering again.

'And don't come back again!' said Maurie.

But I was whistling as I walked out of the shop, and I whistled all the way down the Arcade.

9

I DID nothing but walk around town for an hour and a half, watching Saturday evening begin to happen and the slow queues forming outside the Odeon and the Gaumont. The people walked about as though they were really going somewhere. I stood for a quarter of an hour at a time, watching them get off the buses and disperse themselves about the streets. I was amazed and intrigued that they should all be content to be nobody but themselves.

When it was half past seven I got on a bus myself, on my way to the New House, the pub where I did my club turn. As a rule I could not face this experience without a stiff shot of No. 1 thinking, seeing myself returning to Stradhoughton as the world-famous comedian, doing charity concerts and never losing the common touch. But tonight I did not think about it at all. When Liz was in Stradhoughton I could transport myself from hour to hour like a levitationist, so that all events between one meeting and another were things that happened to other people and not to me.

It was only when I got off the bus at Clogiron Lane and the New House was in sight that I began to unload the ballast and I was left, as usual, with nothing but a kind of desperate inertia.

The New House was an enormous drinking barracks that had been built to serve Cherry Row and the streets around it. The New House was not its proper title. According to the floodlit inn-sign stuck on a post in the middle of the empty car park, the pub was called the Who'd A Thought It. There had been a lot of droll speculation in Man o' the

Dales' column about how this name had come about, but whatever the legend was it had fallen completely flat in Clogiron Lane. Nobody ever called the pub anything but the New House.

There was a windy, rubber-tiled hallway where the children squatted, eating potato crisps and waiting for their mothers. Two frosted-glass doors, embossed with the brewery trademark, led off it, one into the public bar and one into the saloon. It was necessary to take one route or the other to get into the concert-room; the only other alternative was to approach the concert-room direct through its own entrance and run the gauntlet of fat women, sitting in rows with their legs apart, shrieking with laughter and gulping down gin and orange. Either that or climb in through the lavatory window.

I decided on the public-bar route. I smoothed my hair back, straightened my tie, and went in. I preferred the public bar, anyway. The men who sat here were refugees from the warm terrace-end pubs that had been pulled down; they sat around drinking mild and calling to each other across the room as though nothing had changed. 'Have you got them theer, Charlie?' – 'Aye, they're up in our garridge.' – 'I'll come down for 'em tomorrow morning.' They seemed to have secrets between them, and they reunited into a world of their own wherever they went. The few items in the New House that gave it anything like the feel of a pub – the dartboard, the cribbage markers, the scratched blind-box, and the pokerwork sign that said IYBMADIBYO, if you buy me a drink I'll buy you one – were all part of the same portable world, as if they had been wheeled here in prams in the flight from the old things.

Through the smoke, a voice croaked jubilantly: 'Here he is – *the boy!*' and I realized at once that I had made another mistake. From this point I had to walk through a barricade of Formica-topped tables where all these men sat clacking dominoes and making their observations. I waved my hand flaccidly at one or two of the people I recognized. A man called Freddy Platt, who never did anything else but sit around drinking beer all day, started up.

'Nah lad, Billy! Where's thi dog?' The others laughed, and he looked around eagerly for someone to egg him on. 'He's forgotten t' dog ageean! Ask him what he's done wi' t' dog, Sam!'

'Where's thi dog, Billy?'

Once, in some kind of effort to prise myself into this community of theirs, where they were always selling each other things and sharing the same interests, I had asked Freddy Platt if he wanted to take a dog off my hands. For about five minutes it had worked like an open sesame, with everybody in the bar shouting about dogs, and me in the middle of it, but when they found out the truth I had to pretend it was a joke.

'Nay, it's in t' dogs' home!' I called back in the hearty voice. They laughed indulgently.

Freddy Platt winked elaborately at his mates. 'When's ta bahn off to London, Billy?' he called. He started nudging the man next to him and urging: 'Go on, Sam, ask him when he's off to London.'

They were always bringing that one up, too. I had told them months ago, prematurely as it turned out, that I had a job in London waiting for me. I had been gratified, and then alarmed, at the way the story had spread through the pub, like a dangerous fire. They were still at it with the embers.

'When's ta bahn off to London, Billy?'

'I'll be going, don't you worry!' They laughed again, shaking their heads. 'He's a bugger, i'n't he?' said Freddy Platt. 'He is. He's a bugger.' I gave them the deprecating smile, cornered again into the position of village idiot or licensed clown or whatever it was they imagined me to be. Freddy shouted across the room: 'Has ta fetched that stuff down, Walter?' and they were back with their repertoire of secrets.

I walked through into the concert-room, a hideous cork-floored drill hall with buff walls and fancy strip-lighting fitments that looked like rejects from a luxury liner. The concert was already warming up, with the Clavioline thumping away and an Irish labourer, grasping the microphone as though it were a pint pot, singing, *'Blais this house, nya Lard we pray.'* Johnny the waiter moved round the room with his tin tray held high above his head, and the fat women sat at the bowlegged tables eating packets of nuts and knocking back the shorts. Their husbands stood at the long bar at the end of the room, where you didn't have to watch the concert if you didn't want to.

The long bar was where the members of the Ancient Order of Stags or whatever it was gathered on Saturday nights, waiting for their lodge meeting to begin upstairs. They were there now, all lean-faced men calling each other brother, for ever shaking hands and digging in their pockets for penny fines. In their own way they were as bad as Freddy Platt and *his* crowd and I gave them the same limp wave and looked away.

There was a patter of applause for the Irish singer, and Johnny the waiter cried: 'Can I 'ave your orders please before the next *turn*!' He started hustling round the room with his tray under his arm and a fistful of silver. Behind me a ponderous voice said: 'Now then, young man!'

I turned round to see another group of Stags padding in from the saloon bar, all holding pints of beer. In the middle of them was Councillor Duxbury, wearing the chain of past grand warden or something. He did not often come to this lodge, and when he did I managed as a rule to avoid him.

I was not sure what my status with him was after our encounter on Stradhoughton Moor; I played for safety with a non-committal smile.

One of the men he was with said with heavy jocularity: 'Well, is the worthy brother bahn to give us a turn toneet?'

Councillor Duxbury gave me a solemn wink and said: 'Nay, he is but an untutored apprentice, brother deacon.'

Brother deacon winked too. Practically every man in the pub made a practice of winking before he opened his mouth. 'And what about thee, brother warden? Art thou tutored?'

'Aye, it's not me that wants tutoring.' Councillor Duxbury was looking at me pointedly, and I knew that I was supposed to get some kind of hidden message out of what he was saying. I was wondering already what I had found so understanding about him on Stradhoughton Moor. Then it occurred to me that he had probably heard about Shadrack's audit of the postage book since then.

'Tha'rt initiated, then?' said brother deacon, staggering on with the joke. 'Give t' password.'

'At my initiation I was taught to be cautious. I will letter or half it wi' thee, which you please,' recited Councillor Duxbury.

The Stags spent half their time fooling about in this way, and some of them I knew had long ago stopped speaking in any other manner. Councillor Duxbury and brother deacon were settling down for a long, pedantic cross-talk; but before they had the chance to go rumbling through their passwords, the third man in the group spoke huffily: 'The lodge is not yet tiled, brothers!'

Through the crackling microphone, Johnny the waiter announced: 'Quiet, please! *Can* I 'ave a bit of quiet? And now, two very clever young men who've come all the way over from Dewsbury to entertain us tonight, Bob and

116

Harry! Quiet now, please!' Two young men with fresh, eager-to-please faces bounded on to the low platform and started miming facetiously to a record of 'Baby it's cold outside'. They were making an elaborate strong-man-and-coy-girl act of it, fluttering with the eyelids and slapping each other, and I found it embarrassing to look at them.

'Well we'll go up and get t' lodge tiled, then, if tha'rt so particular,' said Councillor Duxbury.

'Shall we tak' t' untutored apprentice up wi' us?' said brother deacon, clawing at me playfully. 'Come on, lad, ther'll be someone tha knows up theer.'

'The craft will keep its omnipotent eye on t' untutored apprentice,' said Councillor Duxbury.

They were all winking at each other like maniacs, and shoving each other's elbows. Filled with an accumulation of nausea I muttered: 'Excuse me,' and sidled out of their way. I meant to take refuge in the saloon bar but, hardly knowing what I was doing, I found myself slipping through the first door I could find, and I was back in the public bar. The old voice cried: 'Here he is again – *the boy!*' I stopped, feeling trapped in the haze of faces. I looked wildly around the bar, searching for a beer barrel or something that I could focus my eyes on without any harm coming from it. I saw an old man like a tramp, hobbling about the room trying to sell an armful of comic papers. I gazed at him steadily as though trying to place his blank face.

Out of one of the close, anonymous groups I heard the honking voice of Freddy Platt: 'Ther's thi paper here, Billy! Give 'im t' paper, Sam!'

'*Billy's Weekly Liar!*' roared somebody else. 'Go on, Sam, give 'im it!'

'He doesn't want it – he's t' editor!'

We had been through this one before, many a time. *Billy's Weekly Liar* was the comic paper that was peddled about the pub on Saturday nights, along with the *War Cry* and the *Empire News*. They would buy one copy between four of them and sit around pointing at the jokes with their stubby fingers. When they saw me coming they would bring out their own old joke.

'*Billy's Weekly Liar*! Here y'are, Billy!' Somebody was trying to shove the paper into my hand.

'Billy Liar!' laughed Freddy Platt. He was shouting at the top of his voice to compete with the noise from the concert-room next door; the miming act was climbing up to a screaming, oscillating crescendo, and it needed nothing but a couple of policemen running about blowing whistles to complete the sudden, hysterical chaos. 'Billy Liar! We'll call 'im that, eh? We'll call 'im that, Sam! Billy Liar. By! Where's thi dog, Billy?'

He did not get any response from me. I could not even see him. I stared sightlessly around the public bar, darting from one object to another without recognizing anything. 'He's a bugger!' shouted Freddy Platt. 'He is, he makes me laugh! By!'

I felt someone prodding me from behind. I staggered a little under the impetus and wondered whether there would be any future in letting myself go on falling until I was flat on my face on the floor and they would have to carry me out into the cool, quiet air. It was Johnny the waiter with his tray loaded with empty glasses and bottle tops. 'You're on next, Billy boy.' Without caring much what I was doing I stumbled back into the concert-room. 'Billy Liar and his talking dog!' shouted Freddy Platt. I whipped round angrily, and saw that the whole lot of them had got up and were following me into the concert-room. I shambled across the cork floor through the troops of women, buckling at the knees in case I should retrieve the idea of dropping in a dead faint.

'All right, now the best of order now! If you please! Next on the bill to entertain us tonight we 'ave a young man who needs no introduction from me. Quiet, please, for our very own Billee *Fish*ah! Break it up small, you lads!'

I climbed up on the platform, with the Clavioline running meaninglessly through the first bars of 'I want to be happy'. I looked out across the concert-room at all the people, trying to remember the first line of my act but knowing perfectly well that, whatever it was, it was nothing to do with them, and, whatever they were, it was nothing to do with me. Some of the women at the round, rocking tables stared at me like cows waiting to be milked, but most of them took no notice at all. Freddy Platt and his friends stood at the end of the room, by the public-bar door, in a swaying, solid group, still swopping their secrets. I was surprised and depressed to see that Bob and Harry, the two young men involved in the miming act, had sat down with a crowd old enough to be their fathers; they were smoking the same Woodbines and drinking the same mild beer. All the people in the concert-room sat so comfortably, as though they had reached a reasonable agreement with life and death, as though they knew all about it, all that there was to know about it.

I put on my funny face and started on the club turn, wishing that I could whistle 'In a Monastery Garden' through my teeth instead, and please everybody.

'*Ah'm coortin'.*'

A few titters from some of the more impressionable women but, on the whole, dead silence.

'*Ah am. Ah'm coortin'.*'

I jerked my head round with the well-staged, well-practised pop-eyed, indignant look, as though expecting scorn or laughter or disbelief or some reaction of some kind or another from the audience.

'*It's a Wakefield lass.*'

I saw the same people, the women, Freddy Platt and Co., and the few customers at the long bar. Most of the Stags had gone upstairs, knocking three times on the door to get themselves let into the lodge; but there was one man standing by himself at the bar counter, dragging on a cigarette and holding his beer as though it had dealt him an injury. I caught his eye and fear, real fear and not a substitute, clutched me. I forgot the act and bent down urgently to where Johnny the waiter was ladling out gin and pep at the table nearest the platform.

'Johnny! Johnny! *What the bloody hell is our old man doing here?*'

Johnny looked up, surprised. 'He's joining t' Stags, it's initiation night,' he whispered. 'Get on wi' t' turn!'

I muttered, 'Jesus Christ Almighty' and straightened up and faced the microphone, feeling as though somebody had just kicked me in the stomach. I had never seen the old man in a pub before, and had come to depend upon him never using the New House. He was looking at me sardonically; so, if it came to that, was the rest of the audience by now. Some of the women were getting restless. I gave the old man a stiff, formal bow and he turned away with a gesture of contempt and embarrassment. Freddy Platt shouted: 'When's ta bringing t' dog on, Billy?' I ran quickly through my lines. Ah'm coortin'. It's a Wakefield lass.

'*She does, she comes from Wakefield. She's a nice lass, only she's got one big fault. She stutters.*'

There was some untidy sniggering from various parts of the concert-room. In so far as the act would come to life at all, it was beginning to warm up.

'*She does, she stutters.*'

I gave them the pop-eyed look again, avoiding the old man's eye. I had just blasted him with the Ambrosian repeater gun; so far as I was concerned he was no longer there.

'But she's a very warm-hearted lass, very warm-hearted. She'll do owt for you. And she likes a cuddle. Oh, yes, she likes a cuddle. Only she stutters.

'We were sitting in t' parlour one night, y'know, just t' two of us, and she were sitting there, and I were sitting here, and she looked at me, she looked at me and she says, would you like a nice cuh cuh cuh cuh cuh cuh cuh cuh –'

The sniggering was well set in by now. The fattest woman of all screamed aloud and the others laughed, this time at her. Freddy Platt was making some kind of noise of his own at the back of the room.

'Would you like a cuh cuh cuh cuh cuh cuh –'

I suddenly realized, with the old sinking feeling, what the low thudding noise I had been hearing for the last minute was. Councillor Duxbury had descended the stairs from the lodge and was clomping deliberately across the concert-room floor towards the gents, the seal of past grand warden swinging round his neck like a prize medal on an old shire horse. He passed within a yard of the old man, but they did not speak to each other.

'Would you like a cuh cuh cuh cuh cup of tea?'

The women shrieked. 'T' record's stuck!' shouted Freddy Platt. I saw Councillor Duxbury off to the door of the lavatory.

'Then she gets all coy and says yes, ah knows thee, ah bet you thought I were going to ask if you wanted a cuh cuh cuh cuh cuh cup of cocoa!'

I got to the end of the stuttering joke, whatever it was. Councillor Duxbury emerged from the gents, buttoning his flies. He walked slowly over to the old man and stood indecisively at the side of him, as though he had forgotten what it was all about.

'But o' course, ah'm a poor man. Ah can't support her. Ah can't support her. Ah only had one clog on me foot when ah came to Stradhoughton. Only one clog on me foot. But very soon ah were riding about in taxis.'

The two of them, the old man and Councillor Duxbury, stood talking for a moment. The old man glanced in my direction once, but not malevolently. He finished his beer and the two of them set off towards the stairs, the old man hanging back to keep pace with Duxbury. I had no idea why he should be joining the Stags, but it was obvious that as one Stag to another Councillor Duxbury would tell him all that there was to be told about me.

'Ah had to take a taxi because ah only had one clog.'

I was back with the fat women and Freddy Platt and his crowd. I brought out the jokes as I remembered them, trying to bring the act to a finish. Some of the women screeched from time to time, but nobody really cared whether I was on or off the platform. They were beginning to turn round to each other and whisper and light cigarettes, and to pour out beer and hold it studiously to the light, as though I wasn't there at all.

'Any road, this feller stuttered as well. So he goes up to this bookie and y'know, it were t' right busy time, just before t' last race, and he says, ah've backed ah've backed ah've backed ah've backed ah've backed ah've backed –'

'Ah've backed a loser!' shouted Freddy Platt.

. . 'Ah've backed ah've backed ah've backed ah've backed. So t' bookie says, gerron wi' it, ah've not got all day –'

('Neither 'ave we!')

'So he says ah've backed ah've backed ah've backed ah've backed. So t' bookie says, come on, nark it –'

'Nark it?' exploded Freddy Platt triumphantly. 'Nark it? That's not Yorkshire!'

'So he says nark it –'

'That's not Yorkshire! That's London talk! He thinks he's in London!'

'*So he says –*'

Freddy Platt's mate, giving an excruciating imitation of a cockney, went: 'Eeyah! Ply the gyme, myte! Caw bloimey!'

The whole thing was getting out of hand. The concert-room was buzzing with talk and laughter, as though they had all just come out of a meeting. They were beginning to nudge each other, nodding in my direction and laughing to themselves. Johnny the waiter was making winding motions with his hand, telling me to get off the platform.

I called back in the bluff, appeasing voice: 'It's all right, ah'm just practising for when ah get to London! Any road, let me finish t' story! *So this bookie says give ower, 'ere's five quid, you can tell me what you've backed after t' race. So t' bloke – this feller – says nay, ah've backed ah've backed ah've backed –*'

There was a gale of laughter, the kind of laugh you get for sheer audacity. Freddy Platt and his friends were beginning to chant: 'Ah've backed ah've backed ah've backed.' Chairs were scraping and people were knocking glasses over and rooting in their handbags. Other people, total strangers, started chanting: 'Ah've backed ah've backed ah've backed.' There was a mood of pandemonium. I was expecting them any minute to start flicking pellets at each other.

'*Ah've backed my lorry through thy window,*' I finished, almost in a whisper. I jumped down from the platform, spraying the lot of them with the Ambrosian repeater gun. There was a trickle of applause from about four people, but most of them did not even realize I had finished. The pianist did not bother to give me a few bars on the Clavio-line, whether of 'I want to be happy' or any other tune. Staggering across the room I tried to remember how many

123

times I had done this club turn in the past; knowing that each occasion would, in retrospect, become a rich, separate source of acute embarrassment. Some of the women looked at me with a kind of compassionate detachment as I passed. They had stared at me in this way before but I had never realized that it was because they knew things I didn't know, because they were involved in basic matters that I had never even heard about.

I made for the nearest door I could see. 'By! *Tha* dropped a clanger there, Billy!' said Freddy Platt. ' "Nark it?" Tha didn't learn *that* in Yorkshire! Tha what? By!'

I raised my fist in what he was to imagine was a playful gesture. Up on the platform Johnny the waiter, trying to mend the broken illusions and turn the place back into a concert-room, announced that somebody or other would sing a laughing song. A middle-aged, cocky-looking man in a cloth cap, a seasoned club turn with a full diary of engagements, took the microphone. He began singing in a broad, confident voice.

> '*Now I think that life is merry,*
> *I think that life is fun,*
> *A short life and a happy one*
> *Is my rule number one,*
> *I laugh when it is raining,*
> *I laugh when it is fine,*
> *You may think I am foolish,*
> *But laughter is my line,*
> *Oh, ha ha ha ha ha ha,*
> *Ha ha ha ha hee,*
> *Ha ha ha ha ha ha,*
> *Ho ho ho ho hee.*'

'When's ta bahn off to London, Billy?' cried Freddy Platt. Some of the women nearest to him turned round and went 'Sssh!' They were all watching the singer, their potato crisps untouched. The place was already transformed.

'Billy Liar and his talking dog, the well-known double act!'

'Sssh!'

> *'Ha ha ha ha ha ha,*
> *Ho ho ho ho hee,*
> *Oh, ha ha ha ha ha ha,*
> *Ha ha ha ha hee.'*

I blundered out of the pub and into the car-park. I did not stop running until I was clear of Clogiron Lane.

I O

THE Roxy was the last splash of light before Stradhoughton petered out and the moors took over. It was supposed to be a suburban amenity or something; at any rate its red, humming neon sign spluttered out the words 'Come Dancing' six night a week, and all the grownup daughters of the cold new houses round about converged on it in their satin frocks, carrying their dance shoes in paper bags advertising pork pies. Youths who had come from all over Stradhoughton for the catch sat around on the low brick banisters by the entrance, combing their hair and jeering at each other.

I approached the place warily, along the shadows, in case Rita was among the girls who promenaded up and down the cracked concrete forecourt, waiting for their escorts to come and pay for them in. I was still full of the evening's fiasco, with selected incidents from it swimming in and out of my head like shoals of bright fish, but as I stepped into the pool of light outside the Roxy I felt an overwhelming relief that another experience was finished with and not still to come. A girl I had once known was waiting by the entrance; I said, 'Hiya, Mavis!' boldly as I passed. I had once written a poem comparing her bosom with twin melons, and it was always fairly embarrassing to meet her nowadays. But it was something fresh to think about anyway. She said, 'Lo, Billy,' and I walked almost cheerfully up to the paybox.

Inside the Roxy it was hot and bright and, as Stamp had once put it, smelling like a ladies' bog. The foyer, separated from the dance floor by a certain amount of cream fretwork and a lot of big plants, was crowded with the same kind of youths I had seen in the X-L Disc Bar earlier; they were all pulling at their tight clean collars and working their heads round like tortoises. Their girl friends queued for the lavatory, and emerged with their zip-boots and their head-scarves discarded, each one making a sort of furtive entry like a butterfly that has turned into a caterpillar. I surveyed this scene with the usual distaste, hunching my shoulders and adopting the attitude of the visiting poet; I was not inclined at this moment towards the bit of No. 1 thinking, fairly standard in this quarter, where I took the floor to a cha-cha with one of the professional exhibition dancers who looked so much like wardresses. I could not see Liz anywhere. I wandered through the fretwork Moorish archway on to the fringe of the dance floor.

The floor was already crowded, with the revolving ball of mirrors overhead catching a hideous violet spotlight and dancing the colours over the pimpled face of, to name the first person I saw, Stamp. He was doing a smirking foxtrot with some girl in a tight, red-wool dress; when he turned her in my direction for a piece of cross-stepping that nearly had the pair of them flat on their backs, I saw that his partner was Rita. From her slightly dazed expression, open-mouthed and cloudy-eyed – a kind of facial rigor mortis that touched her whenever she got inside a dance hall – I guessed that Rita had been here about half an hour. I was a little pained that she had not bothered to wait outside for me – she was, after all, still my fiancée, or thought she was – but I was glad to see that Stamp was taking care of her. He looked a little drunk; but that was his problem and not mine. They glided past without seeing me.

At the bandstand Arthur's friends, the Rockets, blew their muted instruments behind little plywood pulpits, the drummer brushing away and grinning round at everybody as though he knew them. Arthur himself, wearing a blue American-cut suit, was swaying about in front of the stick-shaped microphone, waiting to sing. He looked like Danny Kaye or somebody doing a relaxed season at the Palladium, and I could not help admiring his poise and the professional way he stood there doing nothing. I was glad that he had not seen my performance at the New House. I caught his eye and waved to him, a half-wave arrested before it began. Arthur gave me the same mock bow that, in his situation, I had given to the old man; but he did it with a casual dash that made it part of the act.

The people on the dance floor hung around holding hands limply as one tune finished and the Rockets started on the next. Arthur, splaying his hands out, began to sing. '*Yooo're – my – ev'rthring, ev'ry li'l thing I know-oo.*' He always affected an American accent when he sang. I disliked it, but I had to admit it was good. Then swaying couples brushed past me and, as Stamp and Rita came round for the second time, I began to pick my way upstairs to the balcony.

Liz was sitting by herself at one of the wickerwork tables, gazing down over the dance floor with her chin resting on her plump arms, and smiling happily to herself. I sat down without saying anything to her. She reached out her hand across the table and I took it.

'Late,' said Liz reprovingly as the song finished.

'Yes,' I said. 'I've had an exciting day.'

'I bet you have. Where've you been?'

'Oh, here and there –'

' – up and down,' said Liz, joining in the chant.

' – round and about.' This was a common exchange between us. We used it most when I brushed, without actually asking, on the subject of where Liz kept disappearing to

128

for weeks at a time. I took her hand again. She was still wearing her old black skirt, but with a fresh white blouse. Her green suède jacket hung on the back of the basket chair. I was happy to be with her; it was like being in a refuge, her beaming, comfortable presence protecting me from the others.

'Tell me some plans,' said Liz luxuriously.

'What plans?'

'Any plans. *Your* plans. You *always* have plans. What are you going to do next?'

'I'm thinking of going to London,' I said.

'Only thinking?'

'Well, *going*. Soon, anyway.'

'When's soon?' Liz and I could talk like this for hours, batting the same moonbeams backwards and forwards across the table, enjoying ourselves enormously.

'Well, *soon*.'

'That sounds remote. Why not now?'

'Difficult,' I said.

'No, it's easy. You just get on a train and, four hours later, there you are in London.'

'Easy for you,' I said. 'You've had the practice. Liz –?' We were both leaning over the balcony, our hands dovetailed together. On the packed dance floor, near the bandstand, there was a small arena of space where Stamp and Rita, gyrating dangerously, were working out a dance of their own invention. They were both looking down at the floor to see what their feet were doing.

'Yes?' said Liz.

'Stamp calls you Woodbine Lizzie,' I said.

'You should hear what I call Stamp,' said Liz.

I scanned the dance floor idly, and then sat up with a jolt. I had once read about Shepheard's Hotel in Cairo that if you sat there long enough everyone you knew would pass your table. The Roxy was this sort of establishment too and why someone didn't blow *that* up I could never understand, because the next person I picked out, bouncing along the pine-sprung floor with fresh chalk on his uppers was Shadrack himself, doing the quickstep as it might be performed by a kangaroo. The girl he was with, just to complete the wild pattern of coincidence, was Mavis, the one with the twin-melon bosom I had spoken to outside the Roxy. They were no doubt talking about me. Stamp and Rita were still milling around near the bandstand, and I suddenly knew for certain that somewhere on the premises the Witch, too, was waiting, breathing through her nose and swinging her skirt and looking in general as though she had come to dance the Gay Gordons over a couple of swords.

'Let's go for a walk,' I said.

'Soon,' said Liz, mocking me.

Downstairs the drums rolled and Arthur came to the microphone, lifting his hands to quell the faint suggestion of applause. He put his face close to the mike and, in his half-American accent, began the smooth talk that went down so well.

'*Lazengenelmen, are we all happy? Thank you, madam. Next week at the Roxy we have another all-pop night, feat'ring the Rockets, that golden songstress Jeannie Lewis – Jeannie Lewis, I'm not saying she's fat but she's the only girl I know who when she has a chest complaint, she gets her treatment wholesale – and by popular request, yours truly.* Success! *Lazengenelmen, when I came to Stradhoughton I only had one clog. Now I ride around in taxis. I have to take a taxi I've only got one clog.*'

There were waves of relaxed laughter for Arthur, a cabaret sort of atmosphere that suited him perfectly. Jeannie Lewis, the singer, was sitting on a cane chair by the band, heaving her sequined bosom. Arthur waited for silence, clicking his fingers and smiling confidently.

'*And now a special treat for us all. I want to continue the dance with a little number which I wrote in conjunction with my very good friend Billy Fisher. Where are you, Billy?*' The spotlight played hopefully about the floor, while the Rockets' drummer made a facetious clacking on the kettle-drum.

'That's *you!*' said Liz excitedly.

'I'm all right,' I muttered, hiding my face.

'*Well I know he's out there somewhere,*' said Arthur. '*Maybe he's celebrating the big news, because I know you'll all be glad to know that Billy has just landed himself a big job in London, writing scripts for that verywellknown comedian Danny Boon! I'm sure we wish him all the best in the world.*'

'You stupid *cow!*' I hissed. There was a bit of desultory applause, and one or two of the people on the balcony who knew me slightly looked at me curiously. In spite of it all, I tried to look reasonably famous.

'*Now on with the dance with the little number by Billy Fisher and yours truly — "Can't get along without you"!*' He said it in the coy way that television disc jockeys have, putting the eye on a random girl when he pronounced this soft word 'you'.

'I wish he'd stop calling himself yours truly,' I said through my teeth.

'Shush,' said Liz. 'I want to hear your song.'

The band struck up far too slowly for the number and Arthur, the wry creases in his forehead, began to sing.

> '*Soon you will be saying good-bye,*
> *Just let me mention that I*
> *Can't get along without you.*

> *You seem to have changed with the moon,*
> *Now my heart beats out of tune,*
> *Can't get along without you.'*

I squinted craftily at Liz, hoping she would think the song was dedicated to her. Then I looked down over the balcony at the people dancing below. Nobody seemed to be taking much notice of the song, and in fact Arthur's American accent had become so pronounced that it was difficult to understand what he was singing about. Shadrack and the girl Mavis had vanished, and so had Rita. Stamp was loitering on the brass-rimmed edge of the dance floor, obviously trying to find some way of sabotaging the number. I thought Arthur was doing that effectively himself.

> *'I want to discover*
> *If I'm to blame,*
> *Because as a lover*
> *You're not the same so tell me why.'*

'He's singing it all wrong,' I muttered, getting up. 'Anyway, I suppose I'd better go and congratulate him.' Liz wrinkled her nose at me, and I ran self-consciously down the stairs, keeping my eyes peeled for people who might want to see me.

> *'Please tell me why we must part,*
> *Darling it's breaking my heart,*
> *Can't get along without you.'*

I reached the bandstand as Arthur, his arms outstretched, touched the last note. The Rockets went straight into 'American Patrol' and he jumped down, flexing his shoulders and waving to his friends.

'And then I wrote –' I began, striking a dramatic pose for the beginning of our song-writing routine.

'Ah yes, and do you remember the little tune that went something like this,' said Arthur, clutching his heart with one hand and cupping the other to his ear.

'*You made me love you, I didn't want to do it, I didn't want to do it,*' I sang dutifully in the cracked phonograph voice.

'To think I wrote that song on the back of a menu in a fish restaurant –'

' – and today that menu is worth hundreds of pounds.'

'Yes, the price of fish rose steeply between the wars,' said Arthur, finishing the routine. But it was not the usual thing between me and him; this time he was talking loudly, addressing an audience, the admiring girls who stood around the band giggling and doing little solo jigs.

'And then I wrote –' he said, looking round. I drew him on one side.

'Bloody good, man,' I said. 'How did you manage to persuade them to let you sing it?'

'In your honour,' said Arthur, and now that we had dropped the routine I thought that he was talking in a curiously formal sort of voice.

'Bloody good. Wish you hadn't announced that bit about Danny Boon, though.'

'Why not. It's all fixed up, isn't it?' For the first time, I noticed the slight glint of malice in his eye and the corner of his lower lip twitching.

'Yes, course it is. Only I just didn't want anyone to know just yet, that's all. We ought to get that song recorded and send it up to a publisher.'

'We're going to do it,' said Arthur, meaning him and the Rockets, and also meaning without any help from me.

'Only one thing,' I said in the light voice. 'You want to sing it with a bit less of an American accent.'

133

Arthur turned to me full-face, and I got the whole effect of the studied, indifferent approach.

'I'll sing it with a *Yorkshire* accent if you like.'

I flared up. 'I don't want you to sing it with *any* flaming accent. Just sing it as it's flaming well written, that's all.'

'Listen, boy, if I sang that song the way you wrote it it'd clear the bleeding hall. You've still got a lot to learn, cocker.'

'Oh, for Christ sake –'

Arthur nodded his chin. 'Yes, I can see them taking *you* down a peg or two when you get to London. *If* you get to London, I should say. Anyway, don't tell *me* how to sing, matey. Anyone'd think you were going to work for bleeding Glenn Miller.'

'Oh, it's like that, is it?' I said.

'Yes, it's like that. And another thing. I don't know what bloody crap you've been telling my mother about the Witch being this bloody sister of yours, but she's been doing her nut all afternoon. So bloody lay off, for Christ sake.'

He strode back to the bandstand, grabbing the microphone and switching on the American voice. *'And now folks,* by *request – the Hokey-Cokey!'* I turned away, miserable and depressed.

I had almost reached the stairs to the balcony when I saw Stamp leering over the banisters, beckoning his grimy fingers at me. I swung back abruptly and made for the cafeteria under the balcony, at the side of the dance floor. I meant to lose myself for a few minutes among the squealing girls scoffing cream buns and spilling lemonade down their dresses. I hurried through the rows of enamelled tables towards the dark corner by the band's changing-room, and it was only when I was in the middle of it that I realized what kind of bear-pit I had walked into down here. Immediately in front of me stood the Witch in a revolting green blouse and tartan skirt. She was confronting Rita, and Rita's vivid red dress seemed to have been designed especially to set off the miniature silver cross on its silver chain round her neck, and the engagement ring that she brandished on her finger.

'That's *my* cross,' I heard the Witch say in her loud, clear voice.

My heart, familiar with its duty on occasions such as this, did a full cartwheel. I dodged behind a sort of Corinthian column that was holding the balcony up, but too late to avoid the cold eye of the Witch.

'Talk of the devil,' she said coolly.

Rita turned round. 'Oo, look what's jumped out of the corned beef,' she said in her grating voice. She looked flushed and bewildered.

I said faintly: 'What's this – a deputation?' I skimmed through my mind, more or less in despair, to see if I could find a piece of skilful double-talk, aimed at their different intellectual levels, that would succeed in fooling them both. I opened my mouth to speak but felt the yawn welling up in my throat and I finished up standing there with my mouth open, gaping at them. 'What's up with him, is he catching flies or summat?' said Rita. It was obviously too late for the academic niceties, anyway.

'May I ask why you gave my cross to this – girl?' asked the Witch without any preamble.

My first thought was: 'May I ask why you said you'd given it back to your cousin?' But I still hankered after the subtle approach. 'Yes, it *is* very similar, isn't it?' I said.

'It's my cross. It's got the tooth-mark on it where you bit it that day when you made that ridiculous scene.'

'Do you mean that day at Ilkley, which I am sure Rita is anxious to hear about?' I said, with the intention of embarrassing her.

135

'It's my cross,' said the Witch.

'No it isn't,' I said. 'You gave yours back to your cousin. I just happen to have one similar. If you want to know, your cousin got it from me in the first place.'

'Oh. So you make a *prac*tice of giving these things away, do you?'

'No, I don't make a *prac*tice of it. I just happened to have half a dozen of them to spare. They're what Unitarians wear when they're dead,' I said. It was only a matter of time before the Witch realized who was wearing her engagement ring, and I was beginning to gabble a bit.

'And another thing,' the Witch said. 'Which one of us is supposed to be coming to tea at your house tomorrow?'

'Well neither of you, I'm afraid,' I said, giving them each the frank smile. 'We did hope to have a sort of family party – there were a lot of people coming, including yourselves – only the old man's been called away to Harrogate and he won't be back until Monday.'

'I suppose he's gone to a naval reunion,' said the Witch with her heavy sarcasm. She turned to Rita. 'You know his father's supposed to be a retired sea captain, don't you?'

'Thought he was supposed to be a cobbler or summat,' said Rita.

They started chewing the fat about what the old man did for a living. The Witch, in her bottle-green blouse, stood there looking like the cub-mistress Stamp claimed to have ravished on passion pills. A happy thought struck me, the first happy thought of the evening. I felt in my pocket for the little black beads that were still spilled there. I scooped up a handful, about a dozen or fourteen of them. On the table nearest to us, next to the Witch's handbag and the pile of blood oranges that she had got in as a treat for herself, there was a cup of black coffee, untouched. I moved my hand behind me and, as the two of them got on to the subject of the imaginary budgerigar, I unloaded the fistful of passion pills into the Witch's coffee.

'And now, if it's not too much to ask,' said the Witch, 'perhaps you'll tell us which one of us you invited to the Roxy tonight.'

'Oh, my God,' I said. 'Why don't you ask Rita why she's wearing your engagement ring?' I strode rapidly away, leaving them both open-mouthed as though being filmed at the end of a comedy sequence. I charged through the cafeteria to the foot of the balcony stairs. Stamp, still clinging hold of the banisters, clawed at me as I passed. He was definitely drunk.

'Piss off, Stamp,' I said curtly.

'*You've* had it,' he said thickly, grabbing my sleeve. '*You've* had it.'

'Keep your mucky hands to yourself.'

'You've *had* it,' drooled Stamp. 'Just been talking to Shadrack. You've *had* it, Fisher.'

I pulled his hand angrily off my sleeve. '*Will* you get your hands off my cowing, sodding, frigging *sleeve*!'

'You've had it,' he mumbled, sinking down on the stairs. I ran up two at a time and found Liz still sitting contentedly, looking over the balcony.

'Sorry I was so long. Let's go for a walk.'

She looked up and smiled. 'You're looking het up.'

'I'm feeling het up,' I said. I edged over to where she was sitting to check that she could not have seen what had been going on. 'I've just had an almighty barney with Arthur about the song. He finished up threatening to sing it with a Yorkshire accent.'

'Well he could do worse,' said Liz judiciously.

I sat down, breathing deeply, glad of any opportunity for a bit of normal conversation. The band was playing a soft waltz and there was something soothing about the bobbing heads below us.

'Don't say you're another of these Yorkshire fanatics,' I said.

'No. But there's lots of nice things in Yorkshire. Nice people. To name only one,' she said, squeezing my hand.

'Which is why you keep leaving it, I suppose?'

'Could be.'

To break the silence I said, 'I was talking to that bloke who does the Man o' the Dales column in the *Echo* the other day –'

'Who? Do you mean John Hardcastle?' Liz broke in. 'I *know* him.' She knew everybody.

'That's him,' I said with the sinking feeling. 'At least, I *think* it was him. *One* of the blokes on the *Echo*, anyway. We were going over all this satanic mills lark that he's always doing, and *I* said, Dark satanic mills I can put up with, they're part of the picture. But when it comes to dark satanic power stations, dark satanic housing estates, and dark satanic dance halls –'

'That's good. You ought to use that.'

'So *he* said, That's the trouble with you youngsters, you want –'

'Youngsters? *He's* got a nerve! He's not much older than you are! Are you sure it was John Hardcastle?'

'Oh, for God's sake,' I said desperately. 'A big chap with a moustache – is that him?'

'That's right,' said Liz calmly. 'He's sitting over there.' She nodded casually to a young man with a crowd of people three or four tables away, handlebar moustache and all. Why wasn't Man o' the Dales an old man? And why the handlebar moustache? He looked up, saw Liz and waved. I sat back, exhausted. By now I would not have been surprised to see Councillor Duxbury himself, dancing the Boston Two-Step down below and change out of four-pence.

'Let's go for a walk,' I said weakly.

'Don't you want to have a chat with John?'

Over the tanney, breaking into the music, a crackling voice announced: *'Mist' William Fisher. Mist' William Fisher. Wanted on the telephone. Mist' William Fisher. Than' you.'*

'Mr William Fisher, wanted on the telephone,' said Liz.

My palms gritty with sweat, I gripped the balcony rail and peered into the bright depths of the dance floor. As in some maniac kaleidoscope I could see Arthur, looking belligerent, about to sing; the Witch striding purposefully out of the cafeteria with her handbag swinging on her shoulder; Rita, standing around looking dazed; to the left, Stamp, standing at the bottom of the staircase, and Shadrack brushing past him. I saw them, or thought I saw them, all in the same shrieking moment, and looking up, there was the youthful Man o' the Dales, glaring with what looked like suspicion at our table. I had a sudden histrionic urge to stand up on my chair and shout: 'Ladies and gentlemen, here are my fountain pen and my suède shoes. Crucify me the modern way!'

'Mist' William Fisher, wanted on the telephone.'

'Let's go for a walk,' I said. I felt a hand on the back of my chair. I looked up, and I was not surprised to see Shadrack bending over us, flashing his yellow teeth and breathing his bad breath.

'Could I have a word with you, Fisher?'

I stood up, feeling punchdrunk. 'Next for shaving,' I said hysterically.

Shadrack turned solicitously to Liz. 'You *will* excuse us for a moment?' She smiled at him. He took me over to the top of the stairs, holding my arm in an alarmingly friendly way.

'Look, this is neither the time *nor* the place, of *course*,' he began confidentially. 'But I just thought I'd better have a word with you about our conversation this afternoon.'

'Oh, yes?' I said, swallowing.

'Yes. The fact is, under the circ'stances we think it prob'ly a good idea if you didn't come in on Monday after all. Prob'ly if you didn't come in until we sent for you. I just thought I'd let you know.'

'Oh. Does that mean –'

'No, I'm vair much afraid it doesn't mean you've finished with us. Not by a long chalk. I'm afraid you've still got a lot of explaining to do, Fisher.'

'Oh?' I seemed to be beginning every sentence with 'Oh'.

'Yes, I'm afraid it's come to light that you've been carrying on in an alarming fashion for a vair lengthy period of time. An *alar*ming fashion. To say the least of it. Anyway, the upshot is, we want you to regard yourself as being temp'rarily suspended until we can get it all cleared up.'

He released my arm.

'As I say, this is neither the time nor the place, we realize that. I don't want to stop you enjoying yourself tonight, far from it. But you've got a lot of vair serious explaining to do, sooner or later.'

' "Have a good holiday, Jenkins, I've got some bad news for you when you get back," ' I muttered.

'Wha'? What's that?'

'It was a cartoon,' I said unhappily. 'In the paper.'

'Yes, I'm vair much afraid you think too *much* about cartoons,' said Shadrack. He gave me a strange look and went off down the stairs. I watched the tail of his hacking jacket flapping after him, and murmured '*Bastard*' under my breath.

'*Mist*' William Fisher, wanted on the telephone.'

I beckoned to Liz, and followed Shadrack at a respectful distance down the stairs.

11

I T was quiet outside the Roxy. The evening was warm, but on the crisp side. The sodium lamps were beginning to flicker on and off dismally. The old gaffers who manned the Alderman Burrows memorial bench at the abandoned tram terminus were beginning to crane themselves stiffly to their feet and adjust their mufflers. The last children had left the piles of builders' sand that marked every exit from Stradhoughton, warning of new territorial ambitions in the way of brittle new roads across the moors.

I stood at the entrance to the Roxy, looking at the show-cases full of cracked, shiny photographs and the glue-streaked placards advertising the Autumn Leaf Ball. There was one showcase devoted to the Miss Stradhoughton contest and Rita, with her cardboard crown and her satin sash, smiled toothily down at me. On the broad brick steps, the commissionaire in his threadbare uniform, dry-cleaned to a thin blue and tied with an army webbing belt dyed navy, eyed passing youths with his fixed policeman's stare. Two of them, shiny-haired and wearing dazzle ties, strolled self-consciously up towards the paybox. I recognized them as friends of Stamp from the crowd he had been with at the X-L Disc Bar that afternoon.

The commissionaire moved forward. 'Not tonight, my friends,' he said, putting his arm out. 'Not after last week.'

'Why, what's up?' said one of the youths.

'Never mind what's up, or what's down. You don't come in, that's Mr Bottomley's strict orders.'

'After you with Mr Bottomley,' said the other youth.

'We're not coming in, we just want to get a mate out,' said the first one.

'You're getting nobody out,' said the commissionaire. The two youths retired into the shadows.

I looked up the blue-carpeted foyer at the cluster of girls gossiping outside the Ladies, and saw them part to let Liz through. Some of them stared after her. I noticed, not for the first time, how scruffy she was in her old suede jacket and her dusty black skirt, and it occurred to me that I had rarely, if ever, seen her wearing anything else. She came and went in her green suède coat as though it were a uniform or something, and even when I pictured her at the celebration parade after the November riots in Ambrosia, she was still wearing it.

She came and stood beside me, by the showcases.

'Miss Stradhoughton,' she said mechanically.

'They gave the title to the wrong girl,' I said with a clumsy attempt at gallantry.

We strolled away from the Roxy and the block of tobacconists' shops, chemists and hairdressers that was built in with it, and over the waste ground to the New Road. We walked up New Road past the Houghtondale Arms, the bus sheds and the crematorium and then, where the dump of cracked drainpipes and the crusty little hills of tar marked the last gasp of housing development, we turned into the unadopted road that led down into Foley Bottoms.

At some point during the evening, probably in the flight from the pub concert-room, I had started walking like a man with flat feet, and I was trying hard to stop it. 'Do you find life complicated?' I said as we walked along. I was long past caring one way or the other about anything very much, and what I said was the first thing that came into my head.

'Hmm-hmm,' said Liz happily.

I said: 'I wish it was something you could tear up and start again. Life, I mean. You know, like starting a new page in an exercise book.'

'Well, it's been done,' said Liz. 'Turning over a new leaf.'

'I turn over a new leaf every day,' I said. 'But the blots show through.' I was rather pleased with this.

We came to the end of the unadopted road and crossed over the broken-down chestnut fencing and the backwash of old bricks and bottles that was the entrance to Foley Bottoms.

'Why are you walking like that?' said Liz.

'Like what?'

'Sort of leaning forwards as though you were on roller skates.'

About half a dozen selected falsehoods skimmed through my mind, ranging from bad shoes to middle ear disease. 'I'm pretending I've got flat feet,' I said at length.

'Fathead.'

Stradhoughton clung tenaciously on to the woods for the first few yards: old prams, cement bags flapping, an electricity sub-station, the trees dying on their feet. But wading through the soggy cardboard boxes and the rust-rimmed bicycle wheels we came to the woods with the acorns falling and the ferns waist-high and green about us.

'I turn over a new leaf every day,' I said. 'But the blots show through the page.'

'Well,' said Liz. 'Perhaps a new leaf isn't good enough. Perhaps you need to turn over a new volume.'

She was even better than I was at carrying metaphor to inscrutable lengths. I thought of pursuing the theme a little further, and was weaving a pleasant fancy about trying not only a new volume but a new library, when Liz started on the problem afresh with an entirely new set of illustrations.

'You know, my lad, the trouble with you is that you're –

what's the word – introspective? You're like a child at the edge of a paddling pool. You want very much to go in, but you think so much about whether the water's cold, and whether you'll drown, and what your mother will say if you get your feet wet –'

I hesitated to go with her into the paddling-pool zone, which seemed to me to be fraught with peril, but there was nothing for it but to interrupt her.

'All I'm doing is wondering whether to dive or swim,' I said obscurely.

'Perhaps you need a coach,' said Liz, giving me the sly glance. It was perfectly apparent where this one was leading to, and I decided to leave her floundering in her own paddling pool for the time being. We picked our way over the low blackberry branches in silence.

I searched around in my mind for some fresh nonsense to keep us pleasantly occupied. I felt a quick gust of warmth for Liz for her readiness to go so far with me along the well-trodden paths of fantasy. I decided to try her on the London theme.

'Do you know why I'm so fascinated by London?' I said.

'No, Mr Bones, why are you so fascinated by London?' She was not consciously imitating Arthur.

'A man can lose himself in London,' I said. 'London is a big place. It has big streets and big people –' I tailed off, because she would not be drawn, and in any case I had forgotten the end of the sentence. Liz stopped abruptly, and I turned back to face her, expecting the sudden, rash embrace that was a feature of her impetuous temperament.

But she folded her arms and looked at me with her inscrutable, chubby smile that only faintly looked as though, like the Witch before her, she had practised it in a mirror.

'Billy?'

'Uh-huh?'

'Tell me something?'

I said in the soft voice: 'Of course.'

'Do you really know Man o' the Dales?'

In the hard, defiant voice: 'Course I do.'

'Really and truly?'

'Well, know him, it depends what you mean by *know* him. I've *met* him –'

'Count five and tell the truth,' said Liz. It was an old recipe of hers, and one that I always found distasteful. I said in the high-pitched voice, putting an elaborate hand to my heart, 'I cannot tell a lie, I've never met the man.' The phrase 'I've never met the man' was just not suited to the range of voice I had chosen, and the whole thing sounded forced and ridiculous.

Liz grinned composedly. 'You *are* a fool.'

I wiped the whole matter out with the repeater gun levelled at Man o' the Dales, and we walked on. 'Perhaps I need to turn over a new paddling pool,' I said.

'Write that down,' said Liz, just as Arthur would have said.

Foley Bottoms was largely a botanic clump of nothing, but just before you started getting out of the woods again and on your way to the Strad Lee housing estate – a hideous zoo of orange brick which it would have done Man o' the Dales a power of good to walk through, cobblestones, handlebar moustache and all – there was a knoll or hill of what I always thought of as picnic grass, a kind of lush, tropical green velvet that looked as though you could buy it by the yard in Marks and Spencers. It was a regular custom for me to stop here with whoever it was, Liz, Rita, or the Witch; thereafter the custom would vary according to the personality involved. With Rita, it was the film finale clinch prior to sinking down on the grass; with the Witch, a moment of studied casualness in which we both sat down apparently independently, about a yard from one another. I wondered how the Witch was getting on with her cupful of passion pills. In the case of Liz, part of the regular custom was to hold each other at arm's length, scrutinizing faces and then, as at a given signal, sit down.

'Who d'you love?' said Liz.

'Thee, lass,' I said, finding refuge in the Duxbury dialect.

'Yes, it sounds like it, doesn't it?'

'Ah do, lass.'

'Say it properly, then.'

'I do, Liz, I do,' I said soberly, and wondering if I meant it. I knelt down on the grass and reached my arm up to her. Liz remained standing.

'What about Barbara?'

So rarely did I think about the Witch under her given name that I had to think for a minute who Barbara was when she was at home.

'Well what about her?'

'Well *what* about her?' said Liz. I began pulling at her hands, trying to decide whether to pass the ball back again with another 'Well what about her?' Finally I said: 'All over.'

'You've said *that* before.'

'I know. This time the goose is cooked.' I did not explain whose goose I had in mind. I tightened my grip on her hands and pulled her down, so successfully that she fell on top of me. This should have been the signal for the beginning of some rural by-play but in fact the weight of her knocked me sprawling and by the time I had recovered she was sitting beside me, lighting a cigarette – a delaying trick as annoying in its way as the Witch's oranges.

'I want to marry you, you know, Billy,' Liz said, holding her cigarette to a blade of grass.

I said: 'I know, Liz, I know. We will, one day.'

'Not one day. Now.'

The idea of actually getting married now was so incomprehensible to me that I thought it was part of some new ritual, and I played along with it.

'Tonight?'

'Next week will do. Before you go to London. Or when you get there. Whichever you prefer.'

I began plucking at the glass buttons of her blouse, imagining the court scene where my mother, weeping, opposed my application to marry. The unfastening of Liz's blouse had become a more or less routine affair and it was done in a detached way, rather as if I were helping her off with her coat.

'I think I get engaged a bit too often,' I said.

'I don't want to get engaged. I want to get married.'

'Is that why you keep sloping off every few weeks, because you want to get married?'

'I want to get married,' said Liz stubbornly.

'All right,' I said. 'All right.'

By now I had begun to grow fairly absent-minded in my responses, for it had suddenly struck me that there was somebody in the bushes, listening to us. There was no wind, but every so often one of the rhododendrons behind us would rustle and there would be a crackling of twigs. I looked up sharply, but there was nothing to see.

'How do you mean, all right?' said Liz. 'I've just proposed to you, and you say all right. Aren't you supposed to say this is so sudden, or yes, or something?'

I was groping for some obscure phrase that would comfort her and at the same time leave me uncommitted. I distinctly saw something moving in the bushes behind us. The notion that the Witch had followed us here and was taking everything down in her faultless Gregg shorthand possessed me with an unpleasant vividness.

'If I'm going to dive in,' I said, 'I think it might as well be at the deep end.'

Even if the Witch had got down this remark satisfactorily, there was little that she could make of it in a breach of promise trial. *'Now Mr Fisher, according to these notes you said that if you were going to dive in, it might as well be at the deep end. Now what did you mean by that?'* I got Liz's blouse out of her skirt and began stroking her, like a cat.

Liz screwed her eyes up tightly in the way she did when she was going to say something she thought brazen. Without seeing, she stubbed her cigarette out on the grass.

'You know what you wanted me to do that night on Stradhoughton Moor, and I said another night?'

I remembered very well the cold night on Stradhoughton Moor, in the old folks' shelter, the night before Liz had last disappeared. On that night I had actually proposed, a pretend proposal that we had used for kindling, toasting our hands on it until the early hours when, stiff with cold, we wandered home quietly, the future spent like fireworks.

'I remember,' I said. My heart had begun to beat swiftly. Stamp's phrase, 'Are you getting it regular?' sprang irreverently back into my head. The bushes stirred again, and this time I thought that it might be Stamp himself with his German camera, fitted with infra-red. Either him or the Witch with a portable tape recorder, one or the other.

'Well,' said Liz. 'It's another night tonight, isn't it?'

I kissed her eyes meditatively. So far our relations had been on a thus-far-and-no-farther basis, frustrating to both of us but of such a well-established pattern that it came as a slow shock to suggest that the barriers now be taken down.

'Are you sure?' I said, clearing my throat. She nodded, her face full of meaning. Out in the rhododendron bushes the Witch put on another spool. A new notion, that Shadrack was crouching there with a warrant for my arrest, seized me for a moment, then I put it aside to deal with current problems.

'Er – what do you think we ought to do about, you know, babies?'

'Have them,' said Liz luxuriously. 'Lots and lots of them.'

'No, I mean tonight. I mean, I haven't got – you know.'

'It's all right,' said Liz. I peered unhappily out into the bushes. The Witch turned up her volume control, Stamp changed his film and Shadrack crouched forward in the dusk, licking his lips. Liz nestled plumply up to me and bit my ear. We held each other helplessly, doing nothing, the passion seeping away at a dangerous rate.

Liz said: 'Billy?'

'Uh-huh?'

'Ask you something?'

'Uh-huh.'

She screwed up her eyes again and said: 'Do you know what *virgo intacta* means?'

'Yes.'

'Well. I'm not.'

I sat there quietly, listening. Something had gone wrong with the Witch's tape recorder. Stamp and Shadrack, fiddling with the batteries, were adjusting it for her. 'No,' I said finally. 'I somehow didn't think you were.'

'Want me to tell you about it?'

'No.'

I began to fondle her breast, spanning it in my hand and pressing gently with each finger in turn, compulsively. Liz began to breathe heavily and to tremble out of all proportion to the ardour I thought I was drumming up. 'Tell me about it,' I said.

'No, not now.'

'Tell me about it.'

Liz sat up, almost impatiently, pulling her suède coat

around her. She stared out into the darkness. Then she began to trace little circles in the grass with her fingers.

'You think that's why I'm always going away, don't you?' she said.

I shrugged, saying and thinking nothing.

'Ask me where I've been for the past five weeks.'

'Does the geographical location make any difference?' I said with simulated bitterness, hoping to keep it all on this same sparring level.

'No, I don't suppose it does,' said Liz. I reached out and touched her breast under her coat, but it was cold and lifeless. She began to speak in a rhythmical, reasoning sort of prose, as though she had rehearsed all the words before she met me.

'Every so often I just want to go away. It's not you, Billy, I want to be here with you. It's the town. It's the people we know. I don't like knowing everybody, or becoming a part of things – do you see what I mean?'

We had been over this before, but from a different route. It had never led so beautifully into the point of contact between us. I began to feel excited, as though on the verge of a discovery.

'What I'd like is to be invisible,' said Liz. 'You know, to do everything without people knowing, and not having to worry about them, not having to ex*plain* all the time. That's why I so enjoyed that night on Stradhoughton Moor. We were both invisible. We –'

'Liz,' I said urgently. 'Liz, listen, listen.' I took her hands, trembling almost, and began to speak rapidly, leaving staccato, deliberate pauses between my words.

'Liz, do you know what I do? When I want to feel invisible?' I had no experience of wanting to feel invisible, but the text was perfect. I was doctoring my words as I went along, quickly and carefully. 'I've never told anybody.

I have a sort of – well, it's an imaginary country, where I go. It has its own people –'

'Do you do that? I *knew* you would,' cried Liz triumphantly. 'I knew you would. Why are we so alike, Billy? I can read your thoughts. A town like Stradhoughton, only somewhere over by the sea, and we used to spend the whole day on the beach. That's what I used to think about.'

I was full of excitement, frustrated, painful excitement at not being able to tell her properly, yet at the same time knowing she would understand it, knowing that she would *know*. I wanted to drag her into my mind and let her loose in it, free to pick and choose.

I began counting to myself to slow myself down, and said, only half-feverishly:

'This is more than a town, it's a whole country. I'm supposed to be the Prime Minister. You're supposed to be the Foreign Secretary or something –'

'Yes sir,' said Liz with grave, mock obedience.

'I think about it for hours. Sometimes I think, if we were married, and living somewhere in that house in the country, we could just sit and imagine ourselves there –'

'By a log fire,' said Liz softly. 'And the fir trees all around, and no other house for miles.'

I looked at her squarely. She was as excited as I was in her own settled way. I was tossing a coin in my head, teetering on a decision. Heads I tell her, tails I don't. Heads I tell her this last thing.

'I want a room, in the house, with a green baize door,' I began calmly. 'It will be a big room, and when we pass into it, through the door, that's it, that's Ambrosia. No one else would be allowed in. No one else will have keys. They won't know where the room is. Only we will know. We'll make models of the principal cities, you know, out of cardboard, and we could use toy soldiers, painted, for the people. We could draw maps. It would be a place to go on a rainy afternoon. We could go there. No one would find us. I thought we would have a big sloping shelf running all the way down one wall, you know, like a big desk. And we'd have a lot of blank paper on it and design our own newspapers. We could even make uniforms, if we wanted to. It would be our country.' I stopped, suddenly aware of the cold and the black, peeling branches round about us and the ticking quiet of it all. I had talked myself right through the moment of contact. Liz, her old self, was grinning, pleased with life, seeing it all as our old fantasy, a kind of mental romp in the long grass. 'And let's have a model train, that the kids won't be allowed to use,' she said. 'And a big trench in the garden.'

I sank back, spreadeagling my hands in the grass to rid them of the webbed sensation that was coming back into them like a nervous tic.

'Liz,' I said, all the thoughts exhausted in me. 'Will you marry me?'

She leaned over me and whispered: 'Tomorrow,' in a throaty way. I pulled her down with a feeling of peace and misery, running my hands heavily down her back. She began to kiss me, not knowing that my eyes were open and staring. Her body was warm under the suède jacket and I found some kind of comfort, losing myself, not allowing anything into my head, but sinking into a kind of numb passion. Soon the whole incident had passed into history, to be exhumed and dissected soon, but not now. I felt the black dusty skirt give way as she fumbled at the zipper. I brushed my fingers against the smooth surface of her stomach, feeling her contract gingerly under the touch of them. She rolled over on to her back and I fell on top of her, grateful and easy in my mind, lost in her soft ways.

In the moment of satisfaction I said: 'There's somebody

watching us.' From the bushes there was the sharp crack of breaking twigs and a resounding: 'Tskkkkkkkkk!'

I called: 'Whoever's out there is going to get their bastard teeth knocked down their throat in a minute!'

I scrambled to my feet, gathering my clothes about me like an Arab. Three youths leaped up from behind the bushes and began to run out of the woods, shouting directions at each other. Two of them were the youths who had been turned away from the Roxy while I waited for Liz; the third was Stamp, I raced after them almost as far as the road. Stamp stumbling drunkenly through the ferns, called in falsetto voice: 'Oh, darling – ,' repeating some words I happened to have used a few minutes earlier. I let them go. As if it were far away, I heard Stamp call: 'Can I draw your maps for you, to play with?'

I walked back to the green grass, tucking my shirt into my trousers. Liz was sitting up and combing her hair. 'We should've stayed on the dance floor and let everybody have a look,' she said carelessly.

The idea, fanciful to her, made me go hot all over. Then I shivered. 'Let's go,' I said.

We began to walk back towards the Roxy. 'I'll wrap his cowing posters round his neck, next time I see him,' I said. But the idea of ever seeing Stamp again, or indeed anybody, filled me with horror.

12

THERE was no sense in going back into the Roxy, and so I waited outside while Liz went in to fetch her handbag. It was getting late now, anyway. The commissionaire had changed into civilian clothes and was taking in the sandwich-boards and propping them against the wall inside the foyer. I could hear the Rockets playing tinnily inside, underlined by a steady thump-thump like a ship's engine. After the music there was some announcement over the tannoy which I could not hear. Mist' William Fisher, wanted on the telephone, no doubt; I wondered who had been ringing up for me at the Roxy and why. An inch of white ash fell from my cigarette. I began to walk up and down the parade of shops that lined the Roxy, staring at the gaunt, old-fashioned heads in the window of Molly, hair-stylist, and at the forlorn-looking estate agent's with its little cards buckling in their grained wooden slots. None of the shops looked as though anything had ever happened in them.

I had an instinct that I sometimes used, looking into the future and deciding whether an event would take place or not. I tried to project myself forward, to see whether Liz would come out again. I could not form any definite picture of her coming out and smiling at me, and I concluded that on the whole she would not. I decided to give her five more minutes, counting them off in sixties and folding a finger back for every minute gone. At the third finger I lost count over a commotion behind me. I turned round to see Stamp and his two idiot friends, reeling back from the Houghtondale Arms. Stamp was even drunker than he had been before, and was shouting at the top of his voice: *'To the woods! No, no, not the woods, anything but the woods!'* I stepped back into the estate agent's doorway. The commissionaire had gone round the back of the building with a coke shovel in his hand, and the Roxy was unguarded. They dodged in, giggling and shoving each other. 'Where's yer pass-outs, you two?' yelled Stamp. 'Hey, mister, they're getting in for nix!'

I was dog-tired and feeling gritty round the eyes, and hungry. I walked up to the entrance of the Roxy and looked down the length of the foyer, but I could not see Liz. She was probably already whooping it up with Man o' the Dales inside. At the door of the Ladies, Stamp was talking beerily to Rita, lending her a penny or something. I was hungry and cold and tired.

I walked away, dipping into my mind for a morsel of No. 1 thinking to get me home. Ambrosia was closed for the night, or seemed to be. I came up as chairman of the Stradhoughton Labour Party, in fact M.P. for the division, the youngest member in the House, writing letters to Councillor Duxbury. *Dear Councillor Duxbury, As you know, the proposal to nationalize the undertaking business is already in the committee stage. You are well versed not only in this particular field but in public life also, and before concluding this piece of legislation we would greatly appreciate your comments. (You may remember me as a clerk in your employ, many years ago now....)*

At the corner of Clogiron Lane was a fish shop, a small area of brightness among the discreet drawn blinds and the concrete lamps. I stepped almost automatically over the hollowed step into this tiled, light womb of warmth, and joined the small queue among the Tizer bottles, the stacked sheets of clean newspaper, and the advertisements for cinemas and jumble sales. I leaned in gratitude on the salty marble counter and savoured the high aroma of steam and vinegar and buxom sweat. Written in whitewash on the burnished battery of mirrors above the frying-range was the sign: 'Under completely new management.' The usual fat women were serving in their chip-stained white aprons, but the man at the range, tall and dour like all fishshop proprietors, was a new one. He turned half-round to the trough of batter by his side, and I recognized him instantly as the leading man in an old No. 2 daymare which even now I revived from time to time. Long ago, in a different neighbourhood, I had caused some consternation up and down the street by telling everybody that the man who ran the fish shop had hanged himself. This was undoubtedly the same man. He recognized me too, and gave me one of the keen, contemplative looks that were so much a feature of Stradhoughton life. I had a quick fancy that all my enemies had secretly taken office around Clogiron Lane and were hustling into position, preparing for the coup. I bought a bag of chips and walked out of the shop.

Dear Mr Shadrack, As you know, the nationalization of the undertaking business is imminent, and we are very keen to get someone knowledgeable in charge of casket production. I well remember as an 'old boy' of Shadrack and Duxbury's (I was the wretch who forgot to post the calendars!!!) being shown some drawings of a fibreglass casket which you thought could be produced very cheaply. . . .

The chips lasted me all the way home to Hillcrest. I threw the greasy bag into our own privet hedge, wiped my hands, and lit a cigarette before going indoors. I felt a lot better.

The old man was in the lounge, straddling the fawn-tiled fireplace, the back of his balding head glimmering faintly through what little of the mirror you could see behind its crust of frosted bambis. His certificate of membership from the Ancient Order of Stags, thick with Gothic writing and seals and all the rest of it, was propped up on the mantelpiece. I was surprised to see the old man still up. He stood with his waistcoat open and eyed me as I went into the room.

I said: 'Did you want some chips bringing in?'

The old man said: 'I'm surprised t' bloody chip shop's still open, this time o' night.' He nodded towards the cuckoo clock, swinging its lead weights against the sad wallpaper. He turned to chuck his cigarette end in the fire and said, tossing the remark casually across to me: 'They're down at t' Infirmary.'

'Who is?'

'Your mother and your grandma, who the bloody hell do you think? Your grandma's been taken badly again. We've been trying to get word to you for t' last hour. Where've you been?'

I felt a twinge of alarm at the idea of Gran being carted off to the Infirmary. Normally, after one of her fits, she would sit ticking broodily in a chair until she was more or less normal again. If the fit recurred, it was supposed to be serious or something. I was glad that they had got her out of the house.

I said, harshening my voice to make it acceptable: 'Why, what's up with her?'

'What's up wi' *you*, that's what I want to know,' the old man snarled, beginning to boil up into his slow rage. 'I thought you were off to t' bloody dance hall when you'd been to t' pub. Why don't you go where you say you're going, we've been ringing up half the bloody night.'

'I had a pass-out –' I began.

'Pass-out, you'll do more than pass out if you don't bloody frame! You'd better ring up for a taxi, your mother wants to see you down at t' Infirmary.'

'Why, what's up wi' me grandma?' I said.

'What's allus up wi' your grandma, what do you think? Get ringing up t' taxi!'

Reluctantly, I went into the hall and rang up New Line Taxis. The old man was shouting: 'And bloody come home on a night in future, not at this bloody time!' but there was something oddly restrained and preoccupied about his abuse. I felt that he had something more to say. I put down the telephone and started to walk up the stairs. That was the trigger for it. With a bound of fury the old man reached the hall door.

'*You don't go up there!*'

'Why, I'm just waiting for t' taxi.'

'I said you don't go up there!'

I leaned against the wall, trying to look resigned and reasonable. 'Well ah've got to have a wash, haven't I?'

'You can go mucky. You don't go up*stairs*. We've had enough of you up there, with your bloody hiding and meddling and I don't know what else.'

'What, I don't know what you're talking about,' I said, screwing my face up to look puzzled.

'You know bloody well what I'm talking about.' And then, sharply: 'What have you done with that letter of your mother's?'

I stood, cold, on the stairs.

'Do you hear me? I'm talking to you!'

'What letter?' I said.

'What, what, what,' the old man mimicked, his face cracking into an ugly sneer. 'Don't keep saying bloody what! You know bloody well what letter! That what she gave you to post to t' "Housewives' Choice".'

I leaned back again, my face in a mask of panic, reviewing breakneck all the things they must know if they had found out about my mother's letter.

'I've *told* her once, I posted it,' I said.

'You posted bloody nowt! You've had it in that box! It was given to you to post, you bloody, idle little sod!'

A small wave of relief touched me, at the hope that the old man would put it all down to nothing more than idleness. I said, with desperate nonchalance: 'I *did* post it. That was just the rough copy.'

'What yer talking about, rough copy? It's your mother's letter. How *could* you have posted it?'

I came down one stair to meet him, trying to talk in the patient, explanatory voice. 'Look. The letter my mother wrote was full of mis*takes*, that's all. I just thought it would have a better chance if I wrote it out *again*, properly, that's all.'

'Well who told you to write it out again? And who told you to open it? You keep your thieving hands off other people's things! And where did you get all them bloody calendars from, anall?'

'What calendars?' It was a purely automatic reflex, like kicking up the knee against a hammer. I was trapped without time to think or to stall or to rig the facts.

The old man took a deep breath and started fingering the shredding, concave belt around his trousers. 'By bloody hell, I'll give you bloody what if you don't stop saying what, what, my lad! You know bloody well what! Don't think I've not been talking to Councillor Duxbury, cos I have! I've heard it all. You make me a bloody laughing-stock, you can't keep your hands off owt. And where's that monkey-wrench out of my garage? I suppose you know nowt about *that*?'

'No, course I don't. What do *I* want with a monkey-wrench?'

'What do you want wi' two hundred bloody calendars? And what have you been doing wi' their bloody nameplates anall? You're not right in the bloody head!'

I had no refuge except in rage. '*I'm* not right, *I'm* not right,' I shouted, coming down the stairs at him. '*I* didn't want to work for Shadrack and flaming Duxbury's. You put me there, now you can answer for it!'

'Don't bloody shout at me, you gormless young get! Or I'll knock your bloody eyes out.'

'God give me strength,' I murmured, closing my eyes at the threat.

'God give you strength, he wants to give you some bloody sense! You're like a bloody Mary Ann!' He was slowing down, like a spent volcano. I sat down on the stairs with my head in my hands, trying to look defeated and hoping he would go away. He turned, muttering to himself. 'Well I hope yer mother gets more sense out o' you. And don't go chelping back at her like you chelp at me, else you'll know about it.' He stood at the hall door, fingering the lock, experimenting with the turning mechanism, and trying hard to effect the transition from shouting into normal speech. I tried to help him.

'Well I *told* you I didn't want to work for Shadrack's when I first started, didn't I?'

'You didn't want to work for nobody, if you ask me owt,' the old man said. 'You thought you'd live on me, didn't you?'

'No, I didn't. I could have kept myself.'

'How?'

'Writing scripts,' I said thickly.

'Writing bloody scripts, you want to get a day's work done, never mind writing scripts. Who do you think's going to run *this* bloody business when *I'm* gone?' He jerked his thumb in the direction of the garage outside, and it was so exactly like the trouble at t' mill routine that Arthur and I had between us that the response flicked immediately into my mind '*But father, we all have our lives to lead, you yours and I mine!*'

Aloud, I said: 'You said you didn't *want* me in the business.'

'Only because you were so bloody idle! *Some* bugger's got to carry on wi' it. Who's going to keep your mother?'

Father, the men! They're coming up the drive!

'Why, you're not retiring, are you?' I said with a forced jocularity. The old man turned away in disgust and walked into the lounge. I sat where I was for a minute or so, and then I started to go upstairs. 'And keep out of your grandma's bedroom!' he called venomously.

I tiptoed into my room and went straight over to the Guilt Chest, already convinced that the whole thing had been a gigantic hoax. But the chest had definitely been moved; it was lying slantwise across the linoleum, only half-under the bed, and the stamp edging was gone. It was almost a relief to know at last for certain that they had been into it. I knelt down and pulled the Guilt Chest clear of the bed and lifted the tinny lid. The calendars were still stacked in their heavy piles, though they had been disturbed. The 'Housewives' Choice' letter had gone. I felt under a pile of calendars for the stack of invoices the old man had once given me to post. They were still there. I grabbed them first, the calendars toppling over into the chest, and stuffed them into my inside pocket. Liz's postcards were still there, and so was the copy of *Ritzy Stories*. The letters from the Witch had been interfered with. I ran rapidly through their contents and turned the repeater gun on the Witch and her silly, daft prose.

I sat on the bed, making a weak effort to translate the scene with the old man into No. 1 thinking, with my No. 1 father ushering me into the library for the manly talk. I tried again to project myself into the future. I could see myself, quite plainly see myself, sitting on the train, knocking on a peeling door in Earl's Court, sitting in Danny Boon's office, eating beans on toast in the A.B.C. I took out my wallet and counted the notes again, eight pounds ten now, and seventeen shillings in silver.

I dug out the letter from Danny Boon again and smoothed it out and read it. '*Several of the boys do work for me, you might be interested in this.*' I jumped to my feet and grabbed the old suitcase from under the chest of drawers, throwing out the store of blankets and Polythene-wrapped cardigans my mother kept in it. Pulling open drawers, I began to assemble shirts and handkerchiefs and socks together. I took down my best suit and folded it in two, still on its hanger, inside the suitcase. Then I looked in the Guilt Chest, reckoning that there must be about a hundred and seventy calendars left. I got a great heap of calendars and put them, in three rows, in the suitcase. Then I began packing in earnest, putting a calendar in between each shirt and placing the calendars like lining all the way round the case. The lid would not close. I took out two shirts and one calendar. I tore the calendar out of its envelope and propped it up on the bedroom mantelpiece behind the Coronation tin. I pushed the envelope behind the sheet of newspaper in the fireplace, and got the case shut by pressing on it. There was a rubble of old letters and torn pieces of envelope left in the Guilt Chest. I put Liz's postcards and the letters from the Witch in my raincoat pocket, and left the rest.

I was humming as I went into the bathroom to fetch my toothbrush.

The old man shouted up the stairs: 'Do you hear? T' taxi's come!'

I shouted: 'All right! Just coming,' and put out the light.

13

THE old man did not see the suitcase, and so there was no trouble in getting out of the house. The taxi-driver was one we knew slightly, a man who sometimes came round to Hillcrest to help on jobs. I leaned back against the spent and slithery leather-work, pretending he was a stranger. I clicked without real interest into the piece of No. 1 thinking I always reserved for taxis; my chauffeur-driven Bentley running through the home counties and stopping at the prosperous, half-timbered pub. 'Have you eaten, Benson? Better put the car round the back and join me, hadn't you?'

'What's up, then?' said the real taxi-driver as we turned into Clogiron Lane. 'Is somebody poorly?'

'Yer, me grandma,' I said. 'She's had one o' them turns again.'

'Well, you can expect it, can't yer? She's not getting any younger.'

'No.'

'She's a grand old lass, though, i'n't she?'

'Yer.'

Stradhoughton Infirmary was a white Portland-stone building, rusting round the window-sills and mottled with the bleaching it had had from the so-called brackish air. In the light of the concrete lamps it looked even more like a madhouse than ever. We pulled up outside the scratched swing doors and I told the taxi to wait. I took the suitcase in with me. I was met by the dead smell of lavender polish; it was like breathing through a furry yellow duster. The portraits of aldermen and benefactors looked down over the deserted central hall. I went through the white door into the casualty department.

It was busy in its late-night, sleep-walking way. On the high-backed benches a knot of women were joined in a litany of bad doctors, inadequate pensions, and leaky houses. They whiled away the time indignantly while their husbands had emergency operations or their children suffered. They were the same women, or seemed to be the same women, I had seen earlier in the New House, the ones who knew about life and death and all the rest of it. I no longer envied them. A man with his arm in a sling sat alone and perplexed, wondering why he had come. He was the one I warmed to. Over by the ambulance bay the porters looked as though they did not care about anything, sitting in their little glass office smoking Woodbines crooked in the hollow of their hands. They distended their necks and frowned and altered their mouths into an oblong shape to expel the smoke. A young char in spectacles swilled at the parquet floor. Nurses in white and purple held huddled conferences that were not to do with the dying. The women talked: 'He put me on port wine.'

I found my mother sitting alone in the corridor on a padded bench that had been ripped and sawed at with a knife until the grey stuffing spilled out like brains. I put down the suitcase and went over and stood in front of her. She looked up.

'We looked all over,' she said weakly, and cleared her throat.

'Wher's me grandma?'

She nodded towards the flapping doors where the corridor came to an end. 'They've got that black doctor to her. She can't talk. We're just waiting.' She spoke hoarsely, in a resigned way, yet at the same time excitedly. These were the headlines. I knew, for I had seen her lips moving, that she was already rehearsing the text of this eventful day, plucking at the details of it like pomegranate seeds and stringing them together in a long rosary that would be fingered on and off long after anyone had ceased to care. 'We've been trying to get you since half past nine,' she said. 'I wanted you to come down with me.'

'I know, my dad was saying,' I said, trying to sound like his son. 'He says she's badly this time.'

My mother sucked in her cheeks and moistened her tongue ready for the first run of her long narrative.

'She was all right again at four o'clock, just after you went out,' she began. 'She had a cup of tea at half past, when we had ours, but she wouldn't have any brown bread. Then she had a sleep. And she was all right at *nine* o'clock, when your father got back from the pub, because she woke up and asked him if he were putting t' television on. Then we were all just sitting watching television –' (later she would add the name of the programme and of the singer and possibly of the song) – 'when she just slumped forward in her chair. We thought she were having a fit, but no, she just gave a little jerk with her head, uh, like that there' – she imitated the jerk, and searched with her magpie memory to see if there was some pin she had left unaccounted for in the first five minutes of my grandmother's dying. 'Then she started to slaver. She were just like a baby. It was pitiful. Just like a baby, slavering and gasping for breath.

'Anyway, your father said, if it isn't a fit, we'd better ring for Dr *Mor*gan. So we waited five more minutes and she was still slavering, she wet four handkerchiefs through, them big handkerchiefs of your dad's, so I said "You'd better ring up and get t' doctor".'

The account droned on until we had covered every

paving-stone on the way to the Infirmary. I was not listening but I knew all that she was saying; I responded, Mm, Mm, Mm, at every pause. I did not want the details of it, not every detail, and I began concentrating on objects in the corridor and thinking the wall, the wall, the ceiling, the ceiling, so that the things my mother was saying could ricochet off them and lose what force they had.

'The last thing she said before they got her on t' stretcher was "Where's my Jack". I had to think who she was talking about, then I remembered she must have meant your grandad. Only she always used to call him John. She *never* called him Jack, never. Then she said, *"I love you Jack"* ' – my mother had difficulty in pronouncing this word love. I had never heard her say it before, and it sounded strange on her lips. I tried to imagine it on the lips of the yellow woman on the other side of the swing doors, but it was impossible. I – love – you. My mother said it as though the word had just been invented, like Terylene.

'Oh, before that she said, "What are you thinking about?" I think she must ha' been talking to your grandad.' My mother stopped and took a long breath, the breath coming out in a staircase of sighing. 'But you had to listen close to, to hear what she was saying. She could hardly speak, and by the time we got here she couldn't speak at all. She was just slavering.'

She seemed to have finished. I had been trying on various expressions and by now I was searching feverishly for one that really belonged to me. I found it difficult to feel anything beyond indignation that my grandmother should be seen off with this gossiping commentary. Even as my mother was speaking, the phrases with which Arthur and I dissected the conversations around us kept slotting into my head like price tabs ringing up on a cash register. 'Never use a preposition to end a sentence with.' 'I must ask you to not split infinitives.' I felt disgust at myself but, when I shopped around for some deeper emotion, there was none. I had a nervous urge to laugh, and I found myself concentrating entirely on keeping my face adult and sad.

My mother said: 'They're a long time.' I had no idea how long she had been here, in spite of the time-table she had given me. She stirred on the creaking couch and seemed to shake herself free of her drama. She turned to me, seeing me probably for the first time as her son and not only as a listener.

'Well, you've got yourself into a fine mess, lad, haven't you?' she said.

I got up and stretched, elaborately, turning away from her.

'So it would seem.'

'I'm only grateful *she* knows nowt about it,' my mother said. She was silent for a minute or so. It seemed to me that she did not want to discuss the subject but was pushing herself into it.

'Why didn't you post that letter of mine?'

'I *did* post it. I was telling me dad. I just wrote it out again, that's all.' I had been working on the story since leaving the old man and got it into convincible shape, but I was tired and it no longer seemed to matter.

'What did you want to write it out again for?'

'There were some mistakes in it. I just thought it would stand a better chance if it was better written, that's all.' I was beginning to feel annoyed with her for picking at trivialities at a time like this.

'Yes, well we can't all be Shakespeares, can we,' she said, in a way that was supposed to shame me. She glanced down the corridor at my suitcase against the wall. She showed no surprise, and I knew that she must have noticed it already and decided to say nothing.

'And what have you been saying to Arthur's mother about having a sister?' she said in sharper tones.

'Why, it was only a joke,' I said, not even bothering to try and sound convincing. I did not know how she knew about Arthur's mother, and I did not care.

'A joke, it *sounds* like a joke. And I thought you told me she'd broken her leg?'

'I didn't know you *knew* Arthur's mother,' I said.

'Yes, you don't know who I know and who I don't know, do you? If you want to know, she rang me up. And what did you do with the cardigan she gave you?'

I remembered this. Arthur's mother had once given me a red cardigan for my imaginary sister. I had carted it around town all day and then left it on a bus.

'Gave it to Barbara, thought I told you about it,' I said.

'You tell me nothing. You didn't tell me about giving her cheek outside t' cemetery this afternoon, did you? When you were *with* Barbara. Anyway, she's coming round tomorrow, when Barbara comes for her tea. So you've got a new cardigan to find.'

I decided to speak. She had seen the suitcase, so she knew, but I decided to tell her.

'I won't be here tomorrow,' I said.

My mother sat bolt upright and pursed her lips, pulling in any expression she might have had on her face. She could not disguise a look of restrained shock, as though I had suddenly struck her and she was trying not to show it.

'I'd have gone already if it hadn't have been for me grandma,' I said, as gently as I could.

She looked at me, a long, sorrowing look. 'If you're in trouble, Billy, it's not something you can leave behind you, you know,' she said in a shaky voice. 'You put it in your suitcase and take it with you.'

My mother was so little given to this kind of imagery that

170

I wondered if she had got rush reports on the calendars in my suitcase.

'Well, I'm still going,' I said doggedly. 'I told you I'm going and I'm going.'

The swing doors opened softly. A nurse came padding along the corridor, walking like an actress. She stopped by my mother and said: 'Mrs Fisher?' in the tones of somebody trying to wake somebody else up from sleep. '*Would you come this way?*' Infected by the mood of feigned solicitude, I stood up as my mother, the light of fear in her eyes, rose and walked slowly with the nurse through the swing doors. I sat down, suddenly tense and frightened. I said to myself, clenching my fists, Don't let's have any scenes, don't let's have any scenes, don't let's have any scenes. I wondered rapidly whether to go now, but I knew I would not. I began pawing the floor with embarrassment. I picked up an old newspaper that had been shoved down the back of the bench, and began to read aimlessly. '*Three passengers on a Belfast plane recently were Mr GOOSE, Mr GANDER, and the Rev. Mr GOSLING. They did not know each other.*' Beneath this news item was a cartoon, of a little boy saying: 'Can I see this gab that daddy says you have the gift of, Mrs Jones?' I chucked the paper down and began walking from one side of the corridor to the other, heel to toe as though measuring out a cricket pitch. Don't let's have any *scenes*.

It was only a few minutes before my mother came back, holding her handbag between her hands, her face marked with grief and dignity as she imagined it to be. She was helped as far as the doors by a grave-faced doctor, and it looked to me like some corny act on television. I could not help these thoughts. I prayed: Please, God, let me *feel* something. Let me feel something, only don't let's have any scenes.

'Your grandma died at fourteen minutes past twelve,' my mother said, as though making a formal announcement. I wanted to say: 'I'm sorry' or something, but anything I said would have sounded ridiculous. 'I shall have to sit down,' my mother said. I sat by her, legs apart, head bowed, staring down at my feet and counting the stains on my suède shoes. I examined what I was feeling and it was nothing, nothing.

My mother was already in the luxury of reminiscing. 'She would have wanted it this way,' she said, a platitude so inept that I could only marvel at the clichés that she used like crutches to take her limping from one crisis to another. And at the same time I was relieved to hear her talk like this; I thought, They're as bad as I am, they don't feel it, they only say it. But I did not believe what I was telling myself.

'Do you want to go in and see her?' my mother said. I mumbled 'No', mingling shock and shame.

She sighed, drawing on her gloves. 'Well, we'll have to carry on as best we can,' she said. She stared at the wall, moving her lips again. 'Her last words were just "Jack, Jack, what are you thinking about".'

And she died with a slavered smile and not a genuine thought from anybody. No one had been capable of a genuine thought. All those women, who were supposed to know it all, all about life and death, they didn't know any more than I did.

'Can we get a cup of tea, I've had nothing to eat since half past four,' my mother said.

'Yer, there's a canteen out in the waiting-room,' I mumbled. I hovered about, pretending to help her up, and we walked down the corridor.

'We shall have to ring up Mr Shadrack,' my mother said. I had been fearing this, ever since I had heard that Gran was ill, and often in the past I had worked out how to get out of it if they ever wanted a Shadrack and Duxbury funeral for her.

'You don't want to get them, you want to get the Co-op,' I said.

My mother, speaking as though she was ashamed, said: 'Why, do they pay a divi?' and it was as though her voice was being pulled back on a lead, like a dog.

I said: 'No, but they're better than blinking Shadrack and Duxbury's.'

We were back in the hall of the casualty department. The canteen was still open. I went over to the steamy aluminium-ridged counter with the pale milky rings on it, and ordered sloppy tea in a thick mug marked SGI, Stradhoughton General Infirmary. I took the cup over to my mother and then went back and fetched my suitcase. I stood it almost in front of her and sat down. All the women had gone. There was only an old tramp in a dirty raincoat, his foot bandaged, sitting like a lost man in the corner.

My mother put her cup on the floor, shaking her head. 'I can't drink it.' She twisted her wedding ring.

'What train are you supposed to be catching?' she said.

'I don't know, when there is one.' And then, in the gentle voice: 'I've *got* to go tonight, because I want to see Danny Boon on Monday morning.'

My mother opened her handbag. 'Well you haven't got any money, have you?'

I said, flushing for the first time: 'I've got a few pounds. I've been saving up.' I was beginning to get embarrassed. I wanted to be away and finished with it all. I said: 'You'd better be getting back. I've got a taxi waiting for you outside.'

'I've got some papers to sign first,' my mother said. She stared down at the cup of tea on the floor. 'We don't say much,' she said – a straight lie, for a start – 'but we need you at home, lad.'

The sudden editorial 'we' made me feel uncomfortable. 'Well, I'll be coming home,' I said. With a rush of generosity I added: 'I'll just get fixed up with Danny Boon and then I'll come home next week-end.'

She shook her head slightly from side to side, saying nothing.

'Well, I'll *have* to go, because I don't know what time the train is,' I said. 'T' taxi's just outside, when you're ready.' I shuffled about in front of her, trying to say some words that I had practised for this moment, but I could not say them. I walked away slowly, trying to look as though I were reluctant to go. By the time I reached the white door I was already thinking of Gran as an article in the *Reader's Digest*. '*Ma Boothroyd said what she thought. Everyone feared her blunt tongue. Came the day when Ma Boothroyd had to go into hospital. ...*' Twenty-three, twenty-four, twenty-five. The Lord is my shepherd, I shall not want, he maketh me to lie down in green pastures.

I did not have the courage to turn round and look at my mother, but I knew that her face would be flawed and crumpled like an old balloon, and that for the first time she would be looking as though these things had really happened.

14

THE strange, poppy-like flowers seen nowhere else in the world were in full bloom in Ambrosia, or what was left of it. We had won the elections, and I was pressing forward with my visionary plan to build an entire city over the dunes on a gigantic wooden platform. The reactionary Dr Grover had got a commission set up to investigate me, but I knew for a fact that he had been bribed to put forward a rival plan for another city to the west, over the marshes. In the inner layers of No. 1 thinking, Grover got his way and the houses began to sink, seventy-one dead and fourteen unaccounted for. 'We will rebuild,' I announced in the *Ambrosia Poppy*. 'We will build on the dunes.' Now I was home on a visit to my parents, my full-dress uniform unbuttoned at the throat. The telephone rang, and I spoke rapidly in Ambrosian to one of my lieutenants. '*Monay. D'cra d'njin, intomr nay nay Grover. D'cra Grover, n'jnin repost. Finis.*' My mother was impressed, but no, she was not impressed. How could she be, that one? I tried to fit in my No. 1 mother, but she was a piece from another jig-saw. I began to slide off into some hate thinking about my real mother and her clichés and her knitting, about my dead grandmother snickering 'Good night' at the television set and the old man, stolid and daft, pulling his faces and banging nails all over the garage. '*Dad, I shall want the van. Don't ask questions. There may be people here. You don't know where I've gone or when I'm coming back. O.K.?*' I was sick and tired of it all, of it all.

I walked with my suitcase, following the pitch-pocked

channels in the road where the tramlines had been. I was beginning to feel like a man made entirely of sawdust. I tried to get back to Ambrosia but none of it would click and I had nothing but hate for anybody. I fired off the repeater gun at all the people who knew my secrets, but none of the secrets really mattered, they were like dead wounds with the bandages falling off. I started to get clear, frightening thoughts. Nine pounds. Less the fare, call it seven. Seven pounds. If I can get a room for two pounds ten a week, that's two weeks and a quid a week for food. I can always get a job of some kind, maybe washing-up. I began to imagine myself in the tradition of American writers, driving lorries, sweeping up, South American revolution, soda jerk, newspaper boy. Then the No. 1 thinking switched off, this time at the mains. I knew that it would probably be a job as a clerk, in an office, but by myself, by myself. No Stamps, no Shadracks. I could be an eccentric. The surly one, the man with the past. I began to sing. *'They called the bastard Stephen, they called the bastard Stephen, they called the bastard Stephen, cos that was the name of the ink.'*

Saturday night was over and done with. Along Infirmary Street a low wind caught and held a sheet of brown paper and wrapped it round a lamp-post. I could hear cars whining up Houghtondale Hill two miles away. One or two rashly-hired taxis, piled high with people splitting the fare, ran past me on their way to the Strad Lee housing estate, and I caught the idiot murmur of their radios instructing the drivers as they passed. The late bus went by, looking as though it was the last bus that would ever run again anywhere, its occupants reading the *Empire News* under the blue glare. A dog padded across the road. A man stamped home in his raincoat and I knew that he was counting the lamp-posts to get there quicker. The pavement was dry and hollow, here and there etched with the trickle of long-stale urine. The streets were cold and the girls on the posters were grinning in their sleep.

I walked like a ghost down Moorgate, the suitcase making red ridges on my hand and turning into loot at every sight of a policeman. I turned into Bull Ring, dodging the slow-moving road-sweeper vans emerging like snails from the cleansing department and leaving their trickling smear along the gutters. I walked across Bull Ring into New Station.

The station was ablaze with cold, white light. The booking hall was deserted except for a fleet of electric trollies piled high with newspaper parcels. The last Harrogate diesel was just pulling sleekly away from platform two.

The inquiry office was closed. I walked up to the roller-indicator where the trains were listed: 1.05 Wakefield, Doncaster; 1.35 Leeds (City), Derby, Kettering, London (St Pancras); 1.50 Selby, Market Weighton, Bridlington, Filey, Scarborough. There were no other trains to London that night. All the windows but one at the ticket office were boarded up. I waited under A–G until a tired man in his shirt-sleeves appeared, and I bought a single second-class to St Pancras. It cost thirty-five shillings. I looked up at the big station clock. It was ten minutes to one.

Below the ticket office was the buffet and main waiting-room. The buffet end was closed, its counter still lined with thick cups and the floor littered with crusts of bread, but there were about a dozen people still in the waiting-room, most of them asleep with their feet up on the scratched tubular chairs or their heads down on the rockety tables, among the flattened straws and empty lemon-squash cartons. I went in and stood by the door, under one of the large, empty-looking pictures of fields and hills that lined the walls. A few people were awake: half a dozen soldiers, all in civies, going home on leave, three old prostitutes, a

man in a large black coat. I was sleepy, recognizing everything about five seconds after it happened. I did not see
Rita, or Stamp, until I had settled down on my suitcase and
was lighting a cigarette.

They did not see me either. Stamp, savouring the dregs
of his dull, drunken evening, was leaning against one of the
gilded pillars that separated the waiting-room from the
buffet, sweating and muttering to himself. Rita was pulling
ineffectively at his arm, like a tired wife trying to get her
husband out of the pub. *'Come* on, they're all *look*ing at
you,' I heard her say impatiently. She stood indecisively and
then let go of his arm and said, obviously not for the first
time: 'Oh, well I'm going, you can look after yourself.'
Stamp, lost in the biley swamps of his own suffering,
gripped the pillar for support and comfort, retched,
swallowed, and then, in his thin and watery way, was sick
all over the floor. Rita tutted and phewed and looked
rapidly from side to side to find sympathy for her own
predicament. She walked a few steps away and turned her
back, standing with a formal casualness, pretending not to
be anything to do with Stamp. A few of the sleeping people
stirred. One of them half-woke.

'Christ sake, shift outside if you wanna spew!'

Some of those who were already awake began tittering.
One of the soldiers imitated a man in the toils of sickness.
'Wyyach!' Stamp, clawing at the air, reeling and watery-
eyed, caught some kind of hazy glimpse of me sitting in the
corner, watching him. The image passed straight through
into his subconscious and he peered at me without recogni-
tion, fixing his eyes on me only as an object while he
strained and sweated and gasped for air.

The man in the big black coat, red-faced and beery in
his own right, was enjoying it all. For the benefit of the
soldiers he called: 'Get that man in the guard-house!

C.O.'s p'rade 'morrow morning. Hat off, left right left right left right HALT!' One or two of the soldiers grinned weakly; the one sitting next to me muttered: 'He wants to get back in the effing army if he's so effing keen.'

Stamp, mopping grimly at his damp forehead, staggered to the wall and sat down on the floor under a picture of Lake Windermere, head down like a sleeping Mexican. Rita walked over and began plucking at him again, pleading: '*Come* on, then. You shouldn't drink and then you wouldn't *be* like this.'

In the middle of the room, the tableau changed. The three old prostitutes were haggling with a half-drunk, fair-haired lad who had just come in. 'Well do you want *her*, then? You should have said. *She* doesn't care, one way or t' other.' They were all about fifty years old, and they did not look like prostitutes, more like housewives who baked loaves. They talked like mothers anxious to please their grown-up sons with a good tea. 'Well get a taxi and take her home then. She'll take fifteen shillings, she doesn't care, she doesn't want to skin you.'

The soldiers next to me were muttering. '*He* must be hard up for it, they look like three old grandmothers.'

'Three old grandmothers, bet they'll be getting their pensions in the morning!'

'Ha! Be funny if one of 'em pegged out on the job. Three dirty old grandmothers.'

It was wit to the taste of Stamp, but Stamp saw nothing of what was going on around him. He had got up and was leaning over his pillar again, slavering into the thin green mess which he had padded about the floor with his sick-speckled shoes.

'*Wyyach!*' went one of the soldiers.

'That time me and Jacko got them German drinks. *Wyyach!*'

I got up and walked to the other side of the waiting-room, skirting round Stamp in a broad arc. As soon as Rita saw me I regretted that I had moved.

'Look what's crawled out of the cheese!' she said, neither raising nor lowering her voice. She was wearing a blue swagger coat over her tight red dress. The silver cross was no longer round her neck.

'I should think some people ought to crawl back *into* the cheese,' I said, nodding towards Stamp.

'Oo, where's yer rubber halo?' jeered Rita. We looked at each other, or at least I looked at her. Rita had a habit of looking at nothing, her eyes glazing over with a sort of gormless preoccupation.

'What happened to the Witch?' I said.

She screwed her face up into an ugly scowl. '*Who?*'

'Barbara. Her you were talking to in the Roxy.'

'Don't know, don't care,' said Rita.

'Did she say anything?'

'Ask no questions and you'll get no lies told,' she said in the same level voice.

'I bet she got that cross out of you,' I said recklessly. 'Hope you didn't give her the ring back, did you?'

Rita's voice suddenly took on the same pitch and colour as the voices of the three old prostitutes still haggling away in the middle of the room:

'You what? Do you think I'm daft, or what? It might be her cross, but you gave that ring to *me*!'

I looked around, but nobody was listening.

'I know, only it's a bit of a mix-up,' I said. 'You see, I thought Barbara had broke the engagement off –'

'Yer, well you've another think coming if you think I'm as daft as she is! You gave that ring to *me*, in front of a witness.'

'How do you mean, what's witnesses got to do with it?'

Rita stared at me, thin-lipped like all the people I had known that day. She made as if to speak twice and then, spitting the words out with such force that her head shook, she said in the lowest range of her coarse voice:

'You're just *rot*ten, aren't you?'

I looked wildly across the room to my suitcase, and from my suitcase to the door, planning the shortest route out into the booking hall.

'Y'are! You're rotten! All through! I've met some people in my time but of all the lying, scheming – Anyway, you gave that ring to *me*!'

I said quietly and urgently: 'Look, nobody's asking for the ring. You can have it –'

'Don't talk to me, you rotten get!' Rita's voice was rising with each word, and even the prostitutes were beginning to stare. 'Get back to '*er*! You rotten get! You rotten, lying get! Gar, you think you're summat, don't you? But you're nowt! You miserable, lying, rotten, stinking get!'

White-faced, I turned my back on her and walked quickly towards my suitcase, skidding and almost losing my balance where Stamp had been sick on the floor. 'You think you're it but you're shit!' shouted Rita. One of the soldiers caught my eye and jerked his head up, raising his eyes and going: 'Cuh!' I grabbed my suitcase blindly and made for the door. Two railway policemen walked into the waiting-room, looking ponderously about them, and Rita shut up. One of them walked over to where Stamp was leaning helplessly against the pillar and began talking to him in a low, dangerous voice.

The man in the black coat called: 'Two men, buckets, mops. Floor cleaned. 'Port to me when you've finished. Double!' I slid out of the waiting-room and stood irresolutely in the booking hall, still shaken.

It was just on one o'clock. I stood contemplating the

gigantic advertisement for Ovaltine that filled one whole end of the booking hall. Running my eyes down the wall, I began to count the loaded parcel trolleys that stood around the station. I got up to nineteen, and then the waiting-room door opened again and one of the policemen came out, helping Stamp towards the lavatory. Stamp saw me with his boiled, steaming eyes and muttered through the spit on his face: 'Know somethn bou' you, Fisher. *I* saw you. Wai' Monday, you jus' wai'.' The policeman led him off, as he muttered again: 'Wai' Monday.'

I had lost my place among the parcel trolleys. I began counting the tiles on the dirty, unwashed floor of the station. I counted them in a line, screwing up my eyes, and numbering each tile only with great difficulty after I had passed twenty. Raising my head slightly I saw a pair of heels by the one window of the ticket office that was still open. I opened my eyes again and looked, and there was no mistaking the casual black skirt, the green suède jacket, and the unkempt hair. Liz was just turning away from the ticket office as I picked up my case and began to stumble towards her, walking drunkenly in the manner of Stamp being led off to the lavatory.

She saw me just as she was turning off to make for the platform where the Doncaster train was waiting. I waved, and she came towards me. I flapped my hand again, airily.

'Goin' London,' I mumbled, grabbing her arm and lurching about in front of her. 'You goin' London? I'm goin' London. Go' catch a train. Goin' London.'

'So you keep saying,' said Liz, beaming comfortably.

'You come London, me. Goin' London. Pla'form three, S' Pancra', ge's all London.'

'Where did you get it?' said Liz, still beaming as though she relished the whole thing.

'Where ge' wha'?'

'The booze. Or did you find some little dive to go to after you so mysteriously disappeared?'

'Go' go London,' I said. 'Carn stay Stradanan. Go' go London.'

The station announcer, as inarticulate as myself, crackled out some message about the Doncaster train. Liz looked up at the station clock.

'Well *I'm* not going to London. I've got to go to Doncaster –'

I took hold of her arm again, wagging my head heavily.

'No, you come London. Need you London. Ge' nother ticket, come London.'

Liz gave me one of her long looks, and slowly took hold of me, inspecting me at arm's length.

'Drop it,' she said, stern behind the smile.

I said in my normal voice: 'Drop what?'

'That's better. You may be a brilliant script-writer, Billy, but you're a rotten actor.'

I put on an elaborate mock-sheepish act, standing on one foot, pulling out a grin and spreading my arms about.

'*All* right,' said Liz. 'Now where did you get to tonight?'

'Where did *I* get to? Where did *you* get to?'

Lovingly, in detail, we reconstructed the half-hour I had waited outside the Roxy, charting and justifying our movements, forgiving and understanding, and everything so simple. Liz had been having a long talk with the Witch, whom she had discovered weeping and slobbering and sick on the floor of the Ladies. Everything that could be told had been told.

'Are you really going to London, or just pretending?' said Liz.

I took the ticket out of my pocket and showed it to her. She looked at me steadily and there was love in her dark eyes, the first time I had seen it, a liquid, far-reaching thing, too deep to touch.

'I'm not coming, you know, Billy.'

'Please.'

She shook her head. 'I won't live with you, Billy.'

'Come anyway,' I said. 'Live next door. Blimey, you've been everywhere else, you might as well come and live in –' I broke off as a suspicion crossed my mind. 'Why are you going to Doncaster?'

She grinned again, in the frank manner that gave nothing away.

'Oh, just – Doncaster,' she said, shrugging amiably.

I said bluffly, in the man of the world voice: 'Well whatever you want in Doncaster, they've got it in London. Yes? Yes?

She was shaking her head, smiling.

'One condition,' she said.

I closed my eyes tightly and smote my forehead, teetering on the brink of a decision. All the details of it were there, in a compact parcel of No. 1 thinking, from the registry-office ceremony to the Chelsea attic. All it needed was the decision.

'And I wouldn't want the communal ring,' said Liz. But I did not answer, and she knew that there was no answer.

A porter was rattling the gate at the entrance to the Doncaster platform. Liz picked up her bag, a small, well-worn grip. She regarded me steadily for a few seconds and, standing a foot in front of me, blew me a kiss.

'Postcards?' she said, whispering it.

'Postcards,' I said.

I struck the farewell attitude, legs apart, arms akimbo, the sad figure fading into silhouette as the train steams away. But she did not look back. The porter banged the gate shut and I saw Liz clamber into the last carriage after two soldiers. I watched the train disappear. I knew that she would already be in bright conversation, grinning engagingly at some item of army news.

It was twelve minutes past one. I picked up my suitcase and walked back towards the waiting-room. Rita, the three old prostitutes, and most of the others had gone, and there was sawdust on the floor where Stamp had been. Two soldiers slept on, their feet extended across a couple of chairs apiece. The man in the black coat was still there, but dozing.

I stood by the wall and, raising one leg, balanced the suitcase on my knee. I took out the top layer of calendars and began rooting about among the shirts and socks for more. I stacked the calendars on the tubular table beside me until I had got them all out. Then I closed the suitcase and pushed it under the table. I scooped the calendars up into two heavy parcels, one under each arm, and barged the door open with my back. I looked up and down the booking hall but there was nobody watching. There was a deep wire litter bin, labelled 'Keep Your Borough Clean'. I bent over and tipped the calendars into it. The basket toppled slightly. I gathered up some newspapers from a nearby seat and stuffed them in on top of the calendars.

I turned to go and then, struck by a second thought, I felt in my pocket for the wad of invoices that I should have posted for the old man. I dropped those in the basket too. I found the letters from the Witch, and ripped them in pieces, scattering the bits in the litter bin and on the floor around it. I began going methodically through my pockets, discarding practically everything: the fragment of script for Danny Boon, the letter I had started to write to him, a couple of Stamp's passion pills, a cigarette packet. When I had finished I had nothing left but the note from Danny Boon, Liz's postcards, and my railway ticket. I walked back into the waiting-room and got my suitcase. It needed fourteen minutes before the London train was due to go.

Ambrosia came softly into my head, the beginning of it all, with the march-past and the one-armed soldiers and the flags. I muttered to myself, almost aloud: 'Seventy-eight, ninety-six, a hundred and four, the Lord is my Shepherd, I shall not want, he maketh me to lie down in green pastures, he leadeth me beside the still waters.' The No. 1 thinking fused into a panic-panorama with the No. 2 daymares and the quick sharp shafts of ordinary, level thought. I imagined myself as a modern clergyman, pipe-smoking, twinkling, arranging a contemporary funeral with Shadrack; but nasally he was saying, 'It's vair vair unsatisfactory, vair unsa'sfactory.' I could not summon up my No. 1 mother, only the real one, with her pressed, depressed mouth and her petty frown. Seven pounds, seven pounds ten actually, get a room for thirty bob a week, call it three weeks, three quid left, half a crown a day, egg and chips one and threepence, cup of tea threepence, bus fares a tanner. He restoreth my soul, he leadeth me in the paths of righteousness for his name's sake. I saw Liz in the Chelsea attic, and Rita whoring it in the streets outside, and the Witch as the reactionary Dr Grover's mistress. I tried hard to shut it down and find myself, myself, but not knowing what to do for characteristics. Yea, though I walk through the valley of the shadow of death, I will fear no evil.

The station announcer began to list the stations to London. Leeds (City), Derby, Kettering, London (St Pancras). Change at Leeds for Bradford, Ilkley, Bolton Abbey. The man in the big black coat, chastened now, began to arrange his things. I got up and began to walk hurriedly up and down the waiting-room; I had the sensation of a water-tap running in my stomach. I picked up my suitcase and put it down twice. I took out the ticket and looked at it, vaguely noting the price and the details. I could not think, except in confused snatches. I began to count ten; at the end of the count I would oblige myself to answer one way or the other. One. Two. Three. Four. The train now leaving platform three is the one thirty-five for London, calling at. Five. Six. Seven. There was no need to count to the end. I picked up the suitcase, feeling deflated and defeated. I walked out of the waiting-room and across the booking hall to the ticket barrier on platform three, hoping that I would make a quick decision but knowing that there was no question of it. The man in the black coat and three or four soldiers walked through, showing their tickets.

The ticket collector looked at me.

'You gettin' on this train?' I shook my head, taking a step forward at the same time.

I did not wait for the train to leave. I transferred the suitcase to my left hand and walked out of the station. In Bull Ring I stopped and lit a cigarette and buttoned up my coat. The suitcase felt absurdly light. I began to breathe great gusts of air, but there was little air to breathe.

I walked across Bull Ring and up Moorgate. Suddenly I began to feel excited and buoyant, and I was almost running by the time I reached Town Square. I began to whistle 'March of the Movies' and to march in step with it. There was nobody about. When I came to the War Memorial I transferred my suitcase to my right hand and at the correct moment I saluted with the left – up, two, three, down, two, three, head erect, shoulders back. I brought the whistling to a huffing crescendo and wheeled smartly into Infirmary Street. I dropped into a normal step, and then I began the slow walk home.

BILLY LIAR
ON THE MOON

I

THE only place where you can get a vodka martini in Shepford is just by the M.1 slip road, ambitiously described in the official guide-book as the Highway to Europe. Road maps are not much use to the thirsty traveller, it being the Council's policy to keep one jump ahead of Geographia Ltd. Anyone needing a vodka martini that badly would have to take verbal instructions.

Driving west out of town through the shopping centre – or, for that matter, driving west out of town while still looking for the one-way side street that is the only access to the shopping centre – you come across three or four small brick factories, one of them also mentioned in the guide-book. (It makes plastic weather-shields for offshore generators; thus Shepford, though eighty miles inland, plays its part in the quest for North Sea Oil.) Then there is a patch of rubble where another small brick factory is about to go up or has just fallen down. Then there is the borough's surplus cache of sewage pipes, stacked on what used to be a grass verge. Then there is the road junction with its cluster of signs: this way to the Town Centre, that way to the Abbey, this way to the Castle, this way, that way and the other way to the car parks, and round the back-doubles for the Highway to Europe. This route takes you to the site that was rejected, so they say, by Holiday Inns, but accepted by Heritage Motor Lodges of America.

The Heritage Motor Lodge complex, resembling a Nevada Desert gambling resort that has run foul of the Las Vegas District Council Planning Committee, was but four minutes from the town centre when it was built and is but twelve minutes away since the one-way system was perfected. But it is sufficiently near the motorway to give the discerning visitor a last reviewing the life-style to which he has been reduced by the profit motive, re-packing his case of samples and heading back to London or any point north – in my case, Stradhoughton.

If only I'd left before the second martini, not only would the Helen problem have solved itself, but I could have been driving into the Bull Ring car-stack by half-past nine, throwing-up a Chinese dinner by half-past ten, and still have had ninety minutes to play with before exploring the question I'd often turned over in my mind since leaving Stradhoughton all those light-years ago – did the drunks still race all the way around the Town Hall while the carillon sounded twelve?

I couldn't afford vodka martinis, and neither, I imagined, could Shepford District Council, which paid for them in a roundabout way. I drank them as a gesture to my designer-decorated surroundings – to fit in, as much as possible, with the padded leather bar, the bowls of pretzels, and the old English cross-bows on the bare stone walls. The illusion, for which I was grateful, was of being, if not in New York, then at the very least in downtown Albuquerque, wherever that turned out to be. And anyway, it was not much dearer than the doubles bar which had lately taken possession of the soul of the King's Head in the Cornmarket; and anyway, vodka martinis were what Oscar drank too.

'Nearest place south of Birming-ham where they know how to fix the darn things, Bill. Lemme say this. You British can build the best boats in the world, the best suits in the world and I'd walk a billion miles for an English teacake. But you bet your ass you've never yet built a good barman. No – way.'

'Right.'

Why Oscar spoke like an Australian actor playing an American bit-part in an English television play was because he didn't exist. Sometimes he absolutely didn't exist, for weeks at a time, but he'd been useful with the Helen problem lately and he was often a comfort in other ways, so the least I could do was stand him a drink occasionally. He was an oilman at present, and I was doing him a big favour by introducing him to the only firm in Britain that could turn him out a plastic weather-shield for his offshore generator by the end of the week; but usually he was in public relations and if I played my cards right I would be on Madison Avenue before I was forty. Or should I, I sometimes used to wonder in whimsical moments, and especially when the Helen problem wasn't too pressing, turn Oscar into a six-foot rabbit, like Harvey? That would depend on future access to the vodka martinis.

Who did exist, to the point of occupying Oscar's bar stool and embarrassingly asking for draught Bass, was Purchase, who called himself a colleague of mine and was said to shave his nose.

'You mean the hairs in his nostrils,' I'd said to Hattersley, who had brought me this tit-bit.

'His nose. From tip to bridge.'

'Upward strokes? Sounds improbable.'

'Bridge to tip, then. It's true! I caught him at it in the wash-room – the night we were all going to Pisspot's birthday do. He puts lather all over his nose and then he shaves it.'

'The only man in Shepford with a conk like a baby's bottom.'

Also the only man in Shepford I didn't want to see in the bar of the Heritage Motor Lodge – or, to be fair, going rapidly through a roll-call of about two hundred names and putting asterisks against the dozen or so who might remotely land up there – the last man I wanted to see. Although Purchase could describe himself as a colleague only in the sense that, say, a BBC admin clerk can claim credit for the nine o'clock news – for he was in the Finance Department while I was in Information and Publicity – we were, at least on paper, in line for the same promotion. No *way*, as Oscar would have said.

FOR IMMEDIATE RELEASE. Mr William Fisher, 33, is to be appointed Information Officer and Director of Publicity for the District of Shepford at a commencing salary of about double what he is getting at present, plus entertainment allowance, office car, honorary membership of the municipal golf club, key to the Civic Centre drinks cupboard, and freeloading

*facilities at most official functions. He succeeds Mr R. V. O.
('Pisspot') Rainbell, who is taking up residence in a home for
alcoholics.*

'Be a bit late tonight,' I could hear myself saying. 'Bloody
Mayor's reception. Bloody Japanese trade delegation.'

I could even say the same thing to Helen, if the Helen problem wasn't solved by then.

*Mr Fisher entered local government in the West Riding Borough
of Stradhoughton, where he had been employed as an undertaker's clerk until dismissed for petty embezzlement. After joining the Rates office on forged references, he gained experience in
several municipal departments before transferring to the then
County Borough of Shepford for a motive he finds himself unable to discuss. Mr Fisher has lived in Shepford for eight years,
although it seems like eighty, and has been in the Information
Office for the past five years. He is part-author of* Pageantry
with Progress *(new edition), the official guide-book. Mr Fisher
resides either with his wife and widowed mother on the Fairways estate, or alone in a mahogany-panelled turret overlooking the ancient Cornmarket with its many pavement cafés,
brasseries and bustling restaurants.*

But this was no time for counting golden eggs. If Purchase was
still sitting here humming and hawing over what to drink as a
substitute for draught Bass when Helen walked in ten minutes
hence, there was nothing short of a good shove into the Civic
Centre paper-shredding machine that could prevent his account of the rendezvous reaching the Senior Appointments
Selection Board. Plus, as a bonus, a breakdown of my vodka
martini budget, with informed speculation on how it was
balanced. I could already see his smudgy coloured photograph
in the *Evening Mail*, a news-sheet that seemed to be put together by a hundred monkeys at a hundred keyboards, and the
accompanying text:

Mr James Pugchase, a meber of te District

194

Treasurer's Department ang chairman of the
Shepford Festival Committee ival Committe
shrdlushrdlu has been appointed Mr Purchase,
who is an old boy of Shepford Grammar
Information Officer and Publicity Director
School, Te case was adjourned until Thrusday.

'No draught beer of any kind?' repeated Purchase. The barman, Harry (a name he had drawn from stores along with his white bum-freezer when joining the Heritage Happy Family) had just said that to him, in so many words. Purchase did with other people's sentences what he did with figures all day long at his trestle table in the office next to mine – he checked them for possible discrepancies. I had once made a tape of him cocking-up an interview on the local radio, and he had repeated, word-perfect, a question about the Shepford Festival consisting of fifty-eight syllables. No wonder they called him the human radish, or would do if I had anything to do with it.

'Lager, then,' he said, taking a far bigger handful of pretzels than he was entitled to on such a cheapskate order. The room was too dark to stare at his nose, a spot-check I carried out from time to time. One little nick, or even better, a strip of Elastoplast, would confirm Hattersley's story: I didn't believe all he told me.

'Don't often see you in this neck of the woods,' I said, slipping easily into the council-clerk patois. (If I'd wanted an 'A' for Effort I would have said 'this particular hostelry'.) I cupped my hand around the empty martini glass, wishing I'd ordered it on the rocks so that it would have come in a tumbler and made him believe I was on gin and tonic. As it was, he would have to think it was sherry. With an olive.

'One of your haunts, is it?' A ninety-degree glance around the bar, as casual as a turtle with inflamed neck glands, to indicate that he's only making conversation. You don't catch me like that, Purchase.

'No, it's not really my neck of the woods.' I shouldn't have said that twice; maybe I'm nervous. 'I favour it with the occasional visit.'

'But not often?' No, Purchase, positively not often. Let's hope you gather as much from the half-smile, the deprecatory shrug, the shake of the head, the slight curl of the lip, and the expression, 'No'.

'This on your tab, Mr Fisher?' said Harry the barman. He was English, but American-trained, you bet your ass. He'd worked on a liner, so he told me. It should have been the Titanic.

'No, no, no, wouldn't dream of it,' Purchase protested, now showing further bad taste by digging into his pocket for ten-penny pieces, as if completing a round in a saloon bar. 'Here, let me get you one. I insist.'

He nodded to Harry who, before I could mouth 'Small medium sherry,' commenced an exercise with lemons, olives, ice, vodka, vermouth and shaker that would have won him ten points for style in an International Barman of the Year competition.

'Because,' continued Purchase, after quizzically following Harry's progress for some time in the apparent hope that he was about to produce the flags of all nations out of his cocktail shaker, 'if you *don't* come here often, you *wouldn't* often see me here, now would you?'

Go on, Purchase, let's have it. In a minute you're going to say, 'Not that it's any concern of mine where you spend your evenings,' in a tone that suggests it should be the concern of every right-thinking ratepayer in Shepford. 'Nor is it any of mine where you spend yours,' I could retaliate, leaving him the way open for some cock-and-bull story about being taken short or popping in for a book-match and a packet of Manikins. You followed me here, Purchase. You know it and I know it.

But it wasn't what Purchase was going to say in a minute that immediately worried me, it was what he was going to say any second now when Harry, after pouring my Vodka martini, placed his bill a discreet distance away on the bar counter, though not so discreet a distance that a trained accountant couldn't read it upside down. And it was what he was going to say, if not to me then to himself, and later to everyone listed in the Civic Centre internal telephone directory, when Helen entered in about eight minutes.

'Nice and dry, just as you like it, Mr Fisher,' said Harry, who seemed hell-bent on identifying me as the Heritage Motor Lodge's most favoured son. 'And there's one lined up for her ladyship.'

Thank you, Harry, but surely there are more subtle ways of arousing Purchase's interest? Why not a revolving illuminated sign in the courtyard? HERITAGE MOTOR LODGES OF AMERICA WELCOME WILLIAM FISHER AND HIS MISTRESS, MRS HELEN LIGHTFOOT.

I shrugged him back to his racing paper. Purchase, who had finished the pretzels and was reaching for a bowl of nuts intended for the future occupant of the next bar stool but two, hadn't heard, or pretended he hadn't. His left buttock reconnected with the padded leather, which hissed its dismay, and he turned back to me.

'Not that it's any concern of mine where you – Good – *God*!'

He'd seen the bill. In dramatic terms, his cry of anguish should have been an offstage one, like a crash in a Laurel and Hardy film, and Harry and I could have cringed our shoulders in sympathy. But it wasn't bad as cries of anguish went – rather similar to the one I'd uttered myself on being introduced to my own first Heritage Motor Lodge bar bill. ('Hey, lemme take care of that,' Oscar had said, but I'd already put my hand firmly over the bill, felt in my top pocket for the American Express card that I must have left in one of my other suits, and tossed my last fiver on the bar counter.)

'A pound?' the awestruck Purchase whispered. 'A *pound*? A *POUND*?'

'It includes VAT,' I said. But not service. Odd that despite all my anxieties about Purchase's presence here, my main worry was that he would embarrass me by departing, if he ever got round to departing, without leaving a tip.

'All I can say is if you can afford to drink here, you must have better salaries in your department than we in ours,' said Purchase, who knew to the penny what I earned.

What I could do was slip a few bob on the bar counter near his glass and pretend he'd left it.

'Easy come, easy go,' I said. 'It's not every day I come up on the pools.' You can do better than that, Fisher.

'You say you've come up on the pools?'

Yes, Rastus, I'se come up on de pools. 'Only thirty-eight quid – fourth dividend.' He's going to check that. 'Or at least that's what I work it out at – they haven't coughed up yet. Let me get you another.' Six minutes before Helen was due: the lemming instinct was working well.

'Make it two lagers this time,' I thought I'd better say to Harry. A mistake, probably. I can't drink beer quickly. I could spill most of it over Purchase's trousers, of course, but would that hasten his departure or postpone it while he dried off?

Maybe she'd be late. There was always a sporting chance of a traffic jam on the clearway.

'I'm glad I caught up with you,' said Purchase, another rueful glance at his bar bill indicating that I could take that remark how I liked, 'because I wanted a word in your ear about the Festival.'

Although this was no time for delaying tactics I couldn't resist playing Purchase at his own game: 'When you say you're glad you caught up with me, does that imply you followed me here?'

'I caught sight of your car on the roundabout. I did want a word – it's rather difficult in the office.'

If it's rather difficult in the office, it must be about Pisspot.

'It's about Mr Rainbell. Some of us are *rather* concerned about his drinking.'

'Concerned about him personally, or concerned about his job?' Or after his job, even.

'I'm not in the slightest interested in his personal life.' Only in yours, Fisher. Four minutes to go. 'But when it comes to disrupting committee meetings, arriving late, falling about and having no idea what's going on, then it's very much my pigeon.'

'The poor old sod's only got eighteen months to go,' I said. 'And so far as his work's concerned, Hattersley and I simply carve it up between us. So unless you're tired of picking him up when he falls down the stairs, I don't see what you've got to worry about.'

'What I have to worry about is the Festival. As you know, it's very much my pigeon.' (Making two pigeons so far. Well, it is and it isn't your pigeon, Purchase. You only got the job because your mother had it before you, when Shepford was a grotty little market town and the Festival was no more than a Sunday school float and a couple of sideshows. A classic example of nepotism being all right so long as it's kept in the family.) 'I don't see how we can get through our work if that drunken lout is allowed to disrupt committee meetings, arriving late, falling about –'

Yes, you've already said that, and my time is more valuable than you think. 'So why don't you bar him?' I cut in.

'That's more difficult than you realize. The Festival Committee can't function properly without proper liaison with the Information and Publicity Department.'

Now then, Purchase, you look like a sporting gent. For a fiver, see if you can say this without moving your lips: 'Put properly by Purchase, Pisspot's proper purpose is publicity.' Or rather:

'So Hattersley and I go through the minutes. That's what we always do anyway.'

'There are a thousand questions involving Information and Publicity. The Department must be represented at personal level.'

'So Pisspot sends apologies for absence and Hattersley or I take his place. What's wrong with that?'

'I was hoping you'd say that, Fisher. And rather you than Hattersley, if I may say so.'

I'd drifted off again. Oscar was saying: 'Bill, I wanna put this on the line. One of our team has a drink problem. We have to let him go. Lemme ask you this. Can you telescope your present commitments and be at your desk on the thirty-fourth floor of the Madison Building by nine a.m. Monday? You have to make a decision now.' I frowned Oscar into the leather shadows of some unoccupied booth and looked at the bar clock.

It destroyed the New York or Albuquerque illusion by keeping Shepford pub time and was ten minutes fast. By Shepford pub time Helen should have been here nine minutes ago and so would arrive any second. I knocked back my lager, and heard Purchase continuing:

'Hattersley's a very good man in his way, a good organizer I believe, but we have all the organizing strength we need. What we do need, Fisher, is someone with your flair.'

My flair? But you don't want my flair, Purchase. Considering that we're both after the same job, what you would rather do with my flair is take it out to the council rubbish tip and re-cycle it.

And another thing, stop calling me Fisher, as if you'd been to a minor public school.

'Let me say this.' He can't have got that from Oscar. 'If you can arrange it with Mr Rainbell, we'd be very glad indeed to see you on the Festival Committee.'

Curiouser and curiouser, as they used to say in light fiction. The only thing Purchase had going for him, when it came to stepping into Pisspot's gin-soaked shoes as Information Officer, was that he was chairman of the Festival Committee. Shepford Shows The Way, ta-ra! Exports up by eight point five per cent on some figures we've just made up. He could claim, or certainly would claim, to run the Festival almost single-handed. Why, then, was he tailing me like a private detective with an office over a Soho knocking-shop, only to give me half of the glory with Green Shield Stamps?

It was something I'd have to ponder on later. I had to get him off the premises at once. 'I'll see what I can do,' I said and, making a great show at settling my bill with a handful of silver rather than displaying a bulging money-clip to Purchase's quarterly-audit gaze, I rose from my bar stool, knowing that he would do the same. There was no risk that he was going to sit here by himself, knocking back lagers at thirty-five pence a throw. And indeed, Purchase was also sorting out his loose change; and now he had produced a thin, imitation-leather wallet and was peering into it.

'Fisher,' he said, as I saw Helen arrive at the entrance to the bar, take a step or two towards us, stare hard through the gloom and then disappear with commendable speed into the Ladies, 'could you possibly lend me a pound?'

The plan was simple enough. Wave good-bye to Purchase in the car park, trusting he hadn't registered Helen's bright red Mini parked a lovebird's-breadth away from my old Austin 1100; make a great show, all indicators flashing, of heading for the roundabout and the route home; turn through the back-doubles and be back outside the Heritage Motor Lodge in about two minutes.

But no one driving in Shepford should formulate simple plans without consulting the Highways Department first. The lane running alongside the car was a one-way thoroughfare leading to a T-junction which, to bring it in line with most T-junctions in the district, had recently become a compulsory right-turn. Suspecting that this route incorporated a tour of the sights of Shepford before bringing the bemused motorist to within fifty yards of his starting point, I favoured a policy – and more so favoured it now, since it would have the additional merit of shaking Purchase off my tail – of making an illicit left-turn out of the car park and connecting myself with the obvious route to the roundabout. Disregarding Purchase's scandalized bellows of 'Wrong way! Wrong way!' I did this now, only to find as I turned into the main road that I was confronted by a great scattering of plastic traffic cones, warning lamps, blue-and-white arrows and a sign reading: 'TRAFFIC EXPERIMENT – DIVERSION.' I was led through a bewildering maze of back streets, some of them derelict cobbled alleys that could not have seen wheeled traffic since the last inhabitant was towed away in a horse-driven cortège. As I drove into a reclaimed children's play-street I said aloud: 'One thing, Oscar, we've shaken off that bastard Purchase.' *Right.*

I found myself, in due course, in roughly the area I should have arrived at by taking the proper turn out of the car park. Pulling up at one of the sets of temporary traffic lights that

festooned the streets of Shepford like Christmas lanterns, I saw
that the Ford Popular in front of me contained Purchase. Instead
of he following me, I was now following him. He caught sight of
me in his driving mirror and gave me a stiff, puzzled wave. I
returned the salute, followed him through an obstacle-course
of white-painted railway sleepers that had been arranged along
this section of the route for no clear reason, and took the first
available turning. This was a steep, freshly-tarmaced incline,
hemmed in by new brick walls, and vaguely familiar. It was
only as I reached the top, and saw the blue sign decorated with
kindergarten silhouettes of knives and forks and petrol pumps,
and the legend: 'NEXT SERVICES: 37 MILES' that the feeling
of *déjà vu* completely registered and I realized that I was on the
M.1, heading for Birmingham.

Helen would be ordering her second martini by now. She
would already have received a negative from Harry to the
question, 'Didn't he say anything about coming back?' and
there would be a little pile of twopenny pieces by her glass. On
the third martini, she would go across to the telephone booth at
the end of the bar, ring my number, and hang up when Jeanette
or my mother answered. She would repeat the process on the
fourth. It needed five before she would press home a coin and
deliver some breathless, garbled, drunken and altogether unconvincing message about Mr Fisher being wanted at a Vestifal
meeting – *Festival* meeting, at the Civcensor. Civic Centre.

In times of stress, Helen drank martinis at the rate of one
every eight minutes. I was already two miles up the M.1. An
unbroken length of crash-barrier ran down the central reserva-
tion of the motorway: no prospect of a U-turn. There were no
slip-roads before the promise of knives, forks and petrol pumps
was fulfilled in a transport caff disguised as a primary school
thirty-odd miles further on.

Keep driving, Fisher. A hundred and seventy miles more
and you'll be in Stradhoughton. Book in at the Midland if it's
still standing, and chase yourself round the Town Hall on the
stroke of midnight. You could be a Dick Whittington in reverse.

The image gave me an idea. Was it illegal to reverse down the fast lane of the M.1? Never mind that: was it possible? I decided to have a crack at it, although modifying the attempt (since the rush-hour was not quite over) to the slow lane or better still, in view of the oncoming convoy of juggernauts, to the hard shoulder.

As I backed diagonally across the middle lane a black Cortina, the property of Shepford District Council car pool, and driven in this instance by Councillor Percy Drummond, chairman of the Senior Appointments Selection Board among other senior appointments, skidded out of my blind spot, horn blaring and headlights flashing. A word of explanation seemed necessary. Even if he hadn't seen my face – he'd had to slow down in order to avoid ramming the crash-barrier – he must have registered the car and the Council's 'SUPPORT SHEPFORD FESTIVAL' sticker on the rear windscreen. I leaned out of the window and bawled, '*Gears stuck!*' realizing only as the words were carried into the wind how uncommonly similar they must sound to '*Get stuffed!*'

Owing to some further experimentation by the Highways Department – they had succeeded, at one point, in filtering traffic into a one-way cul-de-sac, a kind of motorized sheep-pen from which it was impossible to escape without technically breaking the law – it was forty minutes past the hour when I got back to the Heritage Motor Lodge. The bar was empty. It nearly always was: but for the hidden subsidy from the Shepford District Council which I passed on twice or three times a week, it would have been converted into a conference lounge by now. There was always room for another conference lounge at the Heritage, which made its living coralling packs of young executives, all with lapel badges stating their names and rank, into compulsory working dinners. Helen and I, arguing in fierce whispers in the corner of the bar, had once surfaced to find ourselves in the middle of a seminar about packaging.

'About twenty minutes ago,' said Harry.

I was about to ask, 'And was she – you know?' accompanying this cryptic inquiry with a vigorous piece of wristmiming that would have suggested a meths drinker knocking back surgical spirit from an eye-bath, when Harry handed me the bill which Helen had left for me to pay. At that price, she must have crawled out of the place on her hands and knees.

'Did she make any phone calls, do you happen to know?' I asked instead.

'She made two or three,' said Harry.

And did she get through to anyone, do you happen to know? Why ask? I'll hear about it sooner or later.

'Oh, I forgot to mention, Mr Fisher,' he went on, mixing a vodka martini on the correct assumption that I looked as if I needed one, 'that other gentleman came back.'

'What other gentleman?'

'Your friend. Who you were talking to earlier. He wanted a copy of his bill, for some strange reason.'

Oh, Christ.

He didn't see Helen, did he? He must have done. Even after being marooned in the Highways Department sheep-pen, and allowing that he'd think twice or three times before driving the wrong way down a one-way street, it couldn't have taken him twenty minutes to get back here.

All right, then, so he saw Helen. He didn't speak to her, did he? You're whistling in the dark, Fisher: he would hardly have cut her dead, now would he?

But he doesn't know her. No, but he's the kind of fellow who'd talk to anybody, provided they were wearing the right clothes. Exchanging a civil word, he'd call it.

All right, then. What kind of civil words did he and Helen exchange?

'Did he speak to Mrs Lightfoot, as far as you know?'

'Did he not!' said Harry, who was quietly enjoying himself. He waited until, deliberately tautening my wrist muscles, I raised the brimming glass to my lips. Then, with what he must have thought was very good timing, he added: 'They got chatting, then of course her ladyship asks him to have a drink. You know what she's like, better than I do. Oh, no, he wouldn't hear of it. "Not at these prices," he says.'

204

'Yes. He would have done.' At times like these, a vodka martini is meant to be swallowed, not sipped. I knocked it back in one, as Harry continued.

' "Ho," she says, "You don't think *I'm* paying for it," she says. Of course, she'd had one or two by then. "Have one on Fisher!" she says. "Fisher always pays."

'Coughing better, Mr Fisher! Let me get you a serviette.'

2

I HAD a whole country once: Ambrosia. Strange blue poppies grew there, and there were cities, fantastic cities such as no one has ever seen the like of, built out on platforms over the sand dunes.

Now there's only one town left, and even that has a slightly second-hand air about it. The sun glinting on the glass roof of the covered market: that's a straight pinch from *The Good Companions*. The trams swaying like galleons: same source. The semi-basement cafés where counting-house clerks and drapers (the salt of the earth, very probably) sit playing chess: that's H. G. Wells, I believe, or is it Bill Fisher when he thought of becoming H. G. Wells?

But the rest of the vision is my own: the Corn Exchange, the old Theatre Royal, the alleys packed with workshops, the Bovril sign in electric light bulbs, the aldermanic statues, the green dome of the Linen Bank, the golden orb over Rabinowitz the jeweller's, and all the people hurrying along the wet streets with their carrier bags – that's mine. Mine, anyway, in the sense that I had a stake in it. It's Stradhoughton, before they commenced to pull it down. Whoever would have thought I'd miss it?

I was President of Ambrosia. Who am I now? The youngest mayor ever, top weight. Gentlemen, I have not become first citizen of this great borough to preside over its demolition. Or perhaps I'm Man o' the Dales of the *Stradhoughton Echo*, ruminating over a pipe and a schooner of sherry in the Wine Lodge. My world is shrinking, as old men shrink when they get older still.

It's not going to happen. It can't happen now. I'm thirty-three. It's too late. It's not too late. It's never too late.

But what was it that was going to happen? I don't think I know.

Helen didn't ring after all, or if she did, she hung up. Which doesn't mean to say she's knocked off for the evening.

And is that all I have to occupy my mind? Yes. That's where the trouble is, Fisher. Life's become day-to-day, hand-to-mouth. It's nearly time for another clean break, or, more likely, another messy one.

'Your mother was just saying,' Jeanette was just saying, 'Akerman's hasn't been open for over a week. We're wondering if they've closed for good.'

'I believe they've gone bankrupt,' I said automatically. Who the hell are Akerman's? The butcher's? The dry-cleaners? The tiny L-shaped corridor of cardboard boxes that tries to pass itself off as a mini-supermarket? Or that place that keeps changing hands – what is it these days, a wool shop or a wine shop?

Akerman's, Akerman's. Why do they give all these shops names, as if we lived in a village? And on the subject of names, why does my wife go around calling herself Jeanette? It may be what she was christened, but does she mean to say there's nothing to be done about it? Negotiations have not been fruitful. She won't let me call her Jean and I won't let her call herself Jeanie. Stalemate.

'Because I haven't seen that ginger cat of theirs for ages, what always used to sit in the window,' my mother said. That rules out the butcher's, then; the wool shop too, unless it's an unusually well-disciplined cat. 'I'm wondering if they've gone back to St Albans, with Mrs Akerman's sister being poorly again.'

Mother, you don't know Mrs Akerman's sister. You've never met Mrs Akerman's sister. All you know about her is her life history.

She had many such vicarious friends. Since the old man had had his final heart attack – nature telling him to drop dead, I'd called it, and felt guilty and depressed when he did – she had cultivated a wide circle of non-acquaintances. We got regular news, for instance, of a family by the name of Baines who lived in Derby. Our only connection with them was that a girl called Barbara, whom I'd been briefly engaged to back in the Ice Age in Stradhoughton, had once met them on holiday in Portofino.

'Talking of cats,' Jeanette said, 'we haven't seen Mr Pussy-paws for a long time.'

No, you wouldn't have done, dear, seeing that Mr Pussy-paws doesn't exist. I'd invented this cat in a spare moment, though not its name, which was supplied by Jeanette. (Not the best of names for a child-substitute, I would have thought, but that was her business.) It was supposed to scamper up and down the eleventh floor balcony chasing moths, and once, so Jeanette believed, I had seen it stretched up on its hind legs, trying to reach the bell-push to summon the lift. Jeanette had heard about so many of these exploits that she'd begun to think she had witnessed some of them herself. Perhaps it's true what the psychologists say about life in high-rise flats: you go potty.

From the living-room window, but for its shroud of lace, it would have been possible to see half-way across the country: the gravel pits, the abandoned quarries, the re-zoned factories, the doomed woods where the new conference hotel would be, the ribbon of wire-netting guarding the pollution-free river; and, far off at the end of a long straight road, the village of Mayfield with its flat-roofed maisonettes, its crescents and cul-de-sacs of clapboard-fronted semis, and its pebbled piazzas of open-plan suntraps including, assuming it was still vacant, the one I had christened Mortgagedene where Jeanette wanted to live.

From the bedroom windows, but for the Venetian blinds protecting my womenfolk from the attentions of peeping toms hovering at 200 feet, you could have looked down on an asphalt quadrangle of garages, pram sheds and laundry rooms, connecting, via a subterranean arrangement of concrete pillars, with the shopping precinct – in other words, a row of eight lock-up shops, including four empty ones permanently barricaded with corrugated iron, and also including Akerman's which was apparently about to suffer the same fate.

Akerman's had not been dropped into the conversation by accident. Neither had the fictitious Mr Pussy-paws. They were twin themes in what, if I cared to listen, would soon develop into an over-familiar fugue.

'It might have got lost,' my mother said. 'It gets into that lift with whoever's going down, then it can't find its way back up.' (She too had delusions of having met Mr Pussy-paws in person.)

'That's why I won't have a cat,' said Jeanette, 'much as I'd like one. It doesn't seem fair, when you're cooped up on the twelfth floor.'

My mother came in counterpoint with: 'It's all right if you're on the ground floor, because then it can come and go. Same as with that ginger cat of Akerman's – it went all over. *I* don't see them opening again, though.'

'That'll be *five* shops that's boarded up. Out of eight.'

'And even them what's left, they won't make the effort. Same as that skirt I took to that cleaner's on Tuesday – it came back worse than it went in.'

'I know. Look what they did to that dark blue suit of Bill's – they just about ruined it. I think I'll start going to that Keen-to-Kleen place in Cripplegate.'

'But it's so far into town, isn't it? And look how long you've got to wait for a bus.'

'*And* the fares are going up again.'

'Tenpence. It's shocking.'

'I don't think it's fair to dump people out here and then leave them with no amenities. It's not as if the demand wasn't there.'

'Ooh, I know, love, I know.'

'You look at Mayfield. It's only been built two years, most of it, and they've got a Boots, they've got a Tesco's, Electricity Board showrooms, Chinese take-away, wine shop, that Baby's Boutique they've got – and they're nearer to Shepford than we are. You could drive to the office in ten minutes, Bill.'

Not bad going, Jeanette. Even working on material far less obscure than the Akerman's and Mr Pussy-paws combine – the size of the kitchenette, for example, or the need, one of these days, for a third bedroom, a sandpit and a play-school occupying rather more permanent premises than an abandoned builders' nissen-hut – I'd known it take up to half an hour's chitter-chatter before they got round to the subject of Mortgagedene.

We are not going to buy a house in Mayfield, Jeanette.

Because we're not.

Because you'd be pregnant before we crossed the threshold.

Because Helen lives in Mayfield, and it is very difficult to ditch your mistress if you are meeting her twice a week at wine-and-cheese parties.

Because I don't like wine-and-cheese parties, Sunday morning drinks, or candlelit sixsomes with vintage car table mats and water-ice served in a scooped-out lemon.

And look at it this way. Even if I get Pisspot's job, we can't afford it. And if I don't get Pisspot's job, I shall be buggering off out of Shepford.

The discourse, both the real and imagined sections of it, got no further. The two-tone doorbell rang – bing-bong! The kind of doorbell they have in situation comedies about this kooky lady who lives next door to her permanently-perplexed husband's ex-wife. She always primps her hair and says, 'I'll get it.'

'I'll get it,' said Jeanette, primping her hair.

My mother, knowing that there has to be a line or two of dialogue before the little woman blazes back in followed by the ex-wife who wants to borrow her ex-husband to fix her fuses – 'O.K., O.K., but this is positively his last and final appearance. And this time he fixes them with chicken-wire' – filled in with:

'I was just thinking, time marches on. The twins'll be four next week.'

Barbara's. Exactly the kind of woman who *would* have twins. And who would file regular bulletins on their progress to her ex-fiancé's mother.

I could see Jeanette doing exactly the same thing, in happier circumstances. Just think, if she'd married Barbara's husband's twin brother they could be living next door to each other in twin bungalows, both scribbling away on their blue crinkled note-paper to be first with the news of the head-on collision of two twin prams on the shopping parade. And Mr Pussy-paws could chase Mr Fluffy-tail up a tree.

'She showed a bit of sense, did Barbara. If you're going to start a family, start it early. Then when they're grown up, the rest of your life's your own.'

Oh, mother, what can you be hinting at? And why isn't the rest of my life my own now?

I needn't have married Jeanette. I needn't even have met her. 'It must have been fate,' she used to giggle in our courting days when, getting nowhere fast on the front-room sofa, I would try to work out the lengthy odds against our having been thrown together. Fuck fate: it was nothing more than a chain of tragic non-events. If I'd uprooted myself and gone to London when I'd meant to, I would never have met her. If I'd stayed as an undertaker's clerk and kept my hands out of the petty-cash box, I would never have met her. If I hadn't gone and worked in the Stradhoughton Rates Office, I would never have met her. Or – given that it was part of the mysterious pattern of the universe that the Stradhoughton Rates Office beckoned me at that time – if I'd habitually used the front entrance instead of the back one, I would have bypassed the open-plan typing pool where she worked and never have met her. Or, since I was compelled by Nemesis to use the back entrance because I was always late for work, and so must inevitably have skirted the side of the typing pool in order to reach my desk unobserved, she could have been sitting somewhere else and I would never have met her. It was because she was one of five typists sitting on the outside aisle, and because I was incapable of entering a roomful of girls without sizing up the talent, that as I walked through the typing pool on my first late morning, I thought, without thinking: 'Not that one, not that one, not that one. That one. She'll do.' And if she had been sitting somewhere else, someone else would have been sitting in her place on the outside aisle, and I would have the thought: 'Not that one, not that one, not that one. That one. She'll do.' Or, if the someone else had been as ugly as the other four, there would have been the canteen, or the office dance, or some other department's office dance, or the social club, or a pub, or a coffee bar, or a bus queue, and I would have thought: 'Not that one, not that one, not that one. That one. She'll do.' Love at first sight, providing I can have the best out of five. And whoever it was, we would have got married because it was the only way I could get away from home; and we would have finished up at my mother's because there was nowhere else to live; and I would have leapt at the job in Shepford with a subsidized flat thrown in; and my mother would have finished up with us because the house was too big for her, so she claimed; and the double of Jeanette and Barbara, looking puzzled, would at this very second be returning to her knitting and box of Maltesers with the message:

'There's nobody there.'

I could have told you that before you went to answer the door, ducky. The drill was this: Helen would by now be skulking by the lift, and in a minute of two she would creep back, or more likely stagger back, and ring again. This time I would be the one to answer it, pursuing my investigations around the bend of the communal corridor on the pretext of breaking some mischievous boy's neck. Helen would beckon me from the fire-door and we would have a hurried conference on the emergency stairs, arranging a rendezvous ten minutes hence by the vandalized cigarette-machine down on the so-called shopping precinct. The last time Helen had pulled this trick she had slipped down a whole flight of stairs and twisted her ankle, so that in addition to finding an excuse for leaving the flat at nearly midnight ('I can hear a mieowing noise. I wonder if that bloody cat's stuck up a tree?') I'd had to smuggle out a tea towel soaked in hot water. I had been living in hopes that this experience would have cured her; but seemingly not.

'It'll be that Charles from the floor below. He's a right handful,' my mother said. Another of her non-acquaintances, much given to breaking windows and getting into scrapes. Actually, I was pretty sure that Charles was one of my own inventions, like Mr Pussy-paws, and that I had called him into being to explain some early escapade of Helen's; but it was equally possible that my mother had overheard his name in the fish queue and now regarded him more or less as her godson. Real or not, I was grateful to him.

My mother had stuffed the communiqué from Stradhoughton back into her handbag. For some reason she would never mention Barbara's name in front of Jeanette, always referring to her as 'that friend of our Billy's what married that accountant'.

'I was saying to our Billy while you were answering the door, that friend of his what married that accountant, her twins'll be four next week.'

Time flies, Jeanette will say.

'Time flies,' said Jeanette, adding, as she always did if we were hovering around the topic of Mortgagedene, 'Isn't that the one who lives in those new bungalows?' You can save your breath for blowing your porridge, my little pot of honey, because the doorbell's about to ring again.

'That's the one. They've done very well, considering they didn't get married till a year after you and our Billy. Because if you ask me, houses cost more up there than what they do down here.'

And the doorbell rang, leaving Jeanette's next sentence ('For what we're paying out in rent and rates, we might just as well have taken the plunge when we first came to Shepford') somewhere between her larynx and her front teeth.

For what we're paying out in rent and rates, may we be truly thankful.

The fire door leading to the emergency stairs was next to the lift, which was next to the staircase proper, which in turn was next to the rubbish chute; a convenient arrangement for an arsonist, I'd occasionally thought when toying with the idea of murdering Jeanette. That arrangement was at present more convenient than it had ever been, for the fire door wouldn't open. I rattled the metal handle which, being of the required specification for one of Shepford's prestigious tower blocks, came away in my hand.

'Then when you complain, they put the blame on vandalism.'

This was from an observer of life's passing show who, in tightly-belted raincoat, hat, gloves and scarf, was waiting for the lift. He looked as if he were going out either to sell insurance or to rape somebody. My mother would have known the biographical details: I recognized him only as one of a multitude of rat-faced neighbours.

'I left my golf clubs inside the door,' I said, in case he felt in need of an explanation.

'Did you now?' he asked keenly. 'When would that have been?' I'll have to give up this habit of making voluntary statements.

'Last night.'

'Because there were definitely no golf clubs there at twenty-past five this morning.'

It was none of my business what a rat-faced neighbour was doing on the emergency stairs at twenty-past five in the morning. Waiting to flash himself at the paper-boy, I shouldn't wonder. I pushed the door handle back on its spindle and waggled it about a bit.

'It seems to be jammed.'

'No, it's not jammed, it's locked.'

'Is it now?' Also, I'll have to stop picking up other people's expressions, like a verbal chameleon. What's it a sign of? Immaturity? Lack of confidence? Desire to ingratiate? Never mind. 'I would have thought there was something in the fire regulations about that.'

'I don't know about the fire regulations,' said Rat-face. 'All I know is it kept us awake from half-past four till twenty-past five. Didn't you hear it, in that gale? Bang bang bang, all night long. That's how the handle's worked loose.' He pressed the bell for the lift which, assuming he'd rung for it already before the start of this dissertation on banging doors, was a long time coming.

'So you got out of bed and locked it?'

'I didn't lock it, no, because I haven't a key. I wedged it with a piece of cardboard. See.' He drew my attention to Exhibit 'A', a folded sliver of cornflake packet on the floor. 'And I expect *that'll* be lying there until goodness knows when, before anyone bothers to sweep it up.'

'But it's not wedged now,' I said, taking my plodding tone from his. 'It's locked.'

214

'Yes, we know it's locked. I had the caretaker up, first thing this morning. It was the only way he could get it to close. Apparently the wood's warped with the damp. It needs planing.'

So Helen wasn't skulking behind the fire door. Then where was she skulking? Either on the stairs or, putting aside the outside chance of her having dived down the rubbish chute, in the lift.

I joined Rat-face at the lift shaft and peered down through the flaking trellis gate.

'No sign of life.'

'I'm wondering if someone hasn't left the gate open on the ground floor. It wouldn't be the first time it's happened.'

If someone like Purchase had been standing where Rat-face was standing now, he wouldn't be wondering about lift gates being left open. He'd be wondering why, since I claimed to have set off to retrieve my golf clubs from behind the fire door, I had now lost all interest in them and was seemingly about to go for a stroll in my shirt-sleeves.

I'm going down to ask the caretaker if he can shed any light on the mystery.

'These golf clubs of yours,' said Rat-face.

'Yes, I'm just popping down to ask the caretaker what he knows about them.'

'I should do. Because as I say, they definitely weren't behind that door at twenty-past five this morning. When did you leave them there? Last night?'

'Yes.'

'About what time last night?'

For God's sake. Five o'clock. Six o'clock. Nineteen and a half minutes to seven. 'About a quarter to six.'

'That's strange. That's very strange. Because my wife often leaves the child's scooter behind that door and I take it in when I come home from business at six o'clock. Are you sure it wasn't later than quarter to six?'

'I don't know. It might have been.'

'Because there were definitely no golf clubs there at six

o'clock. You didn't see anyone hanging about at all? No strange characters?'

Let me see now. There was a one-eyed, hump-backed dwarf who dragged his left foot and had warts all over his face, but I just assumed he was one of the neighbours.

'No, nobody.'

Rat-face, his insurance round or rendezvous on the canal tow-path forgotten, had become totally immersed in the Case of the Missing Golf Clubs. To avoid further questioning I took over the lift-summoning chore, jabbing savagely at the bell-push. Simultaneously, a loud clanging noise started up from several floors below, indicating either that I'd somehow set off the alarm system, or that the martini-sodden Helen had got herself stuck in the lift and had set it off herself, or that the building was on fire. Bearing in mind Rat-face's complicity in the recent breach of the fire regulations, I looked hopefully for smoke.

'That is the fourth time this year, to my knowledge,' observed Rat-face. 'Then when you complain the lift needs overhauling, they fob you off with some cock-and-bull yarn about it receiving regular attention. If it receives regular attention, why does it keep jamming?'

On the landings below us, other rat-faced neighbours could be heard shuffling about in their fleece-lined slippers and rhubarbing about the alarm bell, the alarm bell's culpability in waking up their kiddies, and the methods by which the alarm bell might be switched off. Sundry voices-off chimed in with plot-lines: 'There's someone in the lift' – 'It's down here – half-way past the third floor' – 'Keep calm, my dear, we'll have you out in a jiffy.' A technical adviser offered the opinion that the travelling cable was out of true and had been fouled by some unknown obstruction, probably the counterweight. A shirt-sleeved traffic-warden type, even more rat-faced than Rat-face himself, bounded up from the tenth or eleventh floor, taking the stairs two at a time in his excitement. Ignoring me, he addressed himself to Rat-face, instinctively recognizing him as one of his own kind.

'The Lord help us if there's ever a real emergency in these

flats. Where's the use of everybody running around in circles?'

'It's a job for the fire brigade, I would have thought,' Rat-face said.

'The caretaker, more like! Who else has the master key? He'll have to make his way down from the fourth floor and haul her up through the trap-door.'

'It's a lady, is it? Not of any great age, I hope and trust?'

'We don't know who it is at this stage. All we do know is that the caretaker isn't on the premises, as usual. It's a question of ringing that working man's club on the trading estate. You know he has a part-time job there, don't you?'

'No, I didn't know that.'

'Oh, yes! Part-time waiter, three nights a week.'

'Then when you look for him at eight in the morning, he's still in bed. No wonder,' chuntered Rat-face. Presumably being the owner of a telephone, down which, I was ready to bet, he made breathing noises regularly, he led Rat-face Mark II off along the corridor, pausing to issue an instruction to me.

'You might tell them we're phoning for help, would you?'

'Piss off,' I thought, and considered my position. The trading estate was about three miles away – four, if they'd opened up the new access road by now. Allow twenty minutes for the care-taker to get here, and another five for him to rummage through his large assortment of keys. Say fifteen minutes to half an hour to get Helen out of the lift. Assume the existence of a Rat-face Mark III, with experience in the St John Ambulance Brigade, who would want to treat her for shock: the process of sticking her head between her knees, burning feathers under her nose and giving her cups of sweet tea could take another half an hour or so. It would be quite late before Helen was at large again, by which time her husband would be expecting her home and in any case she would probably have had enough for one evening. I couldn't, of course, rule out the outside chance of Rat-face Mark III topping her up with a swig of medicinal brandy, but if that hideous possibility refused to leave my mind I could always disconnect the door-bell. Sod her.

I went back indoors where, having switched off the hall light to discourage callers, I was surprised to find my female entourage increased to three. Helen, looking only slightly the worse for drink, was sitting between my mother and Jeanette in the armchair I had recently vacated.

3

THIS is no way to carry on at your age, was what skimmed through my mind, among other thoughts: but was I blaming Helen, or myself?

Myself, most likely. One thing about Helen, she had never tried to pass herself off as mature and responsible. Although in calendar years she was slightly older than me – thirty-five next birthday – she was capable of carrying on as if she were four or five years younger. Taking the gloomiest estimate of my own mental age, this put her at about sixteen on some occasions, the present one being among their number.

The other thing was that I had known she would be trouble on first clapping eyes on her – or rather, on her polka-dot knickers, for she was doing handstands at the time, in connection with some office Christmas celebrations in the upstairs room of the King's Head Doubles Bar. The party was that of CCC – Creative City Consortium – a gang of architects and other roving vagabonds dedicated to making Shepford the showplace of their balance-sheet. Helen had worked for them once. I was there as deputy freeloader, representing Pisspot who was freeloading elsewhere that night.

Helen being trouble was the main attraction. Long lunch-time phone calls while the office girls were sunbathing on the Civic Centre roof: 'Was anything said when you got home last night?' Short mid-morning calls while they pretended to be painting their finger nails: 'Can you get out for five minutes? I'm afraid it's urgent.' At least one confrontation with her husband, Geoff: 'I ought to knock you down, Fisher.' – 'Go ahead, if it makes you feel any better.' Adult behaviour.

Jeanette, my mother and Helen were all looking at me, expectantly. The studio laughter died down. Oscar, in his pale-

219

blue Angora sweater and golfing slacks, was the staunch, neutered, bachelor friend, the one you can trust alone with your daffy wife. His grimace said: 'Oh, boy, have you gat problems!'

'Oscar, you keep out of this!'

'Jeanette, I didn't open my mouth!'

'You were *thinking*, though! You were thinking, "Oh, boy, has he gat problems!"'

'Bill, did it ever occur to you that your wife is a remarkable woman?'

'Mrs Winklebaum, you keep out of this too. Bill, I want to know what this – this *creature* is doing in my home. There has to be some *explanation*!'

Oh, there was, there was. Helen hadn't got stuck in the lift after all. Finding the fire door locked, she must have followed the corridor all around the building until it led her back to her starting-point. She would then, in her bemused state, have rung the bell again. My mother or Jeanette, on the way into or out of the bathroom, would have been immediately on hand to open the door before she had a chance to make her getaway. Shocked into comparative sobriety, but not to the extent of reacting like any rational human being with the excuse that she had come to the wrong flat, she must have babbled some story and been invited in on a pretext yet to be revealed. So who was stuck in the lift? Mr Pussy-paws.

'Mr *Pussy*-paws? Is that the best you can do?'

'Oscar! Bill is my husband and he is entitled to a hearing without any interruptions. Mr *Pussy*-paws? Is that the best you can do? You are *pathetic*!'

'Sorry to have been so long,' I said. 'There's half the neighbourhood out with ladders, trying to get that cat out of the lift.'

'Poor thing!' said Jeanette.

'It's a gad job they're sappoosed to hev nine lives, isn't it?' my mother observed, smiling at Helen and talking, for our guest's benefit, in what she thought was a Home Counties accent. A hopeful sign, that. Short of pouring Helen a cup of tea and asking if she took shagger, she couldn't have been more hospitable. Jeanette, too, had expressed her brief sympathy for the plight of Mr Pussy-paws half to Helen, as if to draw her into the family circle. Whatever the confrontation, it was not to be on what's-the-meaning-of-this lines.

'This lady's from the Bedding Council,' Jeanette said, adding to Helen, 'And this is my husband –?' in that irritating way she had of leaving the sentence unfinished, on a rising note, as if there were several more introductions to follow, very likely a string of children with names like Barry and Kevin.

What bloody Bedding Council?

Helen's smile was a piece of artistry: a warm, yet detached social worker's smile that seemed to be appraising a new acquaintance of whom she had heard quite encouraging reports. She let her wedding ring catch the light from the table-lamp next to her: shrewd thinking. The cleavage, I was relieved to notice, had been buttoned away under the navy-blue velvet jacket. She crossed her legs and tugged down her skirt: another good touch, for she was not normally one of nature's tugger-downers.

'The Bedding Advisory Council actually, Mr Fisher. Or to burden you with our cumbersome title, the Council Advisorying the Bedding and Mattress Industries. CAMBY.' Don't push it, baby. And don't slur your words. And for God's sake don't correct CAMBY. 'Do I mean CAMBY?' she went on. 'No. Council Advisorying Mattress Bedding Industries. CABMY. CAMBY.'

'Something about a questionnaire,' put in Jeanette helpfully. She was not looking in the least pissed-off with Helen's performance; looked, in fact, quite eager to have her suburban life brightened up with a bit of consumer research. My mother, who thought this kind of thing was compulsory by law, had put on the intense, I-can-understand-long-words expression she kept for insurance men and council officials.

'We're taking a random sample of two hundred married couples in this area, and names are chosen by computer from the electoral roll. No personal details are included in our reports and the information is confidential, are you sure you have no objection?' She had this bit off pat, having once done a similar job for the Gas Board.

'No objection at all,' said Jeanette.

'None at all,' my mother echoed, looking as if she had just been cautioned by a police-sergeant.

'And it's not inconvenient?'

Just bugger off, Helen. There's no need for this at all.

'Not in the least. We were just sitting here talking.'

'Thank you. It won't take long.'

It had better not. And when you go, Helen, you go for good. This is it. It had already been it before she had started this stupid rigmarole, but at least I had been ready to meet her, explain, face it out. I had even, in a way, been looking forward to the scene: telling your mistress it's all over may be painful but it's a responsible thing to do. I could have done with the credit. Not now, though. Quite definitely sod her.

She had pulled a wad of yellow papers out of her handbag. Her first mistake. I had an idea what they were: handbills for the amateur operatic society where, according to what she told her husband, or at least told me that she told him, she was supposed to be understudying some rat-bag or other in *The Yeomen of the Guard* on evenings such as this. They certainly looked nothing like market research forms, but my mother and Jeanette, both moistening their lips as if being auditioned for First and Second Village Maiden, seemed not to notice.

'Now the first question is about bedrooms. Would you say you had one bedroom, more than one bedroom, more than two bedrooms, more than three bedrooms?'

'Two bedrooms,' whispered Jeanette, nervous. She cleared her throat and went on: 'They're all two-bedroom flats.'

'All in this block,' my mother confirmed, eager to give evidence. 'All two bedrooms.'

'So more than one bedroom. And of beds in use, including spare beds but not convertible sofas or chesterfields, would you say you had one bed in use, more than one bed in use, more than two beds in use, more than three beds in use?'

'Er – more than two beds.' Silly bitch. Trying to fall in with

222

Helen's jargon, Jeanette had got it all wrong. She meant two beds; in other words, more than one bed.

'More – than – two – *beds*,' intoned Helen, scribbling. For Christ's sake, woman, do pack it in. 'And if you don't mind my asking, you live here with your husband and this lady is –?'

Jeanette fielded this one on to my mother with a glance indicating that her version of the relationship would carry more weight.

'I'm Billy's mother. Mr Fisher's mother.' I quite liked that correction, it was the first time my mother had ever called me Mr Fisher. I wished she could have done it with more style.

'So Mrs Fisher senior would occupy a single bed in the smaller bedroom, while you and Mr Fisher share the master bedroom?'

'That's right.'

'In twin beds?'

To make it quite plain to Helen that I was having no part of this inquisition, I had picked up one of the women's magazines which infested the flat. My eye had fallen on the readers' letters page. *'When I am not speaking to my husband I put his slippers in the deep freeze. Don't ask me why.'* Momentarily hypnotized by this, I had missed the significance of Helen's question, only realizing, as I looked up to see Jeanette's blank expression and Helen's social worker's smile, that something had been said that would have been better left unsaid.

'In twin beds?' insisted Helen, and I felt an alarming spasm of pain under my left ribs. Was I too young to be having a heart attack? More to the point, was I too young to *look* as if I were having a heart attack, if I keeled over this very second?

We hardly ever had sex because of Jeanette's headaches and we slept in twin beds : that was what I had told her. And absurd as it seemed even at the time, I had immediately realized that there was another reason why the thing with Helen couldn't go on : for one of these days Jeanette and my mother would take themselves off to a wedding or a christening or a meat tea or something up in Stradhoughton, and Helen would get to know about it and insist on coming to the flat as a change from

Shepford Woods or, if wet, the back of the car; and she would find out that I was lying about the twin beds.

Jeanette, with the slightly incredulous frown of a bright child whose sums have been marked wrong, was saying: 'No-oh. We have one single bed and one double.'

'You and Mr Fisher? In other words, one of you sleeps in the single and the other in the double?' *Cow.*

Jeanette, utterly perplexed, turned to me for guidance; decided, obviously, that domestic conundrums were outside man's domain, and switched the appeal to my mother who, from her vast experience of household trivia, came to the rescue.

'You see, Jeanette, where I think you're getting this lady confused is, you said more than two beds.'

Helen looked apologetic: what-a-little-nuisance-I-must-be. 'That's the answer I've ticked. More than two beds.'

'Oh, I *see*!' Jeanette exclaimed, her face clearing. 'I should have said two beds, shouldn't I?'

'More than one bed.'

The cleared face clouded over again. 'That's right, Jeanette,' my mother said, soothingly. 'Two beds *is* more than one bed, isn't it? More than *two* beds would be *three* beds.'

'I suppose so.'

Helen, ballpoint poised, beamed from one to the other. 'So more than one bed. One single and one double. And obviously Mrs Fisher senior has the single while you and Mr Fisher sleep in the bubble. Double.'

She was pissed out of her mind. Why had I thought she had sobered up? Why had I thought, or even hoped and prayed, that she was going to get away with it? The countdown to disaster, I suddenly realized with a lurching in my stomach, had already begun: it was irrevocable.

As Helen made an elaborate show of correcting her notes, I repeated to myself, like a mantra: '*When I am not speaking to my husband I put his slippers in the deep freeze, don't ask me why, when I am not speaking to my husband I put his slippers in the deep freeze.*' And the ridiculous thing was that in this

224

moment of panic I was staring at her legs, where the light threw a sheen along the dark-blue casing of her shins, and fancying her.

'Now, if we can just move on. This question is about attitudes to beds. Do you think of your bed as primary – pri-*mar*-i-ly – a place to sleep, or would you say it was a centre for various activities?'

Jeanette and my mother exchanged telegraphic glances. Is this woman going too far? Don't know yet. Over and out.

'Such as reading,' added Helen, intercepting the message.

I could get to my feet and tell her to go. 'I'm sorry, I'm afraid these questions are altogether too personal.' But I couldn't see myself saying it, it wasn't my kind of phraseology. And what would Helen think? It would be like a mask coming off – Bill Fisher, exposed as husband, householder and ratepayer. Your John Bull act, she would call it, when we met for just one more time because I fancied her. Do your John Bull act.

I could get to my feet and say something, anyway. Wing it. 'It's getting late,' or something. I half-rose, looking at my watch.

'You've dropped your soup,' said Helen, kindly.

A packet of powdered watercress soup, FREE with this Super Spring Issue, had slipped from the pages of the woman's magazine on my lap. As I stooped to retrieve it, Jeanette drivelled on in released vein about all of us being big readers, her own preference being for the works of Georgette Heyer. The moment had passed or, more accurately, not yet arrived.

'So a centre for various activities. In fact –' although Helen's tone was light and casual I noticed with alarm that she no longer dared look Jeanette in the face – 'the usual activities of a happily married couple.'

'Well,' Jeanette's embarrassment returned, manifesting itself in a short laugh, a slight shrug and a flush around the throat. 'Yes.'

'And would you say these activities took place less than once a week, more frequently than once a week, more frequently than twice a week –'

'Excuse me, young lady!'

My mother's lips had been pursed for some time, and had not become unpursed even during the red-herring interlude about reading matter. She now extended her repertoire of disapproval by folding her arms. 'If you don't mind my asking, just exactly what is all this in aid of?'

With a timid flickering of relief I saw that Helen was losing her alcoholic overdrive. She was swaying slightly in her chair and a faint moustache of sweat had appeared on her upper lip. If she asked to use the bathroom, it would be easy to shuffle her out from there. I had stopped fancying her.

'I'm sorry, I thought I'd made it clear,' she said indistinctly. 'National Bedding Councils –'

'Yes, we know all about that, but where's the point in asking what you've just been asking? I mean, you haven't even shown us any credentials. You could be anybody, for all we know.'

Jeanette, anxious not to be identified with rudeness on quite this scale, said, half-conciliatory: 'Have you got a card, or something like that?' Helen, now looking quite ill, began to rummage aimlessly through her handbag. My mother maintained the folded-arms posture.

'And you, our Billy, I'm surprised *you've* had nothing to say. Do *you* think it's right, people coming into your home and asking your wife that sort of thing?'

But it's only a game, mother! It's only a bloody *game*! Didn't you ever play games? No, we know you didn't. And you frighten me when you say 'your home' like that, pronouncing the aitch, and 'your wife'. You make it sound as if everything's real, as if it matters, as if it's serious. For God's sake, look at Helen – *she's* married, *she* has a home, she cooks breakfast, vacuums, remembers to take her pill, has a bank account, all those grown-up things, and just bloody well look at her!

They did, and Helen had passed out.

We had got her round by shaking her quite roughly, Jeanette's suggestion of black coffee being firmly vetoed by the other interested parties. 'I *though*t she was squiffy when she first came

226

in,' my mother observed. It seemed to wrap up the episode to her satisfaction.

We had steered her across the living room – not without some fear on my part, as she blundered into the sideboard, that she would forget where she was and address me by name. We had got her into the hall. Relieved of helping hands, she leaned against the wall and resumed the vague expedition into the depths of her handbag.

'They shouldn't send them out in that condition,' my mother said. 'You'd think they'd inspect them first.'

'Have you got far to go?' asked Jeanette anxiously, addressing Helen as if she were stone deaf.

Helen had fished out her driving licence. She waved it triumphantly, in answer both to the immediate question and to the earlier one about credentials.

'She's never driving in that condition!' my mother exclaimed.

Jeanette was examining the licence. 'Rookwood Crescent, Mayfield. Do you think you'd better run her home, Bill?'

All right. One last blazing row as we cross town, dump her car by the phone booth at the end of Rookwood Crescent, radio cab home and sod her for all time. I opened the hall door, to be confronted by Rat-face and a young man of about my own age who was wearing a light overcoat and trying very hard to look like a plain-clothes policeman who was trying not to look like one.

'Ah, there you are! Run to earth! I thought this was your flat but I wasn't absolutely sure! This is Detective-constable Carpenter.'

'You're very kind, but I'll catch a bus,' said Helen, once more blessed by a sudden bounty of clear-headedness. 'Good night.' Excusing herself to our new-found friends, she weaved off along the corridor.

'Good-bye,' I said pointedly.

'Take care,' Jeanette called.

'Sorry to disturb you, we're looking into a series of petty pilferings. I believe you're missing some property?' said Detective-constable Carpenter. 'Is that lady all right?'

'That's what *we're* wondering,' my mother said darkly.

I said hastily: 'She'll be all right, she's just had one too many. No, I don't think we've missed anything.'

'I understood you had.'

'Golf clubs,' said Rat-face.

'He doesn't have any golf clubs,' said Jeanette.

'Yes, I bought a set second-hand the other day. They weren't worth much.'

'If I could just have the details,' said Detective-constable Carpenter.

4

Turning into the Cornmarket from the winding alley by the Clock Tower, the visitor may well imagine himself in Brittany. The bustling market place, dominated by Alfred Waterhouse's magnificent Town Hall (see p. 16) is enclosed on three sides by a lively promenade of cafés, brasseries and open-air restaurants. The spacious Café Billard, with its red plush booths and marble-topped tables, is a favourite of Shepford's artists and writers, while the bevelled mirrors of the Relais des Voyageurs next door reflect the town's leading luminaries, such as Councillor Percy Drummond and Detective-constable Carpenter, as they sip their afternoon mazagrans. No need to inquire too closely why Shepford's hosteliers have little trouble with the licensing law!

The question most asked by tourists is how this outpost of Bohemia came to be established in an English market town. The answer is an interesting one. During the Napoleonic Wars, French prisoners were billeted for a time in Shepford Castle. Among them was a certain Henri Gaspard, a pastrycook ...

'Anything for the printer's?' asked Hattersley. *Pageantry with Progress* (new edition) was shaping well to become the department's greatest publishing fiasco since Pisspot's celebrated *Shepford Events* three years ago, which had promised chamber music on the Uniplex sports ground and five-a-side football in the Little Theatre. Yellowing corrected proofs and yellowing uncorrected proofs hung from bulldog clips all around the office walls: no one could remember which was which. Photographs of civic landmarks, historic churches and copper-based alloy factories were stacked on every available flat surface, though many had slithered behind the filing cabinets: no one could remember which buildings were scheduled for demolition before the new guide book was published. A vital block of the Lord Lieutenant opening the Maternity Unit of the Aneurin Bevan Hospital had been missing for two months: it was to be discovered that Pisspot was using it as a paperweight. The quarter-page advertisement for the Shepford Brick Co. still read 'Pricks Are Our Business': we had not yet decided whether to let it through or not. Without a good deal more effort, and some of the overtime that Jeanette thought I was doing already, there was little hope of *Pageantry with Progress* hitting the streets in time for the Shepford Festival; and that, I supposed, could cast some doubt on my ability to hold down Pisspot's job.

I tossed Hattersley a batch of captions. *This monument originally marked the spot where Sir Thomas Bell was killed during the Civil War. It was re-sited outside the new Olympic-length swimming pool when Bell Lane was widened for traffic improvement*

'And there's all that balls about Opportunities for Industry. Where are those bloody girls? They should have had it typed up days ago.'

'Powdering their arses,' said Mattersley. 'Give them a chance, it's only ten to eleven.'

And when they re-emerged from the bog he, although he was technically my junior, would be the one to tell them to get cracking. 'For your information,' they would say, 'we haven't stopped since half past nine.' 'Yes, and for *your* information, the covers are still on your typewriters. Get on with it.' I couldn't do that. The style I had chosen for my dealings with the girls was banter with what I hoped were mildly sexual undertones; I would have found it difficult to switch character. Hattersley, on the other hand, could be discussing their knockers in one breath and making them re-type his letters in the next. It bothered me. Perhaps he had a flair for leadership that I lacked.

'Seriously, though,' he added; and that was something else. He would clown around as if the job didn't matter, and then he would buckle down as if it did. Another schizophrenic tendency I found disturbing: you got it in subalterns who played leap-frog in the mess all night and then led their men over the top at dawn. I work hard and I play hard, was what they said in later life, after they had become chairmen of great industries.

'Seriously, though, we'd better stop pissing about and get this guff organized.' I should have been saying that to him.

'Don't panic, it's getting done.' He should have been saying that to me.

Turning into the Cornmarket past the builders' hoardings surrounding the Clock Tower, the visitor may well imagine himself in a large car park. The arrangement is only a temporary one, however, for as soon as the cobbled market place has been tarmaced over, the Council has it in mind to redeploy it as an overspill bus station. The car park, dominated by the old Town Hall which is now largely used as a linoleum warehouse, is enclosed on three sides by a seedy collection of disgusting pubs, do-it-yourself shops, fried chicken takeaways and electrical appliance establishments, all architecturally undistinguished except the Old Snuffe Shoppe which is about to be pulled down ...

'One of these days,' observed Hattersley, looking over my shoulder, 'some of that shit's going to find its way to the printer's. Then you'll be in it.'

Yes: particularly as the printing firm, up in Birmingham, was owned by Councillor Drummond's brother-in-law, so Helen had once told me. Presumably he had declared his interest when the contract was dished out. (Or possibly he hadn't. 'I'll tell you exactly why you're going to recommend me for Pisspot's job, Drummond. I happen to have paid a little visit to a certain printing firm in Birmingham ...')

The two secretaries, Sheilagh and Patsy, who always made their frequent exits and entrances together, like Siamese twins, came into the office carrying mugs of coffee; their first appearance that morning so far as I was concerned, for I had arrived half an hour late. It was pushing it a bit to call them secretaries –

they were office girls, according to their official grading – but I liked to think of them as such. My secretary. I'll get my secretary to book a table. You can always leave a message with my secretary. If they had been born eight years earlier and had found themselves in the Stradhoughton Rates Office, I could have been married to either one of them by now.

While Hattersley chuntered on about there being such a thing as a fair day's work for a fair day's pay, I winked solemnly at Sheilagh to show that I personally did not give a bugger. I could just about equally have winked at Patsy, for with their long hair, long legs, big eyes and big mouths the two girls were as interchangeable as Cindy dolls; but Sheilagh was slightly ahead on points in not wearing a bra.

Slipping back in the time-machine to the three-and-nines at the Odeon, Stradhoughton, I sometimes dwelt pleasantly on the scope that would have been afforded by a bra-less girl. On the debit side, however, she would have been wearing tights. My mind skipped over a succession of fiancées, steadies and blind dates, all Maidenformed like armadillos above the waist, yet as vulnerable as a whale's under-belly below it. For back-row punters, there must have been a dramatic shift in erogenous zones over the years, a revolution that had passed me by. The thought should have made me melancholy but didn't: I felt like old men who could remember when you got change out of a pork pie for fourpence. Much-needed proof that I was older than I used to be.

Contemplation of Sheilagh's boobs made me feel randy: for a second or two we were surfing off Malibu beach. Oscar, in tartan Bermuda shorts, was Patsy's. Both girls liked older men: we had an air-conditioned Lincoln Continental, a duplex off Sunset and a string of credit cards. We could show them a good time.

They would want to dance barefoot to a combination of voices that somewhat post-dated the Ink Spots. I could only do the quickstep. Where was Helen?

'Any messages?' I asked.

It was now three days since Helen had rolled up at the flat. So far there had been urgent calls from a Mrs Hetherington, a

Miss Springer, a Mrs Mooney, and – an ingenious one, this, better than her recent pose as an assistant at the Reference Library, offering me a map of old Shepford for the guide-book – a voice purporting to be that of a television researcher in Birmingham. I had not yet rung back, and had no intention of doing so except when my resolve was weakened by Sheilagh's bra-less bosom.

'Councillor Drummond's secretary rang,' said Sheilagh. A likely story.

'Was it, er –?' I did some eyebrow-work, intimating to Sheilagh that we were partners in a conspiracy. So far, touch wood, Purchase had been unexpectedly discreet about his encounter with Helen at the Heritage Motor Lodge. Perhaps he had filed it for future reference. Meanwhile, I didn't mind Sheilagh suspecting that an affair was going on or had until lately been going on, so long as she didn't know whom the affair was with. We had never discussed Helen's phone calls, although it was pretty clear from the odd warning nudge when I walked into the office sometimes, that they got freely discussed with Patsy. '– *sounds like a right nut-case*,' I had heard Patsy saying on one of these occasions. Walk tall, Fisher: you have a reputation.

'No, it was her, truly, I know her voice. She's got that stuff typed out, if you want to pop over for it.'

I am not a bloody errand boy, my flower. If there is any popping over to be done, it is for those of popping-over rank to sort out among themselves. On the other hand, half an hour in the King's Head Double Bar on the way back would not be injurious to health. Quandary.

'Oh, and there was another call from Central Police. Would you ring that detective-constable before noon?'

Christ.

'What does he want now?'

'Just said he wanted another word with you.'

Christ.

'Get him on the line, would you?'

Is it possible to experience three sensations at once, one of them pleasurable and the other two not? Yes, it is: for I was fully conscious of and able to isolate and identify my mixed batch of emotions – which, if I wanted to include this analytical process as a sensation in itself, rather than a by-product, brought the count up to four.

The one that ought to have been predominant, but wasn't, was a small wave of panic at the prospect of another interview with Detective-constable Carpenter; subsidiary to that was mild anxiety about my mental stability – the feed back from information collated by the isolating and identifying department, which had quickly spotted that whereas my whole mind should have been filled with apprehension, a large portion of it was in fact filled with something else, this something else being the great bubble of delight that always swelled inside me whenever I said to Sheilagh, 'Get him on the line, would you?'

I have a secretary. I ask her to get me people on the line, and she gets them on the line. I ask her to make tea, and she makes tea. I dictate letters.

I have a cheque book. I have a credit account with a firm of tailors. I have an Access card. If I want to, I can go into betting shops. Landlords do not ask me my age when I buy a drink. I drive a car: I drive a car so unselfconsciously that fellow-motorists do not stare at me and sometimes I can drive for fifteen or twenty miles without thinking 'I drive a car.' I have keys on a key-ring. I have a desk diary in which my secretary writes appointments. My secretary is getting on the line a detective-constable who wishes to talk about golf clubs. It does not seem strange to him that I walk into second-hand shops and buy sets of golf clubs. He believes I play golf: if I told him I played bridge too he would have no reason to doubt my word. He will call me Mr Fisher – probably even Sir.

I lit a cigarette. Look, mummy, I can smoke.

'Mr Fisher?'

'Good morning.' I can make conversation.

'Many thanks indeed for ringing back. I'm sorry to be troubling you again. I'm wondering if you've had any more thoughts about those golf clubs since our telephone conversation yesterday?'

Yes that when I saw Rat-face wondering why I wanted to open the fire-door, I should have left him wondering.

'Well, as I explained the other night and as I think I said yesterday, they were no great loss. In fact, they were in such a tatty condition I can't see a professional thief bothering to take them away.' I can talk man-to-man with detective-constables, but my voice tends to break a little on long sentences.

'You reckon it was one of the local lads, do you?' He knows how to talk like a detective-constable, but shouldn't he be calling me Sir by now?

'It could have been.' And shouldn't I be calling him Officer? He would probably enjoy that: him calling me Sir and me calling him Officer. I remembered our initial interview at the flat after Helen had gone, when he fished out his notebook with some pride and was clearly playing at detectives. To oblige him, I played at witnesses. We were of roughly the same age: if I called him Officer and he called me Sir, we could do wonders for one another's ego.

It could have been, Officer. It could easily have been the young scallywag Charles, the terror of the Fairways estate, if only I could remember whether I had made him up or not.

'It could have been. I don't know. I'm just saying the job wouldn't have been worth a professional thief's while.' *The job*. V. good.

'You'd be surprised, Mr Fisher. You see, you're judging these stolen goods by what you paid for them. You might have got a bargain. They know the market, some of these characters. You'd be surprised.'

I didn't involve myself in the logic of this, if indeed there was any logic. I was waiting for the opportunity to call him Officer which, for the moment, had become my main ambition in life.

'Quite,' I said, for 'Quite, officer' would not have rung true.

'So if you *could* give us more details, especially if you could remember where you bought your golf clubs, it would help us greatly.'

'I'll most certainly try, but at the moment I don't think there's anything I can add to the statement.' I could have done it then. I could have said, 'I'll most certainly try, Officer.' And I shouldn't have said 'the statement'. I should have said 'my statement' or 'my previous statement'.

'Ah, now that's mainly why I'm ringing, Mr Fisher, because technically you haven't made a statement yet. Not that there's any need to at the present moment, but it would save paper work later on if we could get something down on, er –' He's trying to avoid saying 'paper' again. '– If we could get something written down.'

'Any time you like.' I could have slung in an 'Officer' there, but for the feeling in the balls, consistent with having been hit in them with a padded ping-pong bat, which affected my thinking. Does a voluntary statement count as perjury?

'There's no great hurry,' said Detective-constable Carpenter's voice easily – too easily for my liking. Have a cigarette, laddy, and let's go over this yarn of yours again from the top. All that gauche stuff about not being able to say 'paper' again was a blind, in order to lull me. If there was no great hurry about taking my statement, why was it his main reason for ringing?

'If I do remember, I'll certainly call you back.'

My voice was working on too many fronts at once: it was trying to sound normal to myself, trying to impress Sheilagh and Patsy with its sexiness, trying to show Hattersley – who was listening, although pretending not to – that calls from the police were to be taken in my stride like calls from the Town Clerk when Pisspot was out, trying to convince Detective-constable Carpenter that he was talking to an innocent party. The overloading on the system was caused by the entry of Purchase from his rabbit-burrow in the Finance Department next door. I saw him pause at Pisspot's desk, as if expecting a flaccid hand to wave at him drunkenly from one of the drawers; saw him look at me and register me unavailable for immediate consultation; saw him turn to Hattersley as last in order of seniority and hold a murmured conversation with him.

'I wish you would, Mr Fisher,' Detective-constable Carpenter had said; and I heard my own voice, in a choir boy's treble, responding: 'I will indeed – Officer.'

I regretted at once saying Officer. I had self-consciously put verbal quotation marks around the word, making it sound like a foreign expression. Purchase looked at me as if I had mispronounced something from a French menu. Hattersley looked not at me but at Purchase, with a slight cringe of the cheekbones suggesting that elocutionary fastidiousness was perhaps a taste they had in common. Sheilagh and Patsy looked at no one, for they were hammering away at their typewriters as though being clocked by a time-and-motion consultant. Drop in more often, Purchase – you seem to inspire productivity.

Detective-constable Carpenter was saying: 'The thing is, Mr Fisher, what I find a bit puzzling is, there aren't all that many second-hand shops in Shepford,' and I, after wondering fleetingly if it was too late to shift the whole used golf club market to Birmingham or preferably to the larger Midlands conurbation, was saying: 'More than you'd imagine, Officer,' in the choirboy's falsetto range; and he was saying: 'How many would you say exactly with your knowledge of the borough?'; and Purchase, accompanied or rather escorted or more exactly ushered by Hattersley, was proceeding to Pisspot's desk, opening the bottom drawer on the left hand side, and extracting from it the olive-green file containing all the Department's expenses dockets since the start of the financial year.

Christ and double Christ.

'Difficult to say offhand, Officer.' Stop calling him Officer. 'Ten or a dozen. Probably more.'

'As many as that, would you reckon, Mr Fisher?'

To hospitality at the Heritage Motor Lodge for Mr Oscar Seltzer of Time-Life Inc. (London Bureau), in connection with revival of local wood-carving industry: £3.60.

'Oh, easily. Especially if you include that little junk market in the old abbey ruins.'

To hospitality at the Heritage Motor Inn for Mr R. Horniman and Mrs G. Lichfield, BBC representatives, to explore possibilities of TV coverage at Shepford Festival: £5.20.

'But you did recollect you hadn't bought your golf clubs at the junk market, Mr Fisher. Didn't you recollect that yesterday?'

'Oh, quite. Exactly.'

To hospitality at King's Head for Detective-constable Carpenter of Central Police, in connection with publicity for road safety campaign: £1.

'So that narrows down the field quite considerably.'

What I will have to do is bluff it out. Admit nothing. Look, Mr Purchase, all I know is he *said* he was from *Time Magazine* and he had an American accent and of *course* I didn't ask for his credentials, why should I? After all, whoever he was, he wasn't a bloody Russian spy. As for the BBC people, if you doubt my word it's easy to check by ringing round the various studios until you find them.

Entertaining Detective-constable Carpenter was a mistake. *Hospitality, which must not be excessive and which must be authorized in advance by a responsible officer of the Council, is strictly limited to bona fide visitors on official business (including commercial and industrial, housing, foreign deputations &c) where benefit to the Borough might accrue. Hospitality may not be extended to other servants of the Council, tradesmen, industrialists &c, except when officially receiving bona fide visitors as above.* Yes, I know the rules backwards, Purchase, I just bought the poor sod a drink, that's all. Here – there's a bloody pound note. Now we're quits.

Talking of pound notes reminded me that he still owed me one from our recent outing to the Heritage Motor Lodge. I remembered his anguished yelp when he saw his bill, and wished that my own bill for that evening was not now clipped to my latest fiddle-sheet, as evidence of entertaining the Industrial Correspondent of the *Daily Telegraph*.

'Are you there, Mr Fisher? Hello? I was saying, we should be able to narrow the field down to about four or five shops.'

'Yes. Could you hold on a second, Officer? Somebody wants a word.'

Uncradling the receiver from my hunched shoulder, where I was learning to nurse my telephone calls like a junior executive, I covered it with my hand. Purchase, brandishing the incriminating file, was hovering by my desk. Punctilious bugger. Mr

Rainbell is Head of the Department and, in his absence, Mr Fisher, and, in Mr Fisher's absence, Mr Hattersley. If I had been sitting in the bog with my trousers around my ankles, he would have been waiting outside, cracking his knuckles.

'Shall you want a signature for this?'

'I should think Rainbell will. It's his file.'

'It's the Council's file, Mr Fisher. I understand Mr Rainbell is on sick leave. As acting Head of the Department, I'm asking you if you would like a signature.'

No, no, Purchase. What you mean is, I am asking you, as acting Head of the Department, if you would like a signature.

When the judge sentences me to fifteen years, adding that he wishes it were within his power to make it twenty, I shall be standing in the dock correcting his grammar.

'Look, I'm on the phone as you can see. Can you hang on a minute?'

'We all have our business to attend to, Mr Fisher. I'm quite fully authorized to inspect these accounts. I'm asking you again if you require a signature.'

'Forget it.'

'Then I shall send over a pro-forma receipt. Oh, and by the by –' He drew out the imitation-leather wallet and abstracted a clean pound note. 'Many thanks.'

'If you find any of those items puzzling,' I said, 'you'll find there's usually an explanation.'

What I will have to do is acquire a set of golf clubs. If God's in his heaven and I can find a set in one of Shepford's few second-hand shops, I shall buy them, chuck them down a quarry, keep out of Detective-constable Carpenter's way for as long as possible, then tell him I've suddenly remembered where I got them and keep my fingers crossed that the shopkeeper won't recall the exact day of the transaction. If God is not in his heaven and there are no second-hand clubs to be found, I shall have to buy a new set jump up and down on them a bit, sell them to a second-hand shop, go back the next day wearing a false moustache and buy them back – no, wait a minute, don't fall into that trap: wear the false moustache when *selling* the things and remove it when buying them back, in case he gets asked for a description – and then follow the routine as above.

Purchase had departed with his trophy and I was back on the telephone with Detective-constable Carpenter.

'Anyway, Mr Fisher, I won't keep you, and as I say, it's not all that important, but if you *do* happen to find yourself near any of those second-hand shops –'

'Excuse me. Sorry about that.' The telephone receiver back in the crook of my shoulder, had become dislodged and fallen clattering to the floor, dragging the whole instrument with it. I retrieved it and this time held it in the conventional manner.

'– was saying, there aren't all that many of these second-hand shops, so if you *do* find yourself in the neighbourhood of one or two of them, and anything *does* jog your memory ...'

'I'll definitely give you a ring.'

'And we'll keep in touch. Thank you indeed, Mr Fisher.'

'Thank you indeed, Officer.'

The receiver, as I put it down, had the damp imprint of my hand around it. I picked up a sheet of paper at random, saw it trembling like a prize essay being read out to the entire school plus the board of governors, and put it down again. I cleared my throat to dislodge the choir-boy who was still lurking there, and said to Hattersley:

'So what was all that about?'

Hattersley, it gave me comfort to notice, was as worried as I was. Not that he had need to be. Our worry quotient should have been in the ratio of roughly 5:1, if calculated to the proportion by which my expenses regularly exceeded his.

'Your guess is as good as mine,' he said, shrugging too elaborately. 'I suppose he fancies a bit of light fiction to read over lunch.'

'But he's never looked at the swindle sheets before.'

'There's always a first time.'

'I'm not even sure he's entitled to. Why did you give him the file? Why didn't you tell him to wait till Pisspot gets back?'

'Why did you let him *take* the file? You're in charge,' retorted Hattersley. 'Anyway, he reckons he's supposed to see all expense sheets before we get reimbursed.'

'No he isn't. He gets a weekly chit from Pisspot and so long as it's not above a certain level it's none of his twatting business.'

'Don't tell me, friend. Tell him.'

While this edgy bickering was going on, Patsy was waving the tea-money tin under my nose. It was one of the office's jokey traditions that Hattersley and I were supposed to fork out a fivepenny piece every time we called Pisspot Pisspot.

'Ten pee, please. You said it twice.'

'Not this time, Patsy. I need every penny I've got.'

'He's thinking he'll have to start entertaining his lady friends out of his own money,' Sheilagh said, rather surprisingly. I trusted that she was making a harmless joke rather than maliciously aiming to hit nails on the head.

'Have to start giving them luncheon vouchers instead,' giggled Patsy.

'All right, that'll do!' said Hattersley sharply. Curious, come to think of it, that he had never made any oblique reference to Helen himself, since he was not averse to the odd snigger and must have twigged as much as Patsy and Sheilagh that something had been going on. It had crossed my mind more than once that he had his own extra-marital problems on the quiet, and that we were supposed to be observing an unspoken agreement to keep out of the arena of private lives. I could have been wrong, but there had been one or two mornings when I had arrived unexpectedly early at the office, to find him alone and still in his overcoat, making phone calls of the 'Look, I can't talk now, I'll ring you at lunchtime' variety.

'Of course,' he said to me, 'you know why Purchase has it in for us, don't you?'

Yes. No change out of a quid at the Heritage Motor Lodge.

'Has he got it in for us, especially?'

'That story about him shaving his nose. It's got back to him.'

'Not from me, it hasn't,' I said. I had only told it to Ron Casey of the *Evening Mail*, hoping he could drum it up into an interesting paragraph. SHEPFORD MAN SHAVES NOSE.

'And you needn't look at us, either,' said Patsy.

'I *am* looking at you,' said Hattersley.

'Yes, I see you are. Haven't you ever seen a pair of boobs before? We've all got them, you know.'

'If we told people outside this office all that we know,' said Sheilagh, who I hoped was still joking, 'it'd fill the *News of the World*.'

'I said, that's enough! And if you've got nothing to do I can find you something to do. In fact,' Hattersley went on, deliberately addressing himself to the ceiling, 'if we all worked a bit more and talked a bit less, we might get this guide book out before Christmas.'

Cheeky sod.

Turning into the Cornmarket from either of the access roads connecting with the shopping-centre perimeter carstacks, the visitor will find himself in one of the oldest parts of Shepford. Until comparatively recently the commercial hub of an ancient borough that had changed little over the centuries, the Cornmarket has by now outlived its usefulness in a modern industrialized community. The spacious Civic Centre on the edge of Bell Park has superseded the Victorian Town Hall with its draughty chambers and endless, gloomy corridors; while the twice-weekly open-air market has literally 'moved with the times', for it is now housed in the combined wholesale/retail market outlet, with full cold-storage facilities and loading bays, conveniently situated near the new bus station. (A Green Arrow shuttle service between the bus station and the town centre operates during normal shopping hours.)

Although the Cornmarket may have a neglected air at present, the visitor should not be deceived! Plans are well in hand to revitalize the area so that it may once more play a vital part in the ever-expanding business life of Shepford. In a three-phase programme, all the existing shops will eventually be replaced by a linked shopping mall, also comprising offices, flats, restaurants, service areas and underground parking facilities, that will be among the biggest units of comprehensive development in

Europe. The Old Town Hall, at present subject to a Preservation Order, will be completely renovated and adapted to house the long-awaited Agricultural Museum. The market square itself – the original Cornmarket, to be renamed Shepford Plaza – will, when paved and planted with trees ...

The telephone rang. Sheilagh put her hand over the receiver. 'That woman from the BBC in Birmingham again.'

'Who sounds like someone we know?'

She nodded.

'I'm out.' I got up and threw the stuff about the Cornmarket, double-space typed on Planning Department letterheads, over to Hattersley. Let's start pulling a bit of rank, Fisher. 'I can't improve on this piss. See if you can. I'm going over to see Drummond.'

5

'MOMMA WINKLEBAUM, will you please *lissena* me? I am asking why your son – *your son* – is filling my home with *galf* clubs!'

'My son. When there's galf clubs in the broom-closet, he's my son. When he brings home his salary cheque, he's your husband.'

'Jeanette. Mrs Winklebaum. May I have a word?'

'Oh, sure, Oscar, the floor is yours. You practically live here, anyway. As the saying is, *tee off.*'

'Jeanette, all I have to say is that when a normal, healthy guy like Bill takes it into his tiny mind to introduce fourteen sets of galf clubs into the family home – the *family home,* Jeanette, now don't you forget that – there has to be a reason.'

'Oh, sure there's a reason, Mister Oscar Henry Cotton Junior Seltzer, and maybe you can supply it.'

'Now Jeanette! Don't do that, Jeanette! You'll regret it for the rest of your life, Jeanette! Jeanette, put down that galf club!'

'I warned you, Oscar!'

'Jeanette! Never do that again. *Never* hit your husband's best friend with a No. 3 iron.'

I smiled, twisted the lemon peel in my glass, raised the glass to my lips, sipped, and glanced in the frosted mirror opposite my red plush banquette. The Mayor, the Chief of Police, M. le President of the Chamber of Commerce, the Curé, and the owner of the wood-shavings factory who had collaborated with the Germans during the war – all fat, all with napkins tucked under their wobbling chins, all swigging the wine of the house, all sweating away at their Châteaubriants with *pommes alumettes* on the side, were no doubt discussing the scandal of the new public urinal out there in the Cornmarket. All was well. Except ye lord watcheth ye town, ye watchman watcheth in vain – the

244

inscription carved in wood over the Old Town Hall doorway, soon to be picked out again, no doubt, by Arts College students busy with the gold-leaf. Phase one of the three-phase programme. And while they were tarting up the front they would be dismantling the great organ in the Grand Hall and trundling it into a plain van round the back. But all was well for me.

I had been to see Councillor Drummond. Besides being chairman of practically everything it was possible to be chairman of, and as well as being the mayor-elect, he was one of the town's leading solicitors with an office in Shepford's only remaining Georgian terrace on the other side of Bell Park from the Civic Centre. Getting there was something of a rhododendron-hopping adventure, for Helen, who was between jobs, had taken to lurking in the park on the off-chance of seeing me. She had once worked for Drummond's outfit – there were few establishments in the town where she hadn't worked – and I would not have put it past her to have persuaded his secretary to give Sheilagh the popping-over message with the object of waylaying me.

All clear. She was probably sitting at home, either ringing my office under one of her numerous aliases or waiting for me to ring back. I got safely to Drummond's chambers and was shown into a pleasantly-furnished first floor room overlooking the park, with photographs of its occupant bowing and scraping to minor royalty at civic functions and dominated, so far as I was concerned, by a set of brand-new golf clubs in the corner by the drinks cabinet.

'... bound say struck me piece *rather* dangerous driving,' Drummond was saying. He was a difficult person to follow at the best of times: he liked to think he had a reputation as a busy man, and he approached his sentences as he approached his appointments – at the trot, the pronouns and prepositions scattering behind him like dropped memoranda. At present, as he galloped through his reminiscence of my backwards-drive across the M.1, he was even more difficult to follow than usual, for I was mesmerized by his golf clubs.

I pulled myself together and mumbled a few fragments of my well-honed story about the gears having failed, at the same time wondering, as I always did with Drummond, how he managed to make me feel like an inky little office boy.

'Yes. Yes. Yes. Yes. Accept advice, keep off motorway thorough overhaul competent mechanic.' He dismissed the subject from the agenda with a clap of his hands and turned to the next item.

'Now. Rainbell. What can tell about him?'

'I'm not sure. What want know about him?'

'Drinking. Is getting worse, is getting better?'

My eyes, of their own accord, had swivelled back to the corner. Stop it, Fisher. You are not going to steal Councillor Drummond's golf clubs. You are making a simple problem into a complicated one. Besides, it is not a practical proposition.

Mistaking my silence for a decent reluctance to shop Pisspot – of which there were, in fact, small traces – Drummond prompted: 'Can speak freely.'

'Well,' I hedged, 'what can say? At least he doesn't drink in the office.'

'Know doesn't. Never *in* bladdy office.'

Poor old Pisspot.

'Tell truth, think he's slowing down bit lately,' I lied. 'Stopped drinking so much lunchtime, good sign.'

'Hadn't stopped drinking last Festival committee meeting. Tight bladdy owl. Tell frankly, Fisher, want Rainbell off that committee.'

'So Mr Purchase was saying.'

You servile sod, Fisher. Why *Mister* Purchase? Why couldn't you call him Purchase or better still James Purchase or better still Jimmy Purchase? And why can't you call your doctor by his first name, like Hattersley does?

I switched my eyes from the golf clubs, met Drummond's which stared at me unwaveringly, and returned to the golf clubs in some confusion. I know why he makes me feel like an inky little office boy. Because he's a genuine, card-carrying adult, he's not just playing at it. Anyone who can wear a black coat and striped trousers without feeling a pratt, or even looking very much a pratt, must have been a genuine adult since the age of fourteen.

'Believe you, Purchase had words.' A row, does he mean? No, words. *'I'll have words with my master.'* Officer-class talk.

'Yes, there was some idea that I should substitute for Mr Rainbell at the committee meetings, if we can find some way of –'

'Yes. Yes. Yes. Yes. Wish would. Had word with him yet?'

'With Rainbell?' Well done, Fisher. The *Mister* fell away like orange peel that time. 'No, he's on sick leave at moment.'

'Sick leave arse, three-day hangover more like. Well, how manage it own affair, but tell frankly, don't want see bladdy man that committee again. Like bladdy walking brewery.'

How manage it might be own affair, but how *would* I manage it?

I would get Pisspot pissed. Come committee meeting day, I would lead him to the King's Head Doubles Bar at half past eleven in the morning, force-feed him with gin and prize him into a taxi home at three o'clock. Then on to No. 4 Committee Room on the fifth floor of the Civic Centre, the new Shepford Festival whizz-kid whose ideas shoot off like fireworks, yet at the same time has a firm grasp of bread-and-butter detail. Sorry, Pisspot, but if it wasn't me it would be Hattersley. What is it that Oscar says? Somebody loses, somebody wins, somebody wins, somebody loses. That's how you play the game, kid.

But I felt a twinge of shame. Perhaps I wouldn't get Pisspot pissed after all. I would simply refrain from discouraging him getting pissed on his own initiative.

'By by, not problem that direction self, have you?' Drummond asked.

Come again?

'Keep staring drinks cabinet. Golden rule this establishment: sun over yard-arm.'

'Matter fact, looking at golf clubs,' I said hastily. I would need an accomplice. I would need Helen. She knew the routine of Drummond's office: when he would be out to lunch, how to get to his room by the back stairs, thus circumnavigating his secretary. Then one of us would keep a look-out while the other snitched his golf-clubs.

But wouldn't that land me with Helen again? I mentally kicked myself. One stupid remark to a rat-faced neighbour and I am saddled with a mistress I don't want, except when I fancy her, and a bag of stolen golf clubs which are the property, furthermore, of the man on whom I depend for my promotion.

'*You'll have to stop telling all these lies, Billy,*' my mother used to say, all those years ago. Yes, mother. It's just that I'm a slow learner.

'Play?' Drummond asked.

'Knock ball round sometimes,' I said.

'Where play? Must have few holes one Sunday morning.'

'Love to,' I said, astonished; then added quickly, skipping over the issue of where play, 'Trouble is, golf clubs stolen. Bladdy nuisance, big expense buying more.'

You see, mother, if I hadn't told one white lie to a rat-faced neighbour I would have been at a loss for a ready-made excuse when Drummond nearly called my bluff by inviting me to play golf. There is method in my madness, if you hang around long enough.

But never mind that. Drummond was inviting me to play golf. This adult in his black coat and pinstripe trousers was inviting the inky little office boy to play golf. Why?

He must perceive in my make-up something that I cannot yet perceive myself. He must recognize a coming man when he sees one. He would be able to spot my potential where I couldn't, he having the adult gift of insight.

I would learn to play golf. Having stolen Drummond's golf clubs, then jumped up and down on them a bit and sold them to the second-hand shop, then bought them back and thrown them down the quarry, then made certain that Detective-constable Carpenter found them before anyone else – such as the scallywag Charles, if he really did exist – I would reclaim my property at the police station and play golf with Councillor Drummond. Except that Councillor Drummond couldn't play golf, because his clubs would have been stolen.

I decided not to steal his golf clubs and to have nothing more to do with Helen, who could only be an encumbrance on someone recognized as a coming man.

'Back subject Rainbell,' said Drummond, having shunted the golf invitation into a cul-de-sac of vagueness. 'Between four walls, think time closely approaching put pressure consider resigning Director Information. Simply not up to job expanding town this size.'

Yes, Councillor Drummond. That's Purchase's line too. No doubt you'll put the skids under Pisspot between you, him taking one leg and you the other.

'I would have thought as he's only got eighteen months to go –' I began, but Drummond swept on as if I wasn't even in the room, let alone as if I hadn't spoken. Should I put a pencil behind my ear and *look* like the office boy?

'Brings me question successor. Premature ask, of course, but must have considered putting own name forward.'

Me? *Me?* Well, yes, of course I bloody have, but –

Sorry, Pisspot, I'm going to have to get you pissed. I shall lace your gin with white rum.

I am sitting in Councillor Drummond's office and first he has asked me to play golf with him and now he is asking if I have considered putting my name forward for Pisspot's job. There is a catch here and he wants something from me. Or there is not a catch and he wants nothing, but he has marked me down as the best man for the job. I will wear a black coat and striped trousers, Drummond, old man. I will send Oscar packing and I will finish with Helen – I *have* finished with Helen – and I will have Mr Pussy-paws run over and I will not steal your golf clubs.

But what about Purchase? Drummond, obviously, could not yet know that the second favourite was in possession of my swindle sheets. He could know, but apparently didn't, that his ex-secretary Helen had reeled into Purchase at the Heritage Motor Lodge and informed him that the drinks were on Fisher, thus not so much opening up a field for speculation as planting one with landmines. All Drummond did know, and seemed to approve of, was that Purchase had asked me to take Pisspot's place on the Festival Committee, thus doing himself in the eye. There was something that didn't add up here; but I was in no mood for making an audit of Purchase's motives. I was the Shepford District Council Director of Information in black coat and pinstriped trousers, pacing my panelled office where a proper secretary rather than a jumped-up office girl – Helen? – sat with crossed legs and poised pencil while Mr Fisher thanked the Lord Lieutenant and Lady Breezley for their kind invitation to a reception at Breezley Hall on the fourteenth to meet Her Majesty the Queen Mother, but regretted that he would be unable to attend owing to his absence from Shepford on the official Council visit to the City of Prague to examine new methods of industrialized system building.

'By by, this Prague beano,' said Drummond, as if reading my thoughts. While I had been having some of them he had gone on to say that went without saying were several other candidates field, and I had said of course appreciated that, and he had passed on to any other business, i.e. the Prague beano, with the encouraging remark that didn't see why job shouldn't go most qualified man already several years experience Council publicity work.

'This Prague beano,' he said, standing up to indicate that I should do the same and be ready on the starting-line directly he had invited me to piss off. 'Like it played down Press, if all possible.'

Yes, I'll bet you would, you crafty old bugger. The habit of various councillors of swanning off to exotic places such as Prague, Dar es Salaam and Paris on freeloading trips had been getting them talked about in the *Evening Mail*, and Drummond's habit of invariably attaching himself to these expeditions had begun to get him singled out for special mention.

'See what can do,' I muttered.

'Course, trip not till September, some time after Festival. Hope Rainbell gone by then. Great clown, shouting head off, makes these affairs sound flinging ratepayers' money about bladdy orgies. Hope have responsible man by then, point out

250

Press these things fact-finding missions, nothing more. Bladdy hard work.'

There *is* a catch and he wants something from me. I know what you want, Councillor Drummond. You want a yes-man.

'Yes, Councillor.'

6

AND now the Café Billard was filling up with the lunchtime crowd. I hissed at Henri to fetch me one more aperitif – the last one, and then I ought to be getting back to work. No, buggeration to that – I *was* working. I glanced at the sheet of foolscap which Councillor Drummond had given me – the original point of the popping-over expedition. It was his introduction, as Shepford's next Mayor, to *Pageantry with Progress* (new edition), and a fine anthology of platitudes it made. Links with the future just as strong as links with the past ... town proud of its history but even prouder of its place in modern society ... tip-top living conditions ... spacious parks ... factories second to none ... thriving domestic plasticware industry ... exciting plans ... forward-looking ... room for further expansion ... to stand still is to go backwards ... 'Needs tidying up, do with it what will,' he had said. I thought seriously about throwing it in the fire.

I slipped the document back in my pocket and toyed with my half pint of sticky draught lager. The plush banquettes and the mirrors had gone: I was sitting on a cane chair by a Formica-covered table littered with screwed-up crisp packets in a corner of the King's Head Doubles Bar next to the electronic fruit machine that paid out in washers. With only a little more effort the King's Head could have been the foulest pub in Shepford: we used it only because it was marginally less foul than the other pubs in the Cornmarket, our reason for venturing into the Corn-market in the first place being that the new brick shed housing the *Evening Mail* offices was close by, and we could ambush the *Mail*'s reporters with invitations to the sewage-farm open day.

Ron Casey and the rest of the *Evening Mail* patrol were forming their regular semi-circle at the far end of the bar and talking loudly about football. They hadn't seen me yet, and I wasn't

sure that I didn't mean to slide out through the side door that
had once been the entrance to the public bar, before a wave or a
grimace or the mimed up-tipping of a glass beckoned me into
their presence.

There had been a time, back in Stradhoughton, when I had
scraped the acquaintance of newspaper reporters, hovering on
the edge of their company and laughing at their oft-told tales of
how the municipal correspondent came back from lunch and set
his desk on fire. The *Evening Mail* boys were a dull lot in com-
parison, more like clerks: their drinking school was a timid
affair of halves of bitter and shepherd's pie and ploughman's
lunches, and in the early evenings they folded up their unad-
venturous last edition with its green-and-orange photographs of
people shaking hands or wearing knitwear suits now available at
the Cripplegate branch of a third-cousin-twice-removed of the
Bon Marche, Birmingham; and went home to wash their cars.
Another thing: I had been given this impossible mission by my
new patron Councillor Drummond, play down Prague beano
Press, if all possible. How was I supposed to do that? 'Oh, by the
way, I shouldn't make too much of that visit to Prague if I were
you. They'll be travelling economy and taking packed lunches'?
Whatever I said, I could readily imagine the leading article – or
'Viewpoint' as they preferred to call it – in the *Evening Mail*:

> At a time when Shepford ratepayers are onc
> again steeling hemselves form the shock of
> a further massife ingrease dbldbldbldbldbl
> was also among te judges. Wearing a tuqoise-
> set off on another of their expesive jaunts
> to far-away places.
> We repeat the uestion we put to Cllr Drudommn
> and his colllleagues when they spent three
> tatepayers' expense: 'Is your jouney really
> day's at a de-luxe hotel fn Ostend at he
> matching acdessories.

An excited twittering reached my ears from the *Evening Mail*
corner – the dawn-chorus sound, like baby starlings welcoming
their mother with a worm, of apprentice drinkers greeting a

seasoned regular. Young voices trying to sound hearty tried on such expressions as 'Oh, not again', 'Get them in, Casey', and 'Just in time, mate, it's your round'. I looked along the bar, expecting to see the entry of the *Mail*'s only hardened drinker, their crime man Jack Wilmott, perhaps treating them to a mock-cringe and shielding his head with one arm to feign elaborate concern about last night's behaviour at closing-time. Instead, it was Pisspot.

I felt, as I often did when he was sober, a quick surge of what I had once thought was pity but which by now I had begun to recognize as affection. Later, when he was drunk, he would be a bloody nuisance, lurching from side to side like an old Strad-houghton tram as I steered him out into the Cornmarket; thrashing his arms about and knocking tonic bottles over as he made some argumentative point over an absolutely irrevocably final double gin in Shepford's only afternoon drinking club; insisting, perhaps, on staggering back to the office and collapsing in his chair, or worse still on the floor, like a stranded, snoring walrus. But in the mornings, with his glasses slipping off the end of his nose or pushed up to his forehead, a pipe repaired with insulating tape smouldering in one tweedy pocket and a copy of the *Guardian*, looking as if it had recently wrapped lettuce, stuffed in the other, and the strands of multi-coloured wool unravelling from his wrongly-buttoned cardigan, he could look quite touchingly vulnerable – especially against the laminated panels, glass doors and silicone-finished vestibules of the Civic Centre, where he spent the hour before opening-time shambling anxiously up and down like a professor of ancient Greek trapped in a bowling-alley. 'The Shredded Wheat factory,' he called the Civic Centre: the redundant Town Hall, where he had served most of his time in local government, was 'Hatter's Castle'. I was fond of old Pisspot. I went across and joined him.

'The *motor* car,' he was booming as I walked over, evidently to quell the excessively boring debate on miles to the gallon that was the *Evening Mail* crowd's only standby when the topic of Shepford Rovers palled, 'the *motor* car has done more harm – more harm – to the fabric of this town than any intruder since

Oliver Cromwell, with the possible exception of Messrs. Creative City Consortium Incorporated and Limited, and their blasted shopping precincts. And on top of that – on *top* of that, allow me to finish, young man, I believe I have the floor – what you lads won't realize is that the *motor* car is an instrument of repression. Oh yes! I speak among you! Every new mile of road, every lay-by, every car park is land seized from the common people! Yes indeed! If I had my way – if I had my way – if *I* had my way, do you mind, young sir? – if I had my way, no motor car would be allowed in Shepford unless a Labour councillor walked in front of it, singing "The Red Flag". Ah!'

The diatribe was a familiar one and the dragged-in joke an old one and Pisspot was already in danger of losing his audience. The 'Ah!', addressed to me, was exclaimed in some relief. I, at least, would not desert him. There had been times, indeed, when I had been reminded tetchily that it was my job not to.

'Morning, Reggie,' I grinned. 'Enjoying your sick leave?' It was not yet noon and he was already two-thirds of the way through a large gin-and-tonic. A bad sign that, for had he been bent on social drinking rather than serious drinking – not that the two categories were particularly distinguishable as the day wore on – he would have started with a couple of pints of bitter. Perhaps I ought to call Hattersley and warn him that I might be late back.

'Convalescence, dear boy, convalescence. And see –' He returned to the group at large, addressing them as ever like a large public meeting. '– see what happens when I convalesce. Is Arsehole at his desk? No, Arsehole is not at his desk. Does Arsehole hold the fort? On the contrary, Arsehole does not hold the fort. Arsehole at eleven-thirty this morning, I have no doubt, was gasping outside the doors of this very public house with his tongue hanging out, waiting for opening time!'

(He had been calling me Arsehole ever since it had got to his ears that I called him Pisspot. 'Call me Pisspot if you will,' he had said. 'I *am* a pisspot. I am a piss-art*iste*. But so long as you call me Pisspot I shall call you Arsehole, for only an Arsehole would refer to a friend and colleague behind his back as Pisspot. And should you cease to call me Pisspot, I shall nevertheless continue to call you Arsehole. You will be known as Arsehole for all time. You will be remembered as Arsehole. The name will be inscribed on your tombstone: *Arsehole Fishah*!' I was never quite sure whether he was truly offended or not.)

'He was here till closing time yesterday, Reg,' joshed one of the reporters. 'Over to the Lantern Club, back here at five,' supplied another. I let them work this joke to death and then, in case they had planted any small doubts in Pisspot's mind – not that he would have given a toss anyway – explained about my errand to Drummond's office.

'Ah! Bulldog Drummund, the Pooh Bah of Shepford! And did the *bar*stard mention,' asked Pisspot, draining his glass, 'that he is trying to get me fired?'

You sly old sod, you don't miss much, do you?

'Oh yes! Drunk in charge of a publicity department. *And* the *bar*stard wants me off the Festival committee, so my spies inform me.'

You've got friends, Reggie, that's what it is, and I'm one of them, truly I am. But I've got to get you pissed. Not today, though. If I get you pissed today it is only because I'm your friend.

'Let me get a round in,' I said. 'Big one is that, Reggie?'

'Tonic water, dear boy,' pronounced Pisspot importantly – but then he pronounced everything importantly. And he did like his little joke.

'Large gin and tonic,' I ordered.

'*Tonic* water. Slimline – low calorie – Indian – *tonic* water. Containing nought three four calories per fluid ounce. If you please.'

More guffawing from the *Evening Mail* lot as my mouth dropped. 'Look at him, he can't take it in,' 'He's suffering from shock, give him a large brandy,' etc.

'He doesn't drink, Bill,' spelled out Ron Casey. 'Didn't you read it in last night's *Mail*? We put out a special edition.'

'Seen the error of his ways, haven't you, Reg?' said another, as Pisspot bowed complacently, like an old-style ham actor acknowledging his applause.

'Whether my ways were in error, young man, will eventually be judged by a higher authority than ours. However, I am in a position to confirm Mr Casey's announcement. You see before you, my dear Arsehole, a pisspot who is an ex-pisspot. A lapsed pisspot. A reformed pisspot. I am on the proverbial wagon.'

But you can't be, Pisspot! Don't you realize – I've *got* to get you pissed! I've got to get you pissed and wheel you home in a barrow and then take your place on the Festival committee. And I've got to keep you pissed until they throw you out of the Civic Centre and I get your job.

I said, too shaken to imitate his mode of speech, which I often found myself doing despite all my resolutions not to: 'What's brought this on, then?'

' "What's brought this on?" "What's brought this on?" He is given earth-shattering news and he asks "What's brought this on?" Where is your sense of occasion, dear boy? Cause bells to ring! Put out more flags!'

And on and on and on and on, and into the saga of Pisspot's conversion. Three mornings ago – the day he commenced his sick leave – he had woken up not in his bed but in the middle of the bandstand in a public park in Wolverhampton. He had been to an extraordinarily good dinner in Wolverhampton, the retirement dinner of an old colleague of his as a matter of fact, but he could remember nothing beyond the loyal toast. As for claiming to be off with 'flu, he *had* been off with 'flu, having found himself drenched to the skin – the result, he surmised, of having waded through the boating lake at some point. Mrs Pisspot had called the doctor and the doctor had lectured him like the proverbial dutch uncle, and in short he was on the wagon.

'Alcohol,' bellowed Pisspot, 'is a liquid paradox. It is a stimulant, yet a depressant. It is a food, but at the same time a poison. Now to a system such as mine, so I am informed by reliable authorities . . .' And on and on. Most of the young reporters grew bored, as they often did after a few minutes of his company. They began to drift off to the plastic tables with their plates of shepherd's pie. I felt angry with them: the favourite uncle had amused his nephews for a moment with his tricks with pennies and playing cards, but now they were tired of him.

Soon only Pisspot, I and Ron Casey were left at the bar. Only then did Pisspot drop his voice a decibel or so, and the public-orator style with it. 'There's another angle, to this, Ron,' he said, 'but I don't want it publicized at present. Agreed?' You *are* a sly old sod. You drove them away on purpose.

'Agreed,' Ron Casey, the rising star, tried to look like the wise old moon. I wondered if I looked as cross-eyed when doing the same trick.

'You will remember my wheeze or scheme for taking early retirement? Cancel earlier message. Celebratory dinner post-poned. No bodies will be found on bandstands eighteen months hence.'

'Does that mean you're staying on, Reg?' Silly, stupid, wooden-headed, cloth-eared bugger, what do you think it means?

'I'm afraid I'll jolly well have to. Can't afford not to. I took the opportunity while on my bed of pain of peering very closely indeed into the Rainbell coffers. I did not like what I saw. I need the brass, the greenbacks, the *dow* as my Brummingham father used to call it. So I shall work out my full term at the mast and you' – this was to me – 'will have five years to wait before step-ping into dead men's sodden shoes. Sorry about that, my dear old Arsehole, or may I call you Bill? Let me buy you a drink.'

'If I emigrated to the United States, would I have to take my wife?'

Pisspot, having produced a fiver and waved it at the barmaid in a wide circular motion embracing practically everybody in the pub, continued: 'So that is one more reason for the turning over of new leaves. With Master Drummond breathing heavily down my neck I shall probably be best advised to step that little bit more carefully. Not that the *bar*stard could get me out of that office with a crowbar, if it came to a showdown.'

I was reminded of something that the *bar*stard could do, or rather what the *bar*stard's sidekick could do. Excusing myself to

Ron Casey on grounds of private business, I murmured in Pisspot's ear.

'What? What? What? Speak up! Don't mumble!'

'*Pur*chase,' I hissed. 'In our office this morning.'

'Ah! The phantom nose-shaver! Did you know that Purchase shaves his nasal organ, Ron? Good advertising tie-up there: I shave my nose with Wilkinson Sword.'

Covering my mouth, and trying to make it look like a parody of Purchase shaving his nose, I muttered out of the side of my mouth: 'He took away the green file.'

'What green file? Which green file? I have hundreds and thousands and millions of green files.'

'*The* green file. *The one in your left-hand drawer.*'

'Oh, the swindle sheets!' roared Pisspot, completely unconcerned. 'Good luck to him! Which reminds me. Prague,' he went on, turning to Ron Casey; though why it reminded him, I had no idea. Perhaps sobriety was softening his brain. 'You wanted facts and figures on Prague. Subject to audit, I would say it has the makings of our costliest beanfeast yet.'

Pisspot, you silly old fool, we're supposed to be playing it *down*. Or are we? *I* am, but only as a yes-sir-three-bags-full-sir favour to Drummond. Pisspot doesn't do that sort of thing.

'You do know,' I said recklessly, 'that Drummond wants us to nobble the *Mail* to get the whole thing played down?'

'Of course he does, dear boy. The man's not a total nincompoop.'

'Bribes accepted between the hours of twelve and half-past,' said Ron Casey, producing his notebook.

Odd bits of paper, pound notes, pipe cleaners, newspaper cuttings, letters, bills and toffee wrappers were showering to the floor as Pisspot tugged his pockets inside out, his usual mode of finding a missing document. He retrieved a memo stamped CONFIDENTIAL from the torn lining of his jacket and peered at it over his half-moon spectacles.

'Prague, city of, Shepford Council piss-up in, figures relating to,' he announced. 'And it goes without saying, this doesn't come from me.'

Are you a rotten director of publicity, Pisspot, or a very good one? I suspected he was a better one than I would ever have been in what now seemed the absurdly unlikely event of my getting his job; a better one, anyway, than the town deserved. If he didn't give a toss, it was only because there was not very much in Shepford worth giving a toss about; but he had a kind of exasperated, exasperating integrity that I admired, and looked in vain for in myself.

As Pisspot, giving a reasonable imitation of a town crier, dictated the juicier bits from his confidential memo, I leaned against the bar sipping draught lager and idly surveying the lunchtime drinkers through the bank of mirrors behind the bottle-shelves. There had been a time when the original engraved mirrors of the King's Head, advertising gin, port and dinner ale, had put me in mind of the plush saloons of the Café Billard; but when it was tarted up into a doubles bar they were sold to antique dealers, and now, in their place, hung cheap but faithful reproductions of the same mirrors, bought from a flash arcade in Birmingham. It was through the middle one, the one advertising Bass Blue Label, that I saw Helen entering the pub.

She was wearing a yellowish corduroy skirt, a white open-necked shirt, a row of rather unsuitable red wooden beads, and sun-glasses, and she looked stunning. She spotted me at once, but I made a fractional motion of my head towards Ron Casey, moving closer towards him at the same time. Helen, displaying the great sense of which she was intermittently capable, walked to the other end of the bar. Even she, I rightly guessed, did not care to run the risk of Casey's 'Shepford Man's Diary' reporting her as being ust god fiends with the popularBill Fisher of Shepford's ifnormation and puglicity department.

She established herself at a table by the door, fiddling with her beads and sipping what looked to me like a very large vodka and tonic indeed. She would hover there until I left, and catch up with me as I strode across the Cornmarket. Just five minutes, she would say: you do owe me that. What I wanted to do was get her across the table now, and make the white shirt rather more open-necked than it was already, but I had more sense than that; I would leave when Pisspot left, taking him by the elbow and steering him to the office or to the pictures or home or wherever he wanted to go now that he was living his new life of no wine and roses. He would be my shield.

He had finished his conference with Ron Casey, who had pushed his glass away to indicate that no question of another round would arise, in his opinion. Pisspot was cramming the re-claimed litter of his recent excavations back into his accommoda-ting pockets. Helen, ignoring the stares of the *Evening Mail* shepherd's pie set at neighbouring tables, continued to play with her polished red beads, her sun-glasses pushed up to her hair-line and her eyes fixed on me. I shoved my own glass of washing-up liquid aside, partly to indicate to the management that it was washing-up liquid, partly to tell Ron Casey that if he wasn't going to buy a round it certainly wasn't my turn, but mainly to hint to Pisspot that if he was ready, I was ready too.

'Well, my dear Arsehole, I have drunk enough slimline – low calorie – Indian – tonic water to launch a balloon. Do you pro-pose to escort me to Shredded Wheat Towers, or is it your in-tention to be here when the towel is flung over the non-existent barrel?'

God, I fancy you, Helen.

'Come on, Reggie. And by the way. I didn't say it before be-cause I didn't get the chance, but I'm glad you're staying on.'

I'm glad you're staying on, Pisspot.

'I should bloody well hope so.'

You old rascal. By now you should be half-way to roaring drunk and I should be leading you into the Lantern Club and persuading them to make you a life member, if you aren't one already. And having launched you on a seven-day jag, I should be taking your seat at the Festival committee, and thereafter your desk and your job, and telling Hattersley, my number two, that it's the luck of the game you didn't get your full pension. But I'm glad you're on the wagon, Pisspot, and I'm glad you're staying on.

He had little experience of leaving a public house sober and he staggered automatically as he turned for the door. At the same time, Helen's hand tightened on her wooden beads, and they snapped and went rolling across the linoleum floor. I had taken Pisspot's arm with what he must have thought was patronizing solicitude.

'We are no longer an inebriate, my dear old boy.' (It would have helped matters along no end if you were, my dear old Pisspot. I need you senseless.) He shook himself free, walked with exaggerated dignity towards the door, skidded on one of Helen's scattered beads and fell very heavily on his back, knocking himself unconscious against the only remaining iron-legged table in the King's Head Doubles Bar. Ron Casey rang for an ambulance, one of the shepherd's pie crew got a wet towel, and Helen drank up very quickly and walked out, while I, for the sake of appearances, knelt by my fat friend's side, doing nothing in particular, and closing my eyes when I saw blood.

7

IT was not often that my mother and Jeanette were to be found
in the same room after midnight. The former having introduced
the latter to nocturnal pursuits such as knitting bed-jackets or
doing tapestry-work by numbers, they were neither of them
early-to-bedders by inclination; but they had worked out a shift
system whereby one voluntarily clocked off at about eleven
while the other kept the night watch with me.

These vigils gave each of them in turn a regular platform for
personal statements of the type that embarrassment or a sense of
delicacy might have inhibited with the other one being present.
My mother, for example, had once begun a rambling discourse
on the thinness of the walls, and we had discussed modern
building methods for fully an hour before it dawned on me that
what she was trying to get at was that the squeak of bedsprings
sometimes disturbed her dreamless sleep. (You should have
mentioned that to the lady from the Bedding Council, mother,
and then I could have pointed out that the only reason for
bedspring-squeaking on these premises is that we have a
squeaky bed.)

Jeanette, for her part, would use up her allotted time in seeking
advice on whether she should give up the Pill, her belief being
that it brought her out in a rash (Permission refused), or de-
manding assurances that I still loved her (Confirmation post-
poned), or asking how I would react if by chance she found
herself pregnant (Dismissed as hypothetical question), and
similar personal matters. She too would occasionally touch on
the subject of the squeaking bed. She was even more conscious
than my mother of the thinness of the walls and, two years ago,
when her fastidiousness had begun to border on frigidity, we
had switched operations to the bedroom carpet. The eroticism of

this experiment had long worn off and I supposed that I should have got myself down to Pillow-talk (Shepford) Ltd and bought a new bed; but that, like signing the papers for Mortgagedene, would have been forging another link in a chain I wanted to break. The time would come when the bloody bed would fall in altogether, and then I would have to leave Jeanette.

The night shift generally went off duty at about half-past twelve and I would stay up on my own for a minute that became two hours, smoking and listening to the radio, lost in my own thoughts and my own world, a free man for a while, and nobody's hostage. I enjoyed these sessions with myself more than any other part of the day, and it was with some irritation that I realized that tonight's was going to be seriously curtailed. It was my mother's turn on the bridge and Jeanette, according to the custom and etiquette of the house, should have departed for the squeaking bed an hour ago. Instead she was aimlessly pottering about, sorting through magazine racks and making cups of cocoa, while my mother steered herself along one of her frequent exhausting rambles down Memory Lane.

'Then there was another time when his dad's monkey-wrench went missing. And he wanted that monkey-wrench for a special purpose, I forget what he wanted it for, but it was a special purpose, he had to have it that day. Any road, he looks high and low, and *you* know what a temper your father had, our Billy, it was *b* this and *b* that, and oh b h, where's that b monkey wrench, and guess where he finds it. *This* one had it squat away in his bedroom and what he wanted it for I do not know to this day . . .'

You're rewriting history, mother. You're making it sound like an amusing family anecdote but there was a drumhead court-martial when the old man found that monkey-wrench. And you're making it sound as if I was about eleven at the time and I wasn't, I was eighteen. And why did I take the monkey-wrench?

'And the undertaker's shop he used to work for. All them calendars of Mr Shadrack's what never got posted. I bet you don't remember them, do you, our Billy?'

264

'Mm.' And thieving the petty cash, and stealing coffin plates. *'Taking things,'* she used to call it, with the distaste of a maiden lady finding a french letter in her bed. 'What's this I hear about you *taking things* from work?' She had to force herself to say the words and they sounded strange on her lips: they were words like *abortion* and *naked* and *buggery* and *french letter* that she would just as soon not have had in her vocabulary.

She can't be cauterizing old wounds: it was all too long ago for that kind of therapy. She must be expressing relief, heaving a big sigh now that it's all over. Yes, that's what she's doing: everything's turned out all right. I was a little devil in them days but look at me now, all married and wearing a cardigan and settled down and paying the milk bill and the rates and all grown-up. Fancy a game of golf on Sunday, mother? I'll put the green fees on my swindle sheet.

'He was a little devil in them days. Wasn't you?'

Jeanette had been taking little part in the conversation beyond the odd barely-civil monosyllable, and she had by now entrenched herself in an armchair where she sat with arms folded, quite blatantly waiting for my mother to take herself to bed. It was clear to me why she was jumping the night-patrol roster: we were in for an emergency resolution, one of the major set-pieces on the future of our marriage that, once every three months or so, supplemented the usual routine debate about birth-pills and pregnancies.

'I'll see to the cups if you want to go up, Jeanette,' my mother said in the heavy, flat-iron voice that she thought was her diplomatic one. (In her terms, the location of any bedroom, whether in house, bungalow, maisonette or flat, was always 'up'.) She too was plainly hanging about to table an emergency resolution, and I could guess from previous late-night sittings what it was. *Have you noticed how depressed your Jeanette's been getting lately? Well it's none of my business, you suit yourself what you do, but if you want to know what I think, I think it's time she was starting a family ...*

'That's all right, I'm not tired,' said Jeanette, tightly.

Bugger the pair of them. I'll go to bed myself.

I got up, stretched, scratched my hair, yawned a bit, and was digging out the loose change that always slipped down the side of the chair on these domestic evenings, when I saw that my mother had somehow allowed herself to be out-manoeuvred. Perhaps Jeanette had told her to piss out of it in so many words and I hadn't heard; or more likely there had been a slight, rank-pulling frown; at any rate she had commenced to scoop up hand-bags, bottles of pills, hot-water bottles, trashy novels and other bedtime accoutrements, while Jeanette appeared to be saying: 'I should let your mother use the bathroom first.'

I deposited myself back in my chair and, as a gesture of ex-asperation, flicked on the radio at my elbow. Phone-in pro-gramme: men who sounded like London taxi-drivers and women who sounded like Croydon hairdressers, insomniacs all, discussing inflation. '*What I'm tryin to get at ees, Dave, I aven't your gift wiv words, bat, bat, what my question ees, is this, which ees, if that's true what that gentleman jus sayed, if I unnerstan im correctly, what e says ees, ees, that this, where the Common Market is actually keepin prices down so he claims, them was is very words I'm sorry Dave I am very sorry my old mate you don' mind if I call you that only I bin lisseninga your programme for a long time since it started in fact an what I'm tryin to get at ees ...*'

The droning, obsessional voice, echoing slightly and crack-ling with atmospherics as if being bounced by satellite from the suburbs of the moon, induced a zombie-like chilly, three-in-the-morning, fire-out-and-no-cigarettes feeling: my exasperation was replaced by melancholy.

I inhabit a suburb of the moon myself.

Nothing ever happens in this flat. Nothing has ever happened here, save that brief intrusion by Helen from my real life. Noth-ing can ever happen here. It is neutral ground, no-man's-land; it is a waiting room.

'Haven't seen Mr Pussy-paws lately, I hope nothing's hap-pened to him,' Jeanette said, as she often did.

You have never seen him, my blossom, we are dealing with a made-up cat. I made up Mr Pussy-paws for the same reason I

266

stole the monkey-wrench: to relieve the monotony of living on the moon.

Was that a moment of perception I just had?

I didn't reply to Jeanette. She was only marking time until my mother emerged from the bathroom, put her head round the doorway to say Good Night for the second time, put the chain on the hall door, then made her last and absolutely final reappearance with the newsflash that she had just done what she had been doing every night for the last eight years.

'I mean what I mean ees, you know and I know Dave, y'know, it is a definite fact, I mean you ave only got to look at y'know all these different countries . . .'

'I've put the chain on the door. Good night.'

Good *night*, Momma Winklebaum.

Jeanette got up and switched off the radio. She crossed and closed the door which my mother always left slightly ajar. She shut the window which was letting in a small gasp of night air. Whenever Jeanette wanted a serious talk she gave the impression that she was making preparations to gas herself.

It was very quiet. The radiator clanked once. There was an eerie *ping*! from the unplugged television as its electronic innards cooled down.

'You see,' I said, 'it *does* make a pinging noise.'

'Bill. I want to talk to you.'

Oh, Christ. I mean, it comes as no surprise, but oh Christ just the same. Come on then, get it over with.

She took a deep breath and stepped on the diving-board.

'And I want a straight answer to a straight question. *Are you seeing somebody else?*'

Relief.

Are you *seeing somebody else*? What's all this I hear about you *taking things*? The same shame-tinged tone. And I could have laughed aloud. Jeanette, flower of my life, I have been seeing somebody else for the last three and a half years. I have been seeing her twice, three times, four times a week, evenings lunchtimes, Saturdays and Sundays when her husband was away, and you have never suspected a thing. I have come home at two in

the morning stinking of scent and you haven't dreamed I was
seeing somebody else. You have taken a suit of mine to the
cleaners containing a pornographic letter from Helen and you
have not known I was seeing somebody else. You have seen me
covered in scratches, consistent with having spent the evening
in a blackberry bush, and it has not crossed your mind that I
was seeing somebody else. And now, when I have stopped seeing
somebody else – as I positively have – you ask me if I am seeing
somebody else.

'That's a funny question to ask.'

'What's the answer?'

'You know what the answer is. The answer is bloody no.'

Pause for a certain amount of wedding-ring twiddling and
some compulsive straightening of dead matches in an ash-tray.
She went on in a low level, over-calm voice: 'This morning you
said you wouldn't be home until about eight because you had to
go and have a drink with Councillor Drummond to talk about
your guide-book.'

'Well?'

'You said you were meeting him at that wine bar in Cripplegate.'

Mistake, that. Never say where you're going, only where
you've been, and not even that if practical.

'Well?' She knows I wasn't there. That's all right: I met him
somewhere else.

'I was in town this evening, Bill. Late-shopping night. And
I saw the coat I've been looking for in Truelove and Verity's,
but I didn't have enough money. *So*. I went into the wine bar
and Councillor Drummond was there but you weren't. And
he said he hadn't seen you.'

Ah. Now this is a difficult one. The truth is, Jeanette, I was
on an errand of mercy. I went to visit Pisspot in hospital. And
if you don't believe me you can get on that phone now, ring the
Thrisby Ward at the Aneurin Bevan General, and tell the night
nurse to wake the old sod up. And the only reason I didn't tell
you where I was really going was that it would have been a
waste of a perfect excuse. Because one of these evenings Helen is

going to succeed in catching me, and we'll need a last drink to take us through the last argument, and that's going to take two hours minimum, and I'll come home and say I'm sorry I'm late but I had to visit Pisspot in hospital.

But you might have trouble in following that.

'I can tell you exactly where I was this evening. I was visiting Rainbell in hospital.'

'Then why say you were seeing Mr Drummond?'

'Jeanette. Let's establish where I was first. I was visiting Rainbell. And if you don't believe me you can get on that phone now, ring the Thrisby Ward at the Aneurin Bevan General, and ask the night nurse. I got there at half-past six and she came on duty at seven.'

'And you weren't seeing another girl?' Another woman, the expression is, at our age.

'I was seeing Rainbell.' I picked up the telephone receiver, one finger poised on the dial. 'Do you want to check?'

'Don't be silly, of course I don't. What I can't understand is why you didn't tell me.'

Then let me put your mind at rest. I *was* seeing Drummond but he cancelled at the last minute. Then I was going to call you only I remembered it was late-shopping night ...

Sod that. Tell her the truth. Tell her the truth and you could be out of here by morning.

It was my turn to twiddle with spent matches.

'It's hard to explain.'

'What is? What is there *to* explain?'

'Jeanette. Let me give you an example. Did you know I was taking Rainbell's place on the Festival committee?'

'You never told me that. Is that why you had to see him in hospital?'

'No, it isn't why I had to see him in sodding *hos*pital. You're missing the point.'

'What point?' Total bewilderment.

'Of why I didn't tell you. It's because I can't bloody *tell* you things. Anything! Anything at all! About anything!'

'But that's stupid. You *do* tell me things.'

No, I don't, not unless I have to. I can't talk to you without rehearsing the words in my head first. Talking to you is like being interviewed for a job because you don't talk back, you ask questions. And I can't tell you that because I can't tell you things. And I want to leave you because I can't tell you things, but I can't tell you I want to leave because I can't tell you things.

'Is that what's wrong between us, Bill?'

'I don't know what's wrong between us, Jeanette.'

There is nothing between us: that's what's wrong. I would be calling you Jeanie by now if anything had gone right, if we had any hope of making it.

'There's something, I do know that. There's been something for the last few months.'

'There's been something for the last eight years.' I didn't mean to say that aloud, but it was said now. Perhaps I can tell her things.

'What – you mean ever since we got married?'

Yes. We shouldn't have done it, Jeanette. We got married on the wrong terms: yours. I know why I married you but your reasons were just as trivial: wanting a husband. And the deal was that I should behave like one, and if I did, you would become a good and loving wife. But you would have done that for any husband who came your way. And you love me now because you have the responsibility of loving your husband. And you'll cry if I go, but they will only be the mature, slow tears of a reasonable person. It's bloody unfair.

'Well,' I said lamely, 'it's not exactly been a ball of fire, has it?'

'Do you mean you're fed up of me?'

Yes.

'I don't know what I'm fed up of. The whole of bloody life, I think.' I picked up the evening paper. THAT PRAGUE TRIP – CLLR ᗡNOWWUᖉᗡ RELPIES. Go to bed, Jeanette. The moment's passed. No crisis this evening, I've got some things I want to think about.

I thought, as she rose, that she was taking the hint. Instead, she came and curled herself up at my feet, one arm around my

270

knees. I stroked her hair, it having evidently been placed close at hand for that purpose. I was reminded of two old films: *Brief Encounter* and *Lassie Come Home*.

'Do you know what I think, Bill?' Go on, then. Let's have your analysis. Let's see if you can get within two thousand light-years of the true facts. 'I think,' she said with the air of having cracked the Rosetta stone, 'that you tend to over-dramatize.'

I do, I do. And you, my poppet, tend to under-dramatize, which is worse. Nothing ever happens in this flat.

I wonder what Helen's doing at this moment. Screwing her husband in the bath, very probably. 'I'm faithful to you outside home,' she'd once said. 'But I can't help appetite.'

'You think because we don't talk about – oh, world-shattering events, *I* don't know, that we don't talk at all. We do. We talk all the time. About *little* things. *They're* important, Bill.' She made them sound like dwarfs. Come on, Snow White, we haven't got all night. 'And you think because one day's like another, and we lead an ordinary life like the people next door and the people next door to them, you think it's dull. It isn't dull, Bill. *I* don't find it dull. I find it exciting.'

You wouldn't recognize excitement if it chased you down the street.

'Exciting. How?'

'In all sorts of ways. Things to look forward to. Holidays. Outings. Going out for a meal sometimes. In fact, we're always on the go when you think about it.'

'Yes. I suppose we are.' Why am I giving her points? Because she is a good wife, who is ill-used by not having a good husband. It's bloody unfair on her too.

'And you know what your trouble is, don't you, old worry-guts? You don't know when you're well off. You don't, Bill, it's true. But just you look back to where we were when we started and where we are now. Nice job, good money, nice town to live in, nice flat – well I'm saying nice flat, that's because we've *made* it nice. And we can always move – I know you're nervous about taking on new responsibilities but we'd have no trouble in getting a mortgage, and how many couples can say that? And I *know* we've got your mother to put up with but it won't be for ever.'

Why not? Are we going to bury her in the back garden at Mortgagedene? I sometimes dreamed of getting rid of the pair of them like that. Weedkiller, Inspector? Certainly I bought weedkiller. For my new rockery.

She droned on persuasively about the qualities still attaching to a slightly-used marriage, reminding me more and more of the manager of Feet First Shoes when I had tried to return a faulty pair of chukka boots. I had stopped listening. Thinking of police inspectors had reminded me of detective-constables. If I told Jeanette now why I had to find a set of golf clubs, she would look at me as if I were speaking German.

'Aren't we? Bill?'

'Aren't we what?'

'Bill Fisher, you're half-asleep! I thought you wanted to talk!'

One of us did, one of us didn't. 'Sorry. Tired eyes.'

'Well at the risk of repeating myself – don't you agree that we're still good in bed?'

'Well. Let's say on the bedroom carpet.'

She squeezed my leg and smiled up at me, shyly. I could have cobbled together a warm moment for us out of these ingredients, if I'd wanted to. But I held back. I'm not signing anything else. No, we're not very good in bed.

Helen and I had once been supposed to go to a flat that she borrowed sometimes from one of her friends in the operatic society she never went to, only something went wrong and we couldn't get the key. The car was in dock and it was pissing with rain, so to pass the time we sat in the bar of the Heritage Motor Lodge, drinking vodka martinis and working out, on the back of an old envelope, roughly how many hours we'd spent having each other in the last three years or so. And it came to about seven hundred hours or, worked out in days, roughly equivalent to the month of June, which it then was. The image of such a flaming June had not been far out of my mind ever since. I saw myself waking up on that summer morning, the first of the month, with Helen by my side; beginning to touch, explore, kiss, stroke, scratch, bite; through the long day, through the night, bathed in sweat, to the second and third and fourth of the month, through the week and the weekend, through Midsummer's Day, Whit Sunday, Father's Day and the Queen's birthday, through the Test match and Wimbledon: neighbours go on a fortnight's holiday to Yugoslavia and return, a Middle East war is fought and finished, Ford's of Dagenham have turned out fifty thousand cars, and the rhythm continues, this endless song – our faces astonished at what we are doing, as flowers bloom and die, the earth spins, and the moon passes through all its phases. It was a month of life, that was, and we were very good in bed. Sex is a powerful aphrodisiac.

'Well,' said Jeanette in the fullness of time. 'I'm glad we've got all that out into the open.' The marriage had been given its periodic road test, and granted a further certificate. Concessions had been made on both sides. I would tell her more things. She would ask fewer questions. I would be more considerate. She would be more understanding. I would stop leaving the dustbin for her to hump out on Tuesday mornings. She would stop taking the ash-tray out of the bathroom. You wash and I'll dry. Perfection.

I sprawled in my chair, defeated and depressed, while Jeanette detached from its card and popped into her mouth the pill that brought her out in a rash. She kissed me on the forehead and, with quite a successful attempt at huskiness, whispered: 'Don't stay up too long, will you?'

I wouldn't, my little flower, if I thought I'd find you spread-eagled on the bedroom carpet. What are you doing in July?

8

'APOLOGIES for absence, Mrs Drew who cannot be with us, Mr Rainbell who is in hospital recovering from a fall.' The slightest smirk on Purchase's thin lips, and I saw the image that must have formed in his mind of Pisspot still singing as he rolled down three flights of steps. 'I'm sure we all wish him well.'

Year year! from the hypocritical ratbags there assembled.

'Now the question arises of Mr Rainbell's successor, or should I say Mr Rainbell's proxy. We have a slight constitutional dilemma here . . .'

'No constitutional dilemma soever, greatest respect chairman. Standing orders clearly state one representative Information Publicity Department, nowhere specified which particular representative, send whom they please. Sit down, Fisher.'

I had been kept hanging about like a spare part while Purchase sorted out his crisis of protocol. He would have liked to have had me in an ante-room, but as there was no ante-room available and he couldn't very well make me stand out in the corridor, I had been motioned to go and stand by the window, where I was absently watching two workmen in a cradle hosing down the streaked front wall of the Civic Centre, and trying to look as if I were not technically present.

There was one remaining vacant chair at the long conference table: presumably if the absent Mrs Drew had been able to be with us after all, I would have had to squat on the floor. I moved towards it and was about to sit when Purchase, who was poring over some well-thumbed mimeographed sheets that must have been his precious standing orders, held up his hand.

'Before you take your seat, Mr Fisher. With respect, Councillor Drummond, that's not quite the interpretation I would put on standing orders. Standing orders in fact require the Information

274

and Publicity Department to *nominate* one member, and the member it has in fact so nominated is in fact Mr Rainbell.'

This piece of hair-splitting left me in a ridiculous posture, backside poised in mid-air, hands gripping the arms of my chair, as if I were about to do a spectacular forward roll across the table.

'Very well, then propose co-opt Mr Fisher this committee.'

Smart thinking, Drummond. That gets rid of any future appearances by Pisspot, doesn't it, unless we're both supposed to fight for the same chair?

'I'll accept that resolution. It should solve all our difficulties. It is proposed by Councillor Drummond that this committee do co-opt Mr William Fisher as an additional member. Do I have a seconder?'

Nobody twitched a muscle. I remained hovering six inches above the seat of my chair in the attitude of a gorilla waiting for its next banana. Come on, you silly sods.

After what seemed like a full minute, a youngish man in a broad-striped shirt and biscuit-coloured linen suit – Jack Dance, the main-fuse-box live wire of Creative City Consortium – slowly raised his gold pen to the angle of about ninety degrees.

'Seconded by Mr Dance. Those in favour? Against? Then it is resolved that Mr William Fisher be co-opted to the Shepford Festival Standing Committee. Welcome to these proceedings, Mr Fisher.'

Year year. Does that mean I can sit down now?

'I believe you may sit down now, Mistah Fishah,' quavered a leather-faced old ratbag who sounded as if she had been gargling with gin all morning. I bared my teeth at her, nodded stiffly at one or two random faces, and sat, sweeping my agenda to the floor as I pulled in my chair. The smirk played a fleeting return visit to Purchase's face and it suddenly came to me why he'd been so anxious to get me on his committee. He wanted to make me look an idiot in front of Drummond.

'Bill,' Oscar whispered in my ear as I retrieved my agenda. 'He figures you're batting out of your league. Now lemme say this about that. You wouldn't have gatten this far if you hadn't

275

been in the World Series class right from the start. Don't let me down, kid.'

'I now call upon the secretary to read the minutes of the previous meeting,' said Purchase.

The committee secretary, whom I had never met but who looked like retired bank manager material to me, rose to his feet and in a monotonous gabble began to read *War and Peace*. I arranged my agenda, scribble-pad, newly sharpened pencil and other paraphernalia into a pleasing pattern and took in the other faces. I knew most of them through having avoided them in the course of my job. Besides Purchase, Drummond and Jack Dance there were a couple of parsons; an amiable councillor called Hopkinson who seemed to be number two to all the offices that Drummond was number one in; the odd youth leader; a small collection of Rotarians; two bearded men and one moustached woman representing the arts; the distaff side otherwise being catered for by various ratbags from organizations such as the Women's Institute and the Townswomen's Guild. Most of them were fiddling with their pencils and so, even though it meant destroying the symmetry of my arrangement, I did the same. I began to lose my self-consciousness. Nobody was staring at me, wondering what a boy of fifteen was doing at such a gathering. I was unnoticed, unexceptional, adult.

I had been right to wear my dark blue suit – my best one, the one in which the pornographic letter from Helen had once made its undetected journey to the dry-cleaners and back. All the men present, except Jack Dance in his smart linen job, were wearing dark blue suits. I fitted in with them, melted into their company. I was willing to bet, though, that none of them carried in his inside pocket a document featuring the phrase, '*You do not yet know all the things I can do with my tongue.*'

The bank manager type droned on and I felt restless. I patted my inside pocket to make sure that Helen's letter was still there. Although I had congratulated myself on my nerves of steel for keeping such explosive material in so hazardous a hidey-hole, I was in fact on solid ground. Jeanette lacked the instinct of curiosity and she never went through my pockets; it was safer there than hidden in a drawer where it might be found by accident, or locked in my office desk which might be opened with duplicate keys. However, as I clutched feverishly at my jacket, probably confirming my adult status to the rest of the committee in that I appeared to be in the convulsions of cardiac arrest, I realized that I was not on solid ground after all, and that Jeanette's deficiency in curiosity must recently have been remedied, for the letter had vanished.

Christ, double Christ and treble Christ. '... *referred back to the musical events sub-committee,*' drivelled our worthy hon. sec. Shut up, you silly old goat, and let me concentrate. Did I move the letter myself? No, I positively didn't. I checked that it was still there when the suit came back from the cleaners and I haven't even looked at it since. All right, then: has it fallen out of my pocket? Impossible: stop clutching at straws. '... *exploratory discussion with Inspector Corcoran of the Police Band.*' Has my mother found it? Quadruple Christ. Unlikely, though: she never goes into our bedroom. Jeanette has found it, Q.E.D. Jeanette has got my letter.

I now, in retrospect, registered Jeanette's odd behaviour of the last few days. With other things on my mind, I had been vaguely aware that she was acting strangely, without really taking it in. Usually, after one of her in-depth explorations of our marriage, she remained in a state of perkiness for some days, uplifted by all the promises of fresh starts. This time she had reverted quickly to a condition of broodiness, and one evening had alarmed me by emerging from the bathroom red-eyed and puffy-cheeked. To my relief she had gone almost immediately to bed, although it was her turn for the night watch. But then the night watch as an institution seemed to have been abandoned lately. Even though Jeanette or my mother sometimes did still sit up with me, neither seemed to have much to say. That, as I now came to appreciate, was because unknown to me we had not been on speaking terms for a week.

I would bluff it out. After all, the letter didn't have my name on it: 'My darling' could be anybody. It could be Hattersley. Hattersley was having it off rotten with Sheilagh and he had dropped her incriminating letter on the floor of the King's Head Doubles Bar that night when I had got home very late because of the Shepford Publicity Club meeting. We had been having a sandwich and a glass of beer before the meeting commenced, Hattersley had gone on ahead of me to switch off his car lights, and I had found Sheilagh's letter, signed in her middle name of Helen which Hattersley always called her, on the floor. I had put it in my pocket to return to him and then it had completely gone out of my mind.

Jeanette's hash settled, I returned to the business at hand, feeling I had just been through a very white-faced period indeed and wondering if the carafe of water was there for ornament or could you drink it? '... *by a majority of fifteen votes to one to protest vigorously to Shepford District Council, Councillors Drummond and Hopkinson abstaining.*' The panic was not over yet, I could tell by my heart thumping. It wasn't Jeanette, because her hash was settled; it was something else, some other nagging worry that I'd just been reminded of. Sheilagh. Something to do with Sheilagh. Yes. Sheilagh had taken yet another message from Detective-constable Carpenter and would it be all right if he dropped into the office when he was passing this way?

Where was I going to find a set of golf clubs?

'... *make final representations to the Arts Council with the object of extracting a definite yea or nay.*' I had tried every second-hand shop in Shepford (of which there was a far greater number, I might remind Detective-constable Carpenter, than either he or I had imagined). I had scanned the sales and wants columns of the *Evening Mail* which promised Welch dressers and encyclopdldlds as new, but not glof culbs. Finally, clutching my Access card (and pretending it was the American Express card I coveted), I had ventured into the town's only sports shop, prepared to pay full price. They had had golf clubs on order from their depot, but a computer error had sent them cricket bats.

Recognizing an anxiety neurosis when I saw it, I was by now casting about in my mind for other things to fret over while I was about it. The Access card, which should have played only a walking-on part in these ruminations, seemed to linger in my thoughts. It was because I had not had the chance of using it lately; that was what made me feel guilty. I wondered if the Access people were offended. I saw two men at the Access headquarters, quite senior executives they would be, frowning over my statement and asking where they had gone wrong. 'A man in Mr Fisher's position, steady salary, you'd think he'd be glad of the facilities we offer, and yet he hardly uses them at all.' I resolved to run up more credit, to please them. I would buy a biscuit-coloured linen suit like Jack Dance's.

My brow cleared as I disposed of what seemed to be the major of all my worries and I saw that the readings from Tolstoy had ceased and that I was enclosed in a plantation of upstretched hands. I rapidly shot up my own arm, only to receive a withering look from Purchase.

'You must abstain, Mr Fisher. Since you weren't present at the last meeting, you can hardly be expected to judge whether the minutes are correct or no.'

Oh.

'Carried unanimously. Item two, venue. Now I think we must deal with this as a matter of urgency. Are we satisfied with the Cornmarket as the traditional focal point of the Festival, bearing in mind the run-down condition of the area, or do we wish to explore the site adjacent to the Central Bus Station, taking into consideration the difficulty of access from the town centre proper?'

'Well, I may be a bit of an old sentimentalist,' said one of the business types, who looked less of an old sentimentalist than Heinrich Himmler, 'but I do rather look forward to standing on that Town Hall balcony once more, watching the procession go by.'

'And after all, we shan't get the chance next year, way things are going. What say, Percy?' said Councillor Hopkinson.

Drummond shot him a look that seemed to mean something, I couldn't guess what. But then I frequently didn't know why Shepford men gave each other funny looks, or what they were talking about half the time. I comforted myself that this was because they didn't know what they were talking about them-

279

selves, but at heart I suspected that I was not really well-informed enough for my job; and certainly not for Pisspot's job, not that I would ever get it now.

The Cornmarket enthusiasts won over the bus station faction, I once more abstaining, this time on the grounds that it didn't matter to me if they held their Festival in the marshalling yards. There were one or two other items of business, equally uninspiring, then Drummond moved briskly: 'Propose form selves usual working party,' there were some relieved 'Ayes' as the motion was put to the vote, and he and Purchase exchanged chairs. But of course: Purchase was nominally chairman but it was really Drummond who was running the shop, and this was how he swung it. Well, at least we'd get on faster now.

'As chairman working party, must stress time running short, get down nuts and bolts without further ado. Item one, publicity. Believe our newcomer's pigeon.'

A spasm of pain crossed his face as he pronounced the word 'publicity', and he shot me a look containing a fairly high element of personal dislike. Possibly he was thinking of the non-playing-down of the Prague beano by the *Evening Mail*; that kind of publicity, he was sure to believe, would be newcomer's pigeon.

They had all got copies of some balls that Pisspot and I had slung together, largely concerned with fictitious plans to flood the world media with invitations and press passes. In reality, we had long ago stopped bothering, for no one ever came. A man from one of the Birmingham papers had arrived one year, but only, it turned out after we had given him lunch, to visit his sister.

Feeling more nervous than I had judged I would be when rehearsing my speech in the bog earlier that day, I proceeded to guide the ratbags present through the balls in front of them, becoming uneasily aware as I went along that I was doing little more than plough through the stuff verbatim. The meeting grew restive, and I was relieved rather than otherwise when Purchase cut me short.

'While on the subject of television coverage, Mr Chairman,

if I may interrupt, I believe I am not too premature in revealing that we are almost certain of a three-minute item in the BBC-1 news-magazine from Birmingham, at quite a peak hour.'

Cries of 'Good!', 'Excellent!', 'Well done!' etc. The Women's Institute ratbag kept whinnying 'First clarss! First clarss! First clarss!' over and over again, until Drummond banged his gavel.

'I spoke to one of their research people only today about accommodation and so on,' Purchase continued. I saw that he was giving me a crafty look, and after he had gone on for some time in self-congratulatory vein, it was revealed why. 'There *is* one puzzling aspect, Mr Fisher, speaking through the chair. This lady got through to me as Festival chairman only because she had no success at all in getting through to *you*, Mr Fisher. She tells me that despite numerous telephone messages to your office over a period of several days, unfortunately you were unable to find the time to ring her back.'

This didn't go down well with Drummond. It wasn't meant to. Well you see, Mr Chairman, I thought all those calls were from an ex-mistress of mine who I am trying to avoid. Well she *sounded* like this ex-mistress of mine, according to Sheilagh, and Sheilagh should know, she's spoken to her often enough. And anyway, why is a research assistant at the BBC in Birmingham going around sounding like Helen?

I wonder what she looks like. I wonder if we can put her up at the Heritage Motor Lodge. I wonder if she likes vodka martinis.

Wait a minute. If Helen hasn't been calling me for the last three days, disguised as a research assistant at the BBC in Birmingham, what *has* she been doing? A three-day silence: that's unusual. She's up to something.

But personal problems of that kind would have to wait: I had a personal problem. 'I think I can clear that up, Mr Chairman,' I said, noting with satisfaction that the quaver had left my voice. 'It's perfectly true I've been stalling these Birmingham people, because we may have bigger fish to fry. The fact is that we've every hope of being featured on the *Nationwide* programme from London, which of course is networked, er, nation-wide.'

More lawks-a-mussy cries from the gang; a nice line in foiled-again expressions from Purchase; and, more to the point, some congratulatory words from Drummond.

'– feather in cap, certainly would! How soon know one way other?'

'Question really sitting down hammering out details, Mr Chairman. Thought good idea, committee agrees, go up Town discuss personally with producer.'

Most of the assembled ratbags were braying *Year year*, while those with business interests yapped excitely about the need to show something of Shepford industry as well as the lighter side, and the Women's Institute ratbag resumed her chant of 'First clarss! First clarss!' and I saw that as well as doing myself a bit of good with Drummond – not that I any longer had much reason for doing myself a bit of good with Drummond – I had also won myself a free trip to London.

Let Purchase pick the bones out of *that* when he saw it on my swindle sheet. And, when he had tired of the war of nerves he was undoubtedly waging, and it came to the inevitable in-quest on the swindle sheets he had already impounded, let him also pick the bones out of *To hospitality at the Heritage Motor Lodge for Mr R. Horniman and Mrs G. Lichfield, BBC representatives, to explore possibilities of TV coverage at Shep-ford Festival: £5.20.* I should have made it £8.50. How much, I wondered, could I sting them for on the London beano?

I would be able to take Helen. No I wouldn't, because I'd finished with Helen. And another thing, why was she avoiding me, and what the hell was she up to?

My moment of glory passed, and Drummond moved on to the next business, which was pressing need brighten up pro-gramme, all very usual sideshows, *Murder in Cathedral*, knobbly knees contest, egg-and-spoon race what have you, what wanted was something really original, really first-class tip-top original idea.

I decided at first to sit this one out; but then, it seemed, so did

282

everybody else. At any rate there was a profound silence broken only by the sound of a furrow-browed, rat-faced youth leader snapping his pencil in two. He was probably plucking up courage to suggest naked wrestling.

Encouraged by my previous success, but more to say something than because I had anything to say, I opened my mouth and the words 'dog show' came out. I had no idea why I was saying 'dog show', which had entered my mind unbidden. I could equally have said 'Bicycle bell' or 'gas stove' or 'luggage rack'.

'Dog show? Say dog show?' Drummond was looking at me with great distaste, as if I had suggested a ladies' shit-shovelling contest.

'Er – yes.'

'Hardly an original suggestion,' murmured Purchase, examining his fingernails.

All right then, buggerlugs. Let's *make* it original.

'I'm not thinking of the usual dog show,' I said. Aren't I? What kind of dog show *am* I thinking of, then? An *un*usual one, obviously. 'This one would be different.' Oh, yes? In what way?

'In what way?' asked the gin-gargling ratbag.

· 'Well.' And more by a process of elimination than anything else, the idea burrowed desperately through my skull. If not an ordinary dog show, then an extraordinary dog show. If not the kind of hound you got at Cruft's, then the kind of hound you didn't get at Cruft's. If not saddle-faced dog trainers who all seemed to look like the gin-gargling ratbag opposite, then some other kind of trainer.

'A *children*'s dog show,' I said. 'And any child who has a dog, or who can borrow a dog for the day, can enter. And there'd be prizes for the ugliest mongrel, and the spottiest spotted dog, and the most disobedient dog, and the silliest dog, and ...'

I tailed off. It was obvious that everyone present owned a best-of-breed Borzoi. I had not so much lost my audience as never been within ten miles of it from the start. Sod them, then. Let someone suggest hoop-la.

And then the frozen silence was cracked by Jack Dance, speaking for the first time. 'Like it!' he said. 'Like – *it*!'

A buzz of interest. Having made about twenty million pounds in ten years, largely by pulling down most of the shops in Shepford and putting up car-stacks to accommodate the anticipated rise in the volume of shoppers, Dance was widely-respected as a man of vision.

'Mr Chairman,' he began in the mid-Atlantic twang he had brought back with him from a trip to New York a couple of years ago, 'I have some experience of the media – or should I say I have some experience of avoiding the media.' (Sniggers.) 'But I know what the media want. And I am telling all of you present that a children's dog show, on these lines, with the ugliest mongrel and what he said, will hit every newspaper in Fleet Street. Think of the pictures! Five-year-old Suzie Faffernackle and her cross-eyed pooch – first time it's ever won a prize! Mr Chairman, you know me, you know Jack Dance, and Jack Dance tells you, ladies and gentlemen, this is a *winner*.'

As if getting instant playback on a tape-recorder, I was repeating Jack Dance's speech word for word in my mind, but I, not he, was making it and I was on my feet in my biscuit-coloured suit and receiving the *year years* and *splendids* and *first clarsses*, and Drummond was beaming at me (instead of at Jack Dance) and saying asked for tip-top original idea and by golly been presented with tip-top original idea; and then the pandemonium was cut into by the Women's Institute ratbag, who pointed a trembling finger and screeched: 'Good heavens!'

I followed her unbelieving gaze and saw Helen waving at me through the window. This was rather weird, because we were on the fifth floor.

Others looked too. Some rose to their feet. The one or two who were still capable of dashing, dashed to the window. Those with their backs to the wall craned their heads round, just in time to see the workman's cradle in which Helen was precariously balanced being hoisted up out of sight. Fortunately all those who might have recognized her – Purchase, Drummond and Jack Dance, another of her many ex-employers, could only have caught a glimpse of her bottle-green trouser suit.

'What blue blazes that?' barked Drummond.

How did Helen know I was here? Easy: she rang the office and said she was a probation officer involved with the disappearance of my godson Michael, and how could she get in touch with me urgently? But Sheilagh or Patsy would have recognized her voice. Try this, then: she has been rampaging around the office and asking questions. No: because they will still have recognized her voice.

'I believe I can explain that rather startling interruption,' I said. 'I gave permission for a lady photographer from *Time Magazine* to go up to the roof to take some panoramic photographs of the town.'

'Why devil didn't go up lift?'

'She's probably looking for an unusual angle, Mr Chairman – the new Shepford seen with that builder's crane over there in the foreground. That's the kind of symbolic picture they like, and she couldn't have got that shot from the roof. I remember discussing it,' I said, turning to Purchase and speaking quite weightily, 'when I entertained the head of Time-Life London bureau at the Heritage Motor Lodge recently. Of course, you know what these American magazines are like – it will probably come to nothing.'

I know how she knows I was here: it's because she rang Hattersley. But Hattersley recognizes her voice too: he ought to, because he's taken one or two of those calls himself, when the girls have been out in tandem making coffee or having a pee. But he's never asked me what's going on between me and whoever. Why not? Because something is going on between him and somebody, and we have this tacit agreement that we don't talk about it. I've caught him, often enough, and even more often enough in recent weeks, making mysterious phone calls and bringing them to an abrupt end when I've entered the office. So there's obviously somebody: how do I know this somebody isn't Helen? And when I talk about the office to Helen, why does she no longer ask after Hattersley though she always asks after Pisspot and Sheilagh and Patsy? 'I'm faithful to you outside home, but I can't help appetite.' But what if the outside-home supply drops? We haven't had each other for a month.

Stop this silly train of thought, Fisher, it's silly. But watch Hattersley.

The meeting went on: a very long discussion about first-aid tents and ambulance stations that appeared to grip the ratbags among us more than it gripped me. What was Helen doing? Did she intend to throw herself off the roof, or what? No, of course she didn't: but she had got a foothold on these premises. I would have to get her off these premises. If I didn't get her off these premises she was likely to roam anywhere, into Purchase's office even, reminding him as he got back from the committee meeting that they had met once before, when the drinks had been on Bill Fisher. I would have to get up to the roof and confront her, alone and face-to-face at last.

'Other business?' intoned Drummond, closing his folder.

Yes. But it's personal.

It had been a very short interview with Helen, although not the very short interview I had had in mind when belting up the last flight of stairs and on to the roof with a view to kicking her off it. She had been standing on the very edge, facing me as I came out through the skylight door, and I really did think she might fall, if not jump.

'You do owe me five minutes,' she said, as I knew she would. But her seriousness surprised and disturbed me after the prank she had just pulled. She was very sober: I didn't know why I had to assume that Helen must have been drunk to persuade the workmen to hoist her up here.

'All right then, five minutes. Come away from there, for God's sake!' (And I thought: when on roofs, people really do say 'Come away from there, for God's sake!')

'We can't talk here, can we? Won't they be locking up the building soon?'

'Do you want five minutes or five bloody hours?'

'I'd like to see you at the Heritage. Do you mind that? After all, if it's to be the last time, I think you should let me choose where it's going to be. Isn't it the least you can do?'

Possibly. And I'll bet you've booked a bloody room there, under the name of Fisher. I didn't fancy her at all. She didn't know that I'd just passed a test: if I didn't fancy her now, on the roof, which would have been an erotic adventure, then I didn't fancy her.

She had her own car with her, likely parked in the Mayor's reserved bay, so we agreed to meet at the Heritage Motor Lodge in half an hour, give or take ten minutes for possible congestion on Route Four, a new expressway that had recently been bull-dozed through that side of the town. I would have to tell Jeanette I had been visiting Pisspot in hospital.

We went down the lift in silence, I saw her safely out of the building and went back to my office to clear up my desk. Al-though it was not yet six the two girls had skived off, Hattersley was missing also, but Detective-constable Carpenter was present, sitting in my chair and skimming through the dummy copy of *Pageantry with Progress* (new edition) that we had managed to paste together during the week.

'Good evening, Mr Fisher. Sorry for making myself at home – your colleague was sure you'd be back.'

Oh. Yes. Be my guest. And other noises.

'I've been glancing at your guide-book, hope you don't mind.' Not at all. 'Quite interesting, an improvement on last year. Though I couldn't help noticing, why it's printed in Birming-ham. Considering all the number of printing firms in Shepford.'

Oh, indeed, indeed. Almost as many printing firms as second-hand shops and I haven't got your golf clubs and I'm in a hurry.

Try to *look* as if you're in a hurry, and he mightn't ask about the golf clubs.

'Look, I'm sorry –' I began, reaching for my coat.

'Am I keeping you, Mr Fisher? Am I holding you up?' I didn't like his tone, but on the other hand I did. He was trying to sound snide and not quite succeeding. He was young, like me, trying to be grown-up like me, but making nearly the same kind of hash of his efforts. You're playing at detectives, Carpenter, but you can't persuade yourself you're a real one. I hope. No – I don't hope, I know. I recognize the tone of voice, the hackneyed adult phrases, the wooden mannerisms. It's like calling to like.

'Do you think I could possibly –?' Another unfinished sentence from me, this one left uninterrupted. Do you think I could possibly never meet you again? Do you think I could possibly just leave, go, and assume that all this golf club nonsense has been a bad dream? Do you think I could possibly ring you tomorrow? was what I really meant to say, but I was afraid of entering the falsetto register.

He's better at it than I am. He has more nerve, or can see himself in a mental mirror looking as if he had more nerve.

'I'm sure it's inconvenient, Mr Fisher,' said Detective-constable Carpenter, plodding on like Councillor Drummond as if I'd never opened my mouth. 'I was wondering if you could spare five minutes or so for a quick drink.'

'Well, it *is* a bit short notice –' I had hit top C.

'It's not about your golf clubs, Mr Fisher, that can wait. It's about another matter.'

'Oh, yes?' Top G, if there was such a note. 'What's that, exactly?'

'If you *did* have time for a drink. Just a private conversation.'

My God, he's come to blackmail me.

9

HELEN and I, with Detective-constable Carpenter between us, sat in our favourite booth in the Heritage Motor Lodge bar, and Helen did not seem best pleased, for tears were trickling down her cheeks.

Grotesquely embarrassed myself, so that there was a pain in my diaphragm as the result of hunching myself up so tensely, I was glad to see that our plain-clothes gooseberry was equally discomfited. His solution, or attempted solution, to his novel social dilemma was to avoid looking at Helen, to pretend indeed that she was not among those present, and to address his entirely desultory remarks to me. My own policy was to follow his example.

The conversation with Detective-constable Carpenter as I drove him to the Heritage Motor Lodge had been of the what-fine weather and they're-making-a-cockup-of-these-roads variety, the kind of chat you would expect to have with the bank manager before he opened your file. I had been in a state of great apprehension ever since leaving the Civic Centre, and was growing increasingly fearful that he was about to get down to brass tacks, whatever those would turn out to be. (Perhaps he was waiting for Helen to leave, in which case he would wait a long time.) But more than I was growing increasingly fearful, I was increasingly fancying Helen. I always did when she cried. I wanted to lick the tears away, savouring the salt taste on my tongue, then ask her how she felt about a quick bunk-up in London. If we got the first commuter train in the morning we could be in Euston by breakfast-time, find one of those hotels where they make you pay in advance so they don't know or care whether you're staying overnight or not, and crawl back on our hands and knees for the slow train at half-past mid-

night. Allowing five minutes off to ring the *Nationwide* programme to ask how they felt about covering a boring children's
dog show, this would give us thirteen hours and twenty minutes
in bed, thus extending our golden June of shagging into a glorious July.

Whatever Detective-constable Carpenter wanted of me, he
was certainly enjoying his vodka martinis. He and I were near-
ing the end of our second, while Helen, whose dejection had not
affected her thirst, had finished her third (assuming, as I could
not assume, that she had had only one before we arrived), and
was now toying pitifully with her empty glass.

'I don't know what they put in these,' said Detective-constable
Carpenter, 'but they certainly carry a kick. Or is it because I'm
not used to them?'

That's a trick question if ever I heard one. Has Purchase been
on to him, I wondered? Has Detective-constable Carpenter cast
his no-doubt eagle eye over my swindle sheets?

Another tear trickled down Helen's cheek. Don't my love.
Or if you have to, do it in private when you've wiped your eye
make-up off and your bum is nicely settled across two hotel
pillows.

Censoring my words very carefully, I said in my best Publicity Club of Shepford voice, 'They're a very bad habit to
get into, I can tell you. I'm afraid I've been led astray by certain of our American guests.'

'What – dragged screaming to the bar, are you? Spending all
your hard-earned cash on forced entertaining? You can't tell
me! The old swindle sheet – *I* know!' Here it comes.

Not licking my lips, but wanting to, I said as if offended by
the rogueish innuendo: 'It's all very well, but all these visiting
firemen have to be fed and watered, you know.' The pompous
mixed metaphor was borrowed, with gratitude, from Pisspot,
'*And* in our own free time,' I added.

'Get away!' joshed Detective-constable Carpenter with the
off-duty familiarity that he had begun to slip into with his
second martini. 'You enjoy every minute! Expense account,

civic lunches, receptions, trips to Prague and back – I wish I had your job!'

He thinks I'm more senior than I am. But I can't tell him I'm more junior than he thinks. That means he's going to blackmail me for more than I earn, if he's going to blackmail me at all. I wish he would get on with it, one way or the other.

I badly needed another drink but didn't know whether I ought to order another round. For motives too obscure to analyse, I had been trying to put myself over to Detective-constable Carpenter as a two-drink man: probably something to do with the wish to present the image of a solid, upright citizen. I would have been helped in this effort if the solid, upright citizen's mistress could have seen her way to stop weeping into her empty glass.

'What about one for the road, then?' cried Detective-constable Carpenter, rubbing his hands briskly, and that settled it. I made a twirling finger motion to Harry the barman who I was pretty sure would have a substantial batch of martinis already prepared in anticipation of another evening with his couple of lovebirds, as I had once overheard him describing us to one of his clients.

'And then I must go.' What I meant, for Detective-constable Carpenter's benefit, was that whatever he had to say to me he had better get it said; and for my own benefit, that I intended to leave when he did, on the pretext of continuing our conference in the car park. This would be a shitty thing to do to Helen but then I had often done shitty things in my life and I might as well behave in character. Besides, she was sniffling quite noisily now and her nose was reddening, and I had stopped fancying her.

Detective-constable Carpenter, either to hide his embarrassment at her performance or because he was getting to the point of our interview at last, said heartily: 'So you'll be missing your game of golf on Sundays?' And upon this Helen delivered herself of a hiccoughing wail and sobbed: 'He doesn't *per – per – per – play* golf and I wish you'd go *away*!'

'Napkin, madam?' This was from Harry, who had just very smoothly served the drinks. He handed her the tea-towel affair that waiters carry over their arms and she buried her face in it. Harry continued to hang around, evidently hoping for the return of his property. I signalled to him to piss off.

It was impossible to keep up the show of ignoring Helen's distress. I took her hand across the table and repeated, 'Helen, Helen, Helen, Helen,' in what was meant to be a soothing tone, although I failed at keeping a tinge of exasperation out of it. Detective-constable Carpenter assumed a sickly, lopsided grin and in a fairish replica of the heartiness that had kicked off her outburst, observed: 'You'll be watering your dry martini, carry on like that!'

Helen put the mascara-stained cloth aside and dabbed at her nostrils with the crumpled Kleenex that had served her during the trickling-tears period. She took a few deep breaths and seemed to compose herself. She would have been less composed had she known that her face now looked as if she had been delivering coke.

'I'm sorry. I'm all right now.'

'Go and wash the mascara off your face.'

'Yes. In a minute.'

'Never mind, love,' said Detective-constable Carpenter. 'Worse things happen at sea.'

She favoured him with a weak smile and attacked her martini. After some down-the-hatching and first-todaying and all-the-besting, Detective-constable Carpenter did the same.

'No,' he said, to indicate both a change of subject and the dismissal of the painful Helen interlude from his mind. 'You were saying about Councillor Drummond the other day. Quite a character, isn't he? Our future mayor? I expect you see a lot of him?'

My last excuse to Detective-constable Carpenter for not setting off on my long-promised exploration of Shepford's second-hand shops had been that I had a lunch engagement with Councillor Drummond. I might even – for there had been no one in the office to eavesdrop when he telephoned – have expanded on this a little, suggesting that appointments with Drummond were taking up most of my time lately. A little name-dropping, I had reasoned, could do no harm, particularly as Drummond was chairman of the Watch Committee and presumably in a position to get nosey plain-clothes coppers put back on the beat.

I could understand his interest in Drummond – any man of ambition in Shepford had to be interested in Drummond, and I had no doubt that Detective-constable Carpenter had dreams of promotion when the Case of the Missing Golf Clubs was finally cracked. But I couldn't see why he thought this an appropriate moment for vicarious social climbing, when Helen had just told him in so many words to shove off.

He's been tailing me, and he knows I didn't have lunch with Drummond.

'Well, you know what Drummond's like – always busy-busy, rushing about, doing fifteen things at once, cancelling appointments at the last minute,' I said. 'So I don't see all that much of him these days, no.'

'Oh. I somehow had the impression you more or less lived in each other's pockets.'

Yes, I know you did, you snide bugger, and if you fancy yourself as Inspector Hawkeye, give me your theory on the sound we can both hear as of water dripping into a zinc bucket. It is Helen tapping her foot rhythmically against the central metal column supporting our table, and what it means is that if you do not state the purpose of your visit very soon and then clear off, there will be an ugly scene.

'No,' he ploughed on. 'I just wondered, what he's like, that's all. I mean I've *seen* him, to look at, but never to speak to. Just wondered what he's like.'

I gave him some shorthand impressions of Drummond, omitting that I thought he was a self-important twat who made me feel like an office boy; and then I added, in the hope of placating Helen by dragging her into the conversation: 'You should talk to our friend on the right. She used to work for him.'

'*Did* you? Did you really?' He made it sound as if this was very interesting. 'That's very interesting. Very interesting.'

The repetition of the phrase made me suspect that Detective-constable Carpenter was half-pissed on three vodka martinis, but there was no time for speculation on this theme. Helen's foot-tapping came to an end with a crescendo that rocked the table, and she put down, or rather slammed down, her empty glass.

'Tom – is it?'

'Jack.' He had introduced himself to her by his first name, which I remembered thinking had removed any need for calling him officer from time to time.

'Jack. I'm going to be very rude. It must be painfully obvious that you've walked into the middle of a family row. Anyway, a personal row. But you're sitting there, and sitting there, and it's how's your golf and how's Councillor *fuck*ing Drummond, and this, and that, and I'm very sorry but it *must* be obvious, so why – won't– you – *go*!'

'Hel-en!'

'No. No. No. The lady has spoken. Never let it be said that J. Carpenter esquire cannot take a hint.'

'I'm sorry,' said Helen. 'And I must look a mess. I'm off to wash my face.'

Detective-constable Carpenter, who despite his protestations had shown no other signs of leaving, now rose in the kind of ape-crouch he must have learned at Police Federation annual dinners with his lady wife. I did the same, feeling more of a fool than he seemingly did; and as Helen stalked off towards the Ladies I watched her retreating bum, fancying her, I had an idea that I had seen a figure flitting across the archway connecting with the hotel reception area, and that the figure had somehow looked as if it had been hovering there for some few seconds; moreover, that the figure was that of my colleague Hattersley.

We resumed our seats, I puzzled, Detective-constable Carpenter looking less disconcerted than I thought he would have been.

'Quite a lady.'

'Yes. Sorry about all that. She gets a bit hysterical.'

'Oh –!' followed by some deprecatory noises made by the tongue against the roof of the mouth, indicating that he had come across more of these scenes than I had had hot dinners.

What the bloody hell is Hattersley doing here?

'By the way,' I said, 'you won't, er?' With a jerk of my head in what I judged to be a roughly south-easterly direction, embracing the scuffed lawns and weed-grown paths of my home environment, I signified my anxiety about Jeanette learning of the tempestuous assignation just witnessed.

'Oh –!' An identical set of noises, this time accompanied by a screwing-up of the face suggesting that we were both men of the world and that for his own part he was having policewomen and metermaids rotten every day of the week.

Producing a wallet even more wafer-thin than Purchase's, Detective-constable Carpenter now made another sound: 'Ar –?' to ask if he was right in thinking that he would not be pressed too hard for his share of the bill. A succession of 'Tuh-tuh-tuh-tuh!' sounds from me reassured him on that point; whereupon, as he tucked his wallet away and seemed ready to leave, I thought a return to the Queen's English might prove useful.

'So. This has been very pleasant, but I'm still not sure what it's all about.'

'Not about anything. Just thought it'd be nice to have a drink and a chat. Oh, and before I forget – *golf clubs*.'

Shall I tell him the truth? No: he would arrest me for wasting police time or something. I bet he enjoys arresting people, this one. I bet he watches himself doing it. *This is me being a real detective and apprehending a tea-leaf.* A snapshot for his album of adult moments, to remind himself that he has really experienced them.

Reverting to the cough-and-grunt method of communication, I acknowledged the urgency of the golf club question.

'Just where you got them from, that's all, so I can get a proper description from whoever sold them. Sorry to nag, Bill, but out of twenty-nine items nicked out of that Fairfields estate, there's only one that I couldn't identify if I came across it and that's

295

your fizzing golf clubs. "What make?" "*Don't know.*" "What type of clubs?" "*Oh, don't know.*" "What kind of bag, is it zip-up or what?" "*Ooh, think so, but can't remember.*" God blimey, Bill, had you been knocking back these dry martinis when you bought them or what?'

I murmured something about my notorious vagueness when it came to personal property. What was uppermost in my mind was that now that he had started calling me Bill, I would have to start calling him Jack, as soon as possible. And why was I flattered to be called Bill by the police, since it was common knowledge that they always put themselves on first-name terms with criminals?

'But taking your point, *Jack*,' I said doggedly, having acknowledged his lecture, 'you can't tell me you've come all the way down here just to talk about my golf clubs, *Jack*.'

'I didn't come to talk about anything in particular. Told you – I wanted a drink. Even coppers are human, though it may take a bit of believing.'

'But it was about *something*, Jack, wasn't it?' Too many Jacks. 'It was about nothing!'

'Excuse me, gentlemen.' This was Harry the barman, who I had vaguely noticed approaching us after answering his internal telephone. He retrieved his mascara-stained napkin, glanced at me with a sigh and an upward roll of the eyes to convey mutual understanding of the female temperament, and said to Detective-constable Carpenter, 'Was you expecting someone, sir?'

'Yes, I was,' replied Detective-constable Carpenter, to my surprise.

'He's waiting in the Polo Lounge, sir.'

'I'm on my way.'

Detective-constable Carpenter got to his feet. I was gratified to note that I had been right about him not being able to hold his martinis, for he lurched slightly while manoeuvring his way around the table.

'Duty calls,' he said mysteriously, playing at detectives again. Then, having turned away, he turned back, revealing a foxy expression signalling that he was about to take me into his confidence at last.

'For what it's worth, Bill, I'll tell you what it was. *I* thought you knew Councillor Drummond better than it seems you do. And *I* thought if you *did* know him at all well, and you *did* get the chance to throw a word in –. No: the thing is, Bill, you mightn't think it in my type of my job, but my type of job's the same as any other, when it comes to getting on. A word in the right ear – you know? Still. Forget it.'

You're a cheeky cow, Carpenter.

Seemingly even more pissed than I'd thought he was, he staggered off, waving aside my relieved but generalized assurances about words in right ears. Not only a cheeky cow, Carpenter, but a twat, and not only a twat but a fraud. A juvenile lead masquerading as a heavy.

This choice of metaphor pleased me, and I ruminated on its wider implications as, mildly puzzled about something, I crossed to the bar where Harry was polishing glasses. If Detective-constable Carpenter was a juvenile lead, what was I? A juvenile lead too, that went without saying. Helen was a juvenile lead, but my mother and Jeanette were heavies. Drummond was a heavy, Purchase was a heavy, my rat-faced neighbours were all heavies. Hattersley was a heavy trying to look like a juvenile lead. Pisspot was a juvenile lead who could have played the heavy if he'd wanted to. And we were all type-cast in these roles, and nothing that we could do, or resolve to do, could alter the way we played our parts.

'Harry, who did you say was waiting in the Polo Lounge?'

'No idea, Mr Fisher. He just asked for your friend. "Tell him I'm in the Polo Lounge," that's all he said.'

'Did he ask for him by name?'

'No, he didn't, come to think of it,' said Harry with an air of excited mystification that I found too conspiratorial for my taste. Harry was a heavy who would have liked to have been a juvenile lead. ' "The gentleman with Mr Fisher," that's what he called him. "Tell the gentleman with Mr Fisher I'll be waiting in the Polo Lounge." '

'Thanks, Harry.'

He looked at me as if he expected me to slip him a quid for the information: or was it that I would have enjoyed the gesture of giving him one? Anyway, he didn't get it. Behind me, Helen was resuming her place at our table. I told Harry to provide more drinks and headed for the men's room, but made a slight detour once I was out of Helen's eyeline, so that I could peep into the Polo Lounge. Hattersley and Detective-constable Carpenter were sitting in the far corner, both of them crouched over a low coffee table, and they were studying some documents.

One of my problems, Helen, is that whenever I have a problem to face, I always have another problem concurrent with it, which seems to take precedence. So bear with me if I seem abstracted. I cannot give my full attention to anything, because too many things need my full attention. My life has chosen to arrange itself on ramshackle lines, like a badly-wrapped parcel about to burst open; I can secure one corner of it only by disturbing the others, which then must be secured in turn.

'You never told me you played golf.'

'I don't play golf.'

'He said you did.'

'He thinks I do.'

After this exchange from the Shepford Little Theatre production of *Private Lives*, all was silence again until Helen dampened a finger and ran it meditatively along the rim of her glass, producing a piercing hum that, as it was meant to do, hastened Harry to our table with my fifth, and Helen's sixth, martini. I was more sober than I deserved to be at this stage of the evening.

'I reckon Harry's making these to a new formula. One part vodka to six parts ice-water.'

'There's some people at the bar. He doesn't want a scene.'

'If it comes to that,' I said, observing, as Helen hadn't, that the people mentioned were Jack Dance and a woman who didn't look very much as if she were Mrs Jack Dance, 'neither do I.'

'You needn't worry. There won't be one.'

How did Hattersley know where to find Detective-constable Carpenter? Straightforward enough: a message scribbled on his desk-pad while I was out of the office having a pee. But why didn't he come into the bar, instead of lurking about like the Phantom of the Opera, then making cryptic phone calls from the Polo Lounge? And why hadn't Carpenter told me who he was meeting, instead of all that 'Duty calls' stuff? And if they didn't want me to see them together, why meet here? Or was I *meant* to see them together?

Detective-constable Carpenter is playing at detectives, that's what it is. The juvenile lead is playing at detectives. But what's the heavy doing? I would like to know what Hattersley is playing at.

Come on, Helen. Say your piece.

I wonder if Jeanette wonders where I am? Yes: because what with the shock of finding Detective-constable Carpenter sitting at my desk, I forgot to call her to say I was visiting Pisspot in hospital. She must think I am now sitting in a bar somewhere with the author of '*You do not yet know all the things I can do with my tongue.*' I ought to ring her. I could say I'm in the Heritage Motor Lodge with Jack Dance, discussing a children's dog show.

You have to speak first, Helen.

She didn't take a deep breath as I thought she would, or start any kind of speech, she came in at a tangent, speaking in a far-off voice.

'We were so close.'

Yes. We were. We were so close at times that no population census could have categorized us apart.

'Yes. We were.'

'We were one.' She was very calm and articulate, and so direct and reasonable in her approach that anyone who didn't know her might have thought she was talking sense. 'You were me and I was you. We were each other, whenever we made love. We didn't know who was which, it was as close as that.'

Yes. Well. You say these things, Helen, and you're listening to your own voice saying them, but what do they mean, exactly?

We were very good in bed, and on tables, and in the backs of cars, and in haystacks and fields and woods; and we could have been very good on the roof of the Civic Centre, if I'd fancied you, but we were by no means one and by no means close on that particular occasion. Are you sure this isn't simply another miracle of the age of technology – that we are two mass-produced parts, separately drawn from stores, which just happen to interlock to an accuracy of one-thousandth of an inch?

'Yes. It was.'

'Then what's gone wrong?'

Jeanette asked the same question and I couldn't tell her, because I can't tell her things. I can tell Helen anything except the things I don't know, and this is one of them.

'Playing silly buggers, for one thing.'

' "Would you say you slept in twin beds, or not in twin beds?" Answer : not in twin beds.'

I gave her a flinching smile acknowledging this kick in the balls, and she put out her hand and added : '*I'm* sorry, Bill.'

'I asked for it.'

'I mean I'm sorry about that night. I was very drunk. And I panicked when your wife answered the door. I *had* to say something.'

'You could have said good night.'

'Bill, you *know* I'm sorry. And all right. I'm Life President of the Gone Too Far Club. But that's not where it all went wrong, is it?'

'That and other escapades. Bogus phone calls. Careering up and down the walls of the Civic Centre in workmen's cradles.'

'And following you about like a shadow and being a nuisance. Bill, all that was to attract attention, because you were avoiding me. I only behave like that when you *are* avoiding me. So how can you say you don't want to see me because of the stupid things I do when you *have* stopped seeing me?'

You're a logical little devil on the quiet, aren't you, Helen? But there's a flaw in there somewhere.

'I don't know,' I said. 'But it's got to end.'

'What has? Our relationship, or my behaviour?'

'Both.'

'All right.' She drew a deep, resigned breath as if she accepted this ultimatum, which of course she didn't. (Nor did I, at heart, and that was why it all had to end. I had to stop seeing her because I couldn't stop seeing her: another of life's paradoxes.) 'Then tell me *why* it's got to end and I'll go away, and you won't have to worry because I promise I won't do anything silly.'

That's a tempting offer, Helen.

I said nothing, having nothing to say, and she went on: 'Look, Bill. The last time I was supposed to meet you here, and you'd gone, and I went and made that scene at your flat, you were going to tell me something. Tell me now what you were going to tell me then.'

I can't, because I wouldn't have told you anything that night, when it came to it. We would have drunk our martinis and finished up in the back of the car on that old disused road near the brickworks. 'The lay-by', as we have come to call it. That's why it has to end.

Jack Dance and his mistress had finished their drinks at the bar and were going in to dinner. He glanced in our direction and must have recognized us both, although he pretended not to. I wondered if Helen had been his mistress when she worked for him, since having mistresses seemed to be a habit with him.

'Can I ask you something, Helen?'

'That's why we're here, isn't it?'

'While there's been us, has there been anybody else?'

She smiled, too enigmatically for my liking.

'Does it matter?'

'Yes.'

'But I thought our relationship was all over?'

'It still matters.'

'Then whatever you say, it's not all over.'

No: I can see that. And if there *was* somebody else, as it might be Hattersley (what's he up to with Detective-constable Carpenter?), and I found the pair of you at it, I would have to

301

see you again, for the last big scene, and so that you could prove that it wasn't all over.

'Bill. Listen to me. When I fell in love with you I'd had three affairs, and you were the third one. That was all it was going to be; it was fun, it was exciting, and I needed it – not you at first, *it*, the affair – because there was something missing in my life and it was a kind of topping-up process, like the others. And I went through the usual spectrum of emotions – anticipation, pleasure, gratitude, and it should have stopped there, but it didn't. I sometimes wish it had, but it didn't. Because I'd found my missing piece. You complete me, Bill. I'm wildly in love with you.'

Thank you. And now I can answer the question, Helen, about what's gone wrong. It's because you sound as if you mean it; and even worse, as if you are not mistaken in what you say. I complete you and you complete me, insofar as I will ever be complete; and perhaps all that other stuff is true as well, about you being me and I being you, and how close we were and are. And that's why I shy away. I shy away from Jeanette because she never gets near me, and from you because you get too near.

'And no,' said Helen, 'there hasn't been anybody else. And won't be. And couldn't be. And I'm not going to say there's only you, because that wouldn't be enough to keep me faithful. There's only *us*.'

Upon which my spirits rose considerably, and I leaned forward and kissed her on the mouth, out of gratitude: for she was lying.

Had there been a witness present – had Harry, for example, been able to overhear all that we had been saying (and he was trying hard enough as he pottered from booth to booth in his empty bar, distributing and re-distributing nuts and pretzels) – he would have found it impossible to detect where the truth ended and the lie began. She spoke in the same level, serious voice that had pronounced the disturbing testament of her love for me; she spoke in the same style of subdued passion; and nobody who didn't know could have guessed by even the flicker of an eye that here was a married woman who went home each evening to her husband, who enjoyed a normal marital relationship, and who if asked to explain these contradictory roles would say, 'I can't help appetite.'

I knew very little about Helen's husband, except that his name was Geoff, that he was an executive with a pet-food firm, and that he was often conveniently away on business trips. Helen's policy was not to talk about him, at all, ever. If he had to be referred to for any reason, it was in the passive voice: 'I'm expected home early', 'I'm being taken out to dinner.' So the picture I had comfortingly (but unconvincingly) formed of an ineffectual and probably impotent rat-face faded, as it was meant to fade, into a picture of nothing, and I stopped asking myself, as again I was meant to, why a woman like Helen should have married an ineffectual and probably impotent rat-face, which plainly she hadn't. And the only remaining clue was, 'I can't help appetite,' now re-cycled as 'There's only *us*.'

We were juvenile leads after all, and it was light comedy we were playing after all.

'I know what you're thinking, Bill. Do you want me to leave him?'

Quintuple Christ.

No, you don't know what I'm thinking, Helen, you've got your wires crossed. You know what I was thinking a fraction of a second ago, but I've moved on since then. We're juvenile leads. It's comedy.

'I'll tell you what I do want,' I said, 'and that's a drink.'

And I'll drink a toast to you, and what I could have had, if I'd wanted it enough. And then you must go.

I made a tippling motion to Harry and took her hand and squeezed it, and a jaunty voice exclaimed: *'Still here, then? I'm surprised to see you two upright!'*

Detective-constable Carpenter took his light overcoat from the peg where he had left it under the influence of three martinis. 'Don't take that the wrong way, will you? Good night.'

Judging rightly that we were on our last drinks, Harry had restored the vodka quotient and the first sips flooded me with warmth. Helen dug her nails into my palm and laughed as if we'd been having a happy evening. 'I'm surprised to see us upright myself. We're not usually, by this time.'

I'll tell Jeanette I've got to have dinner with Jack Dance. It was only to have been a drink, that's why I've not rung before, but now he wants to make it dinner.

'It's no use, Bill. You still want me, don't you?'

Yes. And need you.

'Yes.'

'What's worrying you?'

'What to tell Jeanette.'

'No, it's something else.'

'Helen. When you used to work for Councillor Drummond, did he always keep his golf clubs in his office?'

IO

'MRS FISHER for you.'

'Jeanette? How many times do I have to ask you not to call me at the ahffice?'

'Oo thoo oo coo roo oonoomoojoosoo!'

'What? What?'

'Son, this is your momma so pay attention. I'm speaking on the extension. Your wife says she thought it was O.K. to call you in an emergency.'

'So hang up, momma, and let Jeanette explain her problem her*self*!'

'She can't do that, son. She trapped her big nose in the vacuum-cleaner nazzle.'

'Bill? This is Oscar? I'm speaking on the extension?'

'You can't be, Oscar. We don't have that many extensions.'

'Bill, I don't know how to tell you this, but I'm speaking on the extension that Jeanette was speaking on when she fainted just now.'

I had made frantic moues to Sheilagh to say I was out: Jeanette's phone calls were always about domestic matters such as radiators blowing up, and tended to be tedious. But Sheilagh kept her hand over the mouthpiece.

'It's not your wife. And it isn't you-know-who. I think it must be your mother, she's phoning from a call-box.'

What the hell does she want? My mother had a morbid fear of telephones and never rang me. Perhaps Jeanette has trapped her nose in the vacuum-cleaner nozzle. Or taken an overdose.

'Hello?' There was a chill in my stomach as I lodged the receiver on my shoulder.

'Hello, Billy! This is your mother speaking. I'm ringing up from the bus station.'

She sounded as if she was ringing up from a tramp-steamer in the North Sea, on what she thought was a bad line.

'What's wrong?'

'Oo, there's nothing *wrong*!' Of course there bloody is, you think the phone is like the old telegram service, to convey bad news; and it's to do with Jeanette, or you would have rung me from home before you came out. It's serious. And I wondered: how can I talk to my mother in what she thinks is my normal speaking voice, when Patsy and Sheilagh will think I'm putting on a broad northern accent?

'It's nothing to be alarmed about, Billy,' she went on, sounding very much as if it was. 'Only I wondered if you could meet me for five minutes, while I'm in town.'

You're not in town mother. The bus indicator said 'Shepford Central' but it didn't mean that, it meant 'Central Bus Station,' meaning the centre of bus-control. Get on the 15A, out there in your tarmac wilderness, and go back home.

Whatever she had to say I didn't want to hear it, and I wanted to say, 'Mother, I'm sorry, but I'm up to my neck in work.' But that would have meant a windfall of flat vowel-sounds for Patsy and Sheilagh to pick up and laugh at. So I said: 'All right. Where?'

'Isn't there a caffy where they sell morning coffee?'

The Café Billard? The Café Sport? The Relais des Voyageurs?

Mother, there are no cafés any more in Shepford. There are no tea shops, supper rooms, chop houses, grills, fish-and-chip saloons, oyster bars, inns or coffee houses. Where do you think you're living? England?

'There's that Pizza Parlour in Castle Street. They might serve coffee.'

I arranged to see her there in half an hour, the time it would take the infrequent Green Arrow to shuttle her from the Central Bus Station, and rang off.

'What are you lot grinning at?'

'Ee, bah goom, lad, oi nivver knew you cum from t' Yorkshire,'

306

mocked Hattersley, in a teeth-grating amalgam of Black Country, West Riding and Mummerset. Even more excruciatingly, Patsy attempted, and botched, a snatch of 'Ilkley Moor baht 'at' while Sheilagh, whose own Midlands accent could have cracked glass, proceeded to gibber incomprehensibly until told by Hattersley to pack it in and get the mail sorted out.

Feeling like an office boy in front of Drummond was one thing, but feeling like an office boy in my own office was not on. I said curtly to Sheilagh, the first time I had ever spoken to her that way: 'And when you've done that, I want these notes typed up.'

'Ooh! Ar! Nay! Ee!'

'They never know when to stop, do they?' sighed Hattersley.

And *you* can mind your own business for a start, Hattersley. But even while getting tight-chested about this assumption of his that he was number one in Pisspot's absence while I was number two, whereas the reverse was true, and about the fact that it was he who had started the girls off in the first place, I felt easier in my mind after his ee-bah-goom bit of ribbing. If you were going to shop someone to the police – grassing, as I believed it was called – you wouldn't make jokes with them, or even about them in their presence, unless you were a professional informer and you were hardened to it. But I still had to know what Hattersley was doing with Detective-constable Carpenter last night.

I was still hanging about the office ten minutes after I should have set off for my mother's coffee morning at the Pizza Parlour, when at last Sheilagh and Patsy, acting as though they had corporate intelligence like ants, rose simultaneously and took themselves off to the Ladies. It was the first chance I'd had of speaking to Hattersley alone.

'You should have come across and had a drink with us last night.'

'Oh. You looked busy.' He tried to look busy himself, not wanting to talk about it.

'It was a bit embarrassing,' I said, without knowing why. Perhaps it seemed an adult-sounding thing to say, implying an instinctive grasp of adult mores. The phrase had floated, like 'dog show', into my mind from nowhere.

'Why should it have been?'

'Well. After all, if you're meeting Bloke A, and he happens to be sitting with Bloke B who's shared the same office with you for years, the least you can do is sit down and have a drink.'

'As a matter of fact I thought I was doing you a favour. I thought you and Helen would want to be on your own.'

Helen? How does he know that name?

He interpreted the question, although I hadn't asked it aloud.

'I have met her, you know. At that party. And it's not exactly a secret, is it?'

Of course he's met her, at the same party where she was standing on her hands and showing off her knickers, all that time ago. He wouldn't have forgotten that, but I had – meaning I'd forgotten he'd been there. And he'd said next morning that she was a 'character'; and I'd thought that he had missed the point about Helen because that night I had driven her home, or rather homewards, and talked with her for hours, and started her third affair and my first one; and she was not a 'character' as I already knew, she was Helen.

And he knew about her all this time, and had pretended not to. And she knew about him, and pretended not to.

'Anyway,' I said, 'What was all the mystery about?'

This is inadmissible evidence, Fisher. All you can pin on Hattersley is a suspicion that he is having it off with somebody. All you have on Helen is that when she says 'There's only *us*', the statement must be expanded to include her husband, wherefore you have a feeling at the back of your mind that it may also have to be expanded to include a third party.

'What mystery?' said Hattersley, stonewalling.

A further thought was swimming against the tide of my immediate anxieties. '*And it's not exactly a secret, is it?*' No: and how have I been able to delude myself for so long that it is? Scores of people must know about Helen. Purchase knows about her. Jack Dance saw us together only last night. There have been occasions without number when we've been recognized, if only fleetingly at traffic lights; and I've always thought, absurdly, it doesn't matter, no one is going to put two and two together.

Shepford was a small town, no matter how desperately it tried to masquerade as a big one. I now faced the reality that there must have been gossip, of which, now that I *was* facing reality, Harry the barman was probably a prime distributor. How far, then, had it gone? Who knew and who didn't know? Had it reached the ears of Helen's husband? Or Jeanette's? No, not Jeanette's, she did not move in informed circles. All Jeanette knew was that I was acquainted with someone who could do peculiar tricks with her tongue.

'You and that tame detective,' I said. 'What did he want you for?'

'Nothing in particular. Just wanted a chat.'

'Yes, well he wanted me for nothing in particular as well. But you were showing him some papers.'

'Was I?'

My mother would be on her second coffee by now and I was growing irritated by Hattersley's wooden attitude.

'Look, I haven't time to play Twenty bloody Questions. All I want to know is, was it something that concerns me?'

'Not directly.'

'It was something concerning the office.'

'Then it does concern me. At least, while Pisspot's away. Look, mate, I'm sorry, but I think I'm entitled to know.' If you're going to be pompous, Hattersley, let's both be pompous.

'And *I'm* sorry, but he told me not to discuss it with anybody.'

'I don't care what he told you. Those papers he was looking at. Did they come from this department?'

'Yes.'

'Right. Who is in charge of this department in Pisspot's absence?'

'You are.'

'Right. Who authorized you to remove those papers?'

'Pisspot did.'

Oh.

My involuntary hissing intake of breath must have sounded to Hattersley pretty much like wind being taken out of sails. I continued, lamely, laboriously and pointlessly:

'You rang the hospital, did you?'

'I did.'

'And Pisspot said it was OK?'

'He did.' A note of amused patience had crept into Hattersley's voice. The bastard was humouring me. I rallied myself for one last despairing canter on the high horse.

'So Pisspot knows what it's all about, and you know what it's all about, and I'm the only one that doesn't?'

'I can tell you what it's *not* all about, if it's worrying you,' said Hattersley, with the air of throwing me a tit-bit. 'It's nothing to do with the swindle sheets.'

You condescending sod. If you'd told me that in the first place I wouldn't be standing here now, utterly humiliated, wondering how to get out of this confrontation with some rag of dignity. 'Thank God for that,' I could have said, and departed for the Pizza Parlour light of heart.

'I don't want to know what it *hasn't* got to do with, I want to know what it *has* got to do with.'

'Sorry. It's confidential.'

'Then bugger you.'

I stormed out of the office, furious with Hattersley but more furious with myself. Any curiosity I felt about his transactions with Detective-constable Carpenter was subordinated to my frustration at being beaten. I supposed I should never have tackled him in the first place: not in that way, anyway, not by trying to come the heavy when it was plain to everybody, even the office girls who thank God had not witnessed the contest, that I was a juvenile lead. Hattersley had taken me on with one hand tied behind his back and whatever it said in the internal telephone directory about who was Pisspot's No. 2 and who was his No. 3, and whatever the differentials in salary, and whatever the dates on our birth certificates, it was now sickeningly, depressingly clear who was really senior to whom.

I put the whole scene out of my mind by starting up an animated conversation with Oscar on our plans for launching an Olde English Tea Shoppe franchise, and after that a chain of cafés, chop houses, grills and oyster bars, but people began to stare at me and I was miserable again as I turned into Castle Street. Entering the Pizza Parlour, I resolved to think seriously about growing a moustache.

I found my mother perched incongruously on an aluminium-and-leatherette mushroom too tall for her dumpy legs, at a kind of circular plastic shelf that served as a table. The shelf was supported by a central column of flexible looking-glass mosaic which made a jigsaw-reflection of her unhappy face as she picked diffidently at a tomato-smothered concoction the size of a dustbin lid.

The town of Shepford shouldn't be doing this to my mother.

'They won't serve coffee by itself, Billy. You're forced to have something to eat.'

A slightly-built, rat-faced juvenile lead in a blue-striped waistcoat affair put a Cellophane-covered menu in front of me.

'Just coffee.'

'No. Am sorree. We don't sairve jus corfee.'

'Why not?'

'Why not, why not? Baycus iss not possibler. You ave to ordair some food.'

Don't wave your arms around at me, short-arse. I pointed at my mother's doughy-looking pizza. 'We've already got enough food to feed ten people.'

'Iss separate owder. You mus choose sometheen yourselv.'

'I want a cup of coffee,' I said, with the deliberation I had observed in others. 'And if you can't or won't get me a cup of coffee, get me the manager.'

'Ees not ere, but ee tell you same ting. Iss cormpenny policee.'

'Listen. I'm with Shepford District Council. Are you telling me it's your company's policy to refuse my order?'

'You jus wan' coffee. Notheen elz.'

'Cor*rect*.'

He shrugged, picked up his menu and retreated. My mother murmured, 'You show me up, you do, our Billy,' but I could see that she was pleased and proud, and that she was filing the incident away in her compendium of anecdotes. I wished that she had numbered Hattersley among her acquaintances.

Now then, mother, what's all this about?

She composed her face into the solemn, formal expression that was only brought out when she had important tidings. She moistened her lips, following this operation by an expectant pause, like a TV-newscaster waiting for his cue.

'I've got to get up to Stradhoughton. Mrs Lacey's passed away.'

Mrs Lacey. Mrs Lacey. Oh, yes. My ex-fiancée Barbara would have been acquainted with a family called Butterfield or Liversedge or something, and these Butterfields or Liversedges would have spent a day at the Ideal Home Exhibition where they were sold a fridge by a man connected by marriage to a Mrs Lacey back in Stradh –.

'You'll remember, Mrs Lacey, Billy. Her that was ever so kind to your Auntie Polly when she had that long illness. She had nobody of her own, poor soul. So I've got to go up, like it or not.'

Not only did I not remember Mrs Lacey, I could not place Auntie Polly either, nor indeed any of my relatives except my grandmother who was dead. A substantial and previously undisturbed nest of kith and kin was flushed out for the funeral, and I could not pick six faces out from the whole pack of them. They posed in front of me in turn, heads cocked whimsically to one side, eyes twinkling, lips pursed: 'See, he doesn't remember us,' said these people of my own blood and they were right, I didn't. I had been to occupied for their meat-teas on Sundays. Now I sometimes wished that I'd tabulated them all when I had the chance: uncles on the beer, aunts with their illnesses, nephews and nieces, great-uncles gone to ruin: I'd had the makings of a rich full family.

'*You're a loner, Bill*,' Oscar said.

My mother wound a skein of congealing melted cheese around her fork, then abandoned the experiment and pushed her plate aside. She seemed nervous about something.

'Still, that's not why I've taken you away from your work.'

I should bloody hope not.

Her voice was pitched higher when she spoke next, and the words came out in a rush. 'I'm thinking of moving back to Stradhoughton for good, our Billy. So now you know.'

You and me both, mother. We could pick up the car and set off now up the M1, and I could be chasing you round the Town Hall by midnight. But you don't want to go back there, you just want to go back, to some ordered existence you think you had once. So do I. And the Town Hall would be there, and the market hall if they haven't pulled it down, and the arcades, and all those blackened buildings: and I'll be so pleased to be back that I'll marry a typist from the Rates Office and emigrate back to the moon.

'Well, lad, don't you want to know why?'

'I should think you're about to tell me, aren't you?' I revolved slightly on my aluminium mushroom. 'That coffee's a long time coming.'

'It's no use blaming the waiter, our Billy, you're forced to have something to eat. You heard what he said, it's the company policy.'

I could go and pick a row with the rat-faced juvenile lead in the striped waistcoat, and put off my mother's forthcoming address by about two minutes. But it wouldn't be much use: I knew, as accurately as if I had a typed transcript in front of me, what she was about to say.

'All right then, why? Why do you want to go back to Stradhoughton?'

'Because I've got eyes in my head, our Billy, and I can see what you can't see, or you won't see, more like. Your marriage is in great danger.'

Great danger. Not an accustomed phrase of hers. Like *taking things*, one that she'd had to borrow from somebody else's vocabulary. It must be more serious than I'd hoped for. Perhaps Jeanette's leaving me. She has found Helen's letter and she's leaving me.

'Why do you say that?'

'Why do I say it, why do you think I say it, because it's true.' Speaking in a half-whisper, her usual volume in any public place, she found it difficult to put across the effect of snapping angrily. 'Because you won't look at a thing till it's pushed in front of your face! You won't, Billy! You haven't the faintest, foggiest idea what's going on in your own home, now have you? Admit it.'

Jeanette hasn't found the letter. It's a more generalized complaint than I can deal with.

'You might well say nothing, but I've got plenty to say and it should have been said years ago. Your Jeanette's very unhappy, our Billy – you know she is, you've only got to look at her.'

Very unhappy. Another one from the library book of words and phrases. I never knew that my mother required happiness as a condition of life, or even that she thought anyone entitled to it. A cow-like contentment, that's all she's ever aimed for. Perhaps it's what she means by happiness.

'And why won't you talk to her? I mean to say, if something's wrong, it's got to be put right. *Has* to. It won't go away, it'll just get worse and worse until you've *got* to do something about it.'

'I *do* talk to her.' I was annoyed to find that I sounded sulky.

'You *don't* talk to her. *You* know what I mean, our Billy, so don't try to look as if you don't. And I'm not putting all the blame on you, it's Jeanette as well, it's both of you. You just won't communicate, and that's half the trouble if you want my opinion.'

Communicate.

I was growing uneasy. She was making sense, so far as her half of the world was concerned, but her half of the world was trying to invade mine, and I'd always thought we had some kind of territorial treaty about that. She was making it sound, with all this talk about *happiness* and *marriage* and *great danger* and *communicate* and all the rest of it, as if other people's lives were somehow my business, as if what I did affected them in some way, shaped them even, as if my actions had consequences. I'm a juvenile lead, mother. Can't you discuss all this with Jeanette and keep me out of it?

To change the subject as far as she would permit it to be changed, I said: 'I don't see what all this has to do with you going back to Stradhoughton.'

'Well it isn't because Jeanette wants to get shot of me, so you can get that idea out of your head for a start. We get on very well together, your wife and me does, and if you'd framed yourself and made a proper go of that marriage, you'd have had your mother for a free babysitter. As it is, you'll have one to pay for, and it's not fifty pee an hour they're asking these days, it's a pound an hour. That's if Jeanette doesn't walk out first.'

'Jeanette isn't going to walk out, nobody's going to walk out,' I said recklessly, even while appreciating what a straw she'd given me to clutch. If Jeanette's thinking of walking out, how much easier to give her an encouraging shove. 'And you're not going back up to Stradhoughton.'

'Oh, but I am. My mind's made up.'

'A minute ago you were only thinking about it.'

'Yes, well I've thought about it.'

'Where would you live?' I knew she meant it, my mother meant everything she said, but I wanted to keep my verbs conditional. I had always found that a good way of staving off the future.

'There's plenty places. Your Uncle Herbert, for one – he's got room, and there's nobody looking after him these days.'

Never heard of him. And even my mother had brought him to mind only because he represented a spare bedroom. She must have gone through the list of relatives, rejecting them in turn, not because she couldn't stand the sight of them but because they would have no room for her; and she would have settled on Uncle Herbert not because of any personal qualities he possessed, but of the spare living room he controlled and the fact that nobody was looking after him these days. It was only one step removed from advertising for companionship, light hsewk & cookg in retn for rm, in the evening paper.

I, Bill Fisher, have done this thing. Actions have consequences. She had been quite happy with Jeanette and me in her cow-like contented way, sucking her sweets and writing her letters and knitting matinee-jackets for children she had never met, and now her suitcases would be coming out of the cistern-cupboard and she would be soliciting my forgotten uncles like a commercial traveller. I have done this thing. I am responsible for this action which is the consequence of the consequence of an action. I have changed her life. I have adult, godlike powers which I do not want.

'Anyway, wherever I go, I shan't be in nobody's way like what I am in yours.'

'Rubbish.' Unconvincing, trying to sound convincing.

'It's not rubbish, Billy. It's ever since you got married, I should have seen it years ago. You've never had a life of your own, the pair of you, I mean to say not as a couple. You've never even got started! I mean to say, you can't even have a proper blazing row, not with me living there.'

Agreed: and it's been a very convenient arrangement.

'Rubbish,' I said again. It was as good a catchword as any.

'You can say rubbish till you're blue in the face, but I'm telling you. It's time you were on your own, with your own wife, in your own home, and sorting out your own future, with nobody else to bother you.'

Future.

That's a large order, mother. That's a very large order indeed.

Twisting uncomfortably on my aluminium mushroom I caught the rat-faced waiter's eye and gesticulated angrily towards the place where my coffee should have been had he brought it when asked. For her part, my mother pushed aside her tomato-and-anchovy circumference of goo to indicate that she had lost her appetite. It was a purely historic gesture, since only a starving navvy could have finished it. She suddenly looked old and tired, a trick that she used to pull on me even in the days when she was neither. It meant she was about to say something disturbing.

'If you could only see that lass of yours, in this last few weeks, after you've gone to work. Crying her eyes out she was, yesterday morning. She was, our Billy! She was sobbing like a baby.'

Don't tell me things like that. I wasn't there, so it didn't happen.

'And *I* know what's wrong and *you* know what's wrong. Or I hope you do, anyway.'

Yes: I can't tell her things.

'She wants loving, our Billy. Any wife does. Just give her a bit of love.'

Love. Loving. The last time I had heard my mother employ that verb had been fifteen years ago, ten minutes after my grandmother died, and she had said it then as if the word had just been invented, like Terylene.

It's more serious than I thought. It's out of my league.

My mother had embarrassed herself by using one exotic expression too many and to cover her confusion she began to assemble the accumulation of paper bags and packages that seemed to attach themselves to her like barnacles whenever she ventured into town. As she was drawing on her gloves, the rat-faced waiter plonked two bills down in front of her. I picked them up.

'What's this thirty pence? *I* didn't have anything!'

'Iss onna menu. Meenimum sharge, thirty penz.'

'Nay! That doesn't seem right! That doesn't seem right at all!' my mother exclaimed, quite loudly. One of the other customers turned round and looked at her.

'Leave it,' I muttered. 'I've not time to argue, I have some business to do.'

I had some business to do. One of the ratbags on the Festival Committee had put me in touch with her ratbag sister who ran a pet shop in Cripplegate, and who had volunteered to organize the children's dog show. As everyone seemed to be taking this event seriously I had thought it was perhaps time I started doing something about it, and so I had made an appointment to see her. I had ninety minutes to kill, but I wanted to get rid of my mother and do some thinking, or avoid doing some thinking. I left her at the corner of Castle Street, headed purposefully towards the nearest car-stack, then, once out of sight, slackened my pace and began to meander aimlessly through the streets.

Most of them were lined with furlongs of bile-green builders' fencing, behind which, in the words of *Pageantry with Progress* (new edition), a forward-looking town was ridding itself of the mantle of a bygone era. The construction cranes were more numerous on the horizon than steeples had once been: the noise of drills and pile-drivers was so familiar by now that it had become an unnoticed backcloth of sound, like waves lapping the breakwaters in a seaside town.

The familiar trademark of Creative City Consortium, the demolition gang headed by Jack Dance, was everywhere: three Cs linked together like a piece of broken chain. If they could only dismantle and redevelop human beings, I could have offered them a fruitful contract.

Love. Loving. I love, I loved, I have loved, would that I could have loved.

I didn't love Jeanette. I didn't love Helen. I didn't love anybody. I fancied Helen, and we completed each other, and she was me and I was her, but we were juvenile leads so it didn't count. Juvenile leads make love, and talk about loving, and they experience the sensations of love, but they don't love.

In my new circumstances, it was going to be very tricky to keep the arrangement with Jeanette going on an even basis, unless I put a bit of effort into it. There would have to be conversations: two-sided ones instead of three-sided ones. Long silences, I supposed, would become more noticeable: I would have to cut down on private thoughts. When I was out, Jeanette would be alone and it would make the hours seem longer, so she would become depressed and might even cry in my presence. She would demand attention and other luxuries that I could not afford to give her. It would be like being married, properly married instead of playing at it. Was it shrewdness, intuition or what that had inspired my mother to place me in this dilemma? Or did she, as she had always claimed, know something about the human condition that I didn't know?

Oscar and an associate of his who had shown interest in the Tea Shoppe franchise idea were waiting for me outside the offices of the Shepford Building Society, so I did not have to think about the prospects of Mortgagedene. We strolled along together, talking business. 'One thing we insist on in all our tea shoppes. No minimum charges.' They left me as I turned into Cripplegate, where the hoardings had come down to reveal a rust-stained edifice like a gigantic, mildewing replica of an architect's model of a shopping precinct. I glanced at my watch and descended, via an escalator that did not work, into the subterranean arcade where the pet shop was located.

For want of specially-ordered materials, so apologetic notices told me, the arcade was not yet completed. Its aerosol-scrawled concrete pillars lacked their tiles, its rough cement floor awaited its finish of old brick, its panel-less ceiling was as yet a confusion of wires and junction boxes, like the inside of a very large transistor radio. I walked along a gangway of planks that led me to the pet shop, where there were kittens playing in the lighted window. The idea crossed my mind that I should perhaps take one home for Jeanette, telling her that Mr Pussy-paws had given birth. It would be company for her on long evenings when I was absent from home, not loving Helen. But the picture of Jeanette weeping quietly to herself as she poured out saucers of milk in the quiet, fluorescent-humming kitchen made me dejected. I dismissed the kitten notion as unworthily sentimental and entered the shop.

A beefy girl in jeans and a sweater that looked as if it were the top layer of fifteen other sweaters was sorting out mice, or doing something with mice that involved transferring them from one sawdust-covered seed box to another.

'Mr Fisher. Oh yes! I'm frightfully sorry, Mr Fisher, but Mrs Mackintosh has had to go down to the kennels rather urgently. I did ring your office but you'd already left.'

319

I murmured something about not worrying, I would drop in again when I was passing.

'But there *is* someone here who'd like to see you. Mr Lightfoot. I should think he's interested in your dog show. It sounds a marvellous idea.'

Lightfoot. I know that name. But I never use it, which is why it didn't register at once.

'Mr Fisher?'

There was a door leading into what looked like a tiny office at the back of the shop, and he had opened it and was standing there; a stocky man of about forty-something in a good suit. Pink, well-shaved face. Not a rat-face and certainly not an ineffective, impotent rat-face. Not a juvenile lead, either. A heavy.

'Would you come in for a moment?'

I went in and he shut the door, remaining with his back to it.

'Now. You've been having an affair with my wife.'

II

REAL things are happening. Not promised, not threatened, they are happening now, in the present tense, and to me, in the first person singular. Actions have consequences. I am experiencing a consequence.

I had imagined this moment from time to time. 'I ought to knock you down, Fisher,' he would say, and my reply – offhand, underplayed – would be, 'Go ahead if it makes you feel any better.' But in that scene, Helen's husband, Helen's nothing husband, had been played by a juvenile lead, like myself. It was light comedy. This was drama. I had opened a door and wandered on to the wrong stage, into somebody else's play.

If he said, 'I ought to knock you down, Fisher,' (and he looked as if he well might before our interview was over) I would not know how to respond. The line I had rehearsed was the wrong one, and there was no prompter to tell me what the right one was. I would lick my lips and avoid his penetrating, decent gaze. That would be the moment when I was exposed as a sham, a shit even, and I would be exposed not only to him but to myself. I didn't want that moment to arrive.

I was afraid: not physically but morally afraid. The knocking-down threat, although it might be delivered, was unlikely to be executed: at least, not here, for the windowless little office was no bigger than a stationery cupboard. The question of what he was doing in it anyway had flickered in my mind and then been extinguished as the least relevant of all the questions I had to find answers to: Helen, when not talking about her husband, might at least have mentioned that his firm owned a chain of pet shops, as a pet food firm well might, and that the absent Mrs Mackintosh was only the manageress.

I was afraid of being afraid. 'Nothing to fear but fear itself' –

well, I feared it. I had much experience of panic, but little of real fear. I wished that I had been frightened more often in my life, that I had been involved in a war or some similar event, where you pick up supplies of moral fibre.

Lightfoot remained with his back to the door. I had my back to a paper-heaped desk. There was two feet of space between us. I leaned back, half-perching on the edge of the desk, to expand this neutral zone to about two feet three inches.

'You've been having an affair with my wife,' he had said. Not, 'I believe you've been having an affair with my wife?' Such niceties had to be taken note of. No question had been asked or implied, so no answer was required. I said nothing, and did not lick my lips. But my heart was pounding and my mouth was dry.

'Well?'

The question had now been posed. I would have to speak, but before I spoke I would have to clear my throat. I did so, then aimed at basso-profundo in the hope that whatever came out would be somewhere in the alto range.

'Is that what your wife tells you?'

Of the hundred or so imbecilic answers that must have flashed through my brain like a computer feedback, I had probably selected the most imbecilic of them all. My thinking, insofar as the jangling sensation in my head could be called thinking, was that it was of the first importance to know how much Helen had told him, if anything. If nothing, then he could only be working on rumour, conjecture and the possible evidence of Harry the barman and a few minor witnesses, in which case I would stand a fair chance of bluffing it out. So to that extent, 'Is that what your wife tells you?' was less imbecilic than, say, 'What are you going to do about it?' which had been considered and rejected.

What I didn't take into account, and should have done, was the effect that such a question would have on a man of his obviously middling-public-school background and intensive training in honour, decency, and not mentioning ladies' names in the mess. I had already been fascinated to observe that a vein was throbbing in his forehead – the first time I had ever come across this phenomenon outside the pages of Sapper – and this alone, never mind his whitened knuckles and the fact that I was clearly dealing with the owner of a cravat and blazer, should have warned me.

'What the *devil* do you mean by that? Are you suggesting that my wife is a liar?'

My brain-computer was issuing a correction. Erase. 'Is that what your wife tells you?' and substitute 'What gives you that idea?' Good thinking: a parry on those lines might have evoked a similar berserk response, but at least it could have yielded some badly-needed information.

But it was too late for that, so I had to make do with: 'I'm not suggesting any such thing.'

'Then what are you suggesting?'

I wished he would stop passing the initiative to me. I tried volleying back with: 'I think we might keep our voices down a little, don't you?' I nodded towards the wall, behind which I had no doubt that mouse-sorting activities had been suspended. There was, I was in process of discovering, no such state as total anxiety: it was as capable of infinite expansion as mother-love is supposed to be; and one of my supplementary anxieties was that when this was all over I would have to make some kind of exit through the shop past the beefy girl in the jeans and sweaters. Would I say 'Good morning,' or nothing, or what?

'You think that, do you? You'd rather no one else heard about your squalid little adventure, would you? I'm afraid you've left it a bit late for that, Fisher, I should think the whole of Shepford knows by now.'

Nevertheless he had taken up my suggestion and lowered his voice, a difficult adjustment to make while indulging in Bulldog Drummond rhetoric; so I surmised – anyway, hoped – that he was exaggerating the Shepford grapevine angle.

He relaxed his knuckle-whitening grip on the door handle and looked as if he would very much like to pace the room, had it been big enough. When he spoke next, in the absence of any further word from me, it was in a deliberate, discoursing manner.

'Last night I had an anonymous telephone call. I was informed that my wife was having drinks with a William Fisher at the Heritage Motor Lodge.' *Hattersley*. 'You won't deny that, I suppose?'

'No.' Bloody *Hattersley*.

'I may say that I've had such telephone calls before. I've chosen to ignore them. I work long hours, I'm frequently away on business, and I see no reason why my wife should be deprived of her social life. She has her own circle of friends, her operatic society activities and so on, and whom she chooses to have drinks with is entirely her business.'

He paused, perhaps wondering, as I often had, why he had never had the simple wit to check up on Helen's almost non-existent operatic society activities. He paused for so long that I thought it was expected of me to come in with some harmless-sounding interjection. With the name *Hattersley* ringing in my head, I did not select carefully enough. I said, 'Quite,' which I should not have done.

'Just keep your bloody mouth tightly shut, Fisher, until I've finished. I say I've never objected to my wife meeting her friends. I know that she's met you on several occasions, and I know in what particular bars and restaurants you've been seen. I took no steps to prevent it. I gave both of you the benefit of the doubt until last night.'

A suspicion was dawning on me, driving *Hattersley* gradually out of my swirling thoughts. Hattersley can wait, this is more important. *Helen's husband has known all along.*

'Apparently last night there was some kind of scene between you. And in bloody public! Is that true or not?'

'I wouldn't say a scene, exactly. It's true that Helen was a little –'

'*What did you say?*' Suddenly it was vein-throbbing time again. He took a step towards me, his face jutting close to mine, and I could see that it was getting perilously close to I-ought-to-knock-you-down-Fisher time also.

What *had* I said, anyway, to provoke this reaction? I succumbed at last to the temptation to lick my lips, and he supplied the answer.

'Don't you *dare* use my wife's Christian name to me! Do you hear? *Do you hear me!*'

'All *right* – I *won't*!'

My initial fear had peeled away, but only to expose an onion-like structure of other layers of fear beneath it. What I was presently afraid of was that I would burst into a nervous snigger, as children sometimes do when harangued by teachers. Helen's husband, although unquestionably a heavy, was coming across as an absurd and even pathetic figure, one who belonged in comic opera rather than straight drama. But it was straight drama we were playing, and I had better not forget it. I sank my teeth into my lower lip to discourage any inclination for it to quiver. Lightfoot, for his part, was doing some work on his cheek muscles with the object of regaining his elusive self-control.

'I say a scene in public, with my wife, in front of a witness. A police officer, if you please! Good God, man, do you know the reputation of the police in this town for gossip and scandal-mongering? The way certain councillors' names have been blackened, for instance – all that comes from your police friends, perhaps you didn't know that! And then you stand there and look bloody astounded when I tell you this story about you and my wife's got round the whole of Shepford.'

Yes, he's known all along all right, but he's chosen not to know, like a Somerset Maugham remittance man whose bridge partners look at him in a certain way when he gets back to his hot-blooded wife after a month up-country. And like the same character, he wouldn't face the truth until he thought he heard sniggers from the club verandah.

'I drove to the Heritage Motor Lodge at eight o'clock last night. My wife was no longer there, as you well know, but her car was. I waited in the car park until you brought her back there a little after eleven. I shan't dwell on the rest. I shan't ask where you took her, because I know where you took her. I know the whole sordid story. We were discussing it at four o'clock this morning.'

Poor Helen. And I was surprised to realize that this was the first time I had given any thought to Helen since entering this small and increasingly stifling room. We had discussed Helen, or rather he had, and I had ill-advisedly spoken her name; but all the time I had been thinking of her not as Helen but as this man's wife, and I had been thinking of him not as Helen's husband but as *a* husband, an aggrieved husband, the cuckolded husband of any wife with whom I might have chanced to have been shacked up at some point.

Looking at him now as the substance of the shadowy figure who gratified Helen's self-confessed appetite, I was conscious that as the layers of fear had continued to peel away, a small core of relief had been revealed. I could identify it now: it was relief that Helen's husband was the man he had turned out to be. He had known about us all along but had done nothing until the fear of public ridicule forced him to take action. If I was the amateur psychologist I thought I was, this would indicate that while not rat-faced and ineffectual, as hoped for, he was almost certainly impotent or near-impotent, as also hoped for. That seemed to fit together nicely enough, although there was one piece of the jigsaw unaccountably left over: what did Helen do with that appetite of hers?

Lightfoot (as I could not imagine myself calling him, for all that he called me Fisher) seemed to have reached the end of the narrative portion of our interview. The vein in his forehead had been brought into play again and he had begun a process of looking me up and down as if I were a cross-bred dog he was thinking of buying or having put down, or a headmaster wondering how to cure me of nose-picking.

'God, you're a swine, Fisher, aren't you?' he now said, or more accurately spat. I felt the nervous snigger fighting for survival behind my clenched teeth, and I clenched them so tightly that my mouth tingled.

'*Aren't you?*'

I didn't know what to say to that, and a reply was plainly expected. I could not bring myself to mumble 'Yes,' and I could not think of any suitable form of words, of the type I would normally use, that would be acceptable. What I very much wanted to do, and what I had to restrain myself from doing, was to copy

Lightfoot's own speech patterns, as I always did with stronger personalities than myself. But that would have meant saying something in the order of, 'Now look here, Lightfoot, we're both men of the world,' and he would have hit me in the mouth.

I struggled for expression and finally came up with: 'I'm certainly not proud of myself, if that's what you mean,' I felt ashamed of myself for saying it, and was uneasily aware that I had got pretty close to the sham/shit self-exposure point, but I knew that he would not settle for much less.

The grovelling admission, or what he accepted at face value as a grovelling admission, seemed to please him; yet it did not seem to mollify him, for he now went on to pose an even more difficult question:

'Do I have your word that you will not see my wife again, or attempt to communicate with her in any way?'

Here again I was in difficulties. The only safe formula was, 'You have my word.' But it was impossible: I tried to speak but my tongue felt swollen.

I would have to get round it somehow, as I always got round saying 'Pouilly Fuissé' when ordering wine.

A muttered, 'I shouldn't worry about that, it's all over anyway,' was the best I could do; and it was not good enough.

'What the hell do you mean, it's all over?'

'It's all over. It's finished. Look –' I could just about spit out the phrase if I put a coarse 'Look' in front of it. 'Look, you have my word that we won't be seeing each other again. All right?'

'Never mind that for the present. It's your use of the word 'all' that I'm querying. *All* over, you say. *All*. You make it sound as if it's been going on for bloody months!'

Quintuple Christ. How long does he want it to have been going on for, then? Weeks? Days? Helen, why didn't you ring me this morning with my side of the story? Or perhaps you did, and I was sitting watching my mother eating pizza and grizzling on about matters of no importance whatsoever.

'Well? How long *has* it been going on?'

The same heaven-sent inspiration that had given me 'dog show' came to my rescue, and I heard myself saying in curt, clipped tones not unlike my inquisitor's: 'I imagine your wife's already informed you on that point.' *Now* who's calling her a liar? Neat.

He took the point, although not in the way I had expected. I was now interested to see that as well as being a master of the vein-throbbing trick, he could also curl his lip.

'You know, of course,' he said – not said: sneered, 'that you're by no means the first one, don't you?'

I felt a vein throbbing in my forehead. The words, 'That's a caddish thing to say about any woman,' were actually forming on my lips. I swallowed them hastily, but I could feel my knuckles whitening.

'I don't think that's any business of mine Lightfoot,' I said stiffly.

'No, I don't suppose you do. Get what you can while it's going, that's your motto! But don't delude yourself that you've been enjoying exclusive rights. You're the fourth one in three years, to *my* knowledge.'

You bloody fool, Lightfoot, *they were all me*! All your anonymous phone calls were about *me*!

In that case, they can't all have been from Hattersley, who appears to have mentioned me by name. Very well: they were from other people, who didn't mention me by name.

I can't help appetite.

At any rate, she has not been having appetites with Hattersley. You don't knock somebody off, then shop her to her husband, even if you're a convoluted sod like Hattersley.

There's only us.

I'm sorry, Helen; I ought to have knocked your husband down, hadn't I?

I experienced a tremor of hope as Lightfoot consulted his watch. Was he timing this, then? Was he fitting me in between appointments? Was it nearly over?

Evidently he still had a few moments in hand, for after wrinkling his brow as if consulting mental notes for anything left unsaid, he asked abruptly: 'You have a wife, don't you?'

'I do.'

'Fine thing if your wife gets to hear about this.' Good. He's not going to tell her. He's not going to do anything, in fact. The incident is almost closed.

'Let's hope she doesn't,' I said. The last onion-skin layers of fear had fallen away, I examined my emotional condition, warily, and discovered that I had pulled through to a state of cautious elation. It was nearly over. Today would pass and tomorrow would come and the day after, and in a few days this real thing happening, this consequence of an action, would no longer be raw in my mind. It would take its place in my memory-bank as an experience I once had, an anecdote to tell myself, with all my present embarrassment skilfully edited out. The day would even come when thinking about it would make me feel cocky. It's not every man who has such a tale to tell.

The re-curling of Lightfoot's lip informed me that I had been premature in my diagnosis, or rather in the symptoms of light-heartedness that the diagnosis had explored. He seemed to have taken exception to my last remark.

'It'll be no thanks to you if your wife *doesn't* hear about it,' he said puzzlingly. Yes it will: I shan't tell her. 'No thanks to your behaviour, I should say. You should be damn well ashamed of yourself.'

I am. I'm ashamed of having said, 'I'm certainly not proud of myself, if that's what you mean,' and I'll try to forget that I ever said it.

'Shouldn't you?'

No, I'm not going to repeat it.

'Aren't you going to say anything, man?'

'What do you want me to say?' That was easy enough.

'Aren't you going to apologize? Aren't you man enough to say you're sorry?'

I wished I could tell him. I wished I could say, Captain Light-foot – for I had begun to think of him as Captain Lightfoot, even though it was improbable that he had ever been more than a conscript second-lieutenant – Look, Captain Lightfoot, where I come from there are certain words and expressions that we have difficulty in using. *Love, loving, taking things, communicate* and

329

happy are examples of these. Another is *sorry*. We may use it in the casual form, when we bump into people in the street for example, and as an expression of sympathy, when we say 'Oh, I *am* sorry' to someone who has been bereaved; but we have great difficulty in pronouncing the word in its formal, apologetic sense, especially to strangers. We do not say, 'I love you,' we do not kiss our mothers, and we do not apologize. I'm very sorry.

But I would have to get something said, and I was thinking up ways of saying it when Lightfoot, uttering an expression of contempt that might well have been 'Tchah!', flung open the door, turned back to face me, and in full view of the beefy girl in the jeans and sweaters, who was now brushing a dog, very unexpectedly spat in my face.

12

HELEN and I were in bed together, or lying across a bed together, and she was doing things with her tongue that I had not previously known she could do, but we were not very much afraid.

We had taken fantastically elaborate precautions. Both of us had independent, cast-iron, watertight, private-investigator-proof, later-checking-up-by-husband-or-wife-proof, legitimate, infallible excuses for being in London.

She had not been working for six months, and at last she had got herself another job. This, so I was informed now that her husband had entered the realm of our common speech, was approved of: he thought another spell in employment would keep her out of mischief.

It was an interesting post, not that it interested me much beyond the scope it gave us for meeting again. The suburb-village, or village-suburb of Mayfield where she lived, and where Jeanette was still pressing me to lay down roots, had been steadily expanding to embrace a suburb-village-suburb or village-suburb-suburb of brick bungalows deployed on carved-up, hard-earth, chicken-wire-separated segments of unadopted half moon crescents following the natural curvature of the earth, or moon. Helen would be a kind of hostess-receptionist, directing the technicians, junior executives, and dental mechanics whom Shepford was trying to lure into its concrete web towards the place where they might vainly try to train roses while reflecting on the error they had made in moving from their university towns or pleasant industrial valleys.

But everything in Shepford that did not belong to Jack Dance and his Creative City Consortium was a branch or subsidiary or offshoot of some company or consortium in London; and the

331

headquarters of Mayfield Properties was in London; and it was there that Helen had to go, and went, cutting two hours off our golden-June-into-glorious July extension, for the interview that would confirm her appointment. A further two hours would be lopped off this evening, when she had arranged to visit her brother in St John's Wood. But that gave her a valid reason for staying in London all day. Cast-iron. Watertight.

As for myself, I had put it about that I was in Birmingham. It was, if anybody cared to check, all down in black and white in the minutes of the last Festival committee meeting: *Mr Fisher was asked what progress had been made in regard to the possibilities of coverage of the Festival by the* Nationwide *television programme. Mr Fisher reported that he had made preliminary contact with a Mr Hellicar of* Nationwide, *who was most anxious for discussions to take place. Since Mr Hellicar would be in Birmingham on the 17th in connection with the BBC training scheme, it was agreed that sooner than incur unnecessary expense by travelling to London, Mr Fisher should arrange a meeting in Birmingham on that date.*

Not only had I put it about that I was in Birmingham, I had been observed departing for Birmingham and had actually set foot in Birmingham. The rendezvous with Helen coincided with my mother's final departure from Shepford to take up residence with Uncle Herbert. I had persuaded her that rather than see her off on the West Riding express from King's Cross, which would have meant us travelling up to London in the same buffet-car as Helen, it would suit my busy schedule better if I drove her to Birmingham where she could catch a not-much-slower train, changing at Leeds. There had been a painfully tear-sodden farewell scene with Jeanette, and my mother had shaken hands with sundry rat-faced neighbours, all of whom had been informed that I was now driving her to Birmingham; I had dumped her at New Street Station and then belted down the M.1, to establish myself in a large, modern, anonymous hotel in the Euston Road under the pseudonym of Midgeley.

It was the first time Helen and I had seen each other since her husband had spat in my face three weeks ago, although there had been three telephone calls of varying degrees of guardedness.

The first was immediately after the pet shop confrontation when, in a fairly traumatic condition, I returned to the office to hear from Sheilagh that the switchboard appeared to be going mad, since the telephone kept ringing every ten minutes and when she answered it there was nobody there.

It rang again as I took my coat off. Hattersley, I was glad to hear, had gone across to the town planning office and would not be back today. I would have had to sit opposite him, seething, the bile rising in my throat as I gathered courage to have it out with him, the chill settling on my stomach as I came to terms with my own cowardice.

'There it is again, you see,' said Sheilagh, hanging up. 'Phone rings – I answer – *click*. Don't suppose by any remote chance it's that friend of yours, is it?'

'I haven't got any friends, Sheilagh,' I said haggardly. I saw her exchange an amused pout with Patsy, and regretted making such a pretentious remark.

I contrived to spend some time at Sheilagh's desk, ostensibly correcting the notes she had been typing up, and probably giving her the impression that I was mesmerized by her nipples producing intriguing indentations in a very marketable new cotton sweater. When the telephone rang again I picked it up, happening to be near at hand.

'Yes? Information and Publicity?'

'Bill!'

'Oh, good afternoon, Dr Hagerty! I was hoping you'd ring.'

'Did he find you?'

'Yes indeed. We had a most interesting discussion.'

'I'm dreadfully, dreadfully sorry I couldn't warn you. He locked me in the bedroom and took the living-room phone off the hook. I couldn't get out until the cleaning lady came.'

Poor Helen.

'I can quite understand that, Dr Hagerty. Perhaps we ought to meet again and talk about it further.'

'We can't meet yet, darling.' Pang. She only ever called me

333

darling in bed. 'We've got to be so, so careful. Can't you arrange to be in the office alone some time, so I can ring you privately?'

'Nine o'clock tomorrow morning. Yes, Dr Hagerty, that would suit me perfectly.'

'He doesn't leave the house till nine. Make it a quarter past. And Bill, I love you desperately and I want you desperately.'

'I look forward to that, Dr Hagerty. Many thanks. Good-bye, Dr Hagerty.'

It was the first time I had ever heard Helen sound hysterical when sober, as she presumably was at that hour. It suited her, and I fancied her strongly. As I put down the receiver my eyes lingered on her surrogate breasts, straining provocatively against Sheilagh's acceptable cotton sweater.

I got to the office at a quarter to nine the next morning and swivelled restlessly in my chair until the telephone rang at twenty-one minutes past. That left us only nine minutes before Patsy and Sheilagh arrived for work: we invested the time in a hurried examination of possible meeting places, discarding all of them as too hazardous and finally settling for London on the seventeenth when Helen, as she had just learned, would be up for her interview. It meant waiting three weeks but we agreed that it would be a useful Caesar's-wife period, during which Helen could lead an ostentatiously pure life of hen parties and operatic society meetings, thus not only calming her husband's suspicions that she might still be seeing me, but also clocking up credit for future assignations when the heat was off. We also agreed that there had better be no more of these early-morning telephone calls, in case the switchboard girls became intrigued by my revised office hours and began listening in.

But there *was* one more call. It came one evening when I was working late, frantically correcting the final proofs of *Pageantry with Progress* (new edition) which was supposed to have been in the printers' hands at the end of the previous month. Sheilagh had suffered a fresh outbreak of 'Phone rings – I answer – *click*' trouble during the day, and I trusted on telepathy to tell Helen that it would be worth her while ringing after the girls had gone home.

334

The message finally seeped through to her at six-thirty. I snatched up the receiver almost before the bell had started to ring and tried to cradle it on my shoulder. Retrieving the instrument from the waste-paper basket I heard Helen's voice crying:

'Hello? Hello? *Is* that extension three nine seven?'

'Helen! Hey – did you know we're telepathic? I've been sitting here, willing you to ring!' No harm in fostering a bit of mystique.

'Oh, *there* you are. May I speak to Mrs Chalmers, please?'

It's all right, Helen, you don't have to speak in code. The switchboard girls have knocked off and we're on a direct line.

'We can talk, love. Everyone's gone home.'

'Oh, it *is* you, Maggie! Darling, I didn't recognize your voice! I'm so glad I caught you and I've got lots of news, but I can't talk now because Geoffrey's just walked in and he wants his dinner. Don't you, Geoffrey?'

Sextuple Christ! Not only is she ringing from home, her husband is in the same bloody room!

You're getting a tremendous kick out of this, aren't you, Helen? I hope you are, because I certainly aren't. And for God's sake watch what you're saying, because you sound half-pissed to me.

'And what if he picks up the extension?' With the receiver close to my mouth, I whispered the words at obscene-telephone-call level. 'Look, Helen, I'm going to ring up.'

'Yes, well I shan't keep you a minute, darling. I just *had* to let you know that I've got you those plants.'

Plants? Plants?

She's getting a kick out of calling me 'darling' too. And isn't she overdoing the gushing a little? I wondered irrelevantly if Helen always talked to her women friends like that.

'What plants?'

'*You* remember, darling. Those sweet little red things we saw growing near the golf course and then you saw them again in Councillor Drummond's window box and you said you *had* to have them.'

Councillor Drummond's golf clubs. Septuple Christ, I had

335

forgotten all about them. Helen had worked out a scheme for purloining them, insisting on carrying it out alone. It was, she had assured me, child's play: all she had to do was loiter on the stairs during Drummond's lunch hour, wait until his secretary came out of the Ladies on the landing, walk into his office, scoop up golf clubs, and make her retreat down the back stairway that led to the mews where her car would be waiting.

But I had thought the plan had been abandoned in the light of our recent troubles. In any case, I was no longer sure that golf clubs were the priority they had once been. Detective-constable Carpenter had stopped pestering me lately, and I had every hope that he had given me up as a bad job.

'Yes, all right, Helen, I'm with you.'

'Well, it turns out that they're a very rare type of paeony, darling, but I've *got* them. Aren't I clever? Now I must ring off because Geoffrey's pacing the room. What do you want me to do with them?'

Why not stick them up his –

'Can you hang on to them?'

'Yes of *course* I can, darling! They'll be quite safe with me. And we'll meet up very soon. Bye bye, darling, and lots of kisses.'

Osculatory sounds reached my ear as she put down the telephone. That had been four weeks ago. And now here we were, in our afternoon hotel, and I was experiencing osculatory sensations of a type new to me.

Little had been said in the first ninety minutes, although many sounds had been made, and a conversation had been held, full of inner meanings and subtleties, as if we had newly-discovered and then quickly mastered a sign language so intricate and comprehensive that it superseded the spoken word.

We lay back exhausted, too exhausted even to reach for a cigarette, and after a long while tried to resume our dialogue, but were too exhausted; and Helen, at last, reverted to standard English.

'Do you want an inquest, Bill?'

'No.'

If she meant an I-was-there account of the night her husband waited for her in the Heritage Motor Lodge car park: no. I had closed that book.

'Thank God. I've been enduring inquests for the last three weeks.'

Poor Helen. But don't tell me about it.

I groped for my cigarettes and succeeded only in brushing the packet to the floor. Lacking the initiative for further movement, I let my arm hang limply over the side of the bed and closed my eyes.

'Who do you think told him, Helen?'

'I've thought about it and stopped thinking about it. I don't *want* to think about it.'

'It was Hattersley.'

'It can't have been. He wouldn't do anything like that.'

I opened my eyes again and wanted to look into Helen's face to see what expression was accompanying this interesting remark. But I didn't. Don't, Fisher, no inquests, she's had enough. And her face will reveal nothing, except love, which is a very effective mask.

'Did he give you a rotten time, Bill?' Her husband, she meant. She was changing the subject.

'Not particularly.'

'I don't know what he said to you and I don't think I want to know, but did he tell you I was promiscuous?' She was not changing the subject after all. Thank you, Helen.

'He said I was the fourth in three years, to his knowledge.'

'Did you believe him?'

'No.'

'I'm glad.'

We reached out simultaneously and clasped hands across the bed. It was a good moment, and I was sorry to destroy it.

'That operatic society of yours. Sometimes you told *him* you were going to it and sometimes you told *me* you were going to it.'

'Well?'

'Well what?'

'You mean well, was I lying to him but not lying to you? Yes. I *had* to go there sometimes, just to have been seen there in case he ever checked up, and whenever I did go, I always got him to pick me up afterwards so he'd know I'd been there. So that on the other nights, when I was out with you, he wouldn't start worrying himself about where I was.'

You must be a very proficient liar, Helen. I bet you could give me lessons. But are you proficiently lying now?

'And Hattersley?' I said.

'I don't know Hattersley.'

'You said he couldn't have made that anonymous phone call. "He wouldn't do anything like that." How do you know he wouldn't, if you don't know Hattersley?'

'Oh, *Bill*!' She rolled towards me and raised herself up slightly, putting both hands on my shoulders and looking into my face. 'I meant I didn't *think* he'd do anything like that, you goose! Someone you work with, someone you've known for years, someone who's got to sit opposite you the next morning and pretend it wasn't him. Impossible!'

Convincing. I smiled at her, and said wryly: 'You don't know Hattersley.'

'No, I *don't* know Hattersley, but before we drop the subject – Geoff *does* think I've had four affairs in three years. However careful I was, he was bound to be suspicious sometimes, and on four occasions I made some silly mistake, told him I'd been where he knew I hadn't been, or whatever, and he knew I was having an affair. But Bill, he thinks they were four separate affairs and they weren't – they were all with *you*!'

My own interpretation exactly, Helen. And I should have knocked your husband down.

'And if I didn't say anything to you about all this,' she went on, answering a question I hadn't asked, 'it was because I didn't want you to worry and perhaps stop seeing me, for fear of – well, for fear of what finally happened three weeks ago. And I *let* him go on thinking there'd been four different men because if he'd ever found out there was only one he would have known it was serious and done something drastic about it.' That was the other unanswered question on the rota.

'And is it *still* serious, after all that's happened?' This one was not on her list. She knew it didn't have to be asked. But I didn't bargain for her answer, which I expected to be as rhetorical as the question.

She looked at me very steadily, cupping my face in her hands. 'It was a game when it started, Bill, and I sometimes behave as if it's still a game, but it hasn't been one for a very long time. I love you, and I want to live with you. I want to be divorced from Geoff and married to you.'

I waited to hear myself say *octuple Christ* and it didn't happen. Very well: then if I was not alarmed there must be some other sensation present – euphoria, perhaps. Helen and I often shared a euphoric five minutes, when we would make impossible, practical, daft, detailed plans to go on holiday together or permanently rent a secret *pied-à-terre* under an assumed name. We enjoyed those moments and I could have done with one now; but euphoria had not happened either. All I could feel was a pleasant numbness, as if I had been lying for a long time under something like a very heavy mattress, which had now been removed. But my mind was not affected and it seemed to be functioning with surprising clarity.

Although I had thought often about leaving Jeanette – or more desirably, about Jeanette leaving me, as half-promised by my mother at our Pizza Parlour *tête-à-tête* – I had never got very much further than the suitcase-packing stage in my planning. Euphoria gave me either a visa to the United States (if I was not fancying Helen) or (when I was), a book-lined suite of rooms in the turret of a non-existent block of Victorian-gothic mansion flats overlooking the cafés and brasseries of the Cornmarket, and there Helen would visit me when she was able; but when euphoria wore off, I was left with a bed-sit over a fruit shop in a condemned terrace, all I could afford if I still had to support Jeanette – but at least Helen would still visit me, and after the golden June had become glorious July, and July August, and August September, she might one evening put on a butcher's apron over nothing else and fix scrambled eggs, before September became October.

'Boy! Does Helen know how to scramble an egg!' Oscar wanted to say, but I wouldn't let him. He had no part in this.

I had never considered being married to Helen, except in the euphoric moments. If the thought ever came into my head at other times, I pushed it out quickly, drawing away instinctively from the sticky preliminaries: the private investigators and the solicitors' letters, *Fisher v. Fisher*, and the divorce judge's disapproving comments, and Jeanette very possibly breaking-down in the witness box, and above all, 'I ought to knock you down, Fisher.' That would be the worst moment – and yet that moment had already been and gone. We were *past* that moment.

It was possible to marry Helen. Such arrangements were being made all the time, by people far more mature than I, who presumably knew what they were doing. We would have to move out of Shepford: that was possible and even desirable, and that too was being done all the time. I would need a job, wherever we went. Washer-up – anything. No, not washer-up, anything: I was being practical now. I had fifteen years' experience in local government; I would see what was being advertised in the *Municipal Journal*. So we would go to Birmingham, or Leeds, or Swindon, but not Stradhoughton; and Helen would work too and supplement my income; but I would have to support Jeanette at her present spin-drier level, out of guilt, so we would live in a bed-sit over a fruit shop, on supermarket plonk and pasta, but our marvellous October would become November. And people, adults, did all these things and changed their lives in this way, and so would we.

'I shouldn't have said that, should I?' Helen had misinterpreted my silence.

Her face was resting on mine by now, her body resting on my body. I began to stroke her hair, but it reminded me of the way I had stroked Jeanette's hair (*Brief Encounter*, *Lassie Come Home*) when I couldn't tell her why I couldn't tell her things. So I stroked Helen's face instead.

'We'd have to move out of Shepford,' I said at last.

340

'Promises, promises.' It was a more lighthearted response than I'd expected. I felt euphoria tingling through her. I rocked her in my arms and started to speak, then stopped myself, and started again, and stopped, and then spoke.

'Helen. I'm going to leave Jeanette.'

'Don't tell me that, Bill. Don't tell me what you mean to do. Don't tell me anything, until it's done. But whatever you do, or don't do, I can cope.'

'Can you?'

'I always have. I always will. I can cope with anything except losing you.'

It seemed like twelve hours later, although it was only half an hour or so, that I was pulling on my underpants by the net-curtained window. Helen was still lying on the bed, looking cherished, and half-asleep from contentment, not from tiredness, for it had been a very gentle half hour. Across the Euston Road I saw a late sun reflecting on the western curve of the glass roof of King's Cross Station.

'I was going to live here once,' I said, for no particular reason: only that I had been reminded that I was going to live here once.

'Mm?'

'When I was about eighteen. I was going to live in London. With a girl.'

'Oh, *were* you?' Not half-asleep at all.

'It seems light-years ago.'

'Were you in love with her?'

'I thought I was, but I couldn't have been.'

'Why not?'

'Because we never got here, did we? She did, but I didn't.'

'That's a *non sequitur*, Bill.'

13

I WAS taking a vicious delight in sending Hattersley on petty errands. Festival week was drawing near. The inspiration that had given me 'dog show' had provided me with several other ideas and gimmicks, and these had won the approval of the linen-suited Jack Dance, with which was automatically bracketed the approval of Councillor Drummond and his sidekick Councillor Hopkinson, and so I had been given responsibilities. One of them was to plan the route for the procession of bands, scout troops, old comrades' associations and assorted rat-faced legions that would converge on the Cornmarket in the last throes of the festivities. Routine tasks such as traipsing round the shops with posters could joyfully be unloaded on to Hattersley. Serve the bugger right.

Sheilagh and Patsy were munching apples at their desks and I was eating sandwiches and poring over the planning office's latest amended amendments to the one-way traffic scheme, and I was fairly well content. My affair with Helen had not become the scandal of the town, as projected by her husband; I got the odd knowing look from time to time, but then I had become used to getting knowing looks during my time in Shepford. Helen's new job had given her mobility, and so we had begun a pattern of weekly meetings near an old windmill by the county border, later to be stepped up to twice a week if there were any unforeseen snags about leaving Jeanette.

Jeanette was behaving well; since my mother's departure for Stradhoughton she had been surprisingly cheerful, imagining, perhaps, that we were in for a new regime. I had been far less tense than anticipated in our new-found privacy. Knowing that I had at last made up my mind to go had relaxed me; I felt quite affectionate towards her, as I might have done to Mr Pussy-paws had there ever been such a cat. (Last night we had even played Scrabble and then made what passed for love, back in the squeaking bed again.) I had rehearsed my abdication speech many times, and now I had but to deliver it, and face her sensible tears.

'Oscar? Oscar? We were *happy*, Oscar. You, and me, and Momma Winklebaum, and – and *Bill*. And then – pow, like a sock in the *jar*!'

Studio silence.

Small voice: 'He'll come back, Oscar? Won't he?'

'Honey, I – Jeanette. Honey? Were you ever smashed out of your mind?'

'I don't think so, Oscar.'

'Can a real friend introduce you to a noo experience?'

There were recognizable sounds of commotion somewhere out in the clinical corridors of the Civic Centre, and soon the glass door of the office was flung open and in staggered, or half-tumbled, Ron Casey of the *Evening Mail*, his crime-beat colleague Jack Wilmott, and Pisspot. Ron Casey was half-pissed, Wilmott was three-quarters pissed, and anyone who didn't know Pisspot would have said that he was entirely pissed, but I could tell that only slimline – low calorie – Indian – *tonic* water had passed his lips. He clutched a walking-stick, although he seemed to have little need of it except for brandishing purposes, and under his arm was carrying – or thought he was, though in fact it was by now lodged precariously under his elbow, and in danger of falling to the ground – a familiar green file.

'Pisspot!'

'Arsehole!'

'*Mister* Rainbell!' Patsy and Sheilagh combined their gleefully shocked welcome with a rattling of the tea-money tin in my face. I happily shelled out my fivepenny fine, while Pisspot dug into various pockets and eventually fished out what looked like his entire wealth in coins, which he flung in the general direction of Patsy's tin.

A sustained hollering of 'Tea! Tea! Tea! Tea! Tea!' sent the girls scurrying off with their in-tray of mugs and milk

343

cartons, and after a report on Pisspot's health – the burden of which was that he had never felt better, and that the Karl Marx Hospital (as he chose to call it) should be renamed the Karl Marx Health Farm – flung out an arm to call my attention to the condition of Ron Casey, who had flopped on Patsy's chair, and Jack Wilmott, who was lying on Hattersley's desk.

'You will observe that our confreres have been celebrating. I, of course, restricted myself to carbonated aitch-two-oh.'

'Reggie, why didn't you let me know you were out and about? I would have come and had one with you.'

'I am not out and about, my dear Arsehole, I am passing through. I suffer from convenient bouts of dizziness which seem to attack me whenever I think of the Shepford Festival. In fact, when I see all that bumph on your desk, I believe I can feel one coming on now.'

'In other words, you're going to skulk at home till the Festival's over. I don't blame you. So what was the celebration in aid of?'

'We were drinking the health of our new Director of Finance. In his absence, needless to say.'

'I didn't know we *had* a new Director of Finance.'

'You know now,' said Ron Casey. 'Three guesses.'

The present rat-faced Director of Finance's rat-faced deputy, I supposed, but I couldn't remember his name.

'No – I give up.'

'The incorrect answer!' boomed Pisspot. 'Your three choices should have been James Purchase, James Purchase and James Purchase.'

'Purchase!'

I looked suitably mind-boggled, as indeed I was. Purchase! Worth a quadruple Christ at least.

Then, even as I mused bewilderedly on Purchase's general inability to run a rats' Christmas club, a fresh wave of incredulity washed over me.

'But I always thought –'

'You always thought, my dear Arsehole, that he was plotting

344

and scheming for my own exalted position. As indeed he was. But if you are offered a plum, the gooseberry loses its flavour.'

'Yes, but even so, Reggie. The phantom nose-shaver of Shredded Wheat Towers?' Don't imitate Pisspot, Fisher. He doesn't intimidate you, he's on your side.

A polysyllabic groan floated up from Hattersley's desk, which the crime reporter Jack Wilmott had transformed into a fair replica of a mortician's slab: '*Drummer wungerfurrer.*'

'Drummond swung it for him,' translated Ron Casey.

'Upon which subject –' roared Pisspot, flinging down on my desk the green swindle sheet file which he had several times dropped and several times picked up, and which I had been hoping he might be getting round to mentioning, '– compliments of the management.'

'Thank God for that. Did you get these back from Purchase?'

'Let us say they were rescued from Master Purchase's pending tray. Your lying swindle sheets have ceased to pend.'

I flipped through the file. *To hospitality at the Heritage Motor Lodge for Mr Oscar Seltzer of Time-Life Inc . . .* All present and correct.

'Do you notice anything, Arsehole?'

'Yes. *Your* dockets are all here, and *my* dockets are all here, and Hattersley's are, but –' I looked up at Pisspot with a diplomatic swivelling of the eyes, meant to take in Ron Casey and the comatose Jack Wilmott.

'We are among friends, my boy! Why do you think the cream of the *Evening Mail* is here? What you observe, and what Mr Wilmott there would love to print but alas would not be allowed to by the craven *bar*stard who calls himself an editor, is that Master Bulldog Drummond's swindle sheets are missing.'

It was true, Drummond, as chairman of about seven thousand Council committees, all of which seemed to be for ever welcoming visiting industrialists and other freeloaders, had long ago established a precedent for extracting part of his entertainment allowance from our department. Diversification, Pisspot had once laconically called it, while initialling Drummond's latest docket. But now his swindle sheets were missing.

'I believe,' continued Pisspot, 'that the trick was invented by the editors of the Great Soviet Encyclopaedia. Read Master Orwell.'

Patsy and Sheilagh, pink from steam and the pleasure of seeing Pisspot again, returned to distribute mugs of tea. It was curious, I reflected as Sheilagh stretched forward over my desk to stir in the required three lumps, that I fancied neither of them, even as stand-ins for Helen, when Pisspot was present. He seemed to reduce them, or perhaps elevate them, to the status of daughters.

He cut short their twitterings about who else took sugar and who didn't with a roar of: 'Ladies! We thank you for your hospitality. Your luncheon awaits!'

'We've had lunch already, Mr Rainbell,' giggled Patsy. He reduced them to giggling too.

'Then have a second lunch! Have a third lunch!' And with a thwack of his walking-stick at Sheilagh's bottom, at which she took no offence at all but merely uttered a schoolgirl shriek, he dismissed them.

'What I can't work out,' I said, feeling like the character in the detective play who says, 'But there's one thing I don't understand, Inspector', 'is how the odd twenty quid on Drummond's swindle sheet makes Purchase Director of Finance.'

'You don't think that's all there is to it, do you?' said Ron Casey, with a rather pitying worldly sneer that I didn't much go for. 'He's been covering up for Drummond for years, hasn't he?'

'Has he? How?'

'You're aware, my dear young innocent Arsehole, that Drummond is about as straight as the proverbial corkscrew?'

'So I've always heard, but has anybody ever proved it?'

'We live in hopes. We live in hopes.'

'*Sollertahnaw!*' This street cry came from the otherwise senseless form of the *Evening Mail*'s crime reporter. The mug of tea which Patsy had thoughtfully placed by his limp right hand had been twitched over, and was dribbling over some quite important files.

'What?'

Ron Casey translated again. 'He's sold the Town Hall.'

'He's done *what*?'

With a monumental effort, as if he were about to make a dying confession, Jack Wilmott raised himself up on one elbow. He spoke with exaggerated clarity.

'He has *sold* the *fuck*ing Town *Hall*!'

Christ and the square root of Christ! And I felt resentfully innocent among these people – my dear young innocent Arsehole, Pisspot had called me, and I deserved the epithet. Ron Casey, who was about six years my junior and who had begun to look even younger as my gullibility was exposed, knew things I didn't know. Jack Wilmott, who had never been known to stand upright after three in the afternoon, knew things I didn't know. Pisspot, dear old bumbling myopic Pisspot, who you would have thought never looked much more beyond his nose than the *Guardian* crossword, knew things I didn't know.

'How do you mean, he's sold the Town Hall? How can anyone sell the Town Hall?'

Wilmott, having got this far on his road to recovery, forklifted himself up to a half-sitting position. Unaware of spilled tea seeping into his trousers, he pronounced in the same spelling-it-out-to-idiots manner:

'He *sold* the fucker to Jack fucking *Dance*, didn't he? Who else would you sell a fucking town hall to?'

'The conference centre of the future, Arsehole! The Tower of Babylon rising on the ashes of Hatter's Castle!'

'But how can he? It's not his to sell!'

I detected pitying glances between Jack Wilmott and Ron Casey. They went Pisspot's way too, but he did not respond, and I felt grateful.

'My dear Arsehole, if in this life you sell only what is yours to sell, you will never dine at the Ritz. We are not speaking of contracts exchanged between solicitors. We are talking about what I believe is technically known as *backhanders*.'

Yes, of course we are. Stupid of me not to have realized. And Ron Casey now looked about nineteen.

I tried to cover my confusion by mimicking Pisspot, which I did clumsily.

'Yes, I'm aware of that, my dear Reggie, but you'll agree that the Town Hall is hardly in the same class as a corner sweetshop. There is such a thing as a Preservation Order.'

'You can't have a Preservation Order on a dangerous structure,' said Ron Casey, aged seventeen, and still my senior.

'Who says it's a dangerous structure?'

'Jack Dance does.'

'Or rather,' came in Pisspot, 'Mr Dance's knowledgeable and independent advisers, who have delivered their report to the District Council, copies to the Department of Environment, and are now refreshing themselves in Bermuda. At Mr Dance's expense, I need hardly add.'

No, you hardly need.

'And Purchase comes into all this, does he?'

'That's what we're working on, sonny boy,' said Wilmott. I remembered the last time I had been called sonny boy, in the back room of a pet shop in an unfinished arcade that looked like a boiler room, and felt myself flushing. But Wilmott, I told myself in self-defence, only spoke like that because he was a heavy and not a juvenile lead, for all that he was drenched in tea and didn't even know it.

Getting the image of Helen's husband out of my head meant putting another image into it, and the one that arrived was of Hattersley and Detective-constable Carpenter, poring over some papers in the Polo Lounge of the Heritage Motor Lodge. I said to Wilmott:

'Do you happen to know a plain-clothes man called Carpenter? Detective-constable?'

'Carpenter. Carpenter. Oh, *Car*penter. *Cunt*,' observed Wilmott, and as if exhausted by his three-minute excursion into coherent English, collapsed across Hattersley's desk again, his final utterance being, '*Noyeytoyla*.'

348

'Noddy in Toyland,' explained Ron Casey. 'He means PC Plod. Carpenter. He's a joke, isn't he?'

Yes he is, you bloody boy scout, and that was my diagnosis the first time I ever met him, so don't look at me as if you were my sodding patrol leader.

I addressed myself carefully and exclusively to Pisspot. 'Reggie, what I'm trying to get at is if any of all this has anything to do with him, joke though he may be. Because you know he was sniffing around here while you were in hospital, and Hattersley showed him some documents?'

'I don't wish to speak ill of a colleague, my dear Arsehole, but Hattersley is a –. No: I contain myself. I do not speak the word. We are in Shredded Wheat Towers: we are not privileged. The expression "cunt", so freely flung about by our somnambulent friend, has not been used.'

I glowed. I hoped that Ron Casey would transmit Pisspot's testimonial to all his shepherd's-pie-scoffing colleagues, and that all his colleagues would spread it throughout Shepford, and that it would eventually get back to Hattersley's burning ears.

'Detective-constable Carpenter is, however, a female organ par excellence. I know the man. I know him well. He once attempted to arrest me for disorderly conduct. I told him that if my conduct was disorderly, his was bloody outrageous, and we left the matter at that.'

Yes, very amusing, Pisspot, and I'd like the full story one day when I have three days to spare, but what's between him and Hattersley?

'Our flat-footed friend's misfortune is that he is permanently behind the times. Long after it had become common knowledge, he made the blazingly obvious discovery that Pilgrim's Progress over there' – (his name for *Pageantry with Progress* (new edition), advance copies of which had just been delivered) – 'was being printed by Bulldog Drummond's brother-in-law. Having relatives of his own in the print, he already knew of the connection between Drummond and brother-in-law, but not of the connection between brother-in-law and Pilgrim's Progress. I believe the revelation came to him in a blinding flash in this very office.'

Yes. And that was why Detective-constable Carpenter was so keen to get me out for a drink. *'I somehow had the impression you and Councillor Drummond more or less lived in each other's pockets.'*

'Going on to put five and five together to make eight, Detective-constable Carpenter then suspected a slight case of hanky-panky, of course knowing nothing of the very large case of hanky-panky already being investigated by his superiors. Friend Hattersley, as one female organ to another, assisted him in his ludicrous investigations by digging out the printing contract, a Xerox of which I happen to know has been in senior police hands for the last six months, since I gave it to them myself ...'

All this swirled in and out of and back in and around my mind, as I tried to pinpoint my reactions to Pisspot's story. Delight: I was delighted that Detective-constable Carpenter had been confirmed, by a higher authority than mine, as a female organ. Satisfaction: I was well-satisfied that Hattersley had been taken in by a female organ, had been defined as a female organ himself by the same higher authority, and was thus relegated from heavy to juvenile lead. But anger: I was angry that all these machinations had gone on above my head, had gone on somewhere outside the realm of all the busy thoughts I had to think each day; that I hadn't been considered worthy of, or fit for, or adult enough to hear about, such semi-public confidences: even by a juvenile lead female organ like Carpenter who had preferred to put his trust in a juvenile lead female organ like Hattersley. *I* could have shown him that printing contract, if he hadn't written me off as useless that night at the Heritage Motor Lodge. I would have been delighted to assist the police in their inquiries.

Except that Detective-constable Carpenter's inquiries were six months behind everybody else's. Pisspot was so indiscreet, and so free with secrets: but he never told me anything.

I said thickly, thinking to myself that this must be what

authors mean when they say someone speaks thickly: 'So what you're saying is that he was wasting his time with Hattersley?'

Pisspot rolled his eyes in a God-help-us manner, and I was sorry to see this time that he rolled them in Ron Casey's direction. Casey, reduced in my eyes to about junior prefect age, piped up:

'PC Plod of the Flying Squad is just about fit for writing out parking tickets. *Every*body knows about that printing contract. What Carpenter doesn't realize, and nobody at Shepford Central dare tell him in case he goes blabbing it around, is that they're hoping to get Drummond on about thirty-five other charges.'

'At least,' I said lamely, not knowing why I was defending Detective-constable Carpenter, 'he's shown a bit of initiative.'

'Initiative bollocks. They're just letting him get on with it to make Drummond think it's a minor inquiry with a schoolboy detective who couldn't even solve a crossword puzzle.'

At this moment Jack Wilmott, who had fallen asleep, rolled off Hattersley's desk and landed on the floor. Cursing richly to himself, he staggered to his feet, and Pisspot took the opportunity of this natural break to invite his guests to leave.

'Well, gentlemen, you have your information about the phantom nose-shaver. Let us hope that one of these days the dam will burst and our investigations will see the light of day. Meanwhile, we all have our routine duties to perform, so as the poet has it, *piss off*.'

They pissed off, and the two of us were left alone. Still wearing the fairly new overcoat that had looked second-hand since the day he bought it, and still clutching his stick, Pisspot was sitting at his desk, which his girth seemed to reduce to the size of a bedside table. It was an absurdly small, drawn-from-stores utility desk for a man in his position. There was an empty panelled room beyond our office, which could have been his own private office had he wished it, with Grade I furniture and a carpet according to his status, but he had never bothered. I would have had that office had I been him, or if I had had his job.

'Well, Bill.'

When we were by ourselves, he rarely called me Arsehole. Nor did he talk as if he were on a convention hall platform. Anyone overhearing Pisspot's private conversation would have thought he was addressing quite a small gathering.

'Well, Reggie.'

We chatted for a while, he asking after Jeanette and I wanting to tell him we were splitting up, but not daring to, for fear of some sage advice coming my way. Partly to change the subject and partly because I genuinely wanted to know, I reciprocated by asking after Mrs Pisspot. I liked his thin, weather-beaten, gardening-gloves wife who treated him like a very old dog that she was still fond of, one that had won prizes for her in its time but had now grown incontinent and daft. She looked and talked and behaved like a Festival committee ratbag but wasn't one, because she had occasionally had Jeanette and me to dinner and had not been patronizing to either of us.

The interval for civilities over, Pisspot humphed and grunted through his accumulation of mail for a minute or two, then peered at me over his half-moon spectacles and asked abruptly:

'How would you like to go to Prague?'

My heart should have jumped and I should have seen myself in Prague even before the words had left his mouth: drinking schnapps or vodka or whatever they drink there, with my gorgeous interpreter, in the great reception chamber of the Hall of Culture, under the chandeliers.

Yet all I thought was: that trip's a long way off, and I may have pissed off with Helen by then.

And a stray aside: if I haven't pissed off with Helen, could I take her with me? She could tell her husband she was exporting English bungalows to Czechoslovakia.

'Do I have to answer that, Reggie? I'd jump at it. Why – can't you go?'

'One of us has to. But the question is, should it be the Dir*ect*-ah of Information or the Dir*ect*-ah of Publicity? Is it our role to inform the benighted foreigner of the delights of this ancient market borough, or to publicize the ceaseless quest for knowledge of building methods by our hard-working city fathers?'

'I'm not with you, Reggie.'

'Then you ought to be with me, young man, because I've given you the broadest of broad hints. The Dir*ect*-ah of Information, or the Dir*ect*-ah of Publicity? Hmm?'

Both of which hats are worn by you, Pisspot. Do stop talking in riddles.

He gave me a weary, petulant sigh, as if feeling put upon because I had failed to read his mind.

'Bill. Or may I call you Arsehole, since we're alone? You know that Bulldog Drummond starts his mayoral year next week, assuming the *bar*stard isn't in Shepford Gaol by then. And you know that Hopkinson takes over as chairman of the Senior Appointments Selection Board. You are with me so far?'

'Go on, Reggie.'

'*One*. Master Hopkinson has had his eye on you at those Festival committee meetings. He is impressed. God knows why he's impressed, but impressed is what he is. *Two*. Master Hopkinson brought grapes to my bedside last week, and we discussed my future.'

I followed what he was saying clearly enough, but none of it was registering. 'About your staying on? Isn't that all settled?'

'It is all settled, but when a man of my age and build skids arse over tit on some blasted female's blasted beads and lands up in hospital with buzzing noises in his head, he begins to consider his position. Whither Pisspot, is the question. Bill, I can still do my job blindfold, and I shall bloody well *have* to do it for the next five years, if Beatrice and I aren't to live on bread and scrape. *But*. I could do it a bloody sight easier without bumph like *this* to cope with.'

He picked up between two fingers, and dropped into the wastepaper basket, the latest copy of the *Shepford Events*, an ill-produced publication put out by our department and subsidized by advertisements from Chinese take-aways. It involved a surprising amount of work, which Pisspot reluctantly supervised.

'Bill, I don't know what you think of Hopkinson. The man is

a female organ, of that there is no doubt. He is certainly not an out-and-out crook like Drummond and Co., and he means well, but he comes high on my list of gullible buggers. He has allowed his head to be stuffed with all that crap and balls about Shepford being the up-and-coming town and Europe-in-a-meadow and suchlike codswallop. And he very much wants to make his mark. So it was not very difficult to persuade Master Hopkinson that an expanding, forward-looking shit-heap such as this should have an expanding, arsehole-creeping Information Department such as the world has never seen. Which, following the usual amoeba-like pattern of such operations, would involve splitting my job in two or if you like hiving half of it off. I would remain Dir*ect*-ah of Information and you would become Dir*ect*-ah of Publicity. What do you think of that? And I'm glad to say he jumped at the notion which of course will be presented as his very own to an astonished District Council.'

No Christs, no euphoria. The same numb feeling as I had felt with Helen. The same clear thinking.

Reggie, if you'd told me all that just over a week ago, you would have seen me standing on my hands. But I shan't be here for your expansion and arsehole-creeping, Reggie. I'm getting out of it with Helen. And even if you *had* told me that just over a week ago, and I'd rushed out into Bell Park yelling that I was going to be the new Dir*ect*-ah of Publicity, it wouldn't make any difference now, because things have happened since that day and I would still be getting out of it with Helen. I'm growing up, Reggie, though you may not have noticed yet. I'm too grown up to accept your grown-up job.

'Well say something Arsehole, even it's only thank you very much!'

I shook my head and grinned, to prove that I was just coming out of a daze.

'That's bloody fantastic, Reggie!'

'I should jolly well think it is. Not that I expect thanks, mind you, since my motives are basefully selfish. And not that you've got the bloody job yet, so don't count chickens. And if you do count chickens, don't expect them to lay golden eggs. Hmm?'

Pisspot examined me quizzically over his glasses, as if assessing my ability to recognize good sense when I came across it.

'Don't fool yourself that this is a plum job, Bill. It is not a plum, it is a gooseberry. If you had any sense you'd turn it down. This is not, repeat not, a town with a future, and if you ever fall for that expanding Shepford crap I will kick you up and down this office until your arse turns blue. It's a glass and concrete excavated ruin we're living in, and if I were your age I'd be out of it on the next train. Except of course, that after the next train whisked you two hundred miles north or a hundred miles due nor' nor' west or wherever, you'd walk out of the bloody station and find yourself back in bloody Shepford. Perhaps the whole country's had it, I don't know. This town certainly has. But don't let the *bar*stards get you down, Bill. And don't let them con you, and don't let them turn you into a piss art*iste*. Here endeth the first lesson.'

Thanks, Pisspot. Thanks for everything, Reggie.

I saw an indistinct, but definitely female shape appear behind the frosted glass door. Not Patsy or Sheilagh; it could be a chit of a messenger girl with the afternoon post. There was a timid knock, suggesting that it was a chit of a messenger girl who had just left school.

'Enter!' roared Pisspot, and Jeanette, my future ex-wife nervously poked her head around the door.

14

'Is it all right? Are you busy?'

'Madame Fisher! Come in, dear lady! Take a chair! Have a cup of exceedingly cold tea!'

I was surprised not only to see Jeanette, since visits to the Civic Centre were discouraged and this was only about her third in eight years, but also by her demeanour. She looked flushed and excited, with a sparkle in the eyes that suggested she was on the verge of some mad adventure such as buying a pair of new shoes. Definitely perky.

After 'He never told me you were out of hospital, Mr Rainbell' and 'You're *looking* well, Mr Rainbell, are you *feeling* well?' and 'How's Mrs Rainbell, Mr Rainbell?' and 'I hope you don't mind my barging in like this, Mr Rainbell' and 'Will you excuse us, Mr Rainbell?' she finally turned to me.

'Bill, you know those new bungalows they're building over in Mayfield?'

Yes, and I know how you came to know about them too, my flower. Helen, bloody Helen, of Mayfield Estates Ltd., had sent us an illustrated brochure about them. The envelope had been in her handwriting and I had uttered some multiple Christs upon finding that it was addressed to 'Mr and Mrs W. Fisher.' 'I thought it was a nice way of telling you I was thinking about you on my first day at work,' she had said when we met by the windmill on the county border.

'Yes?'

'Well you know they're opening a show bungalow, completely furnished, where you'll be able to walk round and see what it'll be like to live there?'

Not what it *will* be like, Jeanette. What it *would* be like.

I'm going to tell you tonight, and I'll be gone tomorrow.

'Well?'

'And you know Mr Richardson?'

Do drop this tiresome style of interrogation, ducky. No, I do not know Mr bloody Richardson.

'Who's Mr Richardson?'

'Did you hear that, Mr Rainbell? Who's Mr Richardson, he says – he's only lived next door but one to us for eight years!'

The fit of asthmatic coughing induced by Pisspot to register dutiful mirth died down, and Jeanette continued. 'Well, Mr Richardson's left Carmichael and Sons, and he's started working in that new office that Mayfield Estates have opened up in Castle Street, and – ooh, Bill, I must tell you this! Do you know who I saw there, this morning? That lady that came round from the Bedding Council that night, and we all thought she was squiffy. I'm *sure* it was her, Bill. She was just coming out of the office as I was just going in.'

And what was she wearing, and did she look happy?

'Did she recognize you?'

'I don't think she even saw me. Anyway, to get back to Mr *Rich*ardson. He's been in charge of getting all the carpets down in the show bungalow, apparently, so of course, he's got his own key. And it's not open to the public until Monday, officially, but Mr Richardson, he said if we didn't tell anybody, and we promised not to disturb anything, he'd lend us his key and we could have a look round it this afternoon!'

Big deal. 'What would we want to do that for?'

'Oh, Bill, you are thick sometimes! Isn't he, Mr Rainbell? I'll *tell* you what we want to do it for – because once the show bungalow opens, that estate's going to be sold like hot cakes! They're going to be showing whole parties round it, Bill! And we could get in first and get our names put down and plonk down a deposit! Don't you see?'

I'll definitely tell her tonight.

'I'm not sure about this key-borrowing lark,' I said, playing dispirited hesitation against her persuasive enthusiasm – a reversal of our usual roles. 'We might get your friend into trouble – you shouldn't really have asked him for it.'

'I didn't ask him, Bill! I just went into the office for another brochure, to send to your mother, and it was Mr *Rich*ardson who made the suggestion. So what do you think?'

'Well, I couldn't get down there this afternoon, for a start. I've got a lot of –'

'*Hogwash!*' Thank you, Pisspot, a fine friend you are.

'No, honestly, Reggie, it's only a few days to the Festival, I've just *got* to –'

'Bugger the Festival! My dear Mrs Fisher, I beg a thousand pardons! You see the effect your husband has on me – he reduces me to a fish porter! Take him away, madam! Lead him from my sight! And don't bring him back until he has bought you all the bungalows you desire.' Thank you *very* much.

I'll tell her this afternoon, then. In a furnished show bungalow, as we peer into its fitted wardrobes and inspect its fitted kitchen, to see what it would be like to live there.

No, that would be cruel. I'll tell her in the car, before we've even picked up the key.

Jeanette's happy prattle about sink units and underfloor heating took us down the lift and into the lobby of the Civic Centre. A burly, public-house-landlord type was standing by the inquiry desk while the rat-faced commissionaire was ringing through to some extension or other on his behalf; the possibility of his being no more a public house landlord than I was, but a plain clothes detective of the heavy rather than the juvenile lead division, was suggested by his general demeanour and also by the bag of golf clubs slung across his broad shoulder.

The rat-faced commissionaire spotted me as I hurried Jeanette towards the revolving doors. Pointing what looked to me like an accusing finger for the non-public-house-landlord's benefit, he shouted in stop-thief tones: 'Mr Fisher! Just a minute!' and I turned reluctantly to greet my visitor as he lumbered across the lobby towards me and dumped the golf clubs at my feet.

'Mr Fisher?'

'Yes?'

'I'm Detective-constable Reid, Shepford Central. This is Detective-constable Carpenter's inquiry really, but he's on day off. I believe you've had some golf clubs stolen?'

'That's right.' If I talk like this all the time, he'll think I have a naturally high voice.

The well-worn bag of golf clubs looked very much as if it had been jumped up and down on and slung down a quarry. But they were not Councillor Drummond's golf clubs. His were practically new, and in any case they were safely locked away, in the boot of Helen's car.

'Do you recognize these, Mr Fisher?'

'Er – I'm not sure. I believe so. In fact – yes. I recognize the grass stains on the bag. And that broken zip.'

Why had I said that? Surely, as far as I was concerned, the case was closed except for tidying up loose ends. All I had to do was jump up and down on Drummond's golf clubs and throw them down a quarry.

'And Mrs Fisher? It is Mrs Fisher? Do you recognize them?'

'No, I'm afraid I've never seen them before.'

Silly bitch. 'I'd only just bought them,' I said, or quavered, hastily, hoping that Detective-constable Carpenter hadn't told him to ask me where. 'So she *wouldn't* recognize them. But they're definitely mine.'

I knew why I'd said it. So he would just get me to sign something, give me the bloody golf clubs, and let us get off. So I could tell Jeanette I wanted a divorce. One problem no longer superseded another in my mind; I was growing up.

If the real owner turned up, would this count as technical theft? Or even non-technical theft?

'Only we raided this flat on the Fairfields Estate – next block to yours, I believe. And it was like Aladdin's Cave in there. Electrical stuff he'd got, radios, fruit bowls, bedside tea-making equipment, you name it. And do you know what he'd the cheek to say, Mr and Mrs Fisher? He said he was opening a second-hand shop, and it was all stock he'd bought!'

What a pity I hadn't known sooner. He could have sold me a set of second-hand golf clubs.

Detective-constable Carpenter's heavy stand-in guffawed.

'Opening a second-hand shop! I laughed! Anyway. It appears no one else has reported golf clubs missing, so we assumed they must be yours. So you can formally identify them, can you?'

'Certainly.'

'Only there's one or two items of gear, well naturally he'd got all his own stuff in there as well, his own household effects, and there's one or two items that we don't know whether he's thieved or not. And what he's claiming is, these golf clubs were given to him by his brother.'

Christ multiplied by fifteen.

'I see. Well, I'm pretty sure they're mine, but I *could* be mistaken. You see, I'd only had them a day or two before they went missing.'

'Only his brother's in New Zealand, so it's going to be a long job checking up.'

Can't I sort this out later, officer? It would be so much simpler. Just leave it for a moment, let me get Jeanette in the car and tell her I want a divorce, then Helen will leave her husband and we'll jump up and down on Councillor Drummond's golf clubs and throw them down a quarry, then I'll come round to the police station and tell you I've made a mistake, this isn't my property after all because there should be a dent in the No. 3 iron, and then we'll bugger off out of Shepford and live happily ever after.

'Oh dear,' I said. 'We don't want to get anyone into trouble, do we, Jeanette?'

'He's in trouble enough already, Mr Fisher. But if you can't be absolutely certain this is your property, we'll have to send a telegram to New Zealand.'

Which is the more serious charge? Wasting police funds and police time, or making a false accusation?

I bent down over the battered old bag of golf clubs and made a great show of scrutinizing it closely.

'Ah. Wait a minute. No, they're not mine. It didn't have this cigarette burn.'

'That could have been made any time, Mr Fisher. He could have made that burn himself.'

Detective-constable Carpenter would never have thought of that. Why does he have to have days off?

'Ah. These irons. I should have looked at these before. There's six irons in this set. Mine had only five, that's why I got them cheap. I can't remember the numbers but there were definitely only five. It wasn't a complete set.'

When we throw Councillor Drummond's golf clubs down the quarry, we'll have to take out one of the irons and put it in a suitcase, and take it with us when we bugger off out of Shepford. Then we can take it to a golf course and throw it in some bushes.

'You're sure about that, Mr Fisher?'

'Absolutely.'

'I think we'd better check with New Zealand just to make sure. He could have found a spare iron and added it to make a complete set, couldn't he? We'll inquire further, Mr Fisher, and let you know what transpires.'

You mean the episode isn't closed? But it must be closed. I've grown up now, and this episode belongs to the days when I wasn't grown up.

I am not thinking about golf clubs. I am thinking about Helen. I am going to tell Jeanette. I am going to begin telling her before we reach that telephone box in the distance.

We had picked up the key to the show bungalow and now we were on the long straight road that led to Mayfield. I had not told her yet, because they had altered the one-way traffic system again and I had been having to concentrate on my driving. But I was going to tell her now.

I had the scenario in my mind, long ago polished into final draft form. It would begin with a discussion of Helen's letter, when the identity of she who could do with her tongue things that a certain person did not yet know about would be formally revealed, as would that of he to whom these things were to be done. I no longer wondered why Jeanette had never said anything about finding the letter. She must have thought about doing so during the weeping period that precipitated my mother's departure for Stradhoughton, and my mother would have counselled her to keep her tongue between her teeth and let this passing infatuation blow over. I could almost hear my mother giving her this advice. 'He's not the first one to go off the rails and he won't be the last. But they never leave home for their fancy women, Jeanette, not unless you make it so they've got to. And then they wish they hadn't, and you've all the palaver of taking them back.'

Had my mother read the letter for herself? When admonishing Jeanette to keep her tongue between her teeth, did she possess new-found knowledge of other uses to which tongues might be put? I was momentarily struck with horror; and momentary horror took me past the telephone box that was my landmark.

I would tell her before we reached that telegraph pole. That second one. That third one. I would tell her now.

'Jeanette, do you remember finding a letter of mine, ages ago?'

'A letter?'

'It was in the inside pocket of my blue suit, when you took it to the cleaner's, and it was still there when you brought the suit back from the cleaner's. Then it vanished.'

'Oh. That letter,' said Jeanette flatly.

We've started. There's no going back now. And I'm more relieved than scared.

'What happened to it, then?'

'Bill.' She drew a deep breath. It was her we've-got-to-have-a-talk deep breath, the one that always heralded the periodic overhauls of our marriage, when she could take it methodically to pieces and lay each part out as if it were a machine stripped down for greasing. Well, this would be the last time.

But then she went on in a small voice: 'I'm afraid I've got a confession to make.'

Yes? *What?* You read it, you didn't read it, you showed it to my mother, you burned it, you kept it, you lost it, you posted it to a sex magazine? *What?*

362

'It *was* in your suit when I brought it back from the cleaner's, because it fell out of your pocket when I was trying to unstaple the cleaning tag. And I was horrified.'

You must have been, but you don't sound horrified now. Continue.

'It was about three or four pages, wasn't it? And written in pen. And all the ink had run, and it was all blurred and soggy and horrible. It must have been the chemicals they used or something, reacting to the ink, because the envelope was quite all right.'

I had not looked in the envelope. I'd felt the envelope to check that the letter was still in it, and I'd kept on feeling it from time to time to see if it was still there, but I hadn't looked at the letter because I knew it by heart. Continue.

'And I felt quite guilty about it, because I should have gone through the pockets before I took the suit to the cleaners, if I'd had any sense. And it might have been an important letter for all I knew.'

'Yes. It was. That's why I'm asking about it.' Continue.

'Well. I left it in your inside pocket, thinking you'd be bound to find it and blow me up about it. But you didn't, and you wore the suit two or three times, and you still didn't say anything about it, so I knew you hadn't looked at it. And I felt even more guilty for not telling you.'

Poor Jeanette. And I thought it in almost the same way as I sometimes thought, poor Helen. Loving sympathy. Warm, affectionate sympathy anyway. To worry so much about nothing, in such a dutiful, wifely way! It was touching, and sad.

'Anyway. You remember that night you went to that big dinner with Mr Rainbell, and you came home a bit squiffy? You threw your jacket over the chair next to the wardrobe, and it slipped off, and the letter must have fallen out of your pocket again, because I found it under the chair next morning.'

'What did you do with it?'

'I'm sorry to say I threw it in the dustbin. I'm sorry, Bill, I know it was a stupid thing to do, but I thought if you saw what condition it was in, you'd be mad at me for not going through your pockets before the suit went to the cleaners, and you would have said *that* was a stupid thing to have done. Which it was. And I suppose I must have panicked, and I'm very sorry.'

Don't apologize, Jeanette, for Christ's sake. We *don't* apologize where we come from, you should know that. And it's so touching, and sad, and even tragic, that you worry about nothing in your dutiful, wifely way.

'Was it a *very* important letter, Bill?'

'Not all that important. Just some stuff about the Festival. Why – didn't you read it?'

'I told you – all the ink had run. It was illegible.'

'It can't have been illegible from beginning to end. Didn't you even *try* to read it?'

'Of course not,' said Jeanette with great wifely dignity. 'I wouldn't dream of reading your letters.'

I wanted to stop the car and hug her, but I couldn't do that, it would give a false impression. But I wanted to do something for her, now, some impulsive thing, to show how moved I was and how much I appreciated her worrying about nothing in her dutiful, wifely way, and how touching and sad and tragic and heart-aching it all was.

We were on the outskirts of Mayfield, passing a row of pink and blue houses that had once been labourers' cottages. On the doorstep of one of them sat a handsome young black and white cat, washing itself with a white-tipped paw. I stopped the car, leaving the engine running, jumped out, scooped up the cat, flung it in Jeanette's lap and drove off, reaching forty in second gear in less than ten yards, and praying that the angry householder reflected in my rear mirror had not got my number.

The cat and Jeanette were staring at each other, both equally astonished.

'It's Mr Pussy-paws!' I gasped as we screeched around a corner. 'They've been looking for him everywhere!'

'Bill! Are you sure?'

'Of course I'm sure! I've *seen* him often enough! So have you!'

'But how did he get all the way down here?'

'They used to live here, years ago. And you know what cats are – they always go back to their old haunts.'

We were speeding along Mayfield's reconstructed High Street, with its village launderettes, its village Electricity Board showrooms and its village secretarial employment agencies. I came down to forty.

'Who's a naughty Mr Pussy-paws?' Jeanette was asking the bewildered cat. 'Who's run away from home, den? But oo'll be *glad* to get home, won't oo, because oo'll have a nice big saucer of milky-wilk.'

God, is she going to talk like that to the bloody animal? Still, it makes no difference to me, I shan't be there to listen.

'Ah, well that's just it,' I said. 'You see, the whole point is, they've moved. They've gone to Norwich.'

'What – and left him behind?'

'Well, he'd vanished, hadn't he? What could they do? I thought you'd heard about it.'

'No – I knew *some*body had moved out of the flats, but I didn't know who it was. Didn't they leave their address with anybody?'

'Not that I know of.'

'Poor Mr Pussy-paws. And such a pretty little thing. Who's doeing to look after oo, den?'

'I suppose he'll have to move in with us.'

'Oh, Bill! Honestly? Could he?'

She hugged the wretched cat to her bosom, whereupon, after an initial struggle, and probably because it had been deprived of affection by the rat-face lately observed in my driving mirror, it eventually settled down and began to purr.

You'll get on very well with Mr Pussy-paws, Jeanette. When I'm gone, you'll have long, daft conversations with him.

And I can't tell you now, but I'll tell you tonight.

We had reached the suburb of the moon where the new bungalows were set out like computerized dots on a map put together from information fed by an unmanned TV satellite. The contours and craters all had names, perhaps given to them by the discoverers who had been here long ago and who had long since left: Milking Green, Meadow Path, Tithe Barn Close, Church Close, Farm Close, The Common, Nettlewood Fold, Bramble Fold, Bluebell Fold. There were, of course, no milking greens or meadows, no tithe barns, churches or farms, no common, no woods where there might have been nettles, brambles or blue-bells. We were in a Legoland of crescents and culs-de-sac with green Lego roofs and red Lego chimney stacks; every bungalow had a Lego porch and a Lego gate and a Lego white fence, and there were new young trees, protected by tubes of wire mesh, growing not far away from where the old trees had been felled, their stumps cleverly converted to accommodate litter bins. And Jeanette, cradling the purring Mr Pussy-paws in her arms, loved it all, uncritically, and so did he.

The show bungalow was at the end of a frying-pan-shaped dead end called Shepherds Croft, without the apostrophe. We walked up its crazy-paving path of imitation quarrystone to the front door of reinforced glass and wrought-iron vertical bars, suggesting an enlightened Borstal. I turned the key that had been lent us by Jeanette's rat-faced friend, and the door wouldn't open.

'That's funny!' And she didn't know it, but I meant that literally.

'Don't tell me after all this he's given us the wrong key!'

'No, it fits all right. But it won't go all the way round in the lock. It seems to be double-locked from the inside.'

'Are you sure it isn't the back door key? Because he didn't say, did he? He just said, that's the key, and be sure to bring it back.'

An extension of the bogus quarrystone paving, which I now saw was more pink in texture than I had previously feared, led us to the back of the bungalow. There did not seem to be a back door, and I had the vaguest idea that we had passed some affair of stripped-pine planks, which we had taken to be the entrance to a fuel-store or laundry room, which might turn out to be the side door. But there was a back window all right, of the picture variety, and looking into it and noting the tasteful bedroom furniture in mainly white painted wood and dull gold fittings, I saw Helen and Detective-constable Carpenter sprawled naked across the candlewick-covered, king-sized divan bed.

I registered, before Jeanette gave a little shriek and the boggle-eyed Mr Pussy-paws mieowed his interest, and they looked up and saw us, that there were still yet things Helen could do with her tongue that I had not known about. Even though the pain in my left side was excruciating, I couldn't help wishing that she had done them with me when the opportunity was still there.

15

THE bunting, which even at the beginning of the Festival had looked like something strung up around the Cornmarket to frighten the starlings, was a sad sight after a week of rain. Last year's plastic replicas of the Shepford coat of arms had been lost, and the dog-eared, paint-streaked substitutes, hanging by string from every lamp standard, had not weathered well. The substantial balcony of the old Town Hall, where my lady wife and I were guests of the new Mayor, had been shored up with tubular scaffolding, a precaution against the recently-discovered shifting of the granite foundations.

The pain in my left side had remained with me in varying degrees all through the week; I could chronicle the progress of the Festival by referring to a mental graph of these degrees of pain. It had been a dull, continuous throbbing all through the gymkhana and display of children's physical training that had started the week; a series of vicious, searing jabs or stabs during the floodlit tattoo; a long, mournful ache, more sorrow than pain, at the exhibition of arts and crafts in the foyer of the *Evening Mail* office; a nagging gripe, like a serious attack of wind, as Old Folks' Day degenerated into mutinous chaos; anguish during the hundred-metre dash in the combined schools sporting events; agony during last night's Son et Lumière at Shepford Castle. And the pain was with me still, it wouldn't leave, as I sat in my canvas chair among all the Festival top brass, rubbing the left side of my chest, my fingers brushing against Helen's letter in the inside pocket where Jeanette would never find it.

I'm sorry, Bill, I'm sorry I'm sorry I'm sorry I'm sorry. Will you see me again? Just once? Please? Please? So that I can explain properly?

Of course I will, Helen, eventually. The scene must be played out, mustn't it? Even juvenile leads are old troupers: the play's the thing, the show must go on.

I had to do it, Bill. You've no idea. He was practically black-mailing me.

No. If what Jeanette and I and Mr Pussy-paws saw was blackmail, Helen, then I'll take up blackmail myself as a living, and my rat-faced, lip-licking victims will hand over their life savings when I've only asked for twenty-five pounds in used notes.

There was nothing else I could do, Bill. He has been pester-ing me ever since that night at the Heritage Motor Lodge – he kept 'happening' to bump into me & wanted to ask questions about Drummond & Jack Dance. I told him there was nothing I could tell him but he was so persistent, he began making sly comments about you & us & talking and obstructing the police in their inquiries & how he could make serious trouble for us both. I was so frightened I agreed to have a drink with him – I met him in the Old Bell at Mayfield because it was convenient for me, he asked me a lot of questions about Drummond & then asked was I going into town & could I give him a lift.

Bill, please please please believe me. I was driving him back to Shepford & we ran over some glass or something & found we had a flat tyre & had to change the wheel. I forgot all about Drummond's golf clubs in the boot & of course he saw them – Drummond had reported them stolen so he knew about them from the police list & there was no use saying they were mine because they were an American make, Jack Dance brought them back for Drummond from New York & you can't get them in this country. I was terrified, Bill. I tried to pretend it was all a silly practical joke & that I meant to return them & he pre-tended to believe me & said what a 'character' I was & was I going to be 'nice' to him. I cringe as I write this down & I shan't write any more of it, you know the rest.

Yes. Do I bloody well not?

Bill, Bill, Bill, darling Bill, forgive me, it wasn't what it must

*have looked like to you, I was acting, I was doing what he asked
me to do because I was terrified & I hated it. Please please let
me see you, Bill, meet me by our windmill again – we've only
been there once & already I think of it as our windmill. Will you
see me there? I know you'll be busy with the Festival but after
that I shall drive there every evening & hope & hope that you'll
come. Will you? Will you?*

I'll be there, Helen. I'll give it about four or five days, I
think, to keep you waiting. Or three days, or two, if the pain has
gone by then: so that I can see you and talk to you and get the
pain back again. And we'll go on meeting and talking, and
exhuming those four affairs that you never had; it'll give our
relationship a new dimension, a kick, a bit of zest that it never
had before. I look forward to it, you probably look forward to it
yourself, it's our big chance. Such fat parts for two juvenile
leads, and such thrilling, unexpected twists in the light comedy.
'Will run and run and run' – *Evening Mail.*

'Rain keeps off, should be colourful occasion,' barked His Wor-
ship the Mayor, adjusting his unaccustomed chain of office for
the fiftieth time. Knowing Drummond, he was probably assessing its troy weight and wondering if he could get away with
reporting it lost.

Next to him sat his ratbag wife, and next to him the new
Director of Finance whose beautifully clean-shaven nose was
disfigured only by a small surgical dressing held in place by
Elastoplast; then came Purchase's ratbag wife, then the rat-faced
Town Clerk and his ratbag wife, then Councillor Hopkinson of
the Senior Appointments Selection Committee and his ratbag
wife, then me, and then Jeanette in her silly little hat and new
clothes. On the mayor's left, and behind us, were various other
rat-faces and ratbags of some standing in the town. There were
two empty chairs: Pisspot's wife preferred to stay at home pottering among her roses, while Pisspot himself was probably
sipping slimline – low calorie – Indian – *tonic* water in the
King's Head Doubles Bar across the Cornmarket, where the
Evening Mail gang, having written their accounts of this last

afternoon of the Festival some hours before, were taking advantage of the all-day extension.

There was a fair number of people in the Cornmarket, thronging the pavements and roadways behind the rope barrier that cordoned off the square itself. Two roads, Cripplegate on the west side of the square, and the meandering shopping-centre access road on the east, had been left clear – the access road for the procession of old comrades, boy scouts and other rat-face patrols that must by now have just about set off from its rallying point at Shepford Castle; and Cripplegate for the triumphal march into the Cornmarket of the Shepford Police Silver Band.

The Police Band, if the schedule I had arranged continued to work like clockwork, should be arriving any minute. Meanwhile those with a taste for music had to make do with the Shepford and District Traffic Wardens' Steel Band, which was playing something of a calypso nature while the gin-gurgling ratbag of Festival Committee fame judged the Spottiest Dog contest.

I was somewhat uneasy about the number of dogs in the Cornmarket, although the protracted event in which they were contenders had been going smoothly enough so far. The children's dog show had produced a remarkable response, yielding a turn-out of some five hundred mongrels, Alsatians, Dalmatians, terriers, bulldogs, and other breeds and half-breeds, all of which, as they strained at their leads or scrabbled frantically in their makeshift orange-box kennels, were kicking up a fair amount of row. It had been my idea to stagger the dog show throughout the afternoon, my theory being that once, say, the Ugliest Dog class had been judged, all those with ugly dogs would then depart the arena, and so on with other dogs in other classes, so that the canine proportion of the crowd would be steadily diminished as the day wore on. This had not worked out in practice. A rat-faced steward was bawling into the Tannoy: 'Can I appeal to all you little boys and girls again! Once your dogs have taken part in their particular section, will you please remove them from the Cornmarket? Please remove your dogs from the Cornmarket, then come back without your dogs to enjoy the fun.' But no one took any notice. For one thing, many dogs would have been entered in more than one class. For another, most dog-escorting children were hemmed in by the great press of adults behind them. But apart from the excessive yapping and the strong smell of unwashed dog that wafted across the square, there had been no trouble so far.

To the cacophony of dogs and steel band, which was ill-rehearsed, there was now added another sound – that of a Sousa march being played rather better than the traffic wardens' rendering of 'Ob-La-Di, Ob-La-Da.'

'Ooh, look, Bill, the police band's coming!' cried Jeanette, clutching my arm in great excitement, as if the police band were making their arrival by parachute.

I craned over the balcony and looked across the Town Hall side of the Cornmarket towards Cripplegate, where I could see the glint of sounding brass.

'Don't they march splendidly!' a County ratbag was saying. 'And then one hears that our police are ill-disciplined! Nonsense!'

I looked at my watch. Spot on time. A rat-face wearing an armband who had been standing at the end of Cripplegate waiting for the band to approach, signalled to the traffic wardens to cease their racket and clear off.

'Wait a minute! They're turning left into St Peter's Street! Why are they turning left into St Peter's Street!'

I craned forward again. Directed by their drum-major with his mace, the police band were indeed wheeling into St Peter's Street, about two hundred yards short of the Cornmarket.

'Of course!' exclaimed Purchase. He had unfolded the street map in his copy of *Pageantry with Progress* (new edition) which had been handed out to the Mayor's guests along with the souvenir programme and other bumph. 'Cripplegate is subject to the revised traffic scheme. There's now a compulsory left turn into St Peter's Street.'

'Damn blast it,' spluttered Drummond. 'Doesn't apply special occasion, surely God!'

'If it applies at all, then it applies *to* all, surely,' croaked the

372

County ratbag. 'If the police take no notice of restriction signs, then who will?'

I had been poring over my own street-map. 'You do realize,' I said, leaning across to Purchase and speaking as if it were his fault, 'that if they're going to obey every road sign they come across, there's a no right-turn in Castle Street so they'll have to fork left as far as the no-entry section, then take a compulsory right into Hill Street which should get them on to the Route Four expressway; and depending on which way they turn there they'll finish up either back where they started from or in Wolverhampton.'

'I'm afraid I'm not responsible for the traffic regulations!' snapped Purchase.

'Well *I'm* certainly not. I worked out this route from the map issued to me by the Festival Office.'

And brought to me, I now recalled, by Hattersley, whom I had dispatched on this little office-boy errand. It would not have been beyond him to palm an out-of-date map on me deliberately.

'Surely a steward can run after the police band and point out that the regulations don't apply to pedestrians?' someone was saying; and someone else was saying, 'At least let the steel band play on a little. We ought to have *some* music, if only to drown the noise of all those blessed dogs!'

But it was a little late for request encores from the steel band. The traffic wardens had arranged themselves in straggling lines of three and were now shambling off to their next engagement, a concert at the old people's home.

As they headed towards the shopping-centre access road there was another diversion. An old Ford van, painted in psychedelic colours and travelling at speed, came tearing out of the access road into the Cornmarket, scattering the battalion of traffic wardens in all directions, steel drums jangling, in fear of their lives. The van screeched to a stop at the edge of the square, its back door was flung open, and two young men in denim suits stitched over with gold and silver stars began to unload amplifying equipment. The legend on the side of the van read in Art Noveau letters, *The Madison* – a combination of talents which had achieved a certain amount of fame in Midlands discotheques and other centres of opinion. I could have told The Madison for nothing, however, that they were in the wrong place, and should have been unloading their gear twenty minutes ago in the disused coke-compound – or Street Theatre, as it was now known – on the industrial side of the town.

Though presumably the hard core of The Madison's following would be waiting impatiently at the coke-compound, many of the teenagers present in the Cornmarket were sufficiently impressed by the sight of them to break ranks and dash across the square brandishing bits of paper, pairs of knickers and lipsticks. More important, The Madison's arrival seemed to have interested the small television unit that had descended on us from Birmingham. (When I had finally got round to ringing *Nationwide* a nice lady had said that it sounded a super idea but unfortunately it clashed with open day at Battersea Dog's Home which they'd already arranged to cover, and if only I'd let them know sooner.) The TV camera zoomed in on our visitors just as the scattered traffic wardens recovered their composure and, with their polished, sawn-off oil-barrels still hanging around their necks, converged on The Madison's van with pencil stubs and pads of parking tickets at the ready.

The effect of the disturbance on the Shepford's Silliest Dog class, which was at that moment being judged, was not a good one. Such silly dogs as had been commanded to sit at their young masters' feet while being examined for cross-eyes, lolling tongues and other points, came lolloping up to join the mêlée surrounding The Madison. The silliest dogs, which could not be trusted off the lead, strained and pulled, barking furiously, in their efforts to join in the commotion. The TV crews, with an escaped Norwich terrier worrying their ankles, panned the camera to take in reaction shots of the set faces on the Town Hall balcony.

'Hmm, I wouldn't describe *this* as very good publicity for Shepford,' grumbled Councillor Hopkinson.

Rat-faced stewards were restoring something like order, mainly by seizing teenagers by the scruff of the neck and frog-

374

marching them back to the rope barrier. Several unleashed dogs were still frolicking about the square, but they were gradually being rounded up by their infant guardians. The driver of The Madison's van was now receiving instructions on the best way to the coke-compound from several of the traffic wardens, who were gesticulating to him to drive up Cripplegate and turn off at Bank Street. This would be a mistake, since Bank Street was now a dead end.

The traffic wardens re-formed themselves in threes and resumed their ragged march towards the access road, one of them peeling off to pursue The Madison's van and point out that as Cripplegate was a one-way street, they could not drive up it but would have to reverse as far as Bank Street.

The crisis more or less over, I sank back into my canvas chair in some relief. At least, I was able to tell myself, it had stopped me thinking of Helen for about ten minutes.

Perhaps feeling that his dignity as Mayor precluded his witnessing such a shambles, Councillor Drummond had studiously ignored the incident involving The Madison and was browsing through *Pageantry with Progress* (new edition). Even as I lit a much-needed cigarette and inhaled gratefully, I heard him explode: 'Good – *God! What devil this!*' Eyes popping, face purple with indignation, he shot out an arm so viciously that it would have sliced the bosom off his ratbag wife had she possessed one, and thrust the guide-book, open at the page that had encouraged this reaction, to Purchase. Purchase looked at it with distaste, exclaimed, 'Inexcusable!' and passed it on. Councillor Hopkinson stared at it without a word, and passed it to me.

The guide-book was open at an obscure back-pages section, an Industrial and Commercial Directory whose closely-printed text had been broken up with single-column photographs of factories and office blocks. The offending page showed a picture of the new chemical laboratory that had been built where the old Assembly Rooms used to be. The caption should have contained some information about the debt owed to the laboratory by the aluminium powder, paper coating and polyurethane paint industries. Instead, it read: '*RAT-FACE HOUSE: where*

*the screams of human guinea-pigs may be heard nightly while
plastic-surgery technicians carry out vivisection-type experiments to produce an improved, forward-looking rat-face for a
go-ahead, forward-looking new Shepford.'*

Christ on crutches.

Bloody Hattersley. I had definitely screwed that bit of nonsense up and thrown it in the waste-paper basket. And just in
case I hadn't definitely screwed it up and thrown it away, I had
checked that caption specifically when going through the final
proofs. And it had not been in the final proofs when they were
handed over to Hattersley to sort out and return to the printers.

'Any explanation of this, at all?' asked Councillor Hopkinson coldly.

'None at all,' I said blandly, restraining the impulse to call
him 'Sir'. 'I simply don't understand it. There must have been a
slip-up somewhere.'

'I should say there *has* been a slip-up. Have these things
been publicly distributed?'

'I'm afraid so.'

'When you see Mr Rainbell, tell him there'll be an emergency
meeting of the Council Publicity Committee tomorrow morning. You'd better come too.'

'Yes, sir.'

Further discussion was prevented by the sounds of commotion
from the shopping-centre access road. The Shepford and District
Traffic Wardens' Steel Band, which should have been half-way
to the old folks' home by now, was shambling back into the
Cornmarket playing an approximate version of 'When The
Saints Go Marching In'. In a moment it was possible to see the
reason for this unscheduled portion of the afternoon's entertainment. The band was being pressed forward – or, from its
own point of view, back – by a great procession of old comrades, ambulance-men, and hordes of other uniformed figures
representing a cross-section of the Shepford community. The
procession had become hopelessly disorganized somewhere
along its winding route, and was marching about twenty deep,
with half the WVS contingent shoulder to shoulder with half

the Red Cross contingent, and the other halves of both contingents pretty evenly distributed among the serried ranks of police cadets, choristers, firemen, non-musical traffic wardens, commissionaires and sundry others who appeared to be taking the cross-section idea pretty literally.

Concurrent with this, the rat-face in charge of the Tannoy system was announcing the grand finale of the children's dog show. '... the moment you've been waiting for, the Disobedient Dog class. Yes, children, we are looking for the most disobedient dog in Shepford. Now let's have all those disobedient dogs in the centre of the arena.'

A rat-face with more knowledge of children would have taken care to say, 'Let's have all those disobedient dogs, *with their owners*, in the centre of the arena.' This important rider was omitted. Several of the smaller children, imagining that the disobedient dogs were required to frisk independently into the arena and demonstrate their bloody-mindedness, let go of their leashes. At this example, other children, who had been coming forward with their dogs firmly under control, hesitated in the belief that they had misunderstood the instructions just announced, then unleashed their dogs or merely let go of their dog's leads. The Disobedient Dog class was a popular attraction and nearly all the dogs present seemed to have been entered for it. As the traffic wardens' band led the limping army of cross-representative, cross-sectionalized, cross-fertilized Shepford citizens towards the square, hardly a square inch of it was visible for the seething mass of yowling, growling, snapping, yapping and above all fighting dogs.

Also concurrently, The Madison's psychedelic van had been observed – by Jeanette, and more importantly, by such teenagers who had not thrown themselves joyfully into the sea of dogs – to re-emerge from the dead-end Bank Street into Cripplegate where, its driver presumably having forgotten whether Cripplegate was one-way going west or one-way going east, it reversed at speed into the Cornmarket.

The TV camera had been knocked off its podium by now; so it was unable to record the great procession entering its final stages of disintegration as, pushed on from behind as in some mad general's battle in the First World War, wave after wave of the cream of Shepford's decent, God-fearing, law-abiding, uniform-wearing youth was thrown into the snarling, slavering pit of dogflesh to which the Cornmarket had been reduced; while the dregs of Shepford's less decent, non-God-fearing, un-law abiding and non-uniform-wearing youth, some with small terriers attached to their lower limbs, had put The Madison's van in a state of siege and, in their anger and disappointment at their idols' refusal to mingle among them and sign autographs, were on the verge of tipping it over. Meanwhile, such members of the Shepford and District Traffic Wardens' Steel Band as were not fighting off Alsatians with their drumsticks, were offering a spirited attempt at 'Cricket, Lovely Cricket'.

Not concurrently, but only fractionally consecutively, there was a kind of sub-disturbance at the corner of the square nearest the Town Hall, where the road had been closed for the benefit of the spectators. The sound of 'Speed Bonny Boat Like a Bird On The Wing', scored for brass, fragmentarily clashed with the calypso-tinted baying and howling of five hundred dogs. I saw several policemen clearing a path through the crowds, incidentally pushing them back into the mass dog fight from which they were trying to escape; and the Police Silver Band came into view.

'Speed Bonny Boat' was naturally arranged as a slow march, and the police band were indeed slow-marching towards their doom, for it had been agreed in correspondence with the Festival committee that this would be a most spectacular way of entering the Cornmarket.

Even more spectacular than the well-disciplined slow march, however, was the fact that the police band had been joined, since last sighted in Cripplegate, by some very senior officers. Walking, rather than marching, several steps ahead of the drum-major, but keeping in step, and maintaining the proper pace, were the Chief Constable of Shepford, uniformed but carrying his gloves; a uniformed superintendent and a uniformed inspector; and someone in a dark overcoat and trilby who, al-

378

though he reminded me somewhat of the man in the Civic Centre lobby who had turned out not to be a public house landlord after all, was plainly his senior by very many ranks.

As a berserk Dalmatian attempted to seize the lead trombonist by the throat, and a nondescript breed that seemed to have a trace of greyhound in it leaped up at, and partly through, the big drum, and the police band ceased to play 'Speed Bonny Boat' – some of its members attempting to restore order, others fleeing in terror, others heading for The Madison's now over-turned psychedelic van with the object of making arrests – the deputation headed by the Chief Constable peeled off, and with eight or nine mongrels chasing after it, made briskly for the steps leading up to the Town Hall balcony.

Councillor Drummond had already gone white and was fingering his chain of office as if telling beads. He ceased to be white, and became the colour of putty, as the Chief Constable and his party, still trying to walk in some kind of formal manner, but having to edge their way through a row of canvas chairs, approached and crowded around him.

'Mr Mayor, are you Mr Percival Walter Angus Drummond?' asked the Chief Constable, at the same time leaning slightly backwards so that his hand could reach and conceal from the ladies' sight the jagged tear in the lower part of his trouser seat.

'Am,' muttered Drummond, eyes downcast, avoiding those of his ratbag wife who was looking as if she feared public rape.

'And do you reside at The Mill House, The Lane, Pontsford St Mary's, near Shepford?'

'Do.'

'I am the Chief Constable as you know, sir, and this is Superintendent Grout who has warrants for your arrest under certain sections of the Public Bodies Corrupt Practices Act, 1889. Will you come along with us now to Shepford Central Police Station, where the charges will be read to you?'

'Would have thought neither time place, surely more suitable occasion?' Drummond, with a new change of hue to that of cigarette ash, was blustering; but the Chief Constable had already turned to Purchase whose clean-shaven nose, I was

379

fascinated to see, had grown damp and pink as if it, and it alone among his features, had just emerged from a turkish bath.

'Are you Mr James Henry Purchase, sir, of number 47 Castle Park, Shepford, and are you the Director of Finance of the District of Shepford?'

'I am James Henry Purchase of that address, but my appointment as Director of Finance has not yet been promulgated,' replied Purchase, punctilious to the last.

'I am the Chief Constable of Shepford, Mr Purchase, and this is Superintendent Grout who has warrants for your arrest under certain sections of the Public Bodies Corrupt Practices Act, 1889. Will you come along with us now to the Central Police Station, where the charges will be read to you?'

Drummond and Purchase, heads bowed, were led away, accompanied by their tight-lipped, blood-drained, ratbag wives and one or two sympathizers or relatives among our little group. The hum of excited or astonished or indignant chatter was cut into by Councillor Hopkinson who, as a lost Afghan hound howled piteously up at him from below the Town Hall balcony, said with hoarse urgency:

'First things first, I think, Fisher. I've seen crowds panic and this crowd's panicking. Do something.'

'What can *I* do?'

'It's your show, Fisher. Get to that microphone and appeal for order. *Move!*'

I pushed my way reluctantly forward to the microphone from which, in happier times, Councillor Drummond would eventually have made the speech of thanks to all organizers worked so hard make Festival first-rate tip-top success been this week. 'Ladies and Gentlemen.' I began, without any notion of what I meant to say; but the microphone was not working, and so I was relieved of that responsibility.

I stared out glassy-eyed at the maelstrom in the Cornmarket, and was somehow able to isolate two clear details, as I remembered being able to pick out details in a crowded picture of Hell that I had once seen in the Stradhoughton Art Galley's collection of Victorian paintings. The first of these was a child of about five, who was being dragged in the direction of Cripplegate by the very large sheepdog which had been number two runner-up in the Silliest Dog class; the child clutched grimly on to the length of rope that served as a lead, but such was the speed and energy of her pet that she was now travelling mainly on her back, like a thrown rider whose foot has caught in the stirrup.

The other detail was Pisspot, who was emerging from, or rather being ejected from, the King's Head Doubles Bar on the far side of the Cornmarket.

Swaying, shouting, and keeping dogs at bay with his stick, Pisspot disappeared into the morass of fighting, knicker-waving, arrest-evading teenagers in the vicinity of The Madison's overturned van; emerged again and kept his head above a fifty-yard heaving slick of small children and dogs; vanished into the tightly-defended human fort that had been formed by the Shepford and District Traffic Wardens' Steel Band; re-emerged, and was now staggering up the steps leading to the Town Hall balcony, bawling: 'Justice has been done! Justice has been done this day!'

The recently-vacated canvas chairs were pushed aside and fell over as Pisspot, drunker than I had ever seen him before, weaved towards me. Scandalized ratbags shrank back; Councillor Hopkinson buried his face in his hands; Jeanette gave Pisspot a nervous, inquiring smile, and I saw her mouthing, 'Good afternoon, Mr Rainbell.'

'My dear Arsehole, why you're not celebrating auspacious day, whorrar you, blurry lily-liller teetotaller? Donyounstan, Arsehole, my dear ol Arsehole, we have won we have won we have fucking WON! The *bar*stard Drummond is in chains!'

He seized my arm, as a master of ceremonies would seize the arm of a winning boxer, and raised it aloft.

'An nother thing, dear ol Arsehole, mus give assemble olpupace goo news.'

He blew like the north wind into the microphone, which had miraculously begun to work again, and steadying himself with one hand against the rock-firm balustrade of the buttressed balcony of the dangerous structure that was the old Town Hall of the ancient Borough of Shepford, he drew breath; and Piss-pot's stentorian voice, drowning even the barking of dogs and the crying of children and the general racket below and beyond us, boomed over the pandemonium of the Cornmarket.

'Ladeez an gennel*men*! May I present to *you*! For the first time in Shep-*ford*! The new, reigning, shit-heat champeens of the British Isles, the firm of Pisspot and Arsehole! Or, if you prefer it, Arsehole and Pisspot!'

16

'THAT'S a pretty little street over there,' Oscar said. 'Yeah, that's real pretty. Now in the Uneye-ed States, you'd never come across a street like that.'

I couldn't see it with his eyes or even with my own, it was my third day of walking aimlessly about and I was exhausted. I remembered dimly what the street had been like, two years or three years or four years ago, when I'd last seen it: more of an alley, really, with some little houses, a very old timbered pub, a villagey-looking post office and one or two villagey-looking general stores. The narrow roadway had been cobbled, like the Cornmarket. There had been a 'Save Green Street' Society which had sent circulars to the Department of Information and Publicity, among other influential bodies, and they had been thrown away unread.

It was all gone now: it was a gap, a rubbled space, with bile-green builders' fencing all around it; but the fencing was half-flattened, because the consortium that was to have built a Georgian-style square of prestige shops here had run out of money, and the patrolling guards and their guard dogs had been withdrawn.

'Real pretty.'

Go away, Oscar, this is serious.

I had not seen Helen yet. This would be her third evening by the old windmill on the county border, if she was still waiting there. I didn't want to see her. It was serious. I was not available for light comedy, nor probably ever would be again.

Hattersley was expected to be the new Director of Information and Publicity. Mr R. V. O. Rainbell had retired prematurely owing to ill-health. I had been given the choice of transferring to the Rates Office or not transferring to it.

There had already been a preliminary interview with the Rating Officer, whom I had better stop thinking of as King Rat.

'I would certainly plump for Rates if I were you, Mr Fisher, even if I had any choice in the matter. I believe you do have some experience in the field, and the opportunities are certainly there. Take Rate Assessment, not that you'd be so high up the ladder to begin with ...'

'Lissena what the man says,' insisted Oscar. 'Oh *kay*, it's a routine *jab*. That's only because up until now it's been done by routine people, Bill!'

Oscar, I have to say good-bye to you. It's been fun while it lasted, but it isn't fun any more. You're a bore even, and an intrusion. Good-bye, Oscar. Thanks.

I couldn't quite make out where I was, although the place seemed familiar. I seemed to be in a graveyard, one that had been abandoned. I was in a walled enclosure, although part of the wall had crumbled to reveal the pretty little street that Oscar remembered and I hardly did. It grew high with grass and the kind of weeds that used to be seen on bomb sites; and dotted here and there, in no particular symmetry, were statues in granite and marble, some upright, some lying on the ground. There was a long dais of planks, raised up on bricks, with a line of busts upon it – they looked as if they had just been potted out and, if anyone still cared for them, would in time grow torsos, legs and arms like the other statues lying all about, and in the fullness of the seasons would sprout scrolls and top hats, their pointing fingers blossoming into heroic gestures.

In the centre of this disused cemetery or whatever it would turn out to be, there was a kind of truncated Stonehenge of marble plinths and podia from which some of the statues now lying on the ground had clearly been removed. Dominating this area, and out of proportion to all its neighbours, was the equestrian statue of the first Duke of Shepford in blackened bronze, the guy ropes still fluttering like streamers from his broad shoulders and from his horse's mane. When I had first arrived in Shepford, this statue had stood in the centre of the

Cornmarket, and I could not remember when it had been removed.

Each morning I had set off on one of these long walks that finished up in strange destinations, telling Jeanette that I had another interview at the Rates Office or that I had to attend the preliminary hearing of the Council's inquiry into the Shepford Festival. Sometimes I mooched about thinking of Helen, sometimes I mooched about thinking of myself; and today I mooched about thinking of myself, Jeanette, and one other.

Last night I had got home late and stood at the window of my book-lined turret, overlooking the steeples and towers and glass arcade roofs and chimney belfries; the sound of 'Tom Bowling' played on the carillon of the covered market died away, and I saw gravel pits, abandoned quarries, rezoned factories, the doomed woods where the new conference hotel would be, the ribbon of wire netting guarding the pollution free river; and far off at the end of the long straight road, the village of Mayfield with its flat-roofed maisonettes, and its new bungalows.

'Bill? Can I say something to you? Are you in a good mood?'

Jeanette had given Mr Pussy-paws his evening tin of something with liver in it. Eventually I would have to ween it, and her, off pet foods manufactured by Helen's husband: silly, painful reminder of a scene that should have been forgotten. But the cat purred contentedly enough as it scoffed this doubtful product. Jeanette seemed happier than I had ever known her.

'I haven't got much to be in a good mood about, have I, Jeanette?'

'Oh, you'll have to stop brooding one of these days, Bill! It could have happened to anybody! And it'll all blow over, and after all, one thing about working in local government, you've still got a job, and the money's not much less, is it?'

'No.'

'Come and sit down, Bill. I've got something to ask you.'

'Ask away.'

'Sit down first.'

'Why – am I going to faint from shock or something?' I'm

picking up her argot, or the husbandly equivalent of it, as I never used to. Does that mean I'm staying with Jeanette after all? And if I'm not staying with Jeanette, where am I going?

'You *might* faint, for all I know. Bill, what would you say if I told you I thought I was going to have a baby?'

Christ. Quadruple, quintuple, octuple Christ.

'You can't be. You're on the pill.'

'The pill isn't infallible, you know. And anyway –' Deep breath. Confession time. '– I haven't been taking my pill. It brought me out in such a rash, and I thought, just for one month, I'll risk it and see what happens. Bill? Is it all right, Bill?'

'It'll have to be all right, won't it?'

Christ in multiples of thousands.

My mother put her up to this.

A baby. A man-child, or perhaps a woman-child. What do you *do* with them?

You give them milk. You take them to zoos and safari parks.

What do you *say* to them?

You tell them stories.

Once upon a time, there was a poor woodcutter, who had but one son ...

'Are you glad, Bill, or sorry?'

'I'm glad.'

I'm glad. It'll be a new experience. I can always do with a new experience.

'You don't sound it.'

'I *am* glad. I need to take it in.'

'Of course, it's not confirmed yet, but if it *is* confirmed, have you made up your mind about the bungalow?'

'Mortgagedene.'

'*What*-dene?'

'Good name for a house, that, Jeanette. I'll sign the papers tomorrow. Mortgagedene.'

'Don't be so daft, Bill Fisher. We'll call it Hillcrest, same as your mother's house. And won't she be glad to hear I've got some news?'

I had walked around the streamered statue of the first Duke

of Shepford three or four times, and now I had placed myself,
I knew where I was.

The walled yard belonged to the Clerk of Works' department
of the district of Shepford; I had been here once or twice on
business, and that was why it seemed familiar, like the cemetery
in Stradhoughton where my grandmother was buried.

I don't love you, Helen. I'm becoming a father this year so I
don't love you. I can accept no more juvenile lead engagements.

Once, before the old terraces had been pulled down, there had
been a fumigating shed here somewhere, and mattresses and
sofas had been put out on this flattened grass enclosure to air
before being returned to their owners. Now the terraces, slum or
otherwise, had gone; the festering mattresses, as well as accumu-
lated junk and solid Victorian furniture, had been tossed into
public bonfires on waste ground before the retreat to the high
blocks on the perimeter of Shepford. Whole streets disappeared,
whole neighbourhoods, and all the statues of aldermen and benefactors, dislodged by demolition or the building of ring roads,
were towed to this place and dumped. At first they were cleaned,
in the belief that they would be found new sites in the beautiful,
rising city; some of the granite statues were scrubbed pink, some
half-scrubbed. The others were black and covered in bird drop-
pings. Slowly it became clear to anyone who cared to notice that
this was to be their last resting place, and as more statues were
tossed in, this walled enclosure had taken on the appearance not
of an abandoned cemetery, as I had previously thought, but of
a knackers' yard.

I can cope, Helen had said. I can cope with anything, I always
have and I always will.

And *I* can cope.

Except losing you, she had said.

You've lost me, Helen. It's serious. It's not light comedy. It's
not even drama. It's life.

I knew where I was and who I was, and I drew in great gulps
of air to show that everything up until now, everything up until
last night when Jeanette had said, 'Can I say something to you?
Are you in a good mood?' was behind me. I was a heavy at last,

or would be, I was grown up, or would be, and it didn't happen by decision, it happened by circumstance.

A telephone message had been taken by Jeanette about some golf clubs. Could I go round and see Detective-constable Reid at Shepford Central? I knew what I meant to do. I would ask for Detective-constable Carpenter, it was his case anyway, and tell him to wind up the matter in any way he chose, or alternatively stick his head up his arse.

Feeling pleased, relieved, relaxed, confident and grown-up, I took a last look at the streamer-tethered statue of the First Duke of Shepford.

'Quite a guy,' a voice said in my head. I ignored it. It would go away. But it didn't; and so it was mainly to drown Oscar's voice that I said aloud to the bronze figure of the Duke of Shepford on his bronze horse:

'Captain Fisher, sir. First Ambrosian Cavalry. We've just got through, sir – it's murder out there.'

But I did not salute, as I would have done once. And I walked, not marched, away.

Discover more about our forthcoming books through Penguin's FREE newspaper...

Penguin

Quarterly

It's packed with:

- exciting features
- author interviews
- previews & reviews
- books from your favourite films & TV series
- exclusive competitions & much, much more...

Write off for your free copy today to:
Dept JC
Penguin Books Ltd
FREEPOST
West Drayton
Middlesex
UB7 0BR
NO STAMP REQUIRED

READ MORE IN PENGUIN

In every corner of the world, on every subject under the sun, Penguin represents quality and variety – the very best in publishing today.

For complete information about books available from Penguin – including Puffins, Penguin Classics and Arkana – and how to order them, write to us at the appropriate address below. Please note that for copyright reasons the selection of books varies from country to country.

In the United Kingdom: Please write to *Dept. JC, Penguin Books Ltd, FREEPOST, West Drayton, Middlesex UB7 OBR*

If you have any difficulty in obtaining a title, please send your order with the correct money, plus ten per cent for postage and packaging, to *PO Box No. 11, West Drayton, Middlesex UB7 OBR*

In the United States: Please write to *Penguin USA Inc., 375 Hudson Street, New York, NY 10014*

In Canada: Please write to *Penguin Books Canada Ltd, 10 Alcorn Avenue, Suite 300, Toronto, Ontario M4V 3B2*

In Australia: Please write to *Penguin Books Australia Ltd, 487 Maroondah Highway, Ringwood, Victoria 3134*

In New Zealand: Please write to *Penguin Books (NZ) Ltd,182–190 Wairau Road, Private Bag, Takapuna, Auckland 9*

In India: Please write to *Penguin Books India Pvt Ltd, 706 Eros Apartments, 56 Nehru Place, New Delhi 110 019*

In the Netherlands: Please write to *Penguin Books Netherlands B.V., Keizersgracht 231 NL–1016 DV Amsterdam*

In Germany: Please write to *Penguin Books Deutschland GmbH, Friedrichstrasse 10–12, W–6000 Frankfurt/Main 1*

In Spain: Please write to *Penguin Books S. A., C. San Bernardo 117–6° E–28015 Madrid*

In Italy: Please write to *Penguin Italia s.r.l., Via Felice Casati 20, I–20124 Milano*

In France: Please write to *Penguin France S. A., 17 rue Lejeune, F–31000 Toulouse*

In Japan: Please write to *Penguin Books Japan, Ishikiribashi Building, 2–5–4, Suido, Tokyo 112*

In Greece: Please write to *Penguin Hellas Ltd, Dimocritou 3, GR–106 71 Athens*

In South Africa: Please write to *Longman Penguin Southern Africa (Pty) Ltd, Private Bag X08, Bertsham 2013*

READ MORE IN PENGUIN

A SELECTION OF FICTION AND NON-FICTION

Yours Etc. Graham Greene

'An entertaining celebration of Graham Greene's lesser-known career as a prolific author of letters to newspapers; you will find unarguable proof of his total addiction to everything about his time, from the greatest issues of the day to the humblest subjects imaginable' – Salman Rushdie in the *Observer*

Just Looking John Updike

'Mr Updike can be a very good art critic, and some of these essays are marvellous examples of critical explanation ... A deep understanding of the art emerges' – *The New York Times Book Review*

As I Walked Out One Midsummer Morning Laurie Lee

As I Walked Out One Midsummer Morning tells of a young man's search for adventure as he leaves his Cotswolds home for London and Spain. 'A beautiful piece of writing' – *Observer*

The Secret Lemonade Drinker Guy Bellamy

Before Bobby met and married Caroline he believed in sex, drink and a good time. He still does... 'Sparkling ... It cracks open a thousand jokes, some old, some new and some blue. As hideously addictive as drink' – *Sunday Times*

A Thief in the Night John Cornwell

A veil of suspicion and secrecy surrounds the final hours of John Paul I, who died of a reported heart attack in September 1978. Award-winning crime-writer John Cornwell was invited by the Vatican to conduct a full investigation and his extraordinary findings are revealed here.

For Good or Evil Clive Sinclair

'The stories are not only very finely poised but genuinely contemporary, stylistically serious... a striking collection' – *The Times Literary Supplement*

READ MORE IN PENGUIN

A SELECTION OF FICTION AND NON-FICTION

Money for Nothing P. G. Wodehouse

Lester Carmody of Rudge Hall is not altogether a good egg. Rather the reverse, in fact. For his intention is to inherit a large sum from the family silver by arranging its theft… 'His whimsical, hilarious stories aimed to do nothing more than amuse' – *Sunday Express*

Lucky Jim Kingsley Amis

'Dixon makes little dents in the smug fabric of hypocritical, humbugging, classbound British society … Amis caught the mood of post-war restiveness in a book which, though socially significant, was, and still is, extremely funny' – Anthony Burgess

The Day Gone By Richard Adams

'He is the best adventure-story-writer alive … Answers to the literary and personal puzzles of the Mr Adams phenomenon lie buried like truffles in his admirable autobiography' – A. N. Wilson in the *Daily Telegraph*

Romancing Vietnam Justin Wintle

'Justin Wintle's journal is a memorable, often amusing, always interesting diary of a tour of duty in a land where sharp-end history pokes round every corner' – *Yorkshire Post*. 'Compelling reading' – *Sunday Telegraph*

Travelling the World Paul Theroux

Now, for the first time, Paul Theroux has authorized a book of his favourite travel writing, containing photographs taken by those who have followed in his footsteps. The exquisite pictures here brilliantly complement and illuminate the provocative, wry, witty commentaries of one of the world's greatest travellers.

BY THE SAME AUTHOR

Waterhouse on Newspaper Style

Keith Waterhouse's classic manual on the use of language in today's tabloids is the standard style guide for journalists, a wide-ranging handbook of popular journalism – and the most entertaining book on the art of clear, correct and effective English you will ever read.

'What Waterhouse has done is to make the teaching of grammar and writing interesting. This is a minor miracle . . . this is also one of the funniest books you are likely to read' – *Daily Mail*

and in Penguin Plays:

Jeffrey Bernard is Unwell and Other Plays
Winner of the *Evening Standard* Comedy of the Year Award

'There is a real Jeffrey Bernard living quietly in Soho. There is also the Jeffrey Bernard he writes about, victim of self-inflicted incendiary disasters, angry women and unreliable horses, who is a national institution in the same way as Falstaff or Mr Micawber. Keith Waterhouse has . . . found ways of turning a confessional monologue into a brilliant comedy' – Irving Wardle in *The Times*